"Are you ready to to me?"

"Promise?" He looked at her blankly.

"You can't have forgotten. You promised you'd wait until I grew up and then you'd marry me."

He was appalled, until he saw her laugh. "What are you trying to do, scare me to death?"

She laughed again.

"So you don't expect me to marry you. Anything else I can do that's not so permanent?"

"As a matter of fact, there is. I want you to help me train my horse, Star. Everyone knows that you're the best there is with horses."

There was no real reason he couldn't help her out, except that it seemed like a commitment and he didn't intend to tie himself anywhere, not now.

"I'd like to help. But I don't know how long I'll be here and—"

"I'll take whatever time you can spare. *Denke*, Aaron. I'm wonderful glad."

He started to say that his words hadn't been a yes, but before he could, Sally grabbed his hand and every thought flew right out of his head.

And he knew in that instant that he was in trouble.

A lifetime spent in rural Pennsylvania and her Pennsylvania Dutch heritage led **Marta Perry** to write about the Plain People, who add so much richness to her home state. Marta has seen nearly sixty of her books published, with over six million books in print. She and her husband live in a centuries-old farmhouse in a central Pennsylvania valley. When she's not writing, she's reading, traveling, baking or enjoying her six beautiful grandchildren.

Leigh Bale is a *Publishers Weekly* bestselling author. She is the winner of the prestigious Golden Heart® Award and was a finalist for the Gayle Wilson Award of Excellence and the Booksellers' Best Award. The daughter of a retired US forest ranger, she holds a BA in history. Married in 1981 to the love of her life, Leigh and her professor husband have two children and two grandkids. You can reach her at leighbale.com.

MARTA PERRY

The Promised Amish Bride

&

LEIGH BALE

His Amish Choice

LOVE INSPIRED
INSPIRATIONAL ROMANCE

LOVE INSPIRED®

INSPIRATIONAL ROMANCE

Recycling programs for this product may not exist in your area.

ISBN-13: 978-1-335-22983-0

The Promised Amish Bride and His Amish Choice

Copyright © 2020 by Harlequin Books S.A.

The Promised Amish Bride
First published in 2019. This edition published in 2020.
Copyright © 2019 by Martha P. Johnson

His Amish Choice
First published in 2018. This edition published in 2020.
Copyright © 2018 by Lora Lee Bale

This edition published by arrangement with Harlequin Books S.A.

For questions and comments about the quality of this book, please contact us at CustomerService@Harlequin.com.

Harlequin Enterprises ULC
22 Adelaide St. West, 40th Floor
Toronto, Ontario M5H 4E3, Canada
www.Harlequin.com

Printed in U.S.A.

CONTENTS

THE PROMISED
AMISH BRIDE

Marta Perry

To Brian, my first and only love.

This is my commandment,
That ye love one another, as I have loved you.
—*John* 15:12

Chapter One

The country road was as familiar as Aaron King's own body, even after all these years away. Here was the spot where his brother, racing a buddy in the family buggy, went into the ditch. There was the bank where they'd picked blackberries, and there the maple tree where he'd stolen a kiss from Becky Esch when they were both fifteen. The maple's leaves were scarlet now that fall was here, but it had just been budding out that spring.

One more bend in the road, and he'd be able to see the family farm. The realization was like a rock in his stomach.

What was he doing? Did he really want to accept the role of the prodigal, returning to the Amish fold in Lost Creek after failing in the Englisch world? That was what they'd think, surely—his two brothers and his uncle. They'd assume he'd messed up, and they'd also assume he'd come back to stay.

They'd be right on the first count—he had to admit it. The memory of the scene that had destroyed his job and the tenuous place he'd made for himself still scalded.

As for coming home to stay...that he wasn't so sure of. To give up modern life, to sink back into the restrictions he'd once left behind, to kneel before the brothers and sisters of the church and confess his wrongs...

The lead weight in his belly grew heavier. He didn't think he could do it. But how many choices did he have left?

He rounded the bend, and the sight ahead of him chased his fruitless thoughts away. A horse reared between the shafts of a buggy, heedless of the efforts of the Amish woman struggling with the lines. Dropping his backpack to the ground, Aaron raced forward. If the horse bolted—

When he reached the animal's head, it was making a determined effort to kick the buggy to pieces, but at least it hadn't run. Sucking in a breath, he lunged, dangerously near the flailing hooves. He caught the leather strap of the headpiece and held on tight, all the while talking in the low, steady voice that could calm the most jittery beast.

"Get away from him before you're hurt. I don't want help." The woman spoke in English, not dialect. She thought him an Englischer, and why not? That's what he was now.

Ignoring her, he focused on the animal, watching the flicker of the ears, the shudders that rippled the skin. He kept his voice low, saying soothing, meaningless words. Slowly, very slowly, the kicks grew halfhearted. They stopped, and the gelding stood, head drooping, shivering a little, but starting to relax.

"There now," he crooned in the still-familiar cadences of Pennsylvania Dutch. "You're all right. Something scared you, yah?"

"Nothing more fierce than a paper cup blowing across the road. Could be he wasn't ready to venture out of the farmyard yet." The light amused voice startled him out of his preoccupation with the animal.

He took a cautious look, his hand still smoothing the gelding's silky neck. The woman set the brake and secured the lines. She jumped down with a quick, agile movement that told him she wasn't much more than a girl.

"Denke. If I'd known it was Aaron King coming to the rescue I wouldn't have told you to go away, that's certain sure." A hint of laughter threaded through her voice.

He frowned. Who was it that knew him right off the bat, even in his jeans and denim jacket? But looking did him no good. Foolish, since she recognized him, but he hadn't the faintest notion who she was.

"Ach, you don't know me, do you? That's a blow to my self-esteem, all right. Here I thought you'd never forget me." A teasing voice, a lively, animated face and laughing blue eyes confronted him. Her silky blond hair was parted in the center and drawn back under a snowy kapp, but… Then she smiled, showing the dimple in her right cheek, and he knew her.

"It's never Sally Stoltzfus." Aaron had to shake his head, even knowing that after nearly ten years away folks would have changed. "You grew up."

"People do." She patted the gelding. "Though I'm beginning to wonder about Star."

"Your daad never picked out a flighty animal like

this for you, did he? He's always been a gut judge of horseflesh. Or is it a husband who did the choosing?"

That gave him a pang, thinking of the little girl who'd had such a crush on him when he'd been a grown-up seventeen and she barely thirteen.

"Not a chance," Sally said, the amusement still in her expressive face. "Everyone knows I'm an old maid by this time, or so my sister-in-law says. And a schoolteacher besides. And no, Daad didn't pick the animal. Star was a present from my onkel Simon."

"That explains it," he said, with half his mind still wondering how that skinny kid had grown into such a pretty woman. "Simon Stoltzfus never could seem to pick a decent buggy horse. So he passed this failure of his on to you, did he?"

It was pleasant standing here talking to Sally, letting the dialect fill his head and come more easily out of his mouth. And incidentally putting off the moment at which he'd have to face his family.

"Some things don't improve with time," she said. "Like Onkel Simon's judgment of horseflesh. Too bad you weren't around to save me from myself when I accepted Star."

"You wouldn't have taken my advice. The Sally I remember always went her own way." The teasing came back to him, lightening his mood. "I don't expect that has changed."

"Probably not. Ach, what am I doing?" Her blue eyes turned serious, her smile slipping away. "I'm keeping you standing here talking when you must be eager to get home. And the family longing to greet you, I'm certain sure. I can get this beast home for myself now."

"I'm not in that much of a hurry," he said, and knew it to be true. "It's gut to catch up a little."

"But they'll be looking for you, ain't so? I'd guess Jessie has been baking half the day with you coming home."

Jessie was his brother Caleb's wife, and he'd never even met her. There were two young ones, his niece and nephew, that he hadn't met either. And his brother Daniel was planning a wedding himself next month. Would there even be a place for him with the family so changed?

"Maybe so. If they knew I was coming." He found he didn't want to see her reaction to that.

"You didn't tell them?" Sally's eyes widened. "Aaron King, why ever not? Don't you know anticipation is half the fun? Your onkel Zeb was just saying the other day how much he wanted to see you. Ever since Daniel visited with you in the spring, he's been hoping to hear word you were coming."

He might have known that folks would hear about his meeting up with Daniel at the racing stable where he'd been working. Nothing stayed secret long in the Amish community. Sally was a close neighbor, of course, but most likely the whole church district knew by now. They'd have had time to talk. To judge.

When he didn't respond, Sally grasped his arm and gave it a shake. "Wake up, Aaron. Why didn't you let them know you were coming? You are staying, aren't you?"

He yanked away from her, suddenly irritated. He should have walked right past and let her manage that nervy horse on her own. Leave it to a woman to complicate matters.

"That's between me and my family." It came out as a snarl, but that was about how he felt…like a wounded animal ready to bite a helping hand.

She took a step back, her hand dropping to her side. "It is. And of course you wouldn't want to say anything to me, knowing that I'll spread it all over the community in the blink of an eye, being such a blabbermaul as I am."

The tart tone and sharper sarcasm caught him off guard. This wasn't the little Sally he'd known any longer. This was a grown woman whose clear eyes, showing every change of mood, were now sparkling with anger.

The realization startled him into a muttered apology. "Sorry. I didn't mean…"

The ready laughter came back into her eyes again. "Yah, you did."

Funny, that she could make him feel like smiling on a day when he'd thought he had nothing to smile about. "Were you always this annoying about being right?"

"I guess you'll just have to strain yourself to remember that, won't you?" She began turning the horse into the lane to the Stoltzfus place, across the road from the King farm. "Star will come along all right now that we're moving toward home. And that's where you need to be headed, as well. Go home, Aaron." She hesitated as if wondering whether to say more. "It will be all right." Her voice was soft. "Go home. You'll see."

Sally forced herself not to look back until she was halfway down the lane toward the farmhouse. Then a quick glance over her shoulder assured her that Aaron wasn't looking her way.

Instead, with his backpack slung on one shoulder, he walked down the lane at the King place, headed for the house and whatever welcome awaited him. Here was the Prodigal Son returning, that was certain sure.

Sally took a deep, calming breath. It had shaken her, seeing Aaron after so many years. Not that she'd forgotten him. A girl never forgot her first crush.

She didn't doubt that Aaron would be welcomed warmly, just as that prodigal had in the story Jesus told. The only reason Onkel Zeb wasn't running down the lane to greet him, like the father in the parable, was that he didn't know Aaron was coming.

Ach, how foolish Aaron was, not to realize they'd be eager to see him. After all, hadn't Daniel traveled all that way out to Indiana just to talk to him once they'd found out where he was?

It was the same with most Amish families who'd had a child jump the fence to the Englisch world. They waited, they prayed and they longed for the time when their child came home. The happy ending they wanted didn't always come, of course. But it looked as if the King family would have their prayers answered, at least for today.

Star nuzzled her as if to ask why they'd slowed down, and Sally patted him absently. Funny that she hadn't seen Aaron for so many years, and yet she'd known him the instant she saw his way with the horse. Aaron had always had that gift—some said he must have been born with it.

That had been what she'd recognized, rather than his face. Her steps slowed again. He'd looked older, of course. She had to expect that. But she couldn't have anticipated those deep lines in his face—lines of bitterness, she suspected. And the golden-brown eyes that once danced with amusement or flashed with lightning anger were now wary and watchful. The charm that had once had all the girls in a tizzy was gone. Aaron had looked braced as if ready for an attack. What had happened out there in the world to change him so?

Sally gave herself a shake. She couldn't stand here dreaming. She had things to do, and even now she saw Elizabeth, her sister-in-law, peering from the window to see what was keeping her. Suppressing any negative thoughts about her brother's wife and her endless curiosity, she hurried on toward the barn.

When Sally entered the kitchen after tending to the horse, Elizabeth was rolling out pie dough. And lying in wait for her, it seemed, as she instantly swung around, a question on her lips.

"Here you are at last. Who was that Englischer you were talking to out on the road?"

Sally had implied to Aaron that she wouldn't spread any rumors about him, but she could hardly deny it was he. And little though she knew the Aaron who'd returned, she could be sure he wouldn't imagine he could keep his being here secret.

"It wasn't an Englischer at all. It was Aaron King, on his way home."

"Aaron King!" Elizabeth's round face flushed with excitement, probably at being one of the first to have the news. She swung round as Ben, Sally's brother, came in the door. "Did you hear that, Ben? Aaron King has come home. With his tail between his legs, I've no doubt."

As usual, Elizabeth managed to rouse Sally's ire in a matter of minutes. Sally took firm control of her tongue, something she'd had to learn to do since her parents went to her sister's for an extended visit and Elizabeth and Ben moved in. School days weren't so bad, since she was out and occupied, but weekends could be difficult.

"I wouldn't say that, Elizabeth. You know Daniel had asked him to come, even if just for a visit. They'll all be so happy he decided to, I'm sure."

Ben, with his characteristic slow reaction, mused for a moment and then smiled. "Aaron finally home. That is gut news, ain't so? It seems like just yesterday that we were walking down the road to school together."

"I don't know what call you have to be so happy," Elizabeth said. "He wasn't much of a friend, never getting in touch with you in all these years."

By the time her parents returned from their lengthy visit and Ben and Elizabeth moved back to their own house, Sally figured her tongue would have calluses from biting it.

"He could hardly be in touch with Ben without letting his folks know where he was," she pointed out.

"That's so," Ben said. "Aaron back again, think of that. Too bad tomorrow is an off Sunday for worship, or he'd have been able to see the whole church at once."

Sally smiled. Ben couldn't imagine that someone might not want to be confronted with the rest of the Leit all at once.

"Maybe it's just as well he has a chance to settle in before greeting the whole community," she suggested.

"Yah, maybe so," Ben admitted. "I heard he was working with horses somewhere out west."

"I don't know about out west, but it looked as if he was giving Sally a hand with that fractious gelding.

That animal's too much for her." Elizabeth frowned, then launched on her repeated refrain about Onkel Simon's gift.

"Star was just a little leery of being on the road, that's all," Sally said, no more eager to get on to this subject of conversation than to talk about Aaron. She wasn't about to admit how scared she'd been before Aaron came to the rescue.

"You're making light of it, but I know what I saw." Elizabeth gave the rolling pin a decided thump. "Ben should have refused that animal for you the minute your uncle showed up with it."

The quick retort she'd been congratulating herself for keeping under control slipped loose. "That was not Ben's decision. It was mine, and I'll thank you to remember it."

She was sorry, of course, the instant the words were out, but then it was too late. She sent up a penitent prayer. Would she ever learn to control her unruly tongue?

Elizabeth swung on her husband. "Tell her, Ben. Tell her that horse is too much for her."

Ben, after a cautious glance at his sister's flushed face, shook his head. Then he sent Sally a pleading look that she could hardly refuse.

She took a deep breath and fought for patience. "Don't worry so much, Elizabeth. I won't take any chances with Star." She'd have to give more, if only to restore peace. "If he's not learned to behave himself by the time Daad gets back, we'll let him decide what to do."

Elizabeth still looked a bit miffed, but she nodded. "I only want you to be safe," she said.

To do her credit, that was probably true. Elizabeth had a kind heart to go with that tart tongue.

"That's settled, then." Relief filled Ben's voice. Poor Ben. He only wanted peace, something he couldn't get with two strong women after him.

But nothing was settled as far as Sally was concerned. She had no intention of giving up the liberty granted by having her own buggy horse. And she'd just had a thought that might well solve her problem.

Aaron King. If anyone could do anything with Star, it would be Aaron. Now all she had to do was convince Aaron of that.

Those moments with Sally Stoltzfus had distracted Aaron from his apprehension, but it had flooded back the instant she turned away. If he'd thought the road filled with memories, it was nothing compared to the flood that threatened to overwhelm him as he walked down the lane to the farm. Every fence post, every tree, every blade of grass even, seemed to be shouting his name.

Welcoming him home? Or reminding him that he no longer had a place here? He wasn't sure. Just as he wasn't sure he even wanted to be here. Or to belong again.

He'd have to make up his mind soon. He could only hope no one would force an answer about his plans. Or be too curious about what had caused him to return now. His mind winced away from that thought.

The field to the left of the lane was planted in corn now. Sere and yellow, it wouldn't be long until they cut the stalks. Behind it, the pasture was filled with the dairy herd that supported the farm. The herd was larger than it had been when he'd left, it seemed to him. The barn and the milking shed looked in good shape, tidy and freshly painted. If the place had been neglected while Caleb recovered from the injury he'd suffered a year ago, it didn't show.

The carpentry shop his brother Daniel ran was a new addition. He only knew about it because Daniel, once he'd learned where Aaron was, had written to him faithfully, as had Onkel Zeb. His oldest brother, Caleb, was never much of a letter writer, but that wasn't the reason for his silence. Caleb, with his high standards and even higher expectations of his younger brothers, would be the least accepting of his return, he expected.

Still, Onkel Zeb had said that Caleb and his wife, Jessie, would like to see him, and Onkel Zeb wasn't one to say things he didn't mean.

As if his thought had brought him, Zeb picked that moment to emerge from the back door of the house. He stared for a long moment, probably not sure who it was he saw walking down the lane. Then, with a loud shout, he ran toward Aaron, beard ruffling in the movement, arms spread wide in welcome.

Once again Aaron dropped the backpack. In the grip of an emotion too fierce to resist, he raced toward his uncle. Zeb's strong, wiry arms went around him, his beard, gray now, brushing Aaron's cheek. The tears in his uncle's eyes made him ashamed—ashamed not of leaving, but of failing to let them know where he was for such a long time. Onkel Zeb, at least, would have worried and wondered.

"Ach, it's sehr gut to see you." Onkel Zeb took a step back, but still held him by the shoulders. "We've been hoping… Why didn't you tell us you were coming? We'd have been ready to give you a fine wilkom."

"This is a fine enough wilkom for me." Aaron blinked rapidly, forcing down emotion. He'd learned, out in the world, not to show his feelings too quickly. It gave the other person an edge, he'd learned. "How are you, Onkel Zeb?"

"Fine, fine. Nothing keeps me down as long as there's work to do. And there's always work on a dairy farm."

"I saw the herd. Looks like Caleb has been doing well." Aaron welcomed the return to a more casual topic. "Still dealing with the same dairy?"

"Yah, that doesn't change. Lots more rules and regulations and paperwork now, but we keep up. But komm, schnell. The others will want to see you." He marched to the bell that hung where it always had next to the back door. Reaching up, he gave it a hearty yank, making it peal across the farm.

They'd all come running when they heard the bell at such an odd time, Aaron knew. He retrieved his backpack, just as glad to hide his face for a moment from Onkel Zeb's keen eyes. His uncle never missed anything, and he'd know the apprehension Aaron felt about coming back.

Zeb had become more of a father than an uncle to the three of them after their mother left. Their own daad seemed to lose heart once Mamm went away, and it was Onkel Zeb who'd stepped in, Onkel Zeb who'd had the raising of them. When Daad passed away they'd grieved him, for sure, but not much had changed. Onkel Zeb was still there.

Aaron straightened. It would have been Onkel Zeb

to be hurt the most when he'd run off, he felt sure. Since his uncle seemed more than ready to forgive and move on, he could indulge in the hope that the others might feel the same.

The house door opened almost immediately, and a woman emerged, wiping her hands on a dish towel. "What's wrong? Onkel Zeb, are you—" She stopped abruptly at the sight of him. She stared for a moment, and suddenly her expression blossomed into a smile. "Ach, you must be Aaron. Wilkom home!"

"Denke. And you must be Jessie, Caleb's wife."

And Caleb's wife was shortly to produce a new baby, it seemed. Obvious as it was to the most casual glance, no one would mention the expected newcomer in mixed company until the babe was safe in its cradle. Things were different in the outside world, but now that he was here, it behooved him to keep Amish customs, so he kept his gaze firmly on Jessie's face.

"Your brothers will be so happy to see you." Seizing the bell, she gave it a few more loud clangs. "If only you'd told me, I'd have had something fancier planned than the chicken potpie we're having."

He grinned at the predictable words. Every Amish woman, it seemed, was born wanting to feed people. "You couldn't have anything I'd want more than genuine Amish potpie," he said. "There's nothing like it where I've been living."

The worry left Jessie's face and she smiled, her hand moving probably unconsciously over her stomach. "That's gut, then. We'll have to feed you up now that we have a chance."

There was a thunder of small feet behind her, and a little boy bolted onto the porch, then stopped short at the sight of a stranger. He was followed a second later by a slightly bigger girl. The boy had to be Timothy, the nephew he hadn't met—straight, silky blond hair, blue eyes that were wide with wondering who he was. The boy was five, from what Onkel Zeb said in his letters. And Becky, at seven looking enough like her brother to be his twin, would be one of Sally's scholars, he guessed.

"Hi, Timothy. Becky." It sounded awkward, and that was how it felt. How did he talk to the niece and nephew he'd never met?

"Mammi?" Timothy clutched Jessie's skirt, and both kinder looked up at her.

"It's all right. This is your onkel Aaron, Daadi's brother. You've heard us speak of him."

The boy nodded, looking at him with those big eyes. "Onkel Aaron," he repeated, but he didn't let go of his mother's skirt. The girl, a bit braver, actually came closer. "Wilkom, Onkel Aaron."

"Wilkom." Another voice repeated the word with a slight edge.

Aaron turned to face his oldest brother, Caleb. He was the one who'd spoken. Close behind Caleb was Daniel, beaming as if it were Christmas. It was Daniel who moved first, throwing an arm across Aaron's shoulders.

"Ach, about time you were getting here. They were all starting to think I'd imagined finding you." He gave Aaron a quick shake. "It's wonderful gut to have you home. Ain't so, Caleb?"

"Yah, for sure." The tiniest of reservations colored Caleb's voice. "Wilkom," he said again. There was a small, awkward pause before he went on. "So, Aaron, tell us. Are you home to stay? Are you ready to be Amish again?"

There it was, the last question he wanted to answer, and the first one anyone asked. *Are you ready to be Amish again?*

He didn't know. He just didn't know.

Chapter Two

For an instant, Aaron felt like heading right back to the road. But before he could frame an answer, Onkel Zeb stepped in.

"Komm, now." He put a hand on Caleb's shoulder. "We asked Aaron to visit, ain't so? If he should be thinking of making that kind of decision—ach, it's not one to make lightly. We will enjoy visiting for now."

There was a hint of sternness in his words, and Caleb looked suitably abashed.

"Onkel Zeb is right, as always." His smile warmed his face. "Wilkom back, little bruder. We're wonderful glad you're here."

"Denke."

Returning the smile, Aaron suspected his brother still wanted to hear an answer to his question, but at least he wouldn't press. Obviously Onkel Zeb still exerted his quiet influence over the family.

Funny, now that he thought about it. Onkel Zeb never scolded or argued, not even when the three of them had been at their most obnoxious. He just had a way of looking at a person and then saying a quiet word. And somehow it always worked.

"You must be hungry," Jessie said quickly as if to do her part to change the subject. "Let me fix you a little something to last you until supper."

Aaron actually found himself relaxing enough to chuckle. "Not just yet, denke, Jessie. I stopped for lunch not long ago, so I'll save myself for your chicken pot-pie. Maybe I can just have a look around."

"For sure." Daniel grabbed his backpack and tossed it on the porch. "Let's have a look at my workshop. That's new since you've been here, ain't so?"

No one else jumped in with a different suggestion, so he figured he wouldn't hurt anyone's feelings by seeing the shop first. "Sure thing. Show me what kind of businessman you are."

It was Caleb's turn to chuckle. "He's a better carpenter than a businessman, ain't so? He loves the building and hates sending the bills."

Daniel just grinned, his placid temperament not easily upset by teasing. "True. That's why I'm marrying Rebecca. I figure the way she runs her quilt shop so well, she'll turn me into a businessman pretty fast."

"You just want her to keep the books for you," Caleb said. "Get on with you and show off your shop. Maybe Aaron can help with the milking later, if he hasn't forgot how."

There might have been a question in the words. "That's not something easy to forget," Aaron said. "It'll come back to me in a hurry."

Caleb seemed satisfied with that answer. Murmuring something about work to be done in the barn, he moved off and Jessie disappeared into the house, probably thinking about supper. That left Onkel Zeb and the kids to tag along as they headed for the shop.

Before they'd gone a few steps, Aaron felt his hand grabbed by Timothy. He glanced down at the boy, a bit surprised that he'd decided to be friends so quickly. Timothy's blue eyes were wary, but he obviously had something to say.

"We're going to have a new cousin," he whispered.

"You are?" The boy was soon going to have a little sister or brother, but what was this about a cousin?

Becky took his other hand, not to be outdone by her little brother. "Yah. A boy cousin." She looked as if she'd prefer a girl cousin. "Onkel Daniel and Rebecca are getting married, so her little boy, Lige, will be our cousin."

"That's wonderful gut, ain't so? You'll get a cousin big enough to play with right away."

Becky mused, her small forehead wrinkled. "You mean he won't be a baby, yah? But he's littler than me. He's in first grade now."

"That means you get to be the big cousin. You can help him with lots of things." From what he remembered, little girls liked that.

She nodded gravely. "I can help him with his spelling. Teacher Sally will like it if I do."

"I'm sure she will." He tried to picture Sally as a teacher and failed completely. He couldn't deny that she'd grown up, but it seemed to him she was much too pretty and lighthearted to be a teacher.

"Teacher Sally is nice," Timothy contributed. Then he glanced at his sister. "Race you to the shop." He took off even before he finished, and she chased after him.

Aaron glanced at Daniel. "Nope," he said after a minute. "I don't see you as a married man."

"That's what we all said until Rebecca came home next door and started her quilt shop. She hired a carpenter and ended up with a future husband." Onkel Zeb chuckled. "Though there were days I thought he'd never make up his mind as ask her."

"I was waiting until the time was right." Daniel pretended to be offended, but it was clear that he was pleased with himself. "You couldn't expect me to ask her until she was settled here at home again."

"I didn't realize Rebecca had been married. Was it someone local?" The man had obviously died. There wasn't another option in the Amish community.

"No. She met him when she went out to Ohio on a visit." Daniel's eyes clouded, as if there were things he didn't want to say. Maybe he regretted not having courted Rebecca before she went away.

But Daniel had been just as cautious when it came to marriage as his brothers had been. They'd lived through the trauma caused by a broken marriage when their mother left. That had been reason enough to take it slowly.

But now that he'd made the decision, Daniel seemed happy. Contented—that was it. He acted like a person who'd found what he wanted.

"So now you're going to be an instant daadi to her little boy. Are you sure you're ready for that?" He said it teasingly, trusting that Daniel still knew him well enough to tell when he was serious or joking.

"Ach, he's already gone a long way in that direction," Onkel Zeb said. "Little Lige was hanging on him in chust a day or two. I'm thinking Lige had a place in his heart that needed filling, and Daniel fit just right."

"I guess it was meant to be, then."

Apparently that was the right thing to say, because Daniel's face lit up. "That's it, for sure. When it's the real thing, you know it's meant to be. I'm thankful to the gut Lord to have a woman like Rebecca and a son like Lige."

Aaron couldn't help but be impressed. It seemed his brother had done a lot of growing up while he was away. "I wish you happiness, all three of you. Now you can use all the things you learned about raising kinder when you practiced on me."

He meant it as a joke, but Daniel gave him a serious look in return. "Seems to me I didn't do that gut a job with you. If I had, you wouldn't have run off without a word to me about it. I've carried the guilt of that ever since."

For a moment he could only stare at his brother. "That's foolishness," he said, wanting to be rid of the uneasy feeling the words gave him. "You couldn't have known. Anyway, when a boy's thinking of jumping the fence, he's not likely to talk to anyone about it. And it wasn't your responsibility."

He half expected Onkel Zeb to say something—to agree with him, at least, that it hadn't been Daniel's fault that he'd run off. Instead they both just looked at him.

"It was my doing," he said, his voice sharper than he meant it to be. "No one else was responsible."

Daniel shook his head. "It was different for Caleb. He had the farm to run. I was the one who was closer to you in age. I should have known. I should have helped you."

Aaron didn't want this conversation—didn't want to know any of it. But he didn't have a choice. When he'd left, he'd told himself it was his decision. Nothing to do with anyone else. But he'd been wrong. He'd hurt people, and he didn't see that there was anything he could do to make it right.

Sally settled into the privacy of her bedroom with Aaron King still on her mind. She glanced around, thinking as she always did how fortunate she was in so many ways.

When she'd expressed her desire to become a teacher, Daadi had insisted on setting up her bedroom accordingly. She had a desk in front of the window with a comfortable chair and a long bookcase that still wasn't quite big enough for all of her books. The file boxes she used for teaching materials were stacked next to the desk.

Each time she walked into the room, she felt a wave of gratitude toward her father. He hadn't waited until she'd obtained the job as a teacher. He'd shown the family's confidence in her even before that happened. Somehow knowing other people believed she could do it had made her believe it, too.

She settled at her desk, trying to focus on her lesson plans for the coming week, but her thoughts kept straying. The arithmetic lesson for her second graders slipped away as she stared out the window and across the road to the King farm. Aaron would be past the initial reactions to his homecoming by now, and she could only pray they'd been everything they should be.

And maybe she ought also to pray about how he'd respond to them. Aaron had always been hard to predict, like a minnow in the creek slipping this way and that, always out of her grasp. Sally smiled at herself, thinking of Aaron's probable response to being compared to a minnow.

Still, even her brief encounter with him was enough to convince her that the Aaron who'd returned wasn't the Aaron who'd left. He'd had a quick temper back then, but it had been as quickly gone, leaving sunshine behind it. Now—well, now he looked like a man with a chip on his shoulder, daring someone to knock it off.

Maybe he'd found that attitude necessary in the Englisch world, but it would be very out of place here. He'd have to get used to the give-and-take of Amish family life in order to get along. To say nothing of the sheer noise with so many people in the house—two kinder and a new boppli soon to arrive. If he'd been living a solitary bachelor existence among the Englisch, he'd find this very different.

And the King household was more than usually wound up at the moment, with Daniel's wedding approaching as fast as Jessie and Caleb's baby. Some days she thought it was turning into a race to see which would be first. But they'd cope, however it turned out. Everyone from the church would pitch in to help, and as neighbors, they'd expect to be called on.

Sally gave herself a little shake and firmly removed her attention from the house across the road. The upper grades needed some extra map work—she'd been appalled at how much they'd forgotten over the summer vacation. Still, it was always the way, and—

Sally's pencil dropped to the desk as she swung around. That sound…what was it? A soft cry? She shot from her chair when it came again…a half-choked sob.

Elizabeth? Hurrying to the door, Sally rushed into the hall. The door to Ben and Elizabeth's bedroom was closed, but it couldn't muffle the noise of Elizabeth's crying.

Tapping at the door, she called out. "Elizabeth? What's wrong? Are you hurt?"

A moment's silence. "No, I… I'm… It's nothing. It…" The words dissolved in tears. Her heart twisting, Sally turned the knob, murmured a prayer for help and walked in.

Elizabeth sat on the side of the bed, her apron askew, a pillow from the bed held against her lips as if to muffle her sobs. Horrified, Sally rushed to her, sitting so that she could wrap her arms around Elizabeth.

"Komm, now, tell me. Something is wrong. Let me help you," she coaxed, keeping her voice soft even as her thoughts tumbled. Should she run to find Ben? This weeping was unheard of for practical, controlling Elizabeth.

"Please, Elizabeth. Tell me why you're crying. I want to help."

"I'm not…not crying." Elizabeth mopped at her eyes ineffectively. "I never cry. I… I just thought for sure I was expecting at last. But I'm not." Tears overflowed again. "Maybe I never will be."

"Ach, no, don't think that." She patted her sister-in-law, hoping that was the right thing to say. "Surely it will happen for you and Ben."

Elizabeth turned her face away, and Sally realized she didn't want anyone to see her like this. But what could she do? She couldn't just go away and pretend it hadn't happened. If only Mammi were here. Mammi would know what to say. She felt very young and very useless for all that she was supposed to be a grown woman.

"Maybe…maybe it's just not time yet," she said. It sounded stupid to her own ears, but after all, some women did take longer to start a family than others. "Or maybe there's some little thing wrong that the doctor can fix. Did you talk to a doctor?"

Elizabeth shook her head, wiping the last of the tears away with her fingers like a child would. "I asked the midwife. She wants me to see a doctor—she gave me the name of someone. A woman doctor, a specialist. But I don't know. Maybe it's not God's will, doing that. Maybe I should just be waiting and praying."

Sally rubbed her back gently, the way Mammi always did when she was hurting. "Surely it can't be wrong just to talk to the doctor." She took a breath. "Why don't you let me call and make the appointment for you? Then I'll go with you, so you won't be alone."

Elizabeth stiffened, drawing away. "Ach, I couldn't even think of letting you do such a thing. What would your mamm say, and you not even a married woman?"

It seemed Sally had gone a step too far, but at least Elizabeth's tears had stopped.

"Mamm would say I should do what she would if she were here, ain't so? Let me do this for you." *And forgive me for all the times my quick tongue let me snap at you.*

Why hadn't she seen or even suspected that this was tormenting her sister-in-law? Was she really so self-centered she couldn't look past her own wants? If she could help now, maybe it would make up for her failures.

"Please, Elizabeth." She clasped Elizabeth's hand.

Elizabeth got up so quickly the mattress bounced. She pulled her hand free and shook out her wrinkled skirt. "What am I doing, sitting here being silly when there's work to be done? Don't you say a word about it. It was foolishness."

"Elizabeth..."

"Forget it. You must get back to your schoolwork. You can't let those scholars get ahead of you, ain't so?"

"That's certain sure." She knew what was happening. Elizabeth had shown weakness, and it embarrassed her. More than that, she didn't consider Sally capable of helping her.

Well, they were agreed on that. She didn't feel capable either.

Aaron had been relieved to learn that the next day wasn't a church Sunday—he'd be spared the task of seeing the entire Amish community until the following week. If he stayed that long.

But he hadn't gotten off entirely. By noon the neighbors were arriving for a picnic, and there was no getting out of it. After all, these were people who'd known him all his life, and they expected to celebrate his return.

Visit, he kept telling himself. *Visit, not return.*

Wondering if Caleb had any chores for him in the barn, he headed out of the house, only to meet Sally, arriving from across the road with a basket in one hand and a bowl in the other.

"Aaron. Just what I need—an extra pair of hands. Grab the potato salad, will you? It's slipping."

Assuming she meant the bowl, he took it from her. "Can I take the basket, as well?" It was only common courtesy to help her, after all.

"I've got it." She looked up at him, her blue eyes dancing. "I can tell you're thrilled to have all the neighbors coming in to have a look at you."

Apparently there was no hiding anything from this grown-up Sally, so he managed a smile. "I guess I can stand it if they can. Is Ben coming?"

"Yah, he and Elizabeth will be along in a minute. She was putting the finishing touches on her salad."

"Judging by the food Jessie has been producing all morning, I'd say there's going to be plenty to eat." He fell into step with her as they headed into the kitchen.

"Did you ever know an Amish meal where there wasn't? Or have you forgotten what it's like in all these years away? Maybe you lived on frozen dinners and fast food out there."

"Maybe," he admitted. "Unless I've forgotten a lot, it seems to me I used to be the one doing all the teasing, not you."

"You'd best hurry and catch up, then," she said, giving him a pert look over her shoulder as she went through the door ahead of him.

Aaron stopped for a second. If he didn't know any better, he'd say that Sally was flirting with him. Worse, that he felt like flirting right back.

Oh, no. He sure wasn't going there. A few quick strides took him into the kitchen and to the counter, where he deposited the bowl. "I'll help Caleb with the tables," he muttered, and scooted out without meeting Sally's glance again.

Caleb and Onkel Zeb were setting up tables on the grass, and he hurried to grab one end before his uncle could reach it. "I'll get it." He glanced across the field. "Looks like some more company on their way."

"Yah, the Fisher family are eager to see you, that's certain sure." Onkel Zeb grinned. "And Daniel is twice as eager to see Rebecca. He's that excited about getting married you'd think no one had ever done it before."

"So Daniel is becoming a daadi. That's still hard to imagine." Aaron was still having trouble just picturing his brother married, let alone being an instant father.

"Like I said, he's gut with little Lige, Rebecca's boy. The child loves him already, and Rebecca... Well, you'll see the way they look at each other." Onkel Zeb gave him a sly glance. "Seems to me it's become a tradition, the King boys getting married."

"Count me out," he said quickly. "It's not for me." Sally's lively face appeared in his mind's eye, and he chased it away.

"More work, less talk," Caleb said. "There's still the benches to set up."

"Right." Aaron picked up one of the benches and carried it to its proper place. He'd be just as happy to have enough jobs to keep him from needless conversation with the neighbors, but he didn't guess that was possible.

In any event, meeting and greeting wasn't as difficult as Aaron had expected, even though he felt foolishly awkward at times. Mostly people hadn't changed much—just gotten older. There was Sam Fisher from next door, who was Caleb's age and had a flock of kids already. He and his Leah must have married early, since their oldest boy was a gangly youth entering his teens and looking much as Sam had at that age.

Daniel's Rebecca had grown up into a beauty, that was for sure. Not lively, like Sally, but with a serene calm that turned into joy each time her eyes met Daniel's. It was oddly disturbing to see that flare of love returned by his easygoing brother. Lige, the little boy, seemed attached to Daniel's pant leg most of the time, chattering away a mile a minute.

Onkel Zeb caught him watching Daniel and Rebecca. "They're gut together, yah? It's a wonder to see Daniel so happy, and Rebecca, too."

"I'm still trying to get used to Caleb being married and having a family. Now Daniel." He shook his head. "I'm not sure what kind of an uncle I'm going to be, but I'm certain sure I won't do as gut a job as you did with us."

"It'll come to you," his uncle said. "Most things are natural when it's family."

He wasn't so convinced of that, but he could hardly argue with his uncle after all Zeb had done for them. His gaze strayed to Sally's brother, Ben, and his wife.

"Ben hasn't changed," he said. "His wife…"

Onkel Zeb grinned. "Tried to get your whole life story out of you, did she? Ach, Elizabeth's a gut woman, but she has an opinion on everything. I expect she and Sally are butting heads plenty these days. Elizabeth and Ben are staying in the farmhouse with Sally while her and Ben's folks are away."

"Sally said something about it." And based on his brief encounter with Elizabeth, he could understand if she got on Sally's nerves.

"Speaking of Sally, here she is," Zeb said. "Are you looking for me or for my handsome nephew, Teacher Sally?"

Sally smiled, squeezing his arm. "You're my sweetheart, Zeb. But it's Aaron I need to see at the moment."

Still trying to get used to the grown-up Sally, he

couldn't find a response for a second or two—long enough for Onkel Zeb to move off. "I'll leave you to talk about it, then."

"I'm not sure what…" he began, but Sally plunged right in.

"Komm, now, Aaron. I thought you might be ready to keep your promise to me."

"Promise?" He looked at her blankly.

"You can't have forgotten. You promised you'd wait until I grew up and then you'd marry me."

He stared at her, appalled for what seemed forever until he saw the laughter in her eyes. "Sally Stoltzfus, you've turned into a threat to my sanity. What are you trying to do, scare me to death?"

She gave a gurgle of laughter. "You looked a little bored with the picnic. I thought I'd wake you up."

"Not bored," he said quickly. "Just…trying to find my way. So you don't expect me to marry you. Anything else I can do that's not so permanent?"

"As a matter of fact, there is. I want you to help me train Star."

So that was it. He frowned, trying to think of a way to refuse that wouldn't hurt her feelings.

"You saw what Star is like," she went on without waiting for an answer. "I've got to get him trained, and soon. And everyone knows that you're the best there is with horses."

"I don't think everyone believes any such thing," he retorted. "They don't know me well enough anymore."

She waved that away. "You've been working with horses while you were gone. And Zeb always says you were born with the gift."

"Onkel Zeb might be a little bit prejudiced," he said,

trying to organize his thoughts. There was no real reason he couldn't help her out, except that it seemed like a commitment, and he didn't intend to tie himself anywhere, not now.

"You can't deny that Star needs help, can you?" Her laughing gaze invited him to share her memory of the previous day.

"He needs help all right, but I don't quite see the point. Can't you use the family buggy when you need it?" He suspected that if he didn't come up with a good reason, he'd find himself working with that flighty gelding.

Her face grew serious suddenly. "As long as I do that, I'm depending on someone else. I want to make my own decisions about when and where I'm going. I'd like to be a bit independent, at least in that. I thought you were the one person who might understand."

That hit him right where he lived. He did understand—that was the trouble. He understood too well, and it made him vulnerable where Sally was concerned. He fumbled for words. "I'd like to help. But I don't know how long I'll be here and—"

"That doesn't matter." Seeing her face change was like watching the sun come out. "I'll take whatever time you can spare. Denke, Aaron. I'm wonderful glad."

He started to say that his words hadn't been a yes, but before he could, Sally had grabbed his hand and every thought flew right out of his head.

It was just like her catching hold of Onkel Zeb's arm, he tried to tell himself. But it didn't work. When she touched him, something seemed to light between them like a spark arcing from one terminal to another. He felt it right down to his toes, and he knew in that instant that he was in trouble.

Chapter Three

Sally found herself fumbling for words. Her brain seemed to have stopped working the instant her hand touched Aaron. That sudden flare of something between them…had he felt it, too? Or was she imagining it? Finally she managed to mutter something.

"Denke, Aaron." Then she fled.

By the time she'd reached the tables, she'd grabbed hold of her self-control. All she could think was that it was good she'd gotten Aaron's agreement before she'd become too tongue-tied to say a word, let alone convince anyone of anything.

Imagine Sally Stoltzfus speechless—no one who knew her would believe it.

She kept walking, moving around the tables and picking up used dishes, mainly because she didn't want to talk to anyone just now. What she needed was a scolding for her foolishness, but only from herself. No one else must know about that abrupt, startling stroke of attraction she'd felt when she'd touched Aaron.

And what were you doing touching him? She'd hadn't thought—she'd just acted out of impulsive gratitude that he seemed willing to help her. And now this happened.

It had been a long time since she'd experienced that wave of…what? Infatuation? She supposed that was it. After what had happened with Frederick Yoder, she'd armored herself against such a thing. After all, for a decent Amish girl to get right up to a few weeks before her wedding and then back out didn't do her reputation any good. She certainly couldn't let any more rumors start about her.

But what else could she have done about Frederick? She'd let herself be carried along on a wave of feeling, happy because everyone else seemed happy for her. Then quite suddenly, between one moment and the next, she'd known it was no good. She liked Fred. He was a fine person. But when she'd thought seriously about spending the rest of her life with him she'd known it wasn't enough.

Mamm and Daad hadn't understood, she suspected, but they'd never let that show. They'd stood by her, apologized to everyone involved and quietly set about the task of living it down.

It had taken some doing, she knew. There were probably still those who blamed her for what she'd done, despite the fact that Fred was happily married now and the father of twins. But the experience had left her wary, and now she had to go and let her guard down. And with Aaron King, of all people.

What if he'd known? Struck with the thought, she stood stock-still, holding an armful of dishes. If she had given herself away, if Aaron had realized what she'd felt—

"Sally, you're looking very red in the face. What's wrong?"

It was Elizabeth, and she couldn't let her guess the reason for her embarrassment.

"It's a hot day for October, ain't so? I was in the sun too long, I think. I'll just take these things into the kitchen."

She hurried toward the house, praying no one would follow her. And that no one was watching her and wondering.

Foolish, so foolish. If Aaron had recognized her reaction to simply touching his hand, there was no doubt what he'd think. He'd be smiling, telling himself she was still the silly little girl who'd had a crush on him all those years ago. Worse, she was starting to feel like that girl, her hard-won poise escaping her.

When the kitchen door closed behind her, Sally let out a sigh of relief. Jessie, sitting at the table, started to get up.

A glance at Jessie's pallor was enough to tell Sally that Jessie had been overdoing it. She put the dishes on the counter and hurried to push her gently back into her chair. First Elizabeth, and now Jessie, driving her into situations she didn't feel ready for.

"Ach, it's that hot out today for October, ain't so?" She talked to cover her concern. "Tires you out, I know. You just sit still, and I'll get you a cool drink. Unless you want Caleb…"

"No, no, don't tell Caleb." Jessie sank back into her seat. "I don't want anyone upset just because I'm a little tired. You won't say anything, will you, Sally?"

"Not if you don't want me to." She was already pouring a glass of cold lemonade. "It seems to me you deserve some fussing over just now, but if you don't want it, that's fine with me." She set the lemonade glass on the table in front of Jessie. "I can understand not wanting all the women clucking over you."

"That's it." Jessie sipped the lemonade. "Goodness, I'm never sick. And I certain sure don't want to make a fuss over something as natural as having a baby. But I confess, I do seem to need a little more rest than usual."

"Well, you just sit there and relax. No need to talk, even." Sally turned the water on and added detergent to the sink. "Pretend I'm not here."

"Denke, Sally. Maybe I will." She leaned back in the chair.

If she were the one expecting a baby, Sally rather thought she'd welcome a little extra fussing over. But Jessie was so determinedly practical and sensible. Sometimes Sally wondered if she was trying hard to be different from the flighty woman, now deceased, who'd been Caleb's first wife.

She swished suds over a serving platter. If she were a bit wiser, maybe she could come up with something comforting to say. Once again, as with Elizabeth, she didn't have the right words.

From the window over the sink, she had a good view of part of the backyard. It just so happened that it was the part that included Aaron. Well, at least here she could watch him without anyone noticing.

If he'd been at all ruffled by what had happened between them, it didn't show. He was smiling at something his little niece had said, his face relaxing. So at least he could relax, when he tried. She'd begun to wonder if that forbidding expression was permanent. Something unpleasant must have put those lines in his face.

Aaron had always been appealing to the girls, maybe especially because they never knew where they were with him. Now he'd added a dangerous edge that ought to warn away any sensible woman. But women were seldom sensible about things like that.

"How is it going since Aaron got here?" she asked, impulse getting the better of her. "I'm sure it was a shock, even if a happy one."

"Yah, that's so." Jessie moved her glass in slow circles on the tabletop, scarred with generations of use. She seemed intent on the pattern of moisture she made. "It's wonderful gut he came home. Everybody feels that way." She almost sounded as if she were arguing with herself.

Sally thought she knew why. Whatever else he might be, Aaron had never exactly been a peacemaker. He'd always been quick to flare up. His sojourn in the Englisch world might have taught him to control that, but somehow she didn't think anyone could count on it.

"Still, it makes a difference, having an extra person in the house. Adds to your work, I'm sure."

"That's no matter," Jessie said quickly, looking up. "I don't grudge an instant of it, and besides, Onkel Zeb is so much help to me." Her face crinkled. "As much help as having another woman in the house, though he wouldn't want to hear me say so."

Sally grinned. "He might not mind. He was pretty much mother and father to those boys after their mamm left."

"That's so." She hesitated, but there was something in her expression that seemed wary. "I worry too much, I know."

All at once Sally knew what it was that put that

look in Jessie's eyes. She was worried about Caleb. She must know that it had apparently been Aaron's frequent clashes with Caleb that had led to his going away the first time.

And if the same thing happened again, would Aaron respond in the same way? Would he go away again, for good this time?

The picnic finally started to wind down, much to Aaron's relief. He was growing tired of answering the same questions over and over. Or maybe tired of evading the answers. Obviously folks who had known him all his life thought they were entitled to hear about his time in the outside world, even if he wasn't ready to talk about it.

If…and it was a big if…he decided he wanted to stay, to become Amish again…well, that would mean kneeling in front of the whole church to confess his wrongs and ask forgiveness. The very thought made his stomach queasy.

He couldn't. It was impossible. The Englisch world wouldn't expect such a thing, but being Amish was to be different. To live by Scripture and the rules of the community. *Impossible*, he told himself again.

Aaron yanked himself out of his self-absorption and hurried to help Onkel Zeb. He and the two children were starting to take the tables down, and he reached them just in time to give his small nephew a helping hand.

The boy frowned. "I have it."

"Sure you do," he said easily. "But I'd best help, or Onkel Zeb might scold me for not doing my part."

Timothy giggled. "He wouldn't scold you."

"Sure I would. He's part of the family, ain't so? When he was a boy like you, I had to scold him plenty." Onkel Zeb hefted the table with surprising ease. He might have aged in appearance, but the strength of his lean, wiry body hadn't changed.

The boy's eyes grew wide. "Was he very naughty?"

"Yah, I was," Aaron said. The child didn't know the half of it. "Sometimes I'd think no one had noticed something I did, but Onkel Zeb always knew. Eyes in the back of his head, I guess."

Timothy gave Onkel Zeb an awed look, and Zeb laughed, shaking his head. "It's just an expression, Timothy. I don't need an extra pair of eyes but I know young ones."

Becky nodded, as if she'd had experiences of her own with Onkel Zeb. She shook the tablecloth out. "Shall I take this in to Mammi?"

At his nod, Becky ran toward the house, taking it for granted that she would help. Caleb's young ones were being raised with a sense of responsibility, it seemed.

"Many hands make light work, yah?" Onkel Zeb said, as if he'd known what Aaron was thinking.

"Are we going to take the tables to the shed?" Timothy flexed his muscles. "I can help."

"We'll just stack them here and put them away later, I think," Onkel Zeb said tactfully. "How about you help your sister clean off the other table? Then we'll soon be done."

Nodding, Timothy scampered off, and Aaron found himself smiling. "They're gut kids. And Caleb is fortunate."

"Yah, that's so. Seems funny when you think that folks used to say that the King men weren't destined for true love. Now Caleb is happily married and Daniel soon to follow."

He'd forgotten that people had once talked that way. Well, his brothers had proved them wrong.

Onkel Zeb raised his eyebrows at Aaron. "And what about you? Is there no woman in your life?"

Aaron shrugged. "Not now." He evaded his uncle's gaze.

"But there was?" Zeb was gently persistent.

"There was." Aaron swung a bench onto the stack of tables. "Not anymore."

The words were enough to put a bad taste in his mouth. He'd thought Diana Lang cared about him. Turned out all she'd cared about was luring him away to train horses for her employer. It was actually kind of flattering, he supposed, that George Norton wanted his services as a trainer enough to go that far. But sulky racing was as competitive as any kind of racing, he guessed.

Maybe he hadn't actually been in love with Diana, but betrayal hurt anyway. To say nothing of humiliation.

Onkel Zeb had said nothing more, but he'd been studying Aaron's face. And Aaron suspected he was coming to his own conclusions. He always did, as much by what Aaron didn't say as by what he did say.

"Maybe you weren't meant to marry an Englischer," Onkel Zeb said at last. "Now that you're home, you'd maybe find someone a lot more suitable as a wife."

Was he thinking of Sally? Granted that his uncle had a gift for knowing what was going on in his nephews' minds, he surely couldn't think that. How could he know about that brief moment of attraction between him and Sally? No, he couldn't.

"I'm a long way from that. I'm not thinking any farther than a visit right now. Just…don't count on my staying. I don't know that it'll happen."

Onkel Zeb didn't seem perturbed. "Listen for God's voice. He'll make it clear, if you'll only listen."

The children came running back at that point, so Aaron didn't have to come up with an answer. Good thing, since he didn't have one.

"We're all finished," Becky announced.

"Gut job. Work is easy because everyone in the family does his or her share, ain't so?"

Aaron didn't know if that was aimed at him or not, but he figured he ought to make an effort. "Think I'll go see if Caleb will let me help with the milking. I believe I remember enough to be useful."

"Yah, you don't forget the things you learned as a boy." His uncle seemed pleased.

"I'll go with you, Onkel Aaron." Timothy grabbed his hand. "Sometimes I get to help a little. Daadi says when I'm bigger I can take over. How big do you think I'll have to be?"

"However big your daadi says," he replied. He wasn't going to start an argument by offering an opinion if he could help it.

Timothy didn't seem upset at the nonanswer. Maybe he hadn't expected anything else. He skipped alongside Aaron, chattering about the dairy herd and how he might have a calf to raise all by himself in the spring.

A nice kid. Caleb had done a fine job with his two, despite the problems caused by his first wife. They seemed to consider Jessie their mammi now, and maybe they didn't even remember much else. From what he'd seen so far, they couldn't ask for someone better. Jessie loved them and took care of them as if they were her own.

How different might his life have been if their father had remarried after they'd learned that their mother had died? But it probably was too late then. He'd already withdrawn from life when she left.

It was impossible to guess how different things might have been. Anyway, they'd had Onkel Zeb, and they'd gotten along all right, hadn't they?

Caleb might have suffered the most, he saw now that he looked at it from an adult viewpoint. He'd not only lost his mother and found his father unreachable, but he'd taken over responsibility for the dairy farm long before he'd normally have been expected to.

Aaron had never thought of feeling sorry for the big brother who'd bossed him around and always seemed so sure of himself. Funny that coming back was changing his ideas about a lot of things.

"Timothy? What are you doing?" Caleb's voice had an edge to it when he turned around and saw them together, and the sympathy Aaron had been feeling vanished.

Timothy didn't seem to notice, because he trotted to his father. "I brought Onkel Aaron to help with the milking, Daadi. He says he remembers how to do it."

"He does, does he?" Caleb patted his head. "We'll have to see if he really does, ain't so?"

Timothy grinned, maybe seeing it as a joke. But Aaron didn't like the measuring way Caleb was looking at him. More, he didn't think it had anything to do with whether or not he could help with the milking.

Caleb hadn't liked seeing his son chattering away to his renegade brother. Well, if that was how he felt about it, then it didn't matter how many times Caleb said he was welcome here, because Aaron would know it wasn't true. Bitterness took another bite out of his heart.

Sally walked home from school on Monday afternoon, with Becky and young Lige Mast skipping alongside her. Lige's older cousins were ahead of them, girls with their heads together, sharing secrets. The boys kicked stones as they went along, playing some game of their own.

Some things never changed. Sally smiled. This little parade of scholars might just as easily have been her, her brothers and sisters, the King boys, and the other neighboring kids, all walking along this same road years ago. As they came to each lane, a few would peel off for home. She glanced at the youngest two walking beside her.

"Don't forget to show your mammi the star you got on your spelling paper, Becky. And Lige, your mammi will be so pleased with the autumn picture you made." Lige had adjusted well to his new life, but he was still a little shy, and she tried always to give him a little extra reassurance.

"I'll show her first thing, Teacher Sally." Becky was looking pleased with herself. "Timothy says he wants to start school so he can get stars on his papers, too."

"I'm sure he will." She hoped so, anyway. Becky was a natural scholar with a love for reading that helped with her schoolwork. Sally would have to find out what young Timothy did well, so she could encourage him.

Lige didn't speak, but he smiled as he looked at the picture he held in careful hands.

"Look, there's Onkel Aaron," Becky exclaimed.

Sally's stomach was suddenly full of butterflies. Aaron leaned against the fence post at the end of her lane, looking as relaxed as if he intended to be there all afternoon. It didn't seem fair that he was so at ease when she felt as jittery as she had on her first day of school.

She watched him exchange greetings with the group of older kids, but he didn't move. He hadn't been waiting for them.

Lige ran ahead to go the rest of the way with his cousins, leaving her and Becky to come up to Aaron by themselves.

"Aaron. Are you waiting to walk Becky home from school?" she asked, reminding herself that she wasn't a giddy teenager any longer.

"Not Becky," he said, straightening. "It would be a pleasure, for sure, but I have other business today." He smiled at Becky, who grinned back.

"No?"

"No. I'm waiting to walk you home from school, Teacher Sally." It was said in his teasing voice, the one that had seemed lost since he'd been away. "Just like I used to."

"You never walked me home from school," she retorted, hanging on to her composure. "You let me tag along behind you and the other big boys, that's all."

"Well, then, it's time I started, ain't so?"

If he was trying to put her out of countenance, he was succeeding. She hoped she wasn't blushing.

Becky giggled. "You should carry her books, Onkel Aaron."

"I knew I was missing something." Before she could react, he'd taken her armload of books. He bent, picking up a faded duffel bag from the long grass. "Shall we go?"

He was trying to tease her, and if she reacted, he'd have succeeded. So she just nodded goodbye to Becky and started down the lane, very aware of Aaron matching steps with her.

When they'd gone a few yards she glanced back to see that Becky was skipping down the King lane, probably eager to repeat her news to the rest of the family.

She turned back to Aaron abruptly. "Enough teasing. Becky is out of sight, so you can give me my books back."

"I don't think so." He held them at arm's length, deliberately daring her to grab them.

She couldn't, because if she did, she risked touching him again. And given what had happened the last time, she wasn't about to take the chance.

"Fine. Carry them if you want to," she said. "But you should know that my sister-in-law is watching from the window."

That sobered him fast enough. He handed the books over. "Does she have binoculars or something?"

"Just a highly developed interest in everyone's affairs." She knew why now, but she couldn't say so to Aaron. Elizabeth was trying to fill up the hole in her heart where a baby should be. "She means well."

"If you say so." His voice held doubt. "Anyway, I have a good reason for being here…a first session with Star."

"Ach, that's wonderful gut." She'd wondered if he'd try to get out of it, but apparently not. "I'll have to run in the house to change my shoes and leave my books. Then I'll get Star from the barn."

She hurried on ahead to the house. Aaron was the answer to all her problems with the horse—she just knew it. Any other reasons for her pleasure in seeing him she'd push down and ignore. At least Aaron had understood why her own buggy horse was important to her, and he wouldn't let her down.

Sally raced into the house, parrying Elizabeth's questions, and hurried upstairs to change out of her school shoes and into the pair she wore in the barn. Then she ran down again, half-afraid he'd get bored and leave if she weren't quick.

No fear of that, she found when she got outside. Aaron had already brought Star out and turned him into the paddock outside the barn. When Sally reached him, he was pulling things out of the duffel bag.

"A lunge line?" she questioned. "Don't you want to harness him up?"

"Nope." He picked up a lunging halter and propped a lunge whip against the rail fence.

"But it's with the buggy that he misbehaves. What's the point of working him on the lunge line?"

Aaron planted his fists on his hips and looked at her with that frozen expression. "Did you or did you not ask me to train this animal?" He waited for her response, and she knew what it had to be.

"Okay. Yah, I asked you. You're the expert. We'll do it your way."

"Gut." He relented, his face relaxing a bit. "If I want to fix Star's problems, I have to go back to the beginning and find out where he went wrong. It might seem like a waste of time to you, but it's necessary. You understand?"

"I guess I do." Once he put it that way, she could

apply the idea to what she did know about. "It's like teaching arithmetic. If a scholar gets in trouble with the advanced steps, it's usually because he or she didn't master one of the elementary ones. So we have to go back and take care of that before we can go on."

"So I'd guess you take your own time to work privately with the kid, right?"

"That's what it means to be a teacher."

Aaron seemed to study her face for a moment before he spoke. "You must be a very good teacher."

She shrugged, unaccountably embarrassed at his praise. "I guess it is like you and Star. If you care about something, you take as much time as you need to get it right, ain't so?"

"It's so." He gave her the first truly relaxed smile she'd seen from him yet, and her heart gave a deplorable flutter.

Fortunately, he didn't seem to have anything else to say, since he slipped between the rails to the paddock, intent now on the horse.

Sally held that warm moment of understanding close while she watched him. She could do it safely, because he was totally preoccupied with the gelding.

It wasn't hard to see how he'd landed in a job training horses for a living. As folks said, obviously that was what he was born to do.

Aaron talked softly to the horse as he attached the lunge line and got Star moving in a circle around him that widened slowly as he let out a little more of the line each time.

Star was skittish at first, inclined to resent the gentle taps of the lunge whip on his shoulder that kept him moving along. But after a few efforts to escape the control of the lunge line, he seemed to start paying attention. The first time he moved along properly, earning a relaxation of the shoulder taps, she wanted to cheer.

She didn't, of course. Nothing should disrupt the work that was going on. Aaron had been right at that. There was little purpose in trying to work the gelding in harness when he hadn't mastered the simplest steps.

Who had trained him initially? Whoever it was must have taken her uncle in completely, convincing him that this was a properly trained buggy horse. She smiled, shaking her head. Simon Stoltzfus was that rare creature—an Amish man without the inborn understanding of animals. Everyone had been right to be skeptical about his unexpected gift.

Aaron was wrapped up in what he was doing, his face intent on the animal, all of his movements steady and sure. His hands—one controlling the line, the other handling the lunge whip—never wavered. When Star, tiring, attempted to bolt, Aaron seemed to know it almost before it entered the animal's head, and he let the line out a few yards before slowly drawing Star's head back around.

She'd always liked watching a person do something well, and Aaron was an expert. More, that quicksilver temper of his had been totally submerged when he worked with the horse. She'd seen others lose their tempers at signs of rebellion, but not Aaron. He just kept bringing Star back to the task at hand, never faltering.

Sally wasn't sure how long she stood there, completely captivated by the dance between man and horse. At last Star was circling the paddock at the length of the line, obedient to the guidance of the line and the sound of Aaron's voice.

Aaron brought Star into a smaller and smaller circle until the gelding stood quietly next to him, letting Aaron pat him and murmur softly, much as he had that day on the road. Then they came toward her.

Sally let go of her grip on the top railing, surprised by the indentations in her palms from the board. She must really have been concentrating not to realize how tight a grip she'd had.

"Wonderful gut," she said when they reached her. She reached out to pat Star's neck. "I can see how you got a job at a racing stable. You'd be an asset to any horse business." She hesitated. "Are they holding your place for you?"

She shouldn't have asked the question—she could see that by the way his face tightened.

"No." He cut off the word.

And cut off, too, anything else Sally might ask. For the past hour he'd been almost transformed as he'd worked with the horse, intent but open. Now that hostile, closed-down look was back on his face.

Something had gone wrong out there in the place he'd made for himself. Something that hurt him. He might think he could outrun it by coming here, but she knew better. Her own experience had taught her a hard lesson. A person couldn't just walk—or run—away from trouble. The only way to get rid of it, to keep it from eating you up, was to face it.

Aaron wouldn't do that unless he had to. Someone would have to push him into it.

Chapter Four

Aaron drew the family buggy up to the back porch the next morning in a driving rain. The wind and thunder of the previous night had passed, but the rain lingered, hard enough that Jessie hadn't wanted Becky to walk to school.

So she'd recruited him. No problem. He'd drop the kids off at the school and be on his way back, probably not even seeing Sally in passing.

It wasn't that he was avoiding her. But…

The back door rattled, and Caleb came out, standing just under the roof overhang. "Sorry," he said, his manner stiff. "Jessie shouldn't have asked you to take the kinder. I can do it."

Once again, it seemed Caleb didn't want him around the kids. What did he think Aaron was going to do? The words hovered on his tongue when Becky came running out, her schoolbooks wrapped in a plastic bag to protect them.

"I'm ready, Onkel Aaron," she sang out.

"Me, too. I don't get many chances to drive a pretty

girl to school." And if Caleb didn't like it, he could be the one to make a move. "Hop on in."

But Caleb apparently didn't have anything else to say on the subject. He hoisted his daughter up the high step and into the enclosed buggy, where she settled on the back seat.

"Mammi says don't forget to stop next door," she said, obviously feeling important that she got to deliver the message.

"I won't, not with you to remind me." He clucked to the mare and she moved on a little reluctantly, no more eager to be out in the rain than anyone else. Apparently the two families shared taking the children to school in bad weather.

With Becky talking away and asking him questions, he didn't have a minute to think until after he'd picked up the youngsters at the Fisher place, including Lige, Daniel's future stepson. Once they'd all piled in, they chattered away together.

Now he had a chance to think about Caleb's reaction to his taking the children to school, and he wasn't sure he wanted to.

Did his brother think Aaron would be a bad influence on them? That becoming close to him might lead them to want to jump the fence? That seemed just plain silly, given how young they were. But what else could it be?

Irritated, he put Caleb's reactions out of his mind. Unfortunately, that seemed to leave room for Teacher Sally to slip in.

Things had turned awkward between them yesterday, and much as he'd like to blame Sally, he had to admit that he shared the fault. Face it, he was supersensitive when it came to the reason he'd left his job. The very subject made him cringe. He wasn't ready to talk about it to anyone, and he didn't know if he ever would be. Sally was just too inquisitive.

But not rude. He was the one who'd been rude, basically snubbing her when she'd asked about it.

By the time he reached the white frame schoolhouse, he'd convinced himself he ought to speak to her, at least. He ought to tell her that he wouldn't be there to work with the gelding today, anyway. Star would have to learn to behave in bad weather eventually, of course, but it was too early to take on that lesson.

So, instead of dropping the kids off, he jumped out and ran through the rain with them, spurting through the door into the vestibule that included places for wet coats and muddy boots. After wiping his shoes on the mat, Aaron opened the door into the classroom.

Instead of the orderly rows of students he expected, they all seemed to be milling around. No, that wasn't it, he realized after he watched for a moment. All of the hurrying around was purposeful, and he understood why when he found Sally struggling with the large bowl she'd pushed under a steady drip of water from the roof.

"That looks bad." He bent to help her position the bowl. "This thing will be full before you know it. Do you have a bucket?"

"Yah, two, thankfully. I sent one of the older boys to bring them from the shed. Denke, Aaron."

She stood up, looking around at the mess caused by water running in, probably since sometime in the night. Her scholars were already organized, some of them removing things from the path of the water while a couple of the older girls had set to work with mops. Apparently he didn't need to come to the rescue. Little Sally was all grown-up now, and she could take care of problems herself. The realization left him feeling oddly useless.

"I'll go outside and see if I can spot the problem." Aaron headed for the door. "It's probably a missing shingle, torn loose in that wind last night."

He ducked back out in the rain, grateful for the protection offered by the black felt Amish hat Daniel had lent him. In fact, Daniel had given him most of what he had on. The clothes he'd left behind had mostly been pitifully small on him now, and it hadn't seemed appropriate to go around in denim.

Aaron had to go around to the side to get a view of the roof, where a quick glance confirmed his suspicions. A good-sized branch had come off the black walnut tree, hitting the roof and taking several shingles with it. Fixing it would be a job for ladders and new shingles, at least.

He returned to the schoolroom to find Sally appointing a couple of the oldest boys to watch the buckets and switch them out whenever one got full.

"Yah, Teacher Sally."

"Yah, Teacher Sally."

Funny to see Sally in the teacher role, but clearly the children accepted her readily. She glanced up and met his eyes.

"How does the roof look?" She came toward him, frowning a little when she took in how wet he'd gotten.

"Nasty. A heavy branch came down on the roof and took several shingles with it. I can't tell how bad it is without going up there."

"Not now." Sally spoke to him in her teacher voice—quietly authoritative.

He found he was grinning. "Not worried about me, are you? I've been on higher roofs than that." It was worth teasing her to see the sparkle in her eyes.

"No one goes up on the schoolhouse roof in the pouring rain," she said. "Including you." She smiled suddenly. "Besides, if you did, I'd have half the boys convinced they can climb up, as well."

"I'd tell them not to." He didn't really intend to go up, knowing there was little he could do without the proper tools and equipment.

"And they'd listen about as well as you did at that age," she retorted.

Aaron realized that Becky was standing at his elbow, looking from one face to another as they spoke.

"Did you go to this school, Onkel Aaron?"

"Yah, of course I did." He pointed to one of the bigger desks in the back row. "I sat right there. And Teacher Sally was on the opposite side almost to the front."

Becky seemed to look at the schoolroom with new eyes. "So you were in school together. That's why you said about walking her home yesterday."

"We all walked to school together," Sally said. "Your daadi and your onkels, and all the kids from the Fisher farm as well as me and my brothers and sisters."

"That's a lot." Her eyes widened. "We don't have so many now."

"Your brother will be coming to school before you know it," Sally said briskly. "Now, I think it's time we got the desks back in place so we can start." She clapped her hands for attention and gave her directions.

That seemed to be the signal for him to leave. He couldn't stand here all day reminiscing.

"I'd best go, unless there's something else I can do to help. I really came in to say we'd better skip working with Star today."

"Yah, I think you'll have gotten wet enough by then," she said. She was walking beside him to the door, and once they were inside the coatroom she paused. "One thing you can do is let Caleb know about the leak. He's on the school board, you know."

"No, I didn't know, but I'll tell him." He wasn't surprised that Caleb would have taken on that responsibility. That was his nature.

He should go, but Aaron found he was studying her face, trying to see the girl he'd known in the teacher. The voices of the children seemed far away.

"Thank you. I appreciated your help." Sally sounded breathless, and her blue eyes darkened under his steady gaze.

So. It didn't even take a touch. That spark of attraction was there even at a look. He'd better get out of range. Maybe the chilly rain would splash some common sense into him.

When the school day had ended Sally lingered, glad to have a little quiet time to clear up and get her school back the way she felt it should be. Her school. At first she hadn't been able to think of it that way, but by the end of her first year of teaching it had become hers.

Now the schoolhouse felt like a personal responsibility—her duty and her pleasure to keep it spotless and welcoming.

The water had splashed some of the books on the

bottom shelf of the bookcase, and she was thankful it hadn't penetrated to the pages. She removed each volume, spreading it out carefully so the binding could dry.

Sally stroked the cover of a copy of *Anne of Green Gables*, long one of her favorite books. She'd always identified with Anne, understanding her lively personality, her vivid imagination and even her irrepressible tongue.

"A favorite book?"

She whirled at the rumble of the masculine voice. Aaron stood in the doorway, watching her with a smile.

"You startled me. I didn't expect anyone."

"Caleb sent Daniel and me to patch up the roof." He gestured toward the open door behind him, and she realized that the King wagon was pulling up to the side of the schoolhouse.

"That's kind of you." She tried to speak evenly, hoping she hadn't given away the wave of sudden pleasure she'd felt at the sight of him.

Aaron's lips quirked. "Daniel's the carpenter. I think he'll let me hold the ladder."

"Aaron, what's keeping you?" Daniel's call floated into the school. "Get out here and help me unload."

He shrugged. "Orders." He turned, and Sally followed him as far as the doorway.

She waved at Daniel. "This is wonderful kind of you both."

Daniel gave her his easy grin. "We can't have our teacher getting wet, now, can we? I told Caleb this roof needs replacing, so we'll be setting up a work frolic soon. Maybe Saturday, yah?"

She nodded, her thoughts hurrying to what she

might have to do to get ready. "You'll tell me what I should move and cover, ain't so?"

"I won't let him make a mess today, at least," Aaron said. He pulled a toolbox from the wagon bed. "Don't worry."

She retreated to the classroom and went back to the books with a wary look at the ceiling. In her experience, when men got working on a project they sometimes didn't pay any attention to the debris they left behind. If they were going to do a work frolic on Saturday to replace the roof, she'd have to ask some of the mothers to help her put things away on Friday.

Working on, she listened with half her attention to the talk between Aaron and his brother. With Daniel, Aaron seemed to have established a quick, easy relationship. It was only with Caleb that she still sensed the tension between them.

As for her... Well, if she could ease his transition back to Amish life, she'd be satisfied, she told herself firmly.

It occurred to Sally that those words sounded very self-sacrificing. Were they? There might be a little self-interest in her longing to have Aaron settled here where he belonged...where she'd see him frequently.

After a bit, the hammering over her head ceased, and she heard the sounds of the ladder being taken down, and a thud as something went into the wagon. It sounded as if they were finished for the moment. She walked to the door to find Daniel coming in search of her.

"That should hold for now. Want a ride home? We can squeeze you in."

"Denke, Daniel, but I still have cleaning up to do. You'll let me know about Saturday?"

"Yah, for sure. We'll be off, then."

But when the wagon drove out, Aaron wasn't on it. He exchanged a few words with Daniel, and then he came back to the school.

"I'll help you finish."

She hesitated, wondering whether being alone in the schoolhouse was the best of ideas. But Aaron didn't wait for permission. He walked into the classroom and picked up the overflowing wastebasket.

"I see what you meant about the mess." He glanced around. "Tell me what to do."

It seemed she didn't have a choice. "If you'll pull that bookcase away from the wall, I'll see if it's wet underneath. I don't want any mold getting into the books."

"Of course not. Always with your nose in a book, that's Sally," he teased. "I remember that about you."

"That's how you learn things," she said tartly. She wasn't the little kid he could tease any longer, and he may as well start remembering it.

His suddenly serious expression caught her off balance. "You were wiser than I was, Teacher Sally. It took me years and some loneliness to find the riches in books."

It was the closest he'd come to being open about his time away, and instinct told her he'd clam up if she made too much about it. "Teacher Esther would be proud of you, no matter how long it took."

He nodded, gazing around the classroom as if seeing it as it had been years ago. "Remember how she used to read poetry to us? I could never see sense to it, until I found it on my own."

Unaccountably moved, Sally struggled for control. She didn't speak until she thought she could sound natural. "Robert Frost was always my favorite. When we have our first snow, I'll read…"

"'*Stopping By Woods on a Snowy Evening,*'" he said, smiling a little. "I know."

"Yah." She was almost afraid to let their eyes meet. It was becoming too dangerous to her peace of mind.

Maybe Aaron felt the same, because his voice changed. "When I sat back there, all I did was watch the clock."

"Or think up mischief," she added. It seemed the right moment to ask the question that troubled her. "Were you planning on leaving even then?"

"Then?" He looked startled. "No, I don't think so. I was a bit older when I started feeling there was more to life than the farm and being bossed around by Caleb."

So. She'd guessed that was at the heart of his relationship with his big brother. She chose her words carefully. "Caleb had a lot of responsibility thrust on him when he was very young to handle it. I guess it's natural that you'd clash."

He'd been gathering up discarded papers, and his hands froze for an instant. Then he pushed them firmly into the trash bag he held. He finished before he let himself look at her.

"You saw a lot, little Sally."

"I keep telling you. I'm not little Sally any longer."

"No, you're not." He studied her for a long moment, and then he smiled. It was the full, genuine smile she kept longing to see, and it moved her entirely too much.

Careful, be careful. A lecture to himself was definitely in order. He couldn't unburden himself to anyone, including—no, make that especially—Sally. A man with nothing to give and an uncertain future might be drawn to her warmth and sympathy, but it was entirely too dangerous.

"Well, this bag is about full." He turned away from her smile. "I'll run it out to the trash cans. Anything else you have ready to go?"

"No, I think that's it." Sally didn't seem to notice the abrupt change in conversation. "I still have to check all the desks that were near the leak to make sure the damp didn't get into anything."

"Didn't you have your scholars check their desks?"

Her dimple returned. "Would you rely on them to be sure nothing was damp?"

"Come to think of it, I guess I wouldn't. At least if they're anything like I was at that age."

Sally was chuckling as he carted the trash bag out. That should mean she hadn't noticed anything about his reaction to her. Good. He deposited the bag in the bin and paused for a moment to scan the still-overcast sky. More rain was probably coming. Daniel's patching might well be tested.

When he got back inside, he found Sally carefully checking everything in a child's desk, touching each item. Following her lead, he started on one of the larger desks.

They worked in silence for a time. When he heard the patter of rain against the windows, he glanced up and saw Sally's look of alarm.

"A gentle rain shouldn't be a problem," he said. "I'd say leave the bucket where it is until morning, though."

She nodded. "Normally I like the sound of raindrops. But not when they're coming through the roof of my school."

"Possessive, aren't you?"

"I guess I am. I've been teaching long enough to feel as if it's mine."

"I can understand that." He glanced across the rows of desks. "Looks like you have more little ones than older scholars this year."

"Yah. It makes it difficult to hold the interest of the older ones when there are so few. But I've found they respond well when I gear their work to what they want to do after leaving school."

The intent look on her face fascinated him. More to see it again than because he was interested in educational theory, he pursued the idea.

"How do you do that? Not bringing in lessons in milking, are you?"

"Very funny." She made a face at him. "No, I stress the importance of knowing how to keep records, figure out profits and assess costs. You might be surprised at all of the book work involved nowadays. If a scholar can see how math and writing will help in his future as a farmer or small business owner, he's likely to stay interested."

He found he was looking at her with respect. "If I'd had a teacher like you, I might have paid a bit more attention in school."

"It's what I'm meant to do, I think." She hesitated. "Just as working with horses is what you're meant to do." She hurried on before he could speak. "I'm not prying about your job or why you left it. Really."

"You don't have to worry. I'm not going to bite your head off again." He frowned, not because he was angry but because he struggled for words. "I don't want to talk because it was a bad experience. It left me feeling… I don't know. Hurt, shamed, I guess. You couldn't understand." And just that much was more than he'd ever intended to say.

Sally stood very still, a book in her hands, her gaze on him. "I understand better than you know." Again she hesitated, almost as if deciding whether she wanted to trust him.

Finally she put the book down and closed the desk. "When I was nineteen, Frederick Yoder asked me to be his wife. You remember him?"

"Freddy Yoder? Isaac's little brother?"

She nodded. "I said yes. I thought… Ach, I'm not sure I thought at all. My friends were pairing off, and I thought I was in love, too. That can happen easily at that age."

If Fred Yoder had jilted her—

But she went on. "Two weeks before the wedding, I woke up and realized what I was doing. I liked Fred. I still do. But I didn't love him, and I couldn't spend the rest of my life with him."

He was swamped with sympathy for her. "You couldn't marry him if you felt that way."

"No. It wouldn't be fair to either of us." Sally took a deep breath. Obviously it still hurt to relive that time. "I told my parents, and I told Fred. It was…hard. But we canceled the plans, told everyone we'd changed our minds."

"And people gossiped. Wondered." He could see that happening. It was the reverse side of the caring in a small, close community.

She nodded. "Word got around, of course. A lot of people blamed me. Called me a flirt and worse." She shrugged, shaking her head. "I survived, thanks to my family. But when it comes to feeling hurt and shamed—yah, I know how that is."

Her voice shook a little on the last sentence. Moved, he clasped her hands in a comforting grip. Anyone would do the same, he told himself. "I'm sorry. It must have been hard for you."

"And for Fred," she added. "But he recovered." Her voice lightened. "He married Peggy Brandt, and they have twin boys now."

"And did you recover?" He studied her face, wondering how much of her pert liveliness was meant to hide her feelings.

"Of course." She said it lightly. Seeming to realize that he still held her hands, she pulled them away. "I learned a lesson. Isn't that what bad experiences are meant to do? Adults always say that. I learned not to let my head be overruled by my feelings."

If she really had learned that, he couldn't help thinking that it was a shame, because if there was ever anyone meant to love and be loved, it surely was Sally.

Chapter Five

Sally decided it was a fine thing that she didn't see much of Aaron for a couple of days. Had she totally embarrassed him, as well as herself, by telling him about Fred?

He'd been sympathetic, that was certain. She could still feel the warm grip of his hands on hers. But had he realized she was just trying to explain why she could understand his feelings? Or had he thought she was trying to draw attention to herself? Her cheeks burned at the thought.

"Sally, are you going to hand me that butter or stand there holding it until supper?" Elizabeth's tart voice brought her back to reality in a hurry.

"Sorry. I was thinking." She handed over the butter, hoping Elizabeth was too busy to wonder what distracted her.

"It must have been something serious to have you that deep in thought. Something about the school? Or that silly horse?"

She should have known better. Elizabeth was never too busy to be curious.

"Yah, something that happened at the school." That was true enough.

"From what your brother says, they'll have that new roof on in no time on Saturday. As if he didn't have enough to do here."

Sally held her breath for a moment. "Everyone wants to help," she said, ignoring Elizabeth's tone. Did she resent the school because she had no children to go there? Somehow the revelation of Elizabeth's disappointment and pain had her thinking twice about everything she said.

"Well, I think…"

Elizabeth stopped, because Sally was already halfway to the door.

"Aaron's on his way. I have to get Star ready." She escaped before Elizabeth could point out that the horse was already in the paddock.

Was she trying to evade Elizabeth or eager to see Aaron? She pushed the question to the back of her mind for consideration later. After all, Aaron was doing her a favor by working with Star. The least she could do was help him.

She reached the paddock at the same time as Aaron. "I wasn't sure you'd come today. If you have things to do at the farm…"

"Not much." He bit off the words, frowning. "But speaking of things to do, you don't need to stay out here. I'm just going to work him on the lunge line again today, anyway."

He didn't need her, in other words. Or maybe didn't want her was closer to the truth.

"Yah, fine." She could be as snappish as he was. She

swung around, but she hadn't taken more than a step before he said her name.

"Sally, wait. Sorry. I guess I got up on the wrong side of the bed today. Forgive me?"

The contrite tone made her smile. "Of course."

Not that she believed his mood had anything to do with which side of the bed he'd arisen from. Something was troubling him, but if he didn't want to tell her, she couldn't pry.

She'd learned her lesson. No more trying to get him to talk to her, but that didn't mean she'd ever stop wondering what had happened to him out there in the Englisch world.

Apparently to make up for his bad mood, Aaron talked as he put Star through his paces, explaining the steps he intended to take with the horse.

"He's responding well to voice commands," he said after an intensive twenty minutes of work. "Let's see how he reacts to the unexpected." He glanced around. "Will anyone care if you break a leafy branch off that lilac bush?"

"Not now. It'd be another story if Mamm's favorite dark purple lilacs were blooming." Seeing what he was about, Sally pulled off a long spray and took it to the paddock.

"Gut. Now when I lead him past, wave the branch off to the side."

Sally obeyed, apprehensive. Sure enough, Star reared at the sight, his eyes rolling. Aaron quieted him with voice and touch.

Catching Sally's expression, he smiled. "He'll do much better with blinders on. I just wanted to see if that side view was what set him off."

They went on to take turns leading Star past a variety of objects. Once he'd settled down, Aaron led him out of the paddock and over to where the buggies were parked, talking casually.

Star stopped, his ears pricking forward, but then he responded to that low, steady voice and walked on. Sally, following, decided it was not too surprising. If Aaron spoke to her in that warm, soft tone, she'd probably do the same.

When they'd circled all the buggies several times, Aaron stopped, letting the rope go slack. Star, apparently deciding he was done, dropped his head and began cropping the grass.

"That'll do for today." Aaron patted the gelding on the shoulder, but his gaze was on Sally. "He's coming along better than I feared. Next time we'll try working him with parts of the harness on. After school all right?"

"I can't be here then." She felt a sharp pang of regret. "Some of the women are coming to help me cover everything in the schoolhouse to prepare for the roof project the next day."

"You don't trust us not to make a mess, in other words." He gave her his rare smile. "You're probably wise. Okay if I work Star anyway?"

"Yah, for sure." She swallowed disappointment. She hadn't realized how much she'd been looking forward to these sessions. Well, there was nothing wrong with that, was there? It was natural to want to spend time with an old friend after all these years.

She was still telling herself that when she waved goodbye to Aaron and headed back to the house and paused to wash her hands at the outside sink. Elizabeth wouldn't want hands smelling like horse in her kitchen.

Elizabeth was setting the table for supper, and she hurried to take the plates.

"I'll take care of that, Elizabeth. I haven't been around much to help you lately."

"You have your work to keep you busy." Elizabeth's normally ruddy face grew a bit redder. "But spending so much time with Aaron King—that's not your job, and it certain sure isn't a gut idea."

Sally counted to five before she spoke. "Aaron is training Star for me without charging. The least I can do is help him, ain't so?"

"Ach, Sally, don't you see what's happening to you? You're always so sensible about men since what happened with Fred, but you flew out of here like a bird when you saw Aaron coming. Don't bother to tell me you're not attracted to him, because I wouldn't believe it."

Only the fact that there was genuine concern behind Elizabeth's sharp voice kept Sally from flaring out at her. This time she counted to ten.

"Aaron is an old friend. If I can do something to ease his way back into Amish life, I should do it."

"What makes you think he wants back into Amish life?" Elizabeth planted her hands on her hips. "He ran away before because he wanted the excitement out in the world. What happens when he starts wanting excitement again?"

"Maybe he won't."

"And maybe he will. You spending time with Aaron is just going to make folks talk. If you don't care about that, your brother and I have to, or what would your mamm and daad say?" Her face softened in time to avert an explosion on Sally's part. "Think about it, Sally. And then about how you'd feel if you gave your heart to him and he went away again."

"That's nonsense." She couldn't listen to any more. "I'm not going to give my heart to anyone. I'm not that foolish, no matter what you think."

Brave words. A month ago she'd have meant them. Unfortunately, she wasn't sure they were true any longer.

Every family in the church district naturally wanted to participate in putting the new roof on their school. Aaron and his brothers and Zeb managed to be the first to arrive on Saturday morning, but a steady stream of wagons and buggies pulled in behind them.

Aaron glanced over the line of buggies. "Almost looks like a church Sunday. We'll have plenty of helpers."

"For sure. We'll get it done in no time." Daniel grinned. "We have enough help that Onkel Zeb doesn't need to go up on the roof."

Zeb gave him a mock glare. "Don't you go saying I'm old, Daniel King. I can work as well as the next man."

"You can, but give the younger guys a chance. They need to show off for their wives and girlfriends, you know."

Aaron slid down from the wagon and led the buggy horse to the improvised hitching post. A buggy pulled in right next to him, and in moments, the normally quiet school was a hive of activity. Ezra Brandt, who claimed to have raised more barns than any man in the county, took charge of organizing the workers and materials.

It wasn't long before Aaron had his assignment. He grabbed a pry bar and started up the ladder behind Daniel. If he hung out with his brother the carpenter, he shouldn't make any foolish mistakes.

Removing the old roof was the first order of business. Shreds of shingles and tar paper began to fly, and Aaron knew Sally had been right to anticipate a mess. Still, no one would leave the site until the school was ready for business again on Monday.

"Done any roofing work while you were away?" Daniel pulled off a long strip of tar paper.

"Nothing like this." He put his back into pulling out a stubborn nail. "I did a little mending now and then when it was needed. Most of the guys would pitch in wherever something had to be done, although some of them didn't know one end of a hammer from the other."

"I trust you showed them." Caleb, working on the other side of him, surprised him by joining the conversation.

"I tried." Aaron shrugged. "Seems like growing up on a farm means you learn how to do a lot of things. I took it for granted that everyone does, too, but they don't."

"They must know horses, if they worked for a stable," Daniel said.

"Most of them had some experience," Aaron admitted. "If they didn't, the boss figured that out fast and got rid of them. But they weren't what I'd call handy."

"I'm glad to know you found some benefit from working on the farm."

He wasn't sure if there was sarcasm in Caleb's comment or not. Remembering what Sally had said about him, Aaron decided to give him the benefit of the doubt.

"That wasn't the only good thing," he said mildly.

The three of them worked in silence for a time, side by side. It was a surprisingly comfortable silence.

Aaron glanced down at the schoolyard. Onkel Zeb was supervising a group of boys who were hauling the debris away and stacking it, while the women and girls were already organizing lunch.

"Seriously, how did you convince Onkel Zeb not to climb up on the roof?" he asked.

Caleb shook his head. "I didn't. That was Jessie. She persuaded him that he was needed more down there."

"He never turns Jessie down," Daniel added. "I think she could ask him anything."

"Yah." Caleb sent a worried glance down at the group of women. "I wish I could have talked her into not coming today, but she was set on being here."

"I'd guess the other women won't let her do too much." Aaron thought that was as close as he should come to mention Jessie's obvious pregnancy.

Caleb nodded, maybe finding comfort in the thought.

The three of them moved to another row of shingles, working steadily. Aaron listened to the flow of Pennsylvania Dutch, punctuated by frequent laughter. There was a reason they called it a work frolic—the Amish found enjoyment in doing a project like this together. He'd forgotten.

It wasn't that folks in the outside world didn't get together to do good things. The boss had organized a crew to work on a Habitat for Humanity house just last year, and most of the guys had contributed their time. Enjoyed it, too.

But that had been something special in their lives. This was routine. If a job needed to be done, the community didn't wait to be asked. They just came together and did it.

Aaron stretched, looking around, surprised by how much they'd accomplished already.

"We're almost ready to start putting the new roof on," he said. "That's fast."

Daniel looked up with his ready smile. "You should have seen us when we raised a barn for Sam Fisher. Now, that was a big project, and it was ready for use by sundown."

Aaron looked suitably impressed. "I noticed the new barn. What happened to the old one?"

"Fire," Caleb said shortly.

"That was when Caleb had his accident," Daniel added.

"Not my favorite memory," Caleb grumbled.

"If you hadn't broken your leg, Jessie wouldn't have come to mind the kinder. And you wouldn't be happily married now," Daniel said. "I'd guess that's worth a broken leg."

"Onkel Zeb said it was God's plan working out." Caleb stopped working for a moment, his expression considering. "I thought maybe He could have found a less painful way."

"Not a chance. You're so stubborn it's a wonder the gut Lord didn't hit you with a two-by-four," Daniel said.

Aaron decided he'd have to give that idea some

thought. In spite of Caleb's grumbling, Aaron knew he'd take a broken leg in a second to have his Jessie.

Maybe God had some plan in mind that included the painful things that had happened to him, Aaron thought. But he'd just as soon decide his future for himself. Wouldn't he?

He edged away from that thought, looking across the group gathered in the schoolyard again. His gaze snagged on Sally. She was bending over Jessie, helping her into a chair she'd brought out from the schoolroom. Caring...that was typical of Sally.

Even as he thought it, Sally looked up as if she'd heard his thought. Her gaze seemed to be drawn to his. Even across the distance between them, he felt its impact.

She turned away to say something to Jessie, so quickly that he felt he might have imagined that moment. He turned resolutely back to the work.

When the men started to come down the ladders, the flow of activity around the tables reached fever pitch. Sally, keeping a wary eye on Jessie, saw neighbor Leah Fisher intercept Jessie when she attempted to pick up a tray. Arm around Jessie, Leah steered her away.

Relieved, Sally grabbed a tray laden with sandwiches and headed for the picnic tables. Obviously other people besides her had noticed how tired Jessie looked. Her thoughts flew to the midwife, and she hoped Jessie's household of men had sense enough to call at the right time.

As she circulated around the tables, Sally made an attempt to speak to everyone, thanking each person for helping out today. Most of them turned her thanks away with a joke or a laugh, but she wouldn't want anyone to think she didn't appreciate their efforts. The school gained its strength from the willing support of the community, and she'd never want that to change.

The King family was sitting at one end of a picnic table—at least the male part of it was. Becky, looking solemn and self-conscious, was carrying away used dishes.

Timothy and Lige, his soon-to-be cousin, seemed equally impressed to be eating with the workers. Sally paused to tap each one on his hat, earning a quick grin from Timothy and a shy smile from Lige.

"I saw how hard you two were working. Onkel Zeb kept you busy, ain't so?"

Zeb, sitting next to the boys, gave them a fond look. "They are gut workers, both of them. I'm fortunate to have two such strong helpers."

Timothy swelled with importance at the words. "We are strong, Teacher Sally. Look at the big pile we made of the shingles and tar paper." He pointed a small finger at the stack of debris, situated so that it could easily be loaded onto a wagon and hauled away.

"That's very impressive. And we'll be sehr glad not to worry about the rain getting into the schoolroom when you're done."

"Yah, we don't want our teacher getting wet," Daniel said, reaching across to rest his hand for a moment on Lige's shoulder.

"Or our scholars missing any class time," Caleb added. "Hope you didn't lose anything important to the water, Teacher Sally."

"Nothing that can't be replaced," she said. "At least the books have dried out without damage."

"We all know how important the books are to the teacher." Aaron's smile seemed to warm her. "She treasures those more than anything."

"Some of us learn to love reading early," she retorted. "And others are late bloomers."

"What's a late bloomer?" Timothy asked.

Caleb chuckled. "I think she means that your onkel Aaron never read anything he didn't have to when he was in school."

Timothy fixed wide blue eyes on Aaron. "But you have some books in your room. I saw them."

"That's right." Aaron actually looked a little embarrassed. "It took me some growing up to learn how much books had to offer me. You'll be better off if you learn to like reading early."

"Mammi reads to us every night," he said. "I'll like learning to read, but…" A trace of dismay crossed his face.

Sally patted him, understanding. "Mammi will still read to you at night, even after you can read for yourself. You don't have to worry about that."

"That's right," Caleb said. "Teacher Sally has the right of it. Mammi loves to read to you."

"Yah." Timothy's face cleared. "She does."

Sally couldn't help glancing at Aaron. He was watching her with Timothy, and his expression was so tender that it made her breath catch. He might not be ready to admit it, but everything he wanted was right here with his family. Whether it included her or not.

She straightened, realizing that Daniel was elbowing Caleb. Oops. She wasn't sure how much they'd noticed, but if she wanted to avoid people talking about her, she'd have to start being careful now.

"I'd best get back to work," she said, giving the kinder a smile. "Everyone needs a hearty lunch in order to finish the roof."

Moving away, she tried not to look at Aaron. She was being foolish, reading so much into every glance. She'd do better to focus on things she could do something about, like taking the desserts around.

A half hour later, most folks had finished eating, and there was a gradual movement back to the work area. Apparently, they were ready to start putting the new roofing in place. It looked as if they'd be finished in time for her and her volunteers to do some cleaning up inside. She'd have to put in as much work as possible today, since tomorrow was the Sabbath.

She'd avoided looking inside the schoolhouse thus far, but finally she just had to take a peek. Standing in the doorway, all she could do was shake her head. Thankfully they'd covered everything, because the tarps and the floor were littered with scraps of tar paper, shingles and the dust that must have been accumulating for a few years.

"I see what you mean about a mess." Aaron's voice, so close behind her, startled her. She swung around to find him inches away.

"I didn't hear you." Sally tried for a natural tone, but the words had come out sounding oddly breathless. "Did…does someone want me?"

Aaron's eyes twinkled. "Probably. But I thought you might want to know how I made out with Star yesterday."

"Oh. Yes, of course." She eased backward a step so she could breathe. "Elizabeth said you'd been there working. How did Star react to the harness?"

He still had an amused look in his eyes, as if he knew full well why she'd backed up. "Better than I thought. He's been harnessed before, so he worked pretty well. He didn't like it when I put the blinders on, though."

"No. He did a lot of head tossing when I tried it."

"A good sign he needs them. He's too distracted by what he sees in his peripheral vision. I worked him for about fifteen minutes on the lunge line with them. He settled down eventually. I'll work him a bit more that way, and then we can try ground-driving him."

She nodded. *We*, he'd said. It sounded as if she'd get to participate. "Sounds gut. Tomorrow's Sunday, so Monday?"

"Yah, I guess." Something wary had crossed his face at the mention of the Sabbath.

Sally hesitated for a moment, but she couldn't seem to help one little question. "Will you be going to worship tomorrow?"

He nodded. "I have to, don't I? I can't be here and stay away."

"You don't need to brace yourself as if it's going to be a battle," she said. "I'm sure everyone will wilkom you."

"Everyone? You really think so?" He sounded skeptical. "I'd guess there will be a few who aren't so eager to see the bad boy back."

"Nonsense." The fear that he might be right gave extra emphasis to her voice. "Nobody would…" The rest of the sentence faded as she saw Elizabeth standing on the porch behind Aaron.

"Sally. We could use your help." She divided a disapproving look between the two of them. It looked as if Sally were in for a lecture.

A wave of defiance swept through her, startling her. She wasn't doing anything wrong, and she wouldn't let anyone make her feel guilty.

Head held high, she marched out of the schoolroom.

Chapter Six

Aaron's stomach lurched as Caleb turned the buggy into the lane of the Miller farm, and it wasn't because of the sharp turn. He was on his way to worship for the first time in more years than he wanted to think about.

As they drove up the lane toward the barn, he saw the lineup of buggies parked along one side of the barn. One after another they stood there, a visible symbol of the Amish at worship. Horses and buggies... Onkel Zeb always said that was one of the things that kept the community together. He hadn't had much time for that idea when he'd been a teenager, longing to be behind the wheel of a car.

As soon as Caleb pulled up near the wide door to the barn, two teenage boys, probably Josh Miller's kids, came running to take the buggy and park it. They'd take care of the horses, as well. The kids in the host family always had plenty to do on worship Sunday. Aaron caught a curious look directed at him, and he figured he'd better brace himself for plenty more.

Sally had been naive when she'd snapped at him on that subject. Or else she was just so tenderhearted herself that she couldn't imagine others wouldn't be as welcoming as she was. But he didn't have any illusions.

The curiosity would be bad enough. He'd be surprised if he didn't encounter outright hostility. Probably a few people had thought "good riddance" when they'd heard he was gone. He'd had a reputation as a teen, and careful families hadn't wanted their daughters anywhere near him.

None of his family seemed to be talking much, making him wonder if they were apprehensive about what was to come. Still, usually folks were fairly quiet when they gathered for worship, as he recalled. Afterward, during lunch, there'd be time for visiting and catching up on all the news.

He followed his brothers and his uncle to the line that was forming along one side of the barn door. Onkel Zeb first, then Caleb holding Timothy by the hand, Daniel, and he brought up the rear. Jessie moved slowly to the line of women along the opposite side, with Becky skipping at her side. Jessie murmured something to her, and Becky slowed to a sedate walk.

Before he'd had a chance to look for familiar faces among the men, their line had begun to move. He was carried forward, taken inexorably along with the others to their seats on the men's side of the rows of benches ready for them. The routine of preparing for worship was as settled as the worship service itself.

The animals had been moved out, and the barn was as spotless as a barn could possibly be. He hated to think of the amount of work that involved. Most folks were glad they didn't have to host worship more than once a year.

He sat, trying to look at ease while he took surreptitious glances along the rows of faces. There was Amos Burkhalter, who'd been his closest friend in his class at school. He sat at the end of the row in front of them, with four little boys arranged next to him like a series of steps.

Was it actually possible that Amos, who'd been as prone to trouble as he'd been, was the father of all those kids? Who had been brave enough to take him on? He'd have to find out after the service.

The two ministers filed in and took their places, followed by Bishop Thomas Braun. Aaron had thought him old when he'd left, but he didn't look any different now. A few more gray hairs in his beard, maybe. Their gazes crossed, and Aaron looked at the floor quickly. He'd have to encounter the bishop sometime, he supposed, but he wasn't eager for the meeting.

The song leader started the long notes of the first hymn, and Daniel stuck a hymnbook into his hands. Actually he remembered the words, but Daniel wasn't taking any chances.

The long, slow cadence of the hymns was oddly comforting. They seemed to settle his mind. He took advantage of the moment to risk a sidelong look at the women's section. Becky was snuggled close to Jessie, and Leah Fisher sat on Jessie's other side. A row ahead of them he spotted Sally, realizing he'd know the back of her neck and her glossy hair under the sedate kapp no matter where she was.

Now, what was Sally doing sitting in the row with the young married women? She ought, by rights, to be with the unmarried girls.

Was this a tacit statement that she considered herself a maidal, an old maid? The anger he felt at the thought surprised him. Sally shouldn't put thoughts of marriage away just because she'd made a mistake once.

He mulled that over as the service moved on, finding no answers. Sally would be a wonderful wife to someone who deserved her. Not him, of course, but someone who would bring a spotless reputation and a heart of devotion.

The bishop began to speak. Aaron, prepared to sleep with his eyes open, found he was listening in spite of himself. He'd been half-afraid the sermon might be on the subject of the prodigal's return, but Bishop Thomas made no reference to him. Good. He didn't need or want to be the object of everyone's attention. There'd be enough of that after worship.

By the time the service had wound to its conclusion, Aaron found that one leg had gone to sleep. He'd lost the knack of sitting through a three-hour worship service, apparently. Timothy, leaning against Caleb, had slept through the last hour, but he woke when his father moved.

In a moment the barn was bustling with activity. The women and girls went out, most to help with the lunch, he guessed. The men, including his brothers, started to work immediately, turning the benches into the tables and benches they'd need for the meal.

He wasn't sure who had invented the convertible tables, but it had been a clever idea. Later they'd be folded up and loaded onto the church wagon, ready to be moved to the next site of worship in two weeks' time.

Once lunch started, folks settled down to talk, catching up on all that had happened since they'd been together. He managed to touch base with Amos, and returned to Onkel Zeb afterward, grinning.

"You found a friend, yah?" Zeb said. "Do you think Amos much changed?"

"He's turned into a pillar of the church, it seems. I don't know how Mary Ann did it. But he's about to get his comeuppance, because those boys of his look as ripe for mischief as he ever was."

His uncle chuckled. "That's always the way. Kinder repeat their parents' deeds. The only hope for a parent is that you'll live long enough to see their kinder do the same to them."

Sally swept past them just then, clearly on her way to the kitchen with a tray. She gave him a nod and kept moving.

What had Elizabeth said to her after she'd found them together in the schoolhouse yesterday? Nothing pleasant, he could be sure. Elizabeth didn't approve of him.

That was okay, because he didn't approve of himself. And if everyone knew what he'd been accused of and why he'd left the Englisch, plenty more would disapprove. He turned, not wanting to be caught staring after Sally, and found the bishop bearing down on him.

Onkel Zeb slipped away, obviously thinking he ought to give them privacy. At the moment, Aaron would rather have protection. A flare of panic struck. What was Bishop Thomas going to say?

People around them drifted away or began loud conversations with each other, obviously following Zeb's lead.

"Aaron." The bishop surveyed him for a moment, and then clapped him on the shoulder, smiling. "It's wonderful gut to see you home again. It's been a long time."

"It has, I know." He took a breath. May as well be honest. "The family would have been disappointed if I hadn't come to worship with them, but I wasn't sure others would feel that way."

"Ach, that's foolishness." His grip tightened strongly, reminding Aaron that in addition to being the bishop, he was also the wheelwright, and he had muscles like iron. "The Leit will always wilkom those who come back to us with an open and contrite heart."

Aaron was at a loss for words. His heart felt like a chunk of rock. He didn't think the bishop would consider that either open or contrite.

"Take your time." Maybe Bishop Thomas saw that he wasn't ready yet. "When you feel like talking to me, you know where I am."

He moved off, leaving Aaron still speechless. Coming back the way the bishop saw it meant confession—meant telling everything, including the reason he'd come back. It meant kneeling in front of the whole congregation and asking to return...to return forever.

He didn't see his way clear to doing any of that. If he couldn't even be open with Sally... But what was he thinking? Of course he couldn't say anything to Sally. She was little more than a kid, and he certainly couldn't burden her with his story. Maybe the best thing he could do for everyone was to walk away again.

Someone touched his arm, and he jerked around. Sally.

"Don't be alarmed," she said quickly, her voice low. "Can you find Caleb for Jessie? There's nothing wrong, but she's tired and needs to go home. We'll be in the kitchen."

He nodded a quick assent, everything else forgotten. Was the baby about to arrive?

Sally hurried back to the kitchen, trying to reassure herself. Everything was fine. Aaron would find Caleb, and he'd take charge of getting his family home.

Jessie sat at the kitchen table where she'd left her, leaning her head on her hand. Becky stood nearby, looking scared.

Sally bent over Jessie, touching her shoulder gently. "I didn't see Caleb, so I sent Aaron to look for him. Don't worry. He'll be here soon."

"I'm all right." Jessie looked up and tried to smile. "Silly of me, but I just felt like I wanted to go home."

"And so you will. In the meantime, if you want to lie down in one of the bedrooms…"

"No, no." She looked horrified at the thought. "I'll just sit here."

She didn't want to draw attention to herself, of course. "Well, it looks as if Mary Miller left everything ready for tea. Shall I make you a cup?"

"That sounds gut." Jessie held her hand out to Becky, who came and gave her a cautious hug. "Maybe a weak cup of tea with sugar for Becky, too. I'm afraid I scared her when I started feeling dizzy."

"I'm not scared, Mammi," Becky said, belying the look in her eyes. "I was just worried." She kept her arm around Jessie's shoulders.

"Two cups of tea coming right up." Sally turned the gas on under the teakettle and took two cups from the tray that was ready. It was sweet to see Becky so attached to her stepmother. She hadn't had much mothering from her own mammi, but Jessie's warm heart was more than filling that gap.

Mary had the water already hot, and it only took a minute to bring it back to boiling. Sally took a quick look out the back window. The women still sat around the tables, having dessert and talking. That was just as well. She didn't think Jessie wanted a lot of people fussing over her.

Still, Jessie could have done better than Sally. Once again she had the sense that she was in over her head. Carrying the cups to the table, she set them in front of Jessie and Becky. Jessie immediately wrapped her fingers around the cup and drank thirstily.

Was tea a good idea if she were going into labor? Sally had no notion, but it seemed to calm Jessie. She smiled, patting Becky.

"Drink up. Your daadi will be here in a minute."

Sally perched on the edge of her chair, not wanting to be too obviously watching for the men. What was taking so long? Most likely, Caleb had walked off to have a look at the Burkhalters' orchard, or their corn crop, or something equally fascinating to him.

Even as she thought that, she saw Caleb and Aaron heading for the porch at a fast walk. At least they had sense enough not to run and get everyone upset. Caleb did run once he got inside, brushing past Sally as if she weren't there to get to his wife.

He bent over her, murmuring softly to her. Aaron paused next to Sally, his hand brushing her arm. "Is she all right?"

"I think so. She felt a little dizzy, but she says she just wants to go home."

He nodded. "Onkel Zeb and Daniel went to hitch

up the buggy. They'll be along any minute now." He gave her a curious glance. "How did you get involved?"

"Becky was frightened, so she ran and got me." She wrinkled her nose. "I guess she thinks teachers can solve anything, but in this case…"

"It looks to me as if you did fine." He squeezed her arm in a quick gesture. "Here comes the buggy. Jessie, shall we carry you out?"

"Ach, no, how silly." Jessie's voice was stronger, and her color was better now that Caleb's arm was around her. "I'm just tired, that's all."

"Are you sure?" Caleb helped her up. "Maybe the midwife—"

"No, not yet." Her voice was firm, and she walked across the kitchen without hesitation. "Denke, Sally."

"Yah, denke," Caleb repeated.

Aaron held the door, and they all went to the buggy where Daniel waited with Onkel Zeb and Timothy. Jessie clearly wanted to get away without causing comment, but folks were bound to notice that they were leaving early.

And ask questions. Once the buggy had pulled out, Sally found herself surrounded. It hadn't occurred to her that she'd be the one they questioned, and she had her work cut out for her parrying all the concerned inquiries.

Before long most people were soon ready to pack up and head for home, while a small group stayed to help clean up and prepare for the young people's singing that evening.

By the time Sally was back in the buggy with Ben and Elizabeth, she was ready for Elizabeth's questions. She repeated all the answers she'd already given.

"I wonder if the boppli…" Elizabeth broke off suddenly. Sally met her gaze and grinned. They were both thinking the same thing. Elizabeth shot a glance at Ben, who was studiously looking elsewhere.

"I guess we'll know soon enough," Sally said. "Especially if we see Anna Miller's buggy coming."

Elizabeth nodded. At least she wasn't carrying on about how unsuitable it was for Sally to be involved. "I wonder…" she began, but her words were cut off when Ben pulled up suddenly.

A car was tipped down over the bank on the right side of the road, up against a utility pole, which tilted at a dangerous angle. Fortunately, the lines it carried were off the road. The driver, a young man who looked to be in his twenties, stood surveying the wreck.

Ben hailed him. "Are you hurt? Can we do anything to help?"

The man scrambled up the bank to the buggy. "Thanks, but I'm okay. I swerved to miss a deer. It's fine, but my car's a mess."

"If we can give you a lift, we will be happy to."

He shook his head. "I already called to report it. But thanks." He stood back, waving as Ben clicked to the horse and they moved off.

Elizabeth glanced back at him. "I hope he's really all right. I wouldn't want to run into something in a car. And young people always drive too fast."

Ben exchanged glances with Sally. "No need to worry. When Frank Williams drives us places, he always goes ten miles slower than the speed limit."

Sally hid a smile. Elizabeth was a born worrier, it seemed. At least the car accident had diverted her attention from Jessie, so hopefully she wouldn't run over there filled with questions and concerns.

"We'd best get home and get ready to leave for your sister's place," Ben said. "Sally, you know they'd be happy to see you if you want to come."

"That's right," Elizabeth echoed.

"I appreciate it, but I have a book I want to read for school this afternoon."

Ben and Elizabeth planned to visit her sister and family this afternoon and stay for supper. It was kind of them to invite her, but the thought of an afternoon on her own was too tempting. Besides, she knew how much Elizabeth looked forward to visiting with her sister. They'd do much better without her.

When Ben and Elizabeth had driven off, Sally settled herself in the living room rocker with a book. She liked to read to her scholars each day after the lunch recess, but it could be a challenge to find something that would interest all ages.

She found it difficult to focus, and she knew why. Aaron had just spoken with the bishop when she'd approached him earlier, and the look on Aaron's face had startled her. He had looked like a man who found himself trapped and was searching for a way out.

But Bishop Thomas hadn't looked stern or forbidding to her—he'd given Aaron a clap on the shoulder in his usual friendly way. Still, something about his words had upset Aaron. If it hadn't been for the necessity of finding Caleb quickly, she'd have tried to find out. Not that Aaron would have been likely to confide.

Sally glanced toward the King farm, wondering about Jessie, and saw a buggy being driven at a fast trot toward her. Dropping the book, she hurried through the house to the back door. Jessie?

Aaron had already flung himself from the buggy when she reached him and was racing for the phone shanty.

"Our phone is out. Does yours work?"

"I don't know." She hurried after him. "Is it Jessie?"

He was already picking up the receiver. Then he slammed it down again. "Dead."

"It must have been the accident. You would have gone past before it happened. A car in the ditch, and the pole knocked sideways. Jessie?"

"She's in labor. I don't know what's wrong, but she wants the midwife right away. Daniel ran to get Leah, and I said I'd call."

She could see the scrap of paper he clutched— presumably Anna's phone number. Sally tried to think what the best possibility would be. The midwife lived even farther out the same road, and her phone might well be affected, too.

"You'll have to go for her," she said. "That's the quickest thing."

"It would be, if I knew where she lived. You forget I've been away a long time."

"No problem." She was already hurrying to the buggy. "I'll go with you."

He hesitated for a moment, as if trying to come up with another option. Then he pulled himself up with an easy motion and grabbed the lines. They were already heading back down the lane before it occurred to Sally that perhaps she should have left a note for Ben and Elizabeth.

It was too late now, and most likely she'd be home

long before they got back. Anna's clinic wasn't that far off, but just far enough that she was in another church district.

"I hope she's home." Aaron sent a worried look back over his shoulder. "If we can't find her... Maybe I should have headed toward town and tried to get the ambulance."

"If Jessie asked for the midwife, then that's what she needs." She prayed she was right. "Anna would leave a note on the door if she went anywhere, and chances are she'll be at home with the family."

Anna had taken over the midwife practice that her mother-in-law had run for so long. Initially there had been those who'd said she was too young, but Anna had proved herself.

Aaron still looked worried. Sally reached out to pat his arm. "It will be all right. You'll see. Leah can handle things until we get back with the midwife."

"I hope you're right," he muttered. "I'd rather have heard about the baby when it was all over."

"You don't mean that. I know you don't. It's a blessing to be able to help at such a time."

"Is it?" He gave her as much of a smile as he could probably manage right now. "You're a nice person, Sally."

She shook her head impatiently. "Anyone would rush to help. I care about Jessie. And so do you."

Aaron's face tightened. "I guess I do. That's the trouble with coming home. It won't be easy to go away again."

Sally's heart seemed to stop for a second. "Are you planning to go away, Aaron?"

"I don't know." His jaw clamped, and his face was suddenly forbidding. "I don't know," he repeated.

Sally clasped the edge of the seat with her fingers, trying to deny the pain she felt. But she couldn't. If Aaron left, she was afraid he'd be taking her heart with him.

Chapter Seven

Aaron's nerves were jangling by the time they neared the farm, the midwife sitting between him and Sally in the buggy. Anna was everything, he supposed, that one would want a midwife to be, with a calm, capable manner and a warm, sweet smile. She seemed to radiate confidence. He wished he felt the same.

Sally and the midwife had been chatting during the ride, but as he neared the lane, Sally leaned forward. "Just drop me here, Aaron. You'll want to get Anna straight to Jessie."

Any other time he might have argued, but he couldn't think of anything else until he'd fulfilled his duty. If only the phones...

He pulled up long enough for Sally to jump down. "Let me know if I can do anything to help," she said.

Aaron turned toward the house, wondering how long it had been. He'd gone as fast as he could, hadn't he?

"I'm sure I'll be in time," Anna said, as if she'd read his thoughts. "First babies always take a while to arrive."

"I hope so, or I wouldn't want to face my brother. Caleb is probably twice as nervous as I am."

"I haven't lost a father yet," she said lightly. He supposed she meant it to be reassuring, but it didn't help him, and he didn't think it would Caleb either.

They came to a stop at the porch, and he hopped down, ground tying the horse. Time enough to unharness once he knew how things were with Jessie.

He followed Anna inside. Caleb was there to meet them, looking as if he'd been dragged through a knothole. He clasped Anna's hands.

"She's upstairs. Leah is with her. I'll show you—"

Anna shook her head. "I'm sure I can find them." Her smile seemed to include all of them. "If I need anything, I'll call you."

As soon as she left the room, Caleb turned on Aaron. "What took so long? It shouldn't have taken you an hour."

He'd snap back, but he could see the worry etched in his brother's face. "All the phones along the road are out. There was a car accident. So I had to go for the midwife."

"An accident? I hope it wasn't bad," Onkel Zeb said, looking up from saying something to the kinder.

"I don't think so. Sally says they passed it on their way home from church. Must have happened not long after we came home."

They heard footsteps. Leah came down the stairs. "It's all right," she said quickly. "Caleb, Anna says you can go up and see Jessie for a few minutes." She caught his arm when he brushed past her, and smiled. "Be calm. Be loving. Don't upset her or we won't let you in again."

"Yah. Right." He hurried off.

Leah looked after him for a moment and then headed for the stove. "Is there coffee hot?"

"Yah, for sure." Zeb seemed to collect himself. "And some sticky buns that Jessie made yesterday. Sit and relax a bit."

"It will be wilkom." She sat at the table with the kinder. "Rebecca is coming over in a bit with supper." She looked from the young ones to the adults with an expression that said she found the grown-ups lacking. "Daniel, isn't there something you and the kinder could be doing outside?"

Galvanized, Daniel got up. "The chickens. We've gotten all behind today, ain't so? Let's go gather the eggs and see to the food and water."

Becky hesitated, looking at Leah. "Can't I see Mammi? I could help."

"I know you're a wonderful gut helper." Leah smoothed back her hair. "Mammi will need you later, after this boppli comes, ain't so?"

Becky didn't look entirely satisfied, but she nodded and left with Daniel and her brother. Leah divided a disapproving look between Zeb and Aaron.

"If you two want to be helpful, you'll keep the kinder occupied so they don't worry."

"I wasn't here," Aaron protested. "I went for the midwife."

"You're right," Zeb said, setting a sticky bun in front of her. "I should have thought." He gave her a rueful glance. "But Caleb has been enough to handle."

Leah sipped her coffee. "I'm sure. Well, you try to keep him busy when he comes back down. Worrying never helped anyone, and Jessie is in gut hands, and everything is going as it should."

"We'll try." Zeb patted her shoulder. "You're a gut friend, Leah."

"Ach, it's what she would do for me." Leah drained her cup and set it in the sink. "I'll go up and chase Caleb down now. Ben and the older boys will be over to help with the milking and anything else you need."

Zeb nodded, accepting it as normal. Aaron turned it over in his mind. Neighbors helped each other in a crisis out there in the world, he was sure, but they seemed to wait to be asked. The Amish were such a part of each other's lives that they didn't need to wait. They'd just be there.

The afternoon wore on. It proved impossible to get Caleb out of the house, so they stopped trying. Deciding to leave him to Zeb, Aaron got up.

"I'll go out and see that everything is ready for the milking."

"You don't have to do that." Caleb's reply seemed almost automatic by now, and Aaron's patience finally snapped.

"If you don't trust me to do it, just say so."

Their gazes met, and for a long moment, he and his brother stared at each other. Then Caleb shook his head. "I thought… I was too hard on you before. Expecting you to do a man's work when you were just a boy. I see that now. I don't want to push you away again."

All of Aaron's preconceptions about Caleb crumbled into dust. "It's not… That's not why I went. Well, not the whole reason, anyway. It wasn't your doing—it was mine. Now that I'm here…" He paused, trying to get it clear in his own mind. "I just want you to treat me like your brother."

The kitchen was so silent they could hear the soft movements from the room over their heads. Caleb's face contorted. Then he grabbed Aaron in a rough hug, shaking him a little. When he drew back, Aaron thought he saw unshed tears in his eyes. He knew there were in his.

"Yah," Caleb said finally. "Get along out to the milking shed. There's work to do."

Grinning, Aaron went.

Aaron stayed busy outside for well over an hour, but by the time he and Daniel returned to the house, he was wondering what they'd find. If the baby hadn't come yet, he'd think it was time to start worrying.

They found Rebecca, Daniel's intended, in control in the kitchen. Caleb was pacing from one end of the room to the other and then back again. Aaron had heard all the jokes about expectant fathers, but he'd never actually expected to see his controlled oldest brother in such a state.

Caleb swung on them. "Is the phone working yet? I think—"

"Hush." Rebecca had paused, one hand on the oven door, seeming to listen to something above them.

And then they all heard it—the thin, protesting wail of the newborn.

There was a concerted rush to the hallway. Caleb had his foot on the first step when Leah came out of the room. "Jessie is fine," she said quickly. She smiled. "You have a son."

"Praise the gut Lord," Zeb said, his face seeming ready to split with his smile. He pounded Caleb on the back. "A new baby. A little bruder for Becky and Timothy."

"I'll show him how to play with my blocks," Timothy said, squirming toward the stairs.

"He won't be ready for that for a long time," Becky said loftily. "I can help Mammi take care of him."

"Me, too," Timothy cried.

Caleb swept them both up in a hug. "We'll all help, ain't so? And we'll all thank God for this day."

Thank You, Lord, Aaron murmured silently. He hadn't done much praying in his recent life, and even those simple words came awkwardly, but he realized he meant them with all his heart.

"We'll put a quart of that vegetable soup in the basket, too," Elizabeth said. She'd started hustling around the kitchen the moment they'd returned and learned of the impending birth. "I wonder…" She glanced in the general direction of the King farm.

"When we take the food over, we'll find out. It's been over two hours since we got back with the midwife."

Sally bent to take the shoofly pies out of the oven. Caleb would be glad of something ready for breakfast tomorrow, and Becky could take a piece in her lunch, as well.

She realized that Elizabeth was watching her, frowning. No doubt she was about to bring up the fact that Sally had gone with Aaron in search of the midwife.

"I wish you hadn't gone alone with him. If you'd just given him the directions…"

"And if he'd failed to find the place?" Sally closed the

oven door a bit more firmly than necessary. "With the baby on the way, I couldn't have done anything else."

"I don't see what all the fuss was about," Ben said. "Sally was just riding in a buggy with him. Any of us would have done the same, with the telephones out and all."

Ben was oblivious of the emotional temperature, as usual, and for once Sally was glad of it. But she suspected that once Elizabeth got him alone, she'd give him an earful.

It was a shame Elizabeth was so busy about Sally's business, but it couldn't hurt her. She could just smile and let it wash over her. Still, she'd be relieved when Mamm and Daad got home.

Elizabeth touched the top of the steak and onion pie she'd made to be sure the dough was done. She turned with a satisfied air. "Everything is ready to pack, I think."

"They'll be sehr glad to see you coming with supper," Ben told her. "Maybe you'll get a look at the new boppli, too."

Elizabeth stiffened. "Sally can take it over," she said quickly.

"But don't you…"

"That's right," Sally said quickly. Ben seemed to have no idea why Elizabeth might find it difficult to go to the King place right now, when they were doubtless rejoicing over a new member of the family.

Sally suppressed an urge to shake him. "I'll be glad to take the basket over." She picked up the basket, and her gaze caught Elizabeth's. They shared an instant of understanding. Then she headed for the door, the loaded basket weighing heavily on her arm.

By the time she'd reached the King place, she'd shifted the basket from one arm to the other several times. She set it down on the porch long enough to rap once and then open the door, carrying the basket to the kitchen.

Here she found Leah in charge and the scent of baking in the air. "I might have known you would beat us here with food," Sally said. "What's the news?"

"It's a boy!" Zeb, clearly elated, grasped her burden and took it to the counter. "A fine, healthy boy, and Jessie is fine, too, thank the gut Lord."

"Ach, that's wonderful gut. I'm sehr happy for all of you."

Zeb nodded. "The Lord does work in mysterious ways, ain't so? There were times I feared Caleb would never be happy again, and now…" He stopped, seeming overcome with emotion.

Sally pressed his arm in understanding. "God has blessed them," she murmured. "Is Caleb up with Jessie?"

"He is." Leah chuckled. "The last time I checked on them, he was sitting there watching them sleep."

"Daniel took the midwife home. Aaron has the young ones helping with chores." Zeb had recovered his usual calm. "And I have been trying to convince Leah that I can handle supper."

"You may as well stop trying. Rebecca and her mamm are taking care of everything there, and you're not getting rid of me until I'm satisfied you're all settled for the night." Leah was firm. "Besides, it smells like Sally has brought most of the supper with her, so it's easily done. Unless you want to push me out the door…"

"Ach, I couldn't do that, now could I?" Zeb took one of the shoofly pies from Sally's basket and sniffed it appreciatively. "You can't lock the doors and windows against kindness—it comes in anyway."

"True enough," Sally said, smiling at the thought. "Is there anything I can do?"

Leah's gaze swept across the various containers on the countertop. "I think we're fine for now with all this food. Denke, Sally. And be sure to thank Elizabeth for us, too."

"I'll be off, then," Sally said. "Ben says he'll be here for the morning milking. Remember to tell Jessie and Caleb we're wonderful happy for them."

She went out, the now-empty basket swinging from her arm. She wasn't, she told herself firmly, upset that she hadn't seen Aaron. That would be silly.

She started down the porch steps just as Aaron came around the large lilac bush at the corner, and her heart gave a glad little leap.

Glancing at her basket, he grinned. "More food. I might have known."

"I think you might," she said, teasing to cover her feelings. "Can you think of an occasion which wouldn't be helped by bringing food?"

"No, I guess I can't. It's kind of you, Sally."

The softness of his glance was turning her to mush inside, and she hurriedly added, "Elizabeth, mostly. I had just started cooking when she and Ben got home, and she swept into action. She's really taken over the kitchen since Mamm and Daad have been away." So much so that sometimes the house felt as if it belonged to her and Ben, instead of being Sally's home.

"Then thank her for us, as well." He was standing very close, and his voice was soft.

"I… I will." She made an effort to control her breath. "So I hear you have a new nephew."

His face lit up. "I never saw such a beautiful baby. Jessie says he looks like Caleb, but I'm not so sure."

"All babies are beautiful, don't you know that?"

"Yes, but it's true about him." He grinned, and Sally's heart seemed to give another shiver of pure joy.

Something was different about Aaron. It was almost, she thought, as if he'd found his place. Her breath caught. If that was true, if he really did think he belonged, then anything might happen. Anything, even for them.

Sally started to walk away, and Aaron realized that he didn't want to let her go. His emotions had been turned upside down today with the worry over Jessie and the baby and the startling conversation he'd had with Caleb. So much had been happening that he hadn't had time to figure it out yet.

But Sally… Sally had somehow seemed to understand his feelings about Caleb even before he did. She'd been the one to point out the thing he'd never taken into account—how young Caleb had been when he'd had to take responsibility for the family.

"Wait."

Sally turned, eyebrows lifted in a question.

"I'll carry your basket for you." He took it from her before she had time to protest. Falling into step, they walked out the lane.

"I could have used you when the basket was filled," she commented.

"Sorry I didn't see you then." He fell silent, not sure how to say what he wanted or even what it was. "You were right," he said finally.

Sally gave him a blank look. "Right?"

"When I was sounding off about Caleb, you said that he'd had to take on a lot of responsibility before he was ready for it." He paused, turning it over in his mind. "I didn't see it at first."

"I know." Her voice was soft, and she seemed to listen intently.

"When our mother left, I was...what? Eight, I guess. I didn't understand what had happened. I just knew that our whole lives had changed in a minute."

"That would be shocking for a child, no matter when or how it happened." Sally's heart was in her eyes. "I imagine a child would feel as if it was his or her fault. And then hide that feeling, for fear of losing the people he had left."

He nodded. Sally's insight astonished him.

"Funny. Now that I think about it, I know I never talked about it to anyone. Daadi didn't tell us anything. It was Caleb who finally told Daniel and me that Mammi had gone away and wasn't coming back."

He heard her sharp, indrawn breath.

"I know." Aaron answered her reaction. "We didn't believe him at first. I remember being so mad I threw my shoe at him. And Daniel ran to the bedroom and hid there."

The memory flooded back...every instant of it. The smell of oatmeal burning on the stove where Caleb had tried to fix it. The cold, hard floor under his stocking feet. The harsh sound of Daniel's sobs. He hadn't consciously thought of it in years, but it was all there, just waiting to spring out and sink its claws into him.

"Surely someone came to help—the neighbors..." Sally's voice died away when he shook his head.

"I guess no one knew at first. Daad just shut himself in the bedroom and locked the door." He drew in a shaky breath. "Caleb did his best to take care of us until Onkel Zeb got here. Onkel Zeb...he made us feel safe. But I still never talked to him about it."

"You couldn't," she said, her voice soft. Gentle. "It probably doesn't help, but that's the way it is with a lot of children when something very bad happens to their family. They can't bring it up because they're afraid that it's their fault, or that if they speak, it will be worse. They need an adult to help them make sense of it."

Aaron gathered his will to push the pain back behind its locked door. When he thought he had it secure, he was able to look at Sally. He studied her face—the warmth in her blue eyes, the caring in her expression.

"An adult like a teacher who cares?"

"Sometimes," she said. "I'd never talk about it, but we often see the results of family trouble in school. At home, everyone's so wrapped up in their own pain they sometimes don't see each other's."

Her words moved through his mind and found acceptance there. Sally had it right. "That's how it was with Daad. He just pulled into himself." He was feeling his way, trying to understand. "Daniel couldn't talk about it... I guess he blamed himself, like you said. And Caleb... Caleb felt he had to take on a man's responsibility when he was just a boy."

It was all becoming so clear to him now. Sally...she

was the one who'd helped him see it. If he hadn't come home, he might never have realized the truth. He'd have gone on blaming everyone else for the breakup of their family and shutting himself away from them.

But he had come back, unwilling, forced into it. Maybe that had all been part of God's plan for him.

Sally was patient, giving him time to think it through without questioning. He managed a wry smile, and her troubled face relaxed.

"It's not easy to look at a child's traumatic event like an adult." Her lips curved a little. "You seem to have come a long way."

"No thanks to myself." His voice was rueful. "I had plenty of help. Like you."

Sally shook her head. "I just listened, that's all. You were ready to talk today."

"Yah, and you know why? Because today of all days I got angry with Caleb. I thought he didn't want me to help out. I thought he didn't trust me, didn't want me back. Turned out he was afraid of pushing me into running away again."

They'd reached the end of the lane, and he paused by the fence post. "Strange. I was looking at everything upside down."

"Maybe you were a bit too sensitive," Sally suggested. "Afraid to believe that they wanted you back. Thinking it was too easy."

"Maybe. And maybe you understand people entirely too well to be comfortable." He'd probably regret showing so much of himself to Sally, but not yet.

She studied his face, smiling a little. "Do I make you uncomfortable, Aaron?"

"On the contrary. It's too easy to talk to you. Makes

me say things I've never said to a living soul." He tried to say it lightly, but it was true.

She reached out to take her basket, their fingers touching, clinging just for a moment. "You were ready to say them. I just happened to be in the right place, that's all."

"Maybe. Or maybe you were the one person I could say all this to." Gratitude swept through him. "Whichever way it was, thank you, Sally. I'm glad to have all of that out, thanks to you."

Her lips quirked with sudden amusement. "You make me sound like a medicine. But I'm glad the medicine helped." With a quick lift of her hand, she was gone.

Aaron stood there, watching her walk away from him, thinking how unexpected it all was. He hadn't even thought of Sally when he'd headed for home, but she'd turned out to be the most important part of his homecoming.

Chapter Eight

Sally had to smile at Becky's chatter as they walked home from school on Monday. She was still so excited about her new baby brother that words just bubbled out of her.

"And he woke up in the nighttime, 'cause I heard him crying. Daadi said he was just hungry."

"I'm sure that's true. The boppli's tummy is so small that he needs to eat more often than you do."

Becky nodded, skipping along a little faster. "I wish I got to stay home today like Timothy did. But Mammi said maybe I could help hold the boppli when I got home."

"That will be exciting."

Had Aaron held his little nephew yet? Her mind returned, as it did so frequently, to Aaron. Bachelors were sometimes reluctant to try, and she'd guess he'd never been around a newborn before.

She ought to put a stop to her tendency to hear his voice in her thoughts…to see his face the way it had looked when he'd confided in her. But she didn't think she could. And besides, what difference did it make?

No one, including Aaron, could guess he dominated her thoughts these days.

"They decided on his name, too."

Sally forcibly removed her errant thoughts from Aaron and brought them back to the infant. She tried to focus on Becky's animated face. Each child deserved that kind of attention from her. "So what is it to be? Caleb, after his daadi?"

"Daadi said no. He'll be William, after Mammi's daadi, and Zebulon, after Onkel Zeb." Becky took a few skipping steps. "But we're going to call him Will."

"That sounds like a fine idea. William Zebulon is quite a mouthful for a little baby."

Not Aaron for a name, of course. A brother came farther down on the list of kin to give their name to a new baby.

Frustrated, she realized she was right back to thinking of him. But really, how *could* she fail to muse about what he'd confided yesterday? He'd said things she didn't imagine he'd said to anyone else.

And he'd felt a sense of relief and release when he'd spoken. She'd known it at once, as if she shared his inner thoughts. Hope blossomed within her. Maybe, with his tension and pain about the past eased, Aaron would think seriously about staying.

Becky giggled and hastened her steps as they rounded the bend in the road and could see the farm lanes. Sally's gaze flew to the spot where Aaron had stood waiting for her. But he wasn't there.

Foolish to be disappointed. He was probably busy at home. One small baby could turn things upside down for everyone in the family. He might have to forget about working with Star for a few days.

"Bye, Teacher Sally." Becky ran ahead, pelting down the lane to her family's farmhouse, obviously unable to wait another moment to see her baby brother.

Sally turned down her own lane, lecturing herself about being disappointed over not seeing Aaron. After all, she'd seen a good bit of him the previous day. She couldn't expect to run into him every day, could she?

She was still arguing her way out of disappointment when she spotted Aaron leading Star out of the barn. Her heart gave a leap. She tried to suppress the happiness that danced along her veins at the idea of seeing him. Silly. She was getting as silly as a thirteen-year-old, giggling in the cloakroom because she'd spotted that special boy.

Waving at Aaron, Sally hurried into the house. For once Elizabeth wasn't in the kitchen, so she was able to leave her things on the table and dash out again.

Aaron was leading Star around the buggies again, and as she came up to them, the gelding danced nervously.

"Komm, foolish one," Aaron chided him. "It's just Sally. You know her."

"That's right." She held out her hand with the carrot she'd grabbed from the bin on her way out the door. "You remember treats, anyway."

Velvety lips moved on her palm, and Star began crunching the carrot noisily. While he chomped, she smiled at Aaron.

"How is it with your new nephew today? All well, I hope?"

Aaron's face relaxed in a grin. "Yah, he seems to be ruling the roost at the moment. Caleb's so delighted he's like a dog with two tails, both wagging. I guess he figured there wouldn't be any more babies after Timothy."

"Until Jessie came along and changed their lives," she finished. "I'm sehr glad. Jessie really longed for a baby, I know."

He raised an eyebrow. "Now, how does a nice young unmarried girl know something like that? I always thought married women were more discreet."

"Some of them are, I suppose." She thought of her sister-in-law, and the attitude that wouldn't let her accept Sally's help. "But Jessie and I have gotten to know each other since she came. She and Leah… Well, they seem to understand that I don't belong with the young single girls any longer."

"You being so very old," he teased.

Before she could find a suitable answer, Star decided to take issue with the wheels of a buggy, trying to back away.

"Enough, you foolish thing." Aaron led him around the buggy again. "Where did Star come from? Was he trained for harness racing?"

"I don't know about his training," she said. "According to my uncle, he was bought off that racetrack out near Scranton."

"He flunked out of racing, in other words." Aaron smiled at her expression. "Don't be offended. Plenty of good buggy horses come from the harness racing world. Star doesn't take to the pacing, though, for all that he looks like a standardbred."

"Would that be why he couldn't make it in harness racing?" She considered Star, liking his smooth, muscular lines and the way he held his head.

"Could be. But it doesn't really matter for a buggy

horse. He's got a nice, smooth trot, and he'd do well enough, if we can get him over shying at anything that distracts him."

"That's what you were doing before you came back, then?" she asked tentatively, knowing his time in the Englisch world was a sensitive topic. "Training racing horses?"

He nodded, but he didn't offer anything else, and she didn't feel brave enough to push the subject. If she was patient, maybe one day he'd tell about his life out there. And how it ended.

Aaron gave the horse a pat on the shoulder. "Let's get him harnessed up, and we'll do some more ground driving. He has to get used to the blinders, or he'll be a danger out on the road." He darted a smiling glance at her. "Don't worry. I don't expect to fail."

"Sure of yourself, aren't you?" she said, teasing.

"Only when it comes to horses," he replied.

She saw the truth of it as they worked. Aaron *was* clearly confident about his ability with the horse. She watched as he put the harness on Star, talking constantly as the gelding, at first a little fractious, calmed down in response and stood quietly.

What a gift Aaron had—he was gentle, steady and patient, everything a horse would respond to.

Or a woman, a little voice in her mind observed. Sally tried to ignore it.

Once Star was standing quietly in full harness, Aaron nodded to Sally to pick up the lines. "I'll walk at his head for a bit while you drive him. You're the boss, and he has to get used to your voice."

She adjusted the lines in her hands, telling herself she wasn't at all nervous, and more than a little aware of Aaron's gaze on her. "Now, Star." She collected the gelding's attention. "Walk on." She accompanied the words with a small movement of her hands.

To her pleasure—and a little surprise—Star walked on quietly. Obviously Aaron's slow and steady training was paying off. Each of her own attempts to drive Star had been a battle from the start.

They walked the horse around and around the barnyard. Understanding what Aaron wanted, she steered Star close to the various obstacles that might be expected to distract him. There wasn't the faintest hesitation as he moved along.

"Gut boy," she said, unable to keep the exhilaration out of her voice. She flashed Aaron a smile. "You really are a wonder worker, ain't so?"

"It's all a matter of patience. And listening to the animal. It tells you what it wants and what it's afraid of if you only listen."

"Well, you clearly heard what Star was saying better than I did."

"Maybe I'm more used to listening." He looked at her, a challenge in his eyes. "Are you ready for me to step away from his head?"

A little flutter teased her stomach as she took the challenge. "For sure. Let's see how he does without you."

Predictably, Star turned his head to watch as Aaron moved away. But when Sally clucked to him, he moved on obediently.

She grinned, picking up the speed a little so that he broke into a slow trot. Sally jogged along behind him, her attention all on the horse. She was doing it. This was going to work out, and she'd have the freedom that her own buggy horse gave her. Exhilaration carried her along.

"Watch out—"

Aaron's warning came an instant too late. She stepped into a depression in the ground and lost her balance, coming down heavily. Even as she saw the ground rushing at her, she held onto the lines and managed to halt Star even as she sprawled in the grass.

Star stopped, standing quietly even though he must have been aware that something was wrong behind him. Sally was so pleased that she hardly noticed her sprawled position until Aaron reached her. He knelt next to her, reaching out to clasp her shoulders.

"Sally, are you hurt? Can you move?" The concern in his voice warmed her.

"I'm fine, I think." She moved her legs and found that everything worked. "Nothing hurt but my dignity."

She could feel his tension relax. "You held on to the lines. That's the most important thing."

"Ach, no. The most important thing is that Star is standing quietly, thanks to you."

She looked up into his face as she spoke, startled to find him so close. It felt as if she could feel the warmth radiating from his skin, and she took in the fresh, masculine scent of him.

Awareness flooded her. She tried to look away, but it was impossible. All she could do was sit there in the grass with Aaron's hands strong on her shoulders and his lips inches from hers.

He sucked in a breath, and his eyes darkened. He drew even closer, until she could imagine his lips on hers, gentle and demanding at the same time.

And then, too quickly, he pulled back, leaving her

with her lips parted and her skin chilled by the sudden loss of his warmth.

"If you're sure you aren't hurt, let me help you up." His hands moved to her elbows. His tone was cool, his face impassive, and her heart winced in pain.

"I can manage..." she began, but he had already lifted her to her feet and taken a step away.

A flurry of movement at the edge of her vision warned her. Elizabeth came running toward them. Aaron must have seen her before Sally did. Relief swept through her.

"Sally, what happened? That horse—"

"No, we can't blame Star. I wasn't watching where I was going, and I stepped in a hole." She looked down, scuffing at the hole with the toe of her shoe. "Next thing I knew I was sitting on the ground, but Star stood perfectly the whole time." She couldn't help the note of triumph in her voice.

"Yah, well, that's a gut thing." It was a grumbling concession, but probably the best Elizabeth could do. She put her arm around Sally's waist. "Komm in the house and let me make sure you're not hurt. You could have twisted an ankle, falling like that. Aaron will take care of the horse, ain't so?"

"Of course." Aaron's tone was carefully polite.

"But we weren't finished—" she protested, but now Aaron interrupted her.

"Just about. I'll walk him around a few more minutes, and then unharness him. Next time we'll hitch him to the buggy."

"Are you sure Star is ready for that?" Maybe Star was, but she had to confess that she wasn't ready for the training to end.

"Aaron is the trainer," Elizabeth said. "I'm sure he knows best. Besides, he'll be wanting to finish up so he'll be free to...do whatever he plans to do next."

They all knew what she meant by that, didn't they? Elizabeth was pushing Aaron for a decision. Was he staying or going? The fact that Sally longed to know the answer didn't make it any easier to forgive Elizabeth for pressing.

"Go along and relax," Aaron said, his voice colorless, his face turned away. "We'll work again tomorrow."

He took Star and began walking him around, leaving her with nothing to say, even if she could have come up with something.

Aaron knew perfectly well what Elizabeth had been doing. She'd seen them close together and come running out to save her sister-in-law from him. Or maybe from herself. He understood, all right.

He swung his leg and kicked a chunk of gravel from the lane, sending it soaring toward a fence post. Unfortunately it missed. He'd have preferred a satisfying plop.

Still, he supposed it was just as well that Elizabeth hadn't been near enough to see their expressions. Then she'd really have panicked. He'd been close to it himself.

Where was the guilt he should feel? Instead of regretting it, all Aaron could do was picture Sally's face so close to his, with her blue eyes filled with longing, her lips...

Now the guilt did wash over him. He'd lived in the outside world too long if he could feel that way for

Sally. What Sally felt was an extension of the hero worship she'd had for him as a child, and that couldn't be a solid basis for anything. In some ways, despite her maturity and her surprising wisdom, she was still that little girl.

Well, maybe not a little girl. Sally had improved with age, but as for him—he seemed to see himself reflected in the clear blue of her eyes. She still saw her hero, but he saw the truth. He was older, worn away by everything that had happened to him. He was no longer capable of being the person Sally needed and deserved. And there was the central, impossible barrier between them—he wasn't Amish any longer.

By the time Aaron reached the farmhouse he was in no mood to inflict himself on the rest of the family. He headed for the barn. There was always something to do there, preferably something that pushed his muscles to their utmost and dulled his mind.

A solid hour of mucking out stalls brought with it a measure of calm. The repetitive movements, the play of muscles against his shirt, the familiar sounds and smells of a stable…they all had the ability to soothe the senses, at least for him. He could even smile at the thought of recommending such therapy for some of the people he'd known.

At least now he was in the proper mood to go inside and inflict himself on other people.

He'd stopped outside the house to scrape the dirt from his shoes when he saw a buggy coming down the farm lane toward him. Automatically he stepped forward to take the horse's head as it reached him.

The driver nodded his thanks, and Aaron's momentary peace vanished at the sight of the bishop. In the next instant Bishop Thomas had turned back to lift down a basket, and Aaron could breathe again. Bishop Thomas had obviously come because of Jessie and the new baby, not him.

"I'll take care of the horse and buggy, Bishop Thomas. You go right on in."

"Denke, Aaron. But you were on your way inside, as well, ain't so?"

It seemed he wouldn't be allowed to slip away out of sight. "As soon as I finish cleaning up." He managed to smile. "Leah's in charge, and she'll kick me out if I bring the stable smell into her clean kitchen."

Aaron delayed it as long as he could. Bishop Thomas was a fine person, but he wasn't ready for any questions about his faith or his intentions. But finally he had to go inside.

He found everyone gathered around Caleb, who held his tiny son while the others clustered around him. Timothy was on the edge, standing on tiptoe trying to see his baby brother, so Aaron picked him up from behind and hoisted, making the boy giggle.

"Is that better? What do you think? Does he look like you?"

Timothy's forehead crinkled as he tried to imagine his image in that tiny face. "I think he just looks like a boppli."

The adults chuckled, but Becky shook her head. "I remember you when you were little, and you looked a lot like Will."

"I wasn't ever that little," he declared.

Caleb grinned and reached out to tickle him. "Yah, you were. But you grew fast."

"Babies have a way of doing that," Bishop Thomas

said, his voice gentle. He reached out to touch the baby's head lightly. "The gut Lord be with you, William."

They were all silent for a moment. Then the bishop stepped back, smiling. "Now I must go, or I'll be late for supper and my wife won't like that. Will you walk out with me, Aaron?"

Caught. Aaron obviously didn't have a choice. He held the door and followed Bishop Thomas outside, bracing himself for whatever words of wisdom the bishop wanted to impart.

Nothing was said as they moved to the horse and buggy together. There Bishop Thomas paused, turning to put a strong hand on Aaron's shoulder. "So, Aaron. How are you doing, now that you have been home for a time?"

Aaron didn't want to meet his eyes, but he couldn't help doing so. At least he didn't read any condemnation there. "All right. But I haven't made any decisions about the future, if that's what you're asking."

It occurred to him that wasn't the best of responses, but Bishop Thomas didn't seem offended. Instead, he just looked curious. "What is it that holds you back, do you think?"

Aaron shrugged, feeling inarticulate. How did he put it into words? "I don't know. It's just…when I think about kneeling in front of everyone, confessing I've done wrong…"

"Ach, Aaron, do you think you're the first to stumble? We have heard worse." He had a rueful smile. "Anyway, that's looking too far ahead."

Aaron could only stare at the bishop blankly. "Too far ahead? That's surely the first step, isn't it?"

"Ach, no." The bishop paused, as if trying to think

how to explain something to a child, and Aaron waited, tense, torn between wanting to hear and wanting to run away.

"If God is calling you back," Bishop Thomas said slowly, "His voice will get so strong that there will be no doubting it. And when that time comes, nothing else will matter the least little bit. You see?"

Aaron shook his head. He didn't see, and he couldn't imagine it.

Bishop Thomas chuckled. "You are like Timothy, unable to see that he'd ever been that small. Just wait, and listen for God's voice. It will come, in His time. And in the meantime, will you commit to living by the Ordnung for a time…say, for a month?"

He was torn, not wanting to commit to anything unless he could be sure. But the bishop was waiting. Finally, reluctantly, he nodded.

"I'll try. For one month."

"Gut." Bishop Thomas clapped him on the shoulder. "Now stop worrying about it. Just listen. God will make it clear."

Aaron wasn't sure whether he hoped the bishop was right or wrong.

Chapter Nine

When Sally had reached the house, she'd made a quick excuse to scurry up to her room, eager to avoid the lecture Elizabeth seemed primed to deliver. She'd said she had to change her muddied dress and do some schoolwork, which was true enough.

But instead of doing so, fifteen minutes later she found herself standing with a clean dress in her hands, completely lost in her thoughts, while Aaron's face filled her mind.

Those moments when they'd looked into each other's eyes—she couldn't be mistaken about what she felt, not now. Dropping the dress, she sank down onto the bed, pressing her palms to her hot cheeks. She loved him. She was in love with Aaron King.

For years she'd convinced herself that she could never risk making a mistake again, but now she knew how foolish she'd been to think she could lock love out of her life.

She hadn't known enough about love. She hadn't realized that love, real love, was like the rush of a mighty river...a strong, deep current that swept away every doubt. No matter what she did or didn't do about it, she loved Aaron.

That love swept away every doubt for her, but what about for Aaron? What she felt didn't matter in the least if Aaron didn't feel the same.

For a moment when they'd touched, when their unguarded gazes had crossed, she'd been sure of what she saw in his eyes. She'd been convinced he loved her, and her heart had sung with the sheer joy of it.

But the moment had passed. He'd backed away first. She couldn't deny that or rationalize it. Aaron had retreated. She'd told herself that he'd stopped because he'd spotted Elizabeth watching them.

But what if she'd been wrong? What if he'd seen the love shining in her eyes and withdrew, embarrassed at the thought that little Sally was in love with him?

The blood seemed to pound in her head, and for an instant her face burned while her hands turned icy cold. Humiliation swept over her, and all her hope seemed to shrivel away to nothing. If Aaron had seen that she loved him and he didn't return her feelings, how could she ever face him again?

Maybe she should be glad that Elizabeth had interrupted them when she did. Maybe that interruption had saved her from still worse embarrassment…the agony of seeing Aaron try to find a way to let her down easy.

Gathering the threads of her confidence together, Sally straightened, her palms pressing into the quilt beneath her. The truth was that she didn't know.

And she didn't have any choice. She and Aaron couldn't avoid each other. They were neighbors, united in so many ways. That meant she'd have to hang on to her self-control regardless of what Aaron might feel.

What would he do? If it had been real, if he'd seen her feelings and returned them, he would speak to her. Naturally he would. And if he didn't? For a moment her mind was blank. She didn't have any illusions that Aaron hadn't seen her feelings—she knew how quick and intuitive he was.

He'd try to spare her. He'd carry on just as usual, as if nothing had happened. He'd want her to be able to save face.

She'd require a lot more control than she'd shown so far if that were to happen. She'd best start practicing. So right now she'd get dressed, go downstairs and hope Elizabeth had been distracted from the lecture she'd been so eager to give.

With a silent prayer for guidance, Sally pulled the dress over her head and smoothed her hair back. She'd make herself presentable, and she'd move forward. She didn't have the luxury of sitting here feeling sorry for herself.

Slipping into the kitchen, Sally found Elizabeth standing at the stove, her back turned. When she didn't immediately spin around and start talking, Sally breathed a sigh of relief. Maybe the worst was over.

With a glance at the clock, Sally pulled plates from the cabinet and began setting the table. Usually this was such a pleasant part of the day—when life was normal, that was. She and Mamm would chatter away about everything and nothing while they got supper on.

Mamm always loved to hear her stories of what had happened at school with the children that day, and Sally knew she could say anything and name names without fear that folks would get to hear about it.

She couldn't do that with Elizabeth. First because

Elizabeth didn't really seem interested in her tales of her scholars. And second, because she didn't feel absolutely confident that something she said might not be repeated. Elizabeth wouldn't do that deliberately, but she liked to talk, and she didn't always stop to think about what was coming out when she did.

The continued silence from Elizabeth began to feel a little ominous. It wasn't like her to hold her fire for this long. She must be really perturbed about what she probably saw as Sally's misbehavior.

Finally Sally moved over next to her. "What can I do?"

"Nothing for supper." Elizabeth shot her a glance. "But you can listen to me instead of running off."

So that was it. There was no point in pretending she hadn't done what she clearly had.

"I'm sorry, Elizabeth. But I didn't want to get into an argument about Aaron." She had to force her voice to remain level when she said his name.

"It's not Aaron I'm worried about." Elizabeth slapped the wooden spoon she was holding down on the counter. "It's you. I looked out the window and what did I see? I saw you down on the ground with Aaron's arms around you."

Sally held on to her tongue with an effort. "I already explained what happened. I stepped in a hole and tripped. Naturally Aaron came to see if I was hurt, just like you did."

"And what about him having his arms around you, and you looking up at him?"

"He was trying to help me up. And I was laughing at my own clumsiness, that was all." That wasn't all, of course, but she couldn't tell Elizabeth the rest of it.

How everything she thought she knew about herself was changed in that instant their eyes met—no, she couldn't tell Elizabeth that.

"What if someone else had seen you?" Elizabeth wasn't accepting it. "What if the bishop had been passing by and had seen you and Aaron with his arms around you? Aaron's just an Englischer now, for all that you were friends when you were a child. You can't get involved with him."

"I'm not involved. I'm just being a friend. And if Aaron wants to repent and come back to the Leit, I won't do anything to make that harder for him." Tears stung her eyes, but she wouldn't let them spill over. "What if everyone acted that way? He'd never want to stay then."

Elizabeth's broad cheeks flushed. "I'm not saying we should be mean to him. I'm saying that you're an unmarried woman and a teacher besides, and you need to mind your reputation. What would your mamm and daad say if they were here?"

"They wouldn't scold me for being kind to an old friend." Her voice was probably a little too tart. "And they'd give me credit for being grown-up enough to make my own decisions."

"Your decisions?" Elizabeth took fire in an instant. "Like throwing over a gut man who wanted to marry you? And taking up with someone who's a runaway and a rebel and thinks and acts like an Englischer? You should be ashamed to cause folks to talk about you."

"You're the only one who's talking about me," she snapped, her control breaking. "You have no business telling me what to do. I'm not your child."

In the instant she said the words Sally wanted them

back. But that couldn't be done. Her unruly tongue had led her into hurting Elizabeth. No matter what the provocation was, she ought to know better if she was as grown-up as she'd declared herself to be.

"I'm sorry." She rushed into speech. "Elizabeth, I didn't mean to say that. I'm so sorry."

Elizabeth clamped her lips closed, shaking her head. She turned back to the stove, but not before Sally saw the tears spill over on her cheeks.

The autumn air smelled fresh and clear the next morning after a brief rain overnight, and the yellows and oranges of the trees on the ridge seemed to shine. Aaron bent to disconnect the battery that ran the electric fence around the west pasture. As often happened, the wire had become grounded somewhere, so he meant to find it before any of the cows decided to go roaming. Usually some wise old cow could find a spot and lean on it until she'd broken through to some grass she thought greener.

"There'll be a small branch down on it somewhere after the rain." Onkel Zeb walked alongside him as they started checking the fence line.

"Most likely." Aaron darted a glance at his uncle. So far no one had asked him what the bishop had said to him, and he'd been grateful. Was Onkel Zeb giving him a chance to talk?

Not that he wasn't willing to tell his uncle, but since yesterday he'd been too preoccupied with his thoughts about Sally to concentrate on anything else. Those moments when they'd been so close to each other… Looking into her eyes had been like sinking into a deep blue pool, leaving him warm and weightless and safe.

Reality had burst in soon enough. Elizabeth had plainly been horrified at the thought of him with her young sister-in-law. Most likely anyone else from the community who saw them would feel the same.

Face it, they would all know he was too old for Sally, both in years and in experience. His time out in the world had changed him.

And yet Sally didn't seem to mind that. She just reached right past the forbidding surface changes and touched his heart. Maybe he could deny what he felt to anyone else, but it was stupid to deny it to himself. He was more than halfway in love with her already.

He came out of his abstraction to see Onkel Zeb kneeling to pull some weeds away from the wire.

"Here, I'll get that." He knelt quickly, annoyed with himself for not doing his job.

"I'm not ready for the rocking chair yet," Zeb said, his tone mild, but he sat back on his heels and made room for Aaron to pull the weeds. But even as he spoke, he reached out to grab the fence post to pull himself up to standing. "Though I won't say a helping hand isn't wilkom now and then."

Aaron grinned at him. "Are you trying to make me feel useful?"

"I don't need to try. It's a fact," Zeb said bluntly. "With Daniel as busy as he is with his carpentry business and the young ones too little to be much help, we need another man around here." He paused as if to let that sink in.

"I'm not sure..." Aaron began, thinking he wasn't that man.

Onkel Zeb swept on. "There's plenty of folks around who'd be interested in a good horse trainer, too, with horses getting so popular among the Englisch. You put up a couple of signs in some stores, and you'd get all the business you can handle."

He didn't know if that was true, but he appreciated Onkel Zeb's effort to make him feel there was a place for him here. "Have you been talking to the bishop, by chance?"

Zeb shook his head. "No, why? Is that what he told you?"

"Not exactly." He hesitated, but he guessed it might as well come out. "He asked me to agree to live by the Ordnung for a month before I made a decision about the future."

The future...and Sally's face forming in his mind, smiling at him.

"Bishop Tom is a wise man. You're taking his advice, ain't so?"

"I guess I am. But I don't know how it will turn out." Aaron hurried to add that, afraid his uncle would read too much into his cooperation. He wasn't even sure if he could do it in the long run.

But if he could, it was so tempting to think he could have a future here.

Onkel Zeb straightened, shielding his eyes as he glanced toward the lane. "There's Ben Stoltzfus coming over." He waved, catching Ben's eye, and Ben left the lane and crossed the field toward them.

"I guess he's looking for us." Aaron stood waiting. And wondering. Was it a coincidence that Ben showed up apparently wanting to talk the day after his Elizabeth had seen Aaron and Sally touching? He didn't think so.

Ben reached them. "Zeb. Aaron. A fine day, ain't so?"

"It is that," Zeb replied. "Are you needing something, Ben?"

Ben looked from Aaron to Zeb and back again, and embarrassment made his already ruddy face a bright red. "Chust a word or two with Aaron, if he can spare the time."

Aaron stiffened. So it was like he'd figured. "I need to walk round the fence line. Come along, if you want."

There was an awkward silence. Finally Zeb seemed to get the idea. "If you've got Ben helping you, I guess you don't need me, yah? I'll go see if there's coffee hot on the stove."

"That's fine. Save some coffee for me."

Waiting until he was sure Onkel Zeb was out of earshot, Aaron pulled a leafy twig off the wire. When he looked up Ben was still standing there, looking like a man who'd rather be anywhere else. Some of Aaron's irritation ebbed.

"Let me guess. Elizabeth wants you to talk to me about Sally."

Ben stared at him for a moment, and then a self-conscious grin spread across his face. "You know women. If they don't have something to worry about, they invent something. I'm that sorry about this."

Aaron shrugged. "No need to worry. I understand. Elizabeth saw me helping Sally up when she fell. Sounds as if she got the wrong idea."

"That's it." Ben sounded relieved. "Sally told her there was nothing to it, but Elizabeth gets nervous. She feels like we're responsible for Sally while the folks are away."

So Sally said there was nothing to it, did she? He was taken aback for a moment. He knew what he'd felt. Surely he didn't imagine what he'd seen in Sally's face. But he ought to be relieved if she didn't make anything of it.

"There's no need to worry about Sally, not where I'm concerned." He walked a few more feet along the fence and pulled out the small branch that had gotten entangled with the wire with one end touching the ground. That was probably the source of the trouble. It didn't take much to cause a problem, did it?

"Well, that's what I thought. I mean, Sally's just a kid."

Aaron looked at him, his eyebrows lifting. "I don't think your little sister is a kid anymore. She's been kind to me since I got back, and I appreciate it."

"Yah, well, Sally has a kind heart." Ben scuffed at a clod of dirt. "I guess it is hard for you, coming back to all this quiet after the life you've had out there."

What kind of life was Ben imagining? Probably nothing close to the truth.

"It wasn't all that different. Taking care of the horses, mucking out stalls…nothing exciting about that."

Ben didn't respond. He'd always been kind of slow of speech, but right now he looked like he was at a complete loss. Aaron sighed. He couldn't expect Ben to understand. All he could do was reassure him.

"Look, the fact is I'm not going to court Sally or anyone else unless and until I make up my mind to stay. So tell Elizabeth she can stop worrying."

The words had come out with an edge, but he couldn't help that. Okay, so Ben was embarrassed, but he'd started it. He couldn't expect Aaron to like having someone else tell him what he ought to do or feel.

Since Ben still seemed bereft of words, Aaron turned away. "If that's all, I need to finish with the fence and get the battery back on again."

"Yah, um, denke." Ben was back to shuffling his feet again. "Denke."

Aaron didn't bother watching him walk away. He was too busy trying to get himself back under control. Okay, it wasn't entirely Ben's fault. He understood that Elizabeth had done most of the pushing. But that didn't mean he had to like having other people interfering in his life. In contrast with this, the total disinterest of most of the people he'd met in the Englisch world looked pretty good to him right now.

As soon as Sally got home, she saw that Aaron had Star hitched up to the buggy already. He hadn't waited for her.

Sally rushed into the house, dropped her books and hurried back out again. But no sooner had she stepped off the porch than her brother appeared, holding out a hand to stop her. "Can we talk for a minute?"

Impatient, she shook her head. "I'm late to work with Star. We'll talk later."

Ben clasped her sleeve. "Wait. I… I have to tell you something."

She read her brother with an experienced glance. Ben was embarrassed, and judging by the way he was hanging his head, he'd done something he wished he hadn't. Something to do with her, clearly.

"Okay. What did you do?"

His eyes flickered toward her and then away. "You're going to be mad, but… I talked to Aaron about you." He held up his hand before she could speak. "I know, I know. You're mad. I guess I shouldn't have, but Elizabeth was so worried—" He stopped abruptly, as if he hadn't intended to say that.

Elizabeth was worried. Elizabeth was also far too fond of interfering in other people's business. But given the hurtful thing she'd said to Elizabeth, she was just as guilty.

She said a quick prayer for calm. "There's no reason for either of you to be worried. I'm all grown-up now, Ben. I know it's hard to believe, but I don't need you or Elizabeth to protect me."

"Yah, yah, but it's not so easy for me." He tried the effect of a smile, but she didn't really feel like smiling back. "You've been my little sister for a long time."

"That doesn't mean you ought to embarrass me that way. Or Aaron. What must he have thought?"

Ben actually looked a little relieved by her scolding words. "Aaron's okay. He didn't get mad. He just said there wasn't anything going on. Said he wasn't courting anybody—he doesn't even know yet if he's staying. So you see, it's all right."

It wasn't all right, but she couldn't see any point to telling Ben so. He'd meant well, she supposed.

"Yah, okay," she murmured, turning away.

But it wasn't all right. Her cheeks were flushed, and her heart was pummeled by a whole mix of emotions— embarrassment, humiliation and disappointment. No, *disappointment* wasn't a strong enough word. All her hope had been dashed to pieces by a few words.

So there was nothing going on between them, was there? She knew what she'd seen in his face, but that didn't matter, not if he chose to ignore it. So it was over before it began, and now she had to face Aaron and pretend she wasn't hurt.

Sally was dreading finding the words to say to Aaron, but he saved her the trouble, pulling Star to a halt and hurrying into speech.

"Star's behaving himself with the buggy. He doesn't seem to object to the harness and blinders at all. You come up and give it a try."

Aaron held out his hand to help her up, but Sally grabbed the edge of the seat and swung herself up easily. So they were going to pretend nothing had happened, were they? In that case, it might be best if they didn't touch.

He handed her the lines. "Just take him up by the barn and circle round. Let's see how he does."

Nodding, Sally clucked to Star and they started smoothly off toward the barn. Star was responding beautifully, but it was hard to concentrate when her mind was filled with so many more important things.

They made a couple of circles before going out the lane, turning and coming back in again. And the whole time Aaron didn't say a word.

Finally he spoke. "Star's turned out to be a quick learner once we got over a few bumps." Aaron was staring straight ahead, over the horse's ears. "Go back out the lane again, and we'll see how he does on the road."

She nodded, circling smoothly before going out the lane. She sent a quick sideways glance toward Aaron. "You don't have to be so careful around me. Ben told me what he said to you. He's downright embarrassed, and it serves him right. I'm so sorry."

"No reason for you to be sorry. Ben's your big brother. He's never going to stop thinking of you as his little sister who needs protecting." The words were spoken casually, but he didn't look at her.

Anger flared, but she controlled it. She was getting tired of everyone referring to her as little. It was bad enough for Ben. Or did Aaron mean that *he* could never see her as anything but Ben's little sister?

Aaron didn't seem to think anything else needed to be said, but she couldn't quite let it go.

"You may be right about Ben, but I'm not Elizabeth's little sister, and I know perfectly well this came from her."

"Turn down toward the school," he said, nodding when Star moved obediently past the spot where he'd thrown a fit that day Aaron arrived.

He waited until they covered a few yards along the road before he spoke again. "Ben says Elizabeth feels responsible because your parents are away."

"In that case, I wish they'd hurry up and come back." Hurt made her voice sharp. Aaron really was acting as if those moments between them had never been.

He chuckled, a low bass note that seemed to set up an answering echo in her.

"All right. I know that sounds childish," she admitted. "I do try when it comes to Elizabeth."

"From what I've seen, it would take a lifetime of patience."

"Something I don't have, I guess. She means well, and she does care about me." She could actually smile with him over Elizabeth's quirks. "Shall I pull in to the school?"

"Yah, let's see what Star thinks of the school grounds."

By the time they'd reached the school, she was congratulating herself on her control. Aaron was behaving normally with her, as if those moments between them had never happened.

So that meant she had to do the same. No one needed to know what she felt about a dream that wasn't going to come true.

And then Aaron's hand brushed hers as he gestured for her to turn, and the warmth of that touch swept along her skin and straight to her heart, and she wanted to cry.

Chapter Ten

Afraid her emotions were going to overwhelm her, Sally pulled up in front of the small porch of the school. "Since we're here, I need to pick up something." She muttered the words, shoved the lines into Aaron's hands and jumped down.

Thank the gut Lord, Aaron didn't question her about the sudden decision. As she hurried inside, she heard him click to Star, and then came the sound of the horse and buggy moving around the schoolhouse.

Sally didn't stop until she reached her desk. Then she stood there, hands planted on the flat surface for support, and fought back the tears that threatened to overflow. A few tears trickled onto her cheeks, and she wiped them away with the back of her hand.

This was so foolish. She'd run out on a reasonable chance of marriage only to fall hard for the one man who wasn't interested. She'd been wrong to think he felt anything. He couldn't possibly be so casual if he did.

Some would say that it served her right to be hurt in the same way she'd hurt Fred. And if she went around moping and showing her feelings this way, soon half the church would guess what had happened between them.

That realization brought her upright in a hurry. Whatever happened, she would not give away her feelings—not to Aaron or anyone else.

Alerted by the thud of footsteps on the wooden porch, Sally managed to be rummaging through a file drawer by the time Aaron came in. He wandered up through the rows of desks, touching one here and there, as if remembering the past.

"Find what you wanted?"

She pulled out a file folder at random. "Yah, this is it. I'm glad we came back this way, or I'd have missed it too late to come back for it."

"Good. Just tell me one thing. Why are there two harrows and a baby crib behind the shed?"

"Oh, no." Annoyance chased away the last of her mood. "I've told people so many times not to leave things here for the auction until the day before. It's just plain dangerous having such things out where the scholars play during recess."

"I don't suppose you want them to play out by the shed, but I get your meaning. Anything like that would have been an irresistible lure when I was a kid."

"Of course. They'd be trying to hitch each other up to the harrow before I knew it." She shoved the drawer closed with a bang. "The auction's not until Saturday. I appreciate having folks bring things for the school auction, but—"

"But you wish they'd follow directions." He smiled. "Shall I go out and drag them into the shed?"

"That's all right. Don't bother. I'll have some of the

older boys do it first thing in the morning. What were you doing out back?"

He perched on the corner of her desk. "Showing Star his accommodations for when you drive him to school. He seems to approve of the stall and the paddock. Acts like he's right at home."

"That's wonderful good news. I was afraid I'd never be able to drive him to school." *See?* she told herself. *You can carry on a perfectly normal conversation with him and not feel so much as a twinge.*

"He's a perfect gentleman. Good, since this is his final lesson."

The words fell on Sally like a blow. "F-final?" She stammered the word. "You're leaving? Going back to your job?"

"No." His face tightened for an instant. "I just meant Star has learned enough to go on with. I don't expect you to have any trouble with him. He deserves a gold star. Or at least a happy face sticker."

Sally managed a smile. How could she be so stupid? She'd best not congratulate herself on her control too soon.

"I think I have some. But he'd probably prefer a bite of apple."

"Most likely." Aaron rose, moving to the chalkboard and back seemingly at random. "Onkel Zeb thinks I can pick up a few more horses to train once word gets around. I'd like that."

He seemed distracted, frowning and tense. Had she said something, done something to bring this on?

Then he swung around to look at her with an air of decision. "You mentioned my job. But I can't go back to it. If I did, I'd probably end up in jail."

Sally, wordless, stared at him, her thoughts tumbling wildly out of control.

"Well?" His face gave a wry twist, maybe to cover pain. "Aren't you going to run away from me?"

She found her voice. "I don't run away from my friends."

"Why not? It's what any respectable Amish maidal would do, isn't it?"

He couldn't hide the pain, not from her. She read it in the darkness of his eyes, the set of his mouth and the tension that radiated from him so strongly it nearly knocked her back a step.

"I've never worried too much about whether folks thought I was respectable or not." She hesitated, knowing she had to say more. Afraid of giving away too much. But Aaron's obvious pain was more important than her feelings.

"Whatever happened, I know one thing for sure. I know that you didn't do anything wrong."

Aaron was stunned into silence. Whatever response he'd expected, it certainly hadn't been that simple, honest statement of faith in him.

"Denke," he murmured.

She nodded. And just stood there, waiting. Not asking anything, not offering advice. Just waiting in case he wanted to tell her more.

To his amazement, for the first time since it had happened, he wanted to speak. He wanted to tell Sally all of it.

He ran a hand through his hair. Where to begin? How could Sally, with no experience of that world, possibly understand?

"Out in Indiana I got a job with a man who ran a racing stable. Harness racing, you know?"

She nodded.

"Albert Winfield, his name is. I was fortunate. I went looking for work without knowing anything about the people, and I ended up with one of the best owners in the business." He paused, thinking of the impression Mr. Winfield had made on him. "A good horseman, but more than that. A good man. Honest, respected."

"The right person for you to work for," she said softly, encouraging him to go on.

"He was in the stables and the training grounds every day. I guess he watched me, and he decided I could do more than shovel stalls." He remembered so clearly the day Winfield had found him working a horse for one of the trainers who was hungover. "Pretty soon I was working as a trainer."

"That made you happy, ain't so?" Again that soft voice, and he realized she was talking to him the way he talked to the horses. And it was having a similar effect. He felt his tension easing and his breath slowing.

"Yah. He had faith in me. After a season he promoted me to head trainer. His horses did well, and he gave me the credit." He shrugged, thinking of the man's generosity. "A lot of the success was in the good, honest stock he brought in. Anyway, we worked together, and I was…" He hesitated, not sure what was the right word.

"Happy?" she suggested.

"Yah, that, but I started to feel like maybe one day I could belong." He let his eyes meet hers. "You don't understand how lost you can be out in the Englisch world. It feels like there's no place you really fit in. Anyway, Winfield did that for me."

He sucked in a breath, feeling the tension returning. How could he say the rest of it to Sally, of all people?

"And then things started to go wrong." Again she didn't ask. She just said the words that made it easier to speak.

"I met a woman—she was involved in the racing circuit. She started showing up to watch me working the young horses. Pretty soon we were seeing each other." He carefully didn't look at Sally. "One night we'd gone out to supper and ran into someone she knew. She introduced me, and next thing I knew we were sitting with him. He was another owner."

"Quite a coincidence," she murmured.

"Yah." He managed a rueful smile. "I was stupid. Flattered that she wanted to see me, that I was sitting there talking to one of the big men in the business. And he made me an offer. Seemed like he knew just what I made, and he topped it. Said we could do great things together—I could help him pick out the best new stock, train them, have things all my way."

He shot a glance at Sally, but she didn't speak.

"So I thought about it. But I liked where I was—liked working with a man I respected. Winfield—he thought more about the horses than the glory of winning. So I said no, I wanted to stay where I was. I figured that was the end of it."

His jaw tightened so much that he could hardly speak. But he had to tell the rest of it. The pressure rose in him to get it out. Sally was safe. He could say anything to her.

"I didn't say anything to Winfield about the offer. I didn't want him to think I was angling for a raise. But

I should have. In the next day's race, one of our horses turned out to be drugged."

Sally didn't say anything, but he heard her sharp indrawn breath.

"Someone had told Winfield about seeing me with the other owner. Winfield…he had a quick temper. He blew up, accused me, didn't give me a chance to defend myself."

He was back in that office again, with Winfield standing behind the big desk. The walls were covered with photographs…some of them horses he'd trained, and there was a shelf full of trophies. The whole place was a tribute to Winfield Stables…to the sterling reputation Winfield had always had in the business. A reputation he thought Aaron had ruined.

He forced himself to go on. "Winfield said he'd bring the police in. I guess I lost it then. I wouldn't even try to explain to someone who judged me like that. I stamped out, packed my gear and left. Everything was gone, and all I wanted was to get lost."

The bitterness was still an acrid taste in his mouth, wounding his soul.

"So you came home."

"Yah. I came home."

He'd spilled it all. It had made him angry and hurt and ashamed all over again, but oddly enough it was a relief…like lancing a boil and letting all the poison out.

Gratitude swept over him. Sally wasn't the little tagalong of his youth or the desirable woman she'd become. She was a source of the belief and comfort he needed more than anything else in the world right now.

He didn't begin to know what to say to her. How to

thank her. He looked at her, to find her frowning a little, a question in her eyes after all that time of listening.

"But, Aaron, didn't you ever tell Mr. Winfield the truth about what happened?"

"He didn't want to hear it." Remembered anger moved in him. "I wasn't going to beg for a chance to explain. He should have known me better than to think I'd do such a thing. Why should I try to explain?"

"I see." She studied his face and then glanced away, as if not liking what she saw there. "You know, your Mr. Winfield sort of reminds me of someone I know. Someone who has a quick temper and flares up and says things he doesn't mean…things he's sorry for later but can't swallow his pride and say so."

Sally knew him too well. She was talking about him, and much as he'd like to deny it, what she said was true.

Well, true or not, the thing was over and done with. "I can't do anything about it now."

She shrugged. "Maybe not. But maybe he's had second thoughts. Maybe after he cooled off, he wanted to hear what you had to say but couldn't, because you'd gone. And he doesn't know how to find you."

"Forget it. I don't need that job any longer." He tried to sound convincing. But somehow he knew that Sally's words had planted a seed. What he did about it was up to him.

Sally studied his face, her heart breaking for him. She longed to reach out, to touch him in comfort, but somehow she knew she had to let him make the first move toward her.

He shook his head as if he tried to shake off the feelings. "Anyway, all that doesn't matter now. But my family…the church…what would they think if they heard about it?"

"They would respond just the way I did." At least, she hoped they would. "They'd know you couldn't possibly have done something like that—you would never harm a horse. It's impossible."

"You might be the exception. Other people aren't so generous." His face darkened. "I shouldn't have told you. Forget it."

The words sounded so familiar. That was what Elizabeth had said when she'd revealed her secret pain to Sally. Now Aaron was embarrassed, wondering why he'd told her something he didn't want anyone to know.

Sally couldn't help it. She had to touch him—just a gentle hand on his sleeve, but she could feel the warmth of his skin through the thin cotton. "I won't say anything. You can trust me."

Aaron swung toward her with an abrupt movement. Before she could identify the expression on his face, he pulled her into his arms. His lips found hers, and he held her as if he were a drowning man and she his only hope of saving.

No, she was the one who was drowning…in overwhelming love and tenderness. Her palms pressed against the strong, flat muscles of his back as she responded to his kiss, feeling the deep need he had for caring.

How foolish she'd been, she thought through the haze that surrounded her, to ever say that what she'd felt before had been love. She'd never known anything like this, never even dreamed that she could feel this way.

Aaron's hand cupped her face so gently, so tenderly.

He brushed a line of light kisses across her cheek and then put his cheek against hers.

"Aaron." She whispered his name. She wanted to stay here, in the warm circle of his arms, forever.

But as if the word had wakened him, Aaron let go of her so suddenly she nearly lost her balance. Groping, her hand found the edge of her desk and gripped it.

"I shouldn't have done it." He seemed to force the words out against his will. "This is wrong."

Sally looked at him steadily, willing him to see what she did. "It's only wrong if you don't feel what I do."

A spasm of pain reflected in his eyes. "I do. You have to know that. What I feel now—I've never felt this way about anyone else. Ever."

Her heart began to beat again. "Well, then…"

"Don't, Sally." He made a sharp, cutting gesture with his right hand. "Don't you see? You're as real and solid as the rich earth and clean air of this place. I love you, but it's no good."

"Why?" Her desperation sounded in the word. She'd been given a taste of everything she could ever want, and now he was snatching it away.

He flung himself away from her. "It's no good because you can't leave. And I can't stay."

The words sliced into her heart like a knife. She shook her head in denial. "Why not? Why can't you stay? Since you've come back, you've fit in here as if you'd never gone away."

"I can't. You know as well as I do that I can't stay unless I'm prepared to be Amish again."

"Why not? You are Amish. You've never been anything else in your heart." Didn't he see that?

"No." The word was sharp. "I'd have to let everyone know what happened to me out there. I'd have to kneel in front of the whole of the Leit and confess what I've done." His quick anger flared in his face. "I can't. I won't have everyone looking at me and pitying me or condemning me. I should never have come back."

Sally pressed her hand against her chest as if she could keep her heart from breaking into pieces. He'd admitted that he loved her, but he wouldn't humble himself to claim her. He was still the boy she'd known...the one with the quick temper and the stubborn pride that wouldn't let him admit it when he'd done wrong.

He'd sacrifice their happiness for that pride, and she could do nothing, because only God could change his stubborn heart.

Chapter Eleven

Somehow Sally got through the next few days. At least she hadn't seen Aaron again, and she supposed that made it easier. No, nothing could actually make it easier. Staying busy just dulled the pain a little.

She glanced around her classroom, checking to see that all of her scholars were occupied in the reading she'd set for them at the end of the school day. Most of the heads were down, although she caught the gazes of one clock-watcher and two daydreamers. A look set them back to their assignment.

She'd formed the habit of this quiet time at the end of the day so that she could look back over the day's activities to see if any concerns had surfaced. In the midst of the busyness of all those children of different ages, something she ought to pay attention to slipped by. Now she could think it through and decide if action should be taken.

It was also a time when any student who was having a problem could come to her for extra help. No one had today, probably because they were excited about the auction coming up tomorrow. It was hard to focus on anything when they could hear the noises made by the parents who were setting up just outside the windows.

She rather wished someone had claimed her attention. Sitting here quietly it was only too easy to let her thoughts wander back a few days, to those moments when she'd stood in almost this spot and heard Aaron say that their love was impossible.

Restless, Sally rose and walked to the window, staring out and barely seeing the men who were putting up a canopy in case of rain for the auction. Aaron had said he loved her, and in the same breath, he'd claimed he couldn't sacrifice his pride for that love. Her heart twisted at the thought. That wasn't love.

Somehow she'd managed to cope, hiding her feelings and getting through the days as best she could. She'd even achieved a measure of peace by telling herself that God's will for Aaron was surely that he stay here.

If so, God would work it out. She could pray for him, and she did, but Aaron had to be the one to open his heart to hear God's will. No one else could do it for him.

A shuffle of feet behind her announced that someone thought it was dismissal time. She turned with a smile. "You may put your work in your desk now." She held up her hand for quiet. "If your family is here and wants you to stay and help, of course that's fine. If not, let's get lined up for dismissal."

They scurried to do as she asked. Those whose parents were outside assumed a self-satisfied look, but it didn't really matter whether parents were here today or not—everyone would show up tomorrow to help with the auction. After all, it was their school that would benefit. People cared about that...the whole church community as well as the parents who had children in the school.

By the time she got outside, quite a few people had gathered, most of them already busy.

"Teacher Sally!" Leah, looking ready to pounce, seemed to have been waiting on the porch, her arms filled with linens. "Can we start setting up inside for displaying the quilts and such?"

"For sure." Sally held the door. "Komm. We'll have to move some desks and chairs around to display them."

Leah hurried inside, waving several helpers to join her, and Sally followed them in. She'd best take a hand before someone decided to put her school supplies someplace where she'd never find them.

Staying busy setting up tables and pushing desks together was a good antidote to thinking about Aaron and wondering if he was among the outside helpers. They began spreading out handmade quilts and place mats.

"This baby quilt is wonderful." She picked up one in shades of palest pinks, greens and yellows that formed a block pattern. "Jessie should have this."

Leah smiled. "She does. That is, Rebecca and I gave her one just like it. Rebecca made them for the quilt shop, and Jessie raved over the pattern so much that we knew she'd love it for her little one."

"Perfect. You know my sister will soon have an addition to her family. I might have to bid on this one." Thinking of her sister, so far away, made her think of Mamm and Daad. And of how much she longed for their steady presence and reassuring love right now.

"Your parents are staying to help out, ain't so?"

Of course Leah was well-informed on what the neighbors were doing. Secrets were hard to keep in the Amish community, and Sally clutched her own close to her heart. No one should know what she felt for Aaron, not now.

"Yah, they're eager to fuss over the new little one." She frowned slightly, remembering Daad's last call. "They like helping to get the new Amish church district started out there, I think. It's a big change from being here. You know they only have ten families?"

"I've heard that." Leah spread out a quilt with careful hands. "Still, ten families is a fine start, especially when most of them are young marrieds who will start having kinder. They'll need a school before they know it."

"Teacher Sally?" The call came from outside. "Where do you want the food stands?"

Leah grinned. "They'll put them where they always do, but you'd best go and direct them, so they can say they asked you."

Sally obediently went outside, giving a cautious look around for Aaron. She'd be bound to see him again soon, but she'd really like enough warning to be sure her armor was in place.

Daniel and his onkel Zeb were present, with Becky and her little brother helping to string a line from tree to tree to mark off space for car parking. There would undoubtedly be some Englisch neighbors come to bid on things, and no one wanted the cars mixed in with the horses and buggies.

But the rest of the King family was absent, and she wasn't sure whether she was relieved or saddened.

"Komm see what we're doing, Teacher Sally!" Becky called and waved.

"In just a minute." First she must meet with those setting up the various food stands.

Sure enough, each of them knew exactly where their stands went…in the same place they'd been the last time. But she solemnly agreed to each placement and expressed her gratitude for their cooperation.

Becky was still waving, so Sally made her way across the schoolyard.

"Very gut work," she said, looking from Becky to Zeb, who was helping her tie off a streamer. "Looks like you're planning on lots of folks with cars tomorrow."

"Sure enough," Zeb said. "It's going to be a sunny day, and I've even heard the men at the feed mill talking about the sale. It'll be a gut sale, that's certain sure."

"I hope you're right. The roof repair took a bite out of the budget."

Zeb's leathery face split in a grin. "So Caleb keeps reminding us. He's bringing a wagonload of things later, and Jessie says she's making an extra batch of whoopie pies."

"That's wonderful kind of her, but she shouldn't be doing too much." Not so soon after having a new baby, she thought.

"Ach, there's no stopping her, but I made her promise to leave the icing. Becky and I will finish them when we get home."

Becky nodded. "I love making whoopie pies."

"And eating them," Timothy said, making them all laugh.

No mention of Aaron, so apparently he wasn't showing up to help, at least not today. She would not let herself feel disappointed.

Zeb nodded back toward the schoolhouse. "Looks as if your brother is looking for you."

Sure enough, Ben came hurrying toward her. She went to meet him, praying nothing was wrong to put him in such a rush. But he was smiling when he came up to her.

"You missed a call from Daad. He forgot about it being the day before the sale, or he'd have known you'd be here late. He says he's sorry not to talk to you, but he'll call back tonight after supper."

"That's gut. There's nothing wrong, is there?"

His grin reassured her. "He says Mamm thinks the boppli will be coming soon. He didn't know why she thinks that, because he says the first one is usually late."

"I'd guess Mamm knows more about it than he does. I think I'll go with her opinion." Happiness bubbled up at the thought of her little sister becoming a mammi. Impossible, that's what it seemed. She focused on Ben. "Did you tell Elizabeth?"

He stared at her. "Yah, for sure. Why wouldn't I? She's happy about it."

Was he trying to deny what was so obvious to her? Or did he really not see it? Sally bit her tongue to keep the words in. She'd promised Elizabeth she wouldn't say anything, so she couldn't. But the urge to give her brother a shaking had never been so strong.

Poor Elizabeth. Another baby in the family, and still none for her after six years. If Mammi were here...

Sally realized abruptly that it wasn't only Elizabeth

who needed to talk to Mammi right now, as close as she was to her mother-in-law. Sally needed it even more.

There was no one, no one at all, that she could talk to about her feelings for Aaron. The girls who had been so close during their teen years had moved on to marriage and children of their own. Much as she loved them, she couldn't talk to them. And she certain sure couldn't talk to Elizabeth about Aaron.

Mammi was the only person she might have confided in, and Mammi was far away and preoccupied with the coming baby. So she not only had to hold her secret to herself, she had to put on her usual upbeat face and never let anyone know.

Aaron arrived early at the schoolhouse the day of the auction with Daniel, since his brother had volunteered him to help get everything ready. Daniel nudged him as they pulled in.

"What's wrong with you? Still sleepy? Wishing you'd waited to come later with the others?"

"I'm fine." Aaron ground out the words, finding his brother's teasing more annoying than usual today. "You go see who needs help. I'll take care of the mare and the buggy."

Nodding, Daniel hopped down. "Don't put her next to that bad-tempered mare of Gus Albright's. Those two hate each other."

"Will do." In his opinion, Daniel's Queenie was the one with the bad temper, but it wouldn't do to say that to his brother, since Daniel had raised her since she was a filly.

Relieved to have an excuse for not joining the people who were hustling around the schoolyard, he took his time about the task. He knew perfectly well what had caused his shortness with his brother. He'd avoided Sally all week, but he couldn't possibly keep from seeing her today.

It hadn't been easy, doing without her. He'd missed her teasing smile and the flash of her dimple, to say nothing of the bright curiosity in her blue eyes and the glow of warmth and concern in her face. But it was for the best that he stay away from her.

He'd said too much, revealing his inner thoughts and torments in a way he'd have said was impossible. And after that kiss that had rocked him right down to the ground, what was there to do? He had no choice— he had to either ask Sally to marry him or to pretend it hadn't happened. And he couldn't ask her to marry him.

So there wasn't really a choice at all.

He couldn't deny that she'd known him only too well, though. She'd compared Mr. Winfield's quick temper to his own. She'd said he should give the man a second chance. She hadn't pointed out that he himself had been given a second chance by the community. She'd trusted he'd see that for himself.

It made too much sense to ignore, and he'd begun to feel as if it was the Lord rapping at his thoughts, urging him to take action. So he'd written to Albert Winfield.

No pleading. Just a simple telling of everything that had happened. He hadn't wanted to confess about his foolishness in trusting the wrong woman, but he'd told it all.

He hadn't asked for his job back…didn't even know if he wanted it. But he'd felt better when the letter was written and in the mail. Then it was too late to change his mind. Maybe Winfield would tear up the letter unread, but he'd done what he could.

When he rejoined his brother, he was immediately swept into helping set up the speaker system the auctioneer would be using. Isaiah Byler had been running auctions in Lost Creek, Pennsylvania, ever since Aaron could remember. His reddish beard had plenty of gray in it now, and his voice might be a little weaker, but he was still master of the rapid-fire patter folks expected from an auctioneer. Aaron suspected some people came just to be entertained by him.

It took some time to have everything set up in the way Isaiah wanted it, but Isaiah finally nodded in satisfaction.

"I'm picky, ain't so? But we have to get it right, you know." He gave Aaron a friendly clap on the shoulder. "I don't have the volume I used to, so I need the help."

"Daniel says you still have the stamina you used to, though. According to him, you won't stop until every single thing finds a new home."

"Got to raise the money for the school, ain't so? Can't have the kinder running out of books and such." Isaiah glanced over Aaron's shoulder. "There's Teacher Sally coming now. That's never that spooky gelding Simon Stoltzfus bought at the livestock auction, is it?"

"That's Star, all right." He schooled himself to bear the sight of Sally, weaving her buggy competently through the busy grounds.

"Aaron had the training of him," Daniel put in. "Or retraining, I guess you'd say."

Isaiah grinned. "For sure any horse Simon trained or even picked out would need that. Never saw an Amishman so lacking in horse sense. But I'd have said that animal never could be trained. Too skittish by nature." He looked at Aaron with a tinge of respect in his face. "It's gut to see you developed your promise as a horseman."

"I worked with a harness racing outfit out west," he said, as briefly as possible.

"You know, I've got a two-year-old filly that needs training. Pretty flighty, and I haven't got the time or patience to work with her. Think you might be interested in taking her on?"

Aaron hesitated. He'd been on the verge of leaving for the past few days, but somehow he hadn't been ready to do it. Besides, he'd given his word to Bishop Thomas that he'd live by the Ordnung for a month. He couldn't back out now just because staying had become difficult. The reason for that had nothing to do with the Ordnung.

The lure of working with Isaiah's horse called to him—the greater the challenge, the better. And a lot could happen in three weeks.

"I'll give it a try, if you want. At least I can give you my opinion on her."

"Gut. Stop over any morning this week, and we'll see what you think." He looked around at the gathering crowd. "Looks like we're about ready to start. See you soon, yah?"

Aaron nodded. Like he'd told himself, a lot could happen in three weeks.

He and Daniel wandered through the crowd, taking a look at the items on display. Daniel was on the lookout for any tools he might be interested in, and Caleb, once he showed up, would have an eye out for farming implements. He'd been muttering something about a harrow when they'd left this morning.

As for him…well, there was nothing he needed in his footloose life, was there? Still, he ought to support the sale. He'd take a look through the toys and books. Maybe there'd be something Becky or Timothy might like. Or something for the new baby.

If…when he left, he'd like it if they had something to remember him by.

He turned to point something out to Daniel and nearly bumped into Sally. She looked as startled as he felt.

But it only lasted an instant, and then she was back to her usual smiling self. "So, what are the two of you doing? Bidding on anything?"

"Still looking," he said, trusting he sounded normal. "Hope it's a great moneymaker for the school."

"Bound to be," Daniel said. "Look at the crowd. Nobody would dare leave without buying something. And it's brought Aaron benefit already. He's picked up work training another horse, thanks to you and Star."

"Thanks to us?"

"Yah. Isaiah spotted you driving Star this morning and decided Aaron was just the man he needed."

"That's wonderful gut. I'm glad we brought you some business already." It was said with a quick smile for Aaron. He was probably the only one who could tell that her smile wasn't quite as usual.

"We'll be sehr glad to get him out of the house again," Daniel teased. "He's been moping around bored as can be without seeing you and Star every day."

The color came up in Sally's cheeks, and Aaron felt like clouting his brother. He couldn't have said anything worse if he'd planned it ahead of time.

Before Aaron could come up with something to distract Daniel, it was done for him.

"That looks like a tool chest over there. I have to have a look." Daniel headed off, intent.

"I'm sorry." Aaron rushed the words off. "He didn't know... I mean, nobody suspects anything. I wouldn't talk about it."

"It's all right." The pink had washed out of her cheeks, leaving her looking a little pale. "I understand. Daniel would never say anything like that if he knew."

Sally's response was so heartfelt that it was a separate little barb in his heart. She understood. She always had, and she always would. That was what made this whole thing between them so hard.

She seemed to sense his inner struggle. "It's all right," she said, her soft words meant only for him. "We were friends first of all, and that doesn't change. We're still friends."

"Denke." He should be grateful that Sally was being sensible about the situation. So why should that annoy him at the same time? Was he mean enough to want her to show the world a broken heart?

Chapter Twelve

Sally leaned back in her spot at the kitchen table with a sigh of satisfaction. Supper had been a light meal of Elizabeth's homemade vegetable soup, and it had been just right after a long day spent at the school auction.

"I wouldn't be surprised if today was the best school auction we've had in years." She smiled at Ben and Elizabeth. "Thanks to all the support we had."

"Yah, it was gut. Caleb said he'd try to have the totals by tomorrow." Ben's gaze turned toward the harness that was slung over the back porch railing, clearly visible through the screen door.

"You can't wait to get that harness polished up," Elizabeth said, topping off his coffee. "I see you eyeing it. I think you men are even worse than women when it comes to finding a bargain."

"It's not for me," Ben protested. "It's chust what Daad needs for the pony cart. He wouldn't want me to pass it by when it's in such fine shape."

"I guess not." Elizabeth patted the fat brown teapot she'd found. "I never thought I'd find the perfect teapot. And so cheap, too."

Sally's lips curved. That was the great thing about a sale…everyone donated and then they all went home with something they needed. The school made money for repairs and equipment and, she hoped, some new books she'd had her eye on.

"I don't think there was a thing left at the end," she said. "Elizabeth's pies disappeared in no time at all. Folks knew something good when they saw it."

Elizabeth brightened, but only for a moment. Her gaze moved back to the back door, left open so they could hear the phone from the phone shanty. Daad had said he'd call tonight. Maybe he'd have news of Alice's baby.

Elizabeth would try to be happy for Alice. She *would* be happy. But Sally understood now how each new baby reminded her of her loss. She'd felt the same each time she'd seen a courting couple walking around the sale, eyes only for each other. Each glimpse had been a fresh pain in her heart for what could never be.

Sally had gotten up to put her dishes in the sink when they heard the sound they'd been waiting for. The phone rang, and since she was already on her feet, she beat Ben to the back door. They jostled each other, each trying to get to the phone shanty first.

Sally snatched up the receiver, edging Ben out by a step. "Hello. Daadi?"

Her father's deep voice boomed from the phone, and she held it so the others could hear.

"Gut news! Our Alice has a baby girl—chust as sweet and pretty as can be. They're both fine, thank the gut Lord."

Sally breathed a silent prayer of thankfulness.

"That's wonderful. How much does the little one weigh? Does she have hair?"

Daad chuckled. "A little wisp of hair so light it's almost white. Mammi says it will darken up. And she weighs almost seven pounds."

"Tell them we're wonderful happy for them," Ben shouted into the receiver. Like Daad, he seemed to think yelling helped the telephone carry his message.

"Yah, yah, I will. Your mammi says to tell you all she misses you."

"We miss you, too, Daadi." They couldn't know how much Sally longed to have them near enough to confide in. "When will you be coming home?"

"As for that, I don't know. There's lots to be done here with getting the new church district organized. These young folks actually seem to appreciate having us old people around to advise them."

A whisper of concern ran along her nerves. Daadi almost sounded as if he were growing attached to that new place. He was always one who liked a challenge. Maybe he felt as if life here in Lost Creek had gotten stale.

"We need you here, too." She couldn't say more, much as she'd like to. That would be selfish. "So come back soon. Give our love to everyone."

Sally handed the phone over to Ben to say his goodbyes, trying not to let dismay get the upper hand. Maybe she was being selfish, but if Mamm and Daad decided to stay out there, what would become of her?

Her gaze caught the expression on Elizabeth's face, and she felt ashamed of her own self-centeredness. Elizabeth was struggling with a far deeper pain, and

Ben, being more obtuse than usual, didn't even recognize it.

She slipped her arm around Elizabeth's waist as she turned toward the kitchen. "It's getting chilly out here now. Let's get inside and try out that new teapot of yours. Want to split one of those whoopie pies we brought home?"

Elizabeth seemed grateful to have something else to focus on. "Yah, I'd like fine to give it a try. Denke, Sally."

They went inside, closing the door against the evening chill. Ben stopped inside the door and stretched. "Ach, what an end to a busy day, ain't so? We had a wonderful gut sale, and our little Alice has a new baby girl. Quite a day."

"Yah, it was." Sally sent him a warning glare, but he didn't seem to get the message.

"Sounds like he and Mamm are really enjoying life out there. Could be they'll decide to stay."

She'd hoped she was reading too much into Daad's comments. But if even Ben, obtuse as he was, had noticed it, it could be real.

Elizabeth turned away from the kettle and came to put her arm around Sally's waist in much the same gesture Sally had used. "Don't worry about it. I think they'll be eager to get home before long. And if they don't, you know you always have a home with us."

Naturally that was what she'd say. It was automatic in any Amish family. But Sally heard the real caring that underlay the words, and though it wasn't the life she would have wanted, she was comforted.

The next week went quietly for Aaron. He started working with the new filly, and between that and the farm work, he kept busy. But not quite busy enough, since he found he was thinking of Sally too much.

Still, it was better not to see her. Better for both of them, he felt sure. But it was a long week.

Worship was held the following Sunday morning at the home of a distant cousin of the King family, Elijah Esh. That meant that Aaron and his brothers arrived early to help with the final setup for worship.

Elijah and Mary had a large prefab shed that they used when they hosted worship, and it was easy to see that the family had been hard at work removing the equipment that usually lived in the shed and scrubbing the space until it shone.

The church wagon was pulled up next to the shed, and Aaron joined Daniel and Onkel Zeb in pulling the benches out and carrying them inside. Timothy scurried along behind them, eager to help, while Caleb took Jessie and the baby into the kitchen to wait until time for worship. Becky marched along with them, proudly toting the diaper bag.

Onkel Zeb grabbed one end of a bench before Aaron could beat him to it. "I told Caleb to wait and bring Jessie and the baby a bit later. It's a mite cold out this early for such a little one."

"I'm sure Jessie will enjoy a quiet gossip with Mary in a warm kitchen before everyone comes flooding in." Aaron swung his end around so that he was the one to walk backward.

"Yah, I guess so." Zeb shook his head at the teenage boy who tried to take his end of the bench. "Ach, I'm not that old yet. Aaron, you remember Elijah and Mary's oldest boy, Adam, yah?"

The boy grinned at him. "I've changed since you last saw me." His voice was as low as his father's.

"You have. I'd say the least Onkel Zeb could do is let you carry a bench, given how big you are."

"Yah, that's so. Timothy and I can take it, ain't so, Timmy?"

Timothy's small chest expanded. "Sure thing. Let us, Onkel Zeb."

Zeb handed it over. "What can I do, with two young men eager to help?"

Relieved, Aaron saw Onkel Zeb move off to greet Elijah's father. Always so eager to carry his share of the load, that was Zeb, but it was time he took things a little easier.

And if you leave again? The small voice in the back of his mind asked the question. *Who will be around to lend a helping hand until Timothy and his baby brother are old enough to step in?*

He didn't want to go where that question led him. He hadn't even thought about things like that before his world had fallen apart around him, and he felt a flicker of shame. It was one thing to pursue his call to the outside world and another thing entirely to cut off the family he'd left behind.

That realization clung to his mind like a cobweb he couldn't wipe away. Why had he given so little thought to them?

At first it had been a necessity, he knew. If he'd thought too much about his family and his home, he'd have given up and gone home. Those first months had been hard, and it was only his pride that had kept him from heading back.

Eventually he'd pushed his family so far back in his

mind that he'd barely thought of them at all. There'd been nothing and no one to remind him that he'd once had another life.

Now…now he couldn't forget. If and when he left again, there would still be an unbreakable cord attaching him to this place and these people. And to Sally.

Helping Adam arrange the benches kept his body occupied, but it didn't do a thing to stop his thoughts. Images of her tossed and tumbled through his mind… Sally laughing, Sally pensive and even Sally looking at him with her blue eyes filled with love.

How could he leave, knowing he'd never see her again? But how could he stay, seeing her and knowing she'd never be his?

Once the service began, Aaron forced himself to concentrate on the songs and prayers. At first it was difficult, but he found his agitated thoughts mellowed by the long slow notes of the songs. His mind automatically made the adjustment to the High German that was used in worship and scripture. He found the familiar words of the readings resonated, waking his mind to their meaning.

Odd, how he'd have said he'd forgotten all this during his years away. It wasn't forgotten; it had simply been stored temporarily, ready to come back the moment he needed it.

The longer sermon was given by the youngest of the ministers, a boy he remembered from school, only a few years older than he was. He'd never have said that Jacob Beiler had it in him to be a minister, but the call of God fell without the intervention of anyone else. God had chosen Jacob, and he'd grown into the job, it seemed.

When the service had ended and the tables had been set up, he found himself sitting across from Ben. Aside from a little initial uneasiness the first time they'd met after he'd asked Aaron about his relationship with Sally, Ben had gone back to his usual manner. Today he was even a little more animated than usual.

"Did you hear our news?" he asked around a large bite of sandwich. "Our Alice has had a baby girl."

"No, I didn't know." He'd guess Sally was relieved if that meant that her parents would soon be coming home. "Your mamm and daad must be happy."

"Ach, wonderful happy. Daadi called us last night, and he couldn't stop talking. Seems like she's the prettiest baby girl he's ever seen, by the sounds of it."

If the birth of a new niece made Ben think of his own childless home, he didn't let it show. And since Ben wasn't subtle enough to hide his feelings, Aaron would guess that his happiness was genuine.

He'd guess Elizabeth might be feeling differently. Sally had given him the idea that she was struggling when it came to that subject.

It seemed a shame, given how many unwanted babies there were in the world, that good people like Elizabeth and Ben should be childless.

Ben turned away to greet Bishop Thomas, who'd stopped at the end of the table, and regale him with their news. After congratulations and best wishes for the family, the bishop asked the question that Aaron had been wondering.

"Does this mean we'll have your mamm and daad back with us soon?"

Ben's plain, open face clouded over. "I don't know. Seems like they've really gotten involved in helping that new community get on its feet. There aren't so many Amish down in that part of southern Ohio, from what Daad says."

The bishop didn't offer an opinion, but then, that wasn't his way. He rested his hand on Ben's shoulder for a moment. "You'll tell them we're missing them, yah?"

Ben nodded and then turned away to answer a question about Alice from the woman who'd just put a full serving plate on the table. That left Bishop Thomas free to turn his attention to Aaron, who began to wish himself elsewhere.

"I've been hearing about you, Aaron."

It swept into his mind to wonder who'd been reporting on him to the bishop before he realized Bishop Thomas was smiling.

"Something gut, I hope."

"Ben says he had his doubts that gelding of Sally's was even trainable, but I hear you've got him behaving like a lamb."

Aaron's face relaxed. "I wouldn't say Star was exactly lamblike, but I don't think Sally will have any more trouble with him."

"You always did have a gift where horses were concerned."

He'd said what everyone did, and Aaron realized that coming from the bishop, the fact gratified him. Whatever else folks said about him, there was at least that positive thing.

"Star just needed retraining, that's all. Some folks skip past the fundamentals when it comes to horses."

"Some folks skip past the fundamentals when it comes to a lot of things," Bishop Thomas said. "It never does work out, not in the long run. We just have to go back to the beginning—to the things we learned first."

He gave Aaron that characteristic pat on the shoulder and moved off before Aaron could respond. He sat still for a moment, pondering those words.

Had the bishop been thinking of faith when he'd said that? Somehow that seemed to echo his feelings when he'd slipped back into the familiar worship without needing to consider it. Those, he supposed, were the beginning things—the things that a person knew in his heart without struggling.

He wasn't sure how long he'd have sat there, lost in thought, but one of the teenage girls who'd been pressed into service swept his plate out from in front of him. He realized that everyone else was getting up, so he followed suit. He'd have to leave deep thinking for another time.

No one was in any hurry to clean up and get back on the road except perhaps for those teenage girls. They were probably eager to finish their work so they could gather in giggling groups, eyeing the boys who tended to talk a little louder and gesture a little more broadly when the girls were watching. He smiled, remembering what it felt like to be one of them, so caught up in what your peers thought that you didn't have room for anything else.

"Have some dessert?" Sally appeared next to him, carrying a tray with various kinds of cake and pie slices. "The lemon squares are all gone, but there's plenty of chocolate cake."

"Thanks." He picked up a slab of chocolate cake with what looked like caramel icing. If Sally could behave normally around him, the least he could do was follow suit. "I hear you have a new little niece."

Her smile sparkled. "A beautiful girl, so we hear. I wish I could go and see her. Maybe over Thanksgiving, when we have a few days off school."

"Your mamm will be eager to head back and see how she's grown by then." It occurred to him that it might not be the most tactful thing to say, especially when a tiny wrinkle appeared between her brows.

"If they've come home by then. I keep fearing they'll say they've decided to stay out there."

"Surely not. Their lives have been here. To say nothing of their other kinder."

"I hope you're right." She seemed to shake herself. "That sounds selfish."

"But understandable." He couldn't help thinking about that promise he'd once made to marry her when she grew up. If Sally were married, she wouldn't have to worry about living with her brother and his wife for good.

But there was no sense in thinking about something he'd already decided was impossible. "If they stayed out there, are you thinking that you might join them? Their community will probably need a teacher."

Now, that sounded as if he were trying to get rid of her. Why was he being so awkward around her?

"No, I won't do that." Sally spoke with certainty. "I know where I belong, and it's here."

Simple, it seemed, to her. Sally knew where she belonged. Too bad he couldn't say the same.

She started to turn away, and he spoke abruptly.

"There's something I ought to tell you."

She looked back at him, blue eyes questioning.

"What we talked about…about why I left my job. I started thinking about what you said, and I decided I should write to Winfield. Just to tell him what happened from my side."

"And did you?"

He gave a rueful smile. "It wasn't the easiest thing I've ever written, but I did it. Then I wanted to snatch it back from the mailbox a half a dozen times, but I didn't. I actually felt relieved when I saw the mail truck carry it down the road."

She nodded, but her face, usually so expressive, didn't give away her feelings. "Are you hoping he offers you your job back again?"

"No, not exactly. I don't know that I'd want to go back. But after what you said… Well, I couldn't just leave it."

"I see." Sally managed a slight smile, but there was something more in her eyes, something he didn't quite understand. "I'm glad you were able to put your pride in your pocket when it came to making things right with Mr. Winfield."

She turned and was gone, carrying her tray like a shield, before he could respond.

Once again he was left thinking, wondering and trying to puzzle out the meaning behind her words.

Chapter Thirteen

Sally should have gotten used to not seeing Aaron waiting for her at the paddock when she got home from school. He had finished his job and moved on. That was all anyone needed to know. Sally drove Star up to the hitching rail outside the barn, wishing she could convince herself.

No, she didn't want that. She wouldn't give up those moments of closeness. That was all she'd have.

When she'd walked away from Aaron the previous day after church, she'd told herself that was an end to it. She didn't have to be hit with a two-by-four to know when something was over.

She slid down from the buggy and began to remove the harness from Star. Aaron had told her more than he realized when he'd said that he'd written to his former employer to defend himself. He'd been willing to humble himself for a man she'd never seen, but not for her. That said everything.

And she'd best take her time about unharnessing, or she'd be walking into the house with a face that would give her away to anyone as sharp as Elizabeth. She had to stop thinking about Aaron, or she'd have half the church feeling sorry for her while the other half considered that it served her right.

Well, maybe not the second part of it. There might be a few people who still blamed her for jilting Fred, but not many. Not when he was so obviously happily married. And the father of twins, no less.

But she still had no desire to let folks know how she felt. What happened would stay between her and Aaron, and it was obvious that Aaron had successfully put it behind him.

Sally hung the harness on its rack and proceeded to brush Star down. She hadn't driven that far and the day was cool, so it wasn't really necessary, but she found the smooth, even movements as soothing as Star did. Bending, she checked Star's hooves. Daadi had taught her to drive, not entirely trusting Ben to do it, and he was always particular about how the horses were shod when they were used on the hard road surface.

Everything seemed to conspire to remind her of things she'd rather not think about. If Mammi and Daadi did decide to relocate out to Ohio, she'd have to find a tactful way of making a change in her living arrangements. It would be unheard of for a woman her age to live alone, but whether Ben and Elizabeth moved back to their own house or more liking stayed here, they'd expect her to live with them. Maybe they'd agree that she could have the grossdaadi haus, next to the farmhouse. At least that would give her a little more privacy. And Ben and Elizabeth might well feel they wanted privacy, as well.

When she walked back to the house, she gave a considering look at the grossdaadi haus, empty for several years now. She and Mamm always kept it clean and tidy for company, and it wouldn't require any changes for her to move in. The living room and kitchen downstairs and two bedrooms and bath upstairs would be more than enough space for her.

With that to occupy her mind, Sally could push the memory of Aaron's kiss far enough back to ignore it, at least. One day she'd get over him.

She went inside and found Elizabeth peeling potatoes for supper.

"Just let me wash up, and I'll do those." She lathered her hands and wrists thoroughly, not wanting to carry the scent of horse into their supper.

"Denke, Sally." Elizabeth surrendered the peeler to her. "That would be a help."

Sally darted a glance at her sister-in-law. Elizabeth sounded as if she were trying hard to be cheerful, but other than that, she could see no signs that Elizabeth was feeling depressed. If Mammi were here, she thought for the hundredth time, she'd know what to do about Elizabeth.

She hesitated, trying to think of a neutral topic of conversation, but Elizabeth saved her the trouble.

"The school auction was wonderful gut, ain't so? I heard that was the most money we've raised at one auction in years."

It seemed to Sally that Elizabeth was watching her, trying to measure her feelings. Maybe Elizabeth was checking her for signs of depression, just as she did with Elizabeth. The thought amused her for a moment, but she wondered what it might mean.

"Yah, that was a blessing for sure, especially with the cost of the new roof."

"You'll be able to get some new books. And I told Ben we should see about replacing those bookshelves that got wet when the roof leaked."

Sally blinked. Elizabeth had expressed more interest in the school in the past few minutes than she had all year. It was almost as if she thought Sally needed cheering up, or...

Then she got it. Elizabeth always kept an eye on her when Aaron was around. She had probably been watching when Sally had stalked away from Aaron yesterday after church. So she hadn't hidden her emotions as well as she'd thought.

"Star has been going fine for you since Aaron finished with her. He does a gut job with the horses, I guess." Elizabeth must be concerned if she were willing to go to the extent of complimenting Aaron. Sally didn't know whether to laugh or cry.

"Yah, he has." She took a breath, trying to sort out the confusion in her own mind. And then the words spilled out before she could censor them. "I'm glad Aaron had time to train Star before he goes away again."

"Is he going away?"

"I think so." She choked up suddenly, turning her face so that Elizabeth couldn't see her expression.

Her sister-in-law came close, gently taking the peeler from her hand. "It will be all right." She stroked Sally's back, patting her the way Mammi would. "It will."

A jumble of thoughts crowded her mind, and out of it one thing became clear. She accused Aaron of being prideful, but wasn't she doing the same thing, loath to show Elizabeth her suffering? She was trying to hold on to her own pride instead of practicing the humility that was a cornerstone of Amish faith.

She turned into Elizabeth's arms, feeling them soft around her, hearing the words of comfort that fell on her like a gentle murmur of peace. She could surrender her own self-will, but it was one thing no person could do for another. As long as Aaron clung to his pride, there could be no future for them.

Eventually she was cried out. She drew back, mopping her eyes, trying to smile. "I got you all wet."

"Ach, that's nothing." She pressed a fresh tea towel into Sally's hand. "Use that."

With a shaky laugh, she complied. "I'm sorry. You tried to warn me, but I didn't listen."

"Ach, I should have saved my breath. No one in love wants to hear it." She paused and then added, "Is there no chance he'll stay?"

"Very little." Sally sucked in a breath. Her eyes burned and her face felt hot, but the hard knot in her chest had dissolved. "I'll be all right. I have plenty to keep me busy."

She didn't really believe that, but it might help Elizabeth to hear it.

"About that…" Elizabeth stopped, as if struggling with the words. "I have been thinking about that special doctor. I… I would be afraid to go myself. But if you will go with me, I can do it."

Sally nearly burst into tears again. Was Elizabeth trying to distract her? Or had she somehow, through her suffering, become what her sister-in-law needed just now? She didn't really need to know why—just to accept that some good had come from suffering.

She wrapped her arms around Elizabeth, holding

her tight. "I would love to. We'll call the doctor and set it up."

A few tears slipped out then, but it didn't matter. Elizabeth was crying, too, but for both of them, they were tears of hope.

Aaron knelt beside the front porch steps, giving the railing a tentative wiggle. Sure enough, it was loose, and they couldn't risk someone getting hurt.

As he opened the toolbox, he found he was glancing toward the mailbox. Here it was Thursday, and all week he'd been first to check the mail just in case he heard back from Albert Winfield. It was too soon, he knew that. And even if he heard the best possible response, he didn't know that he'd be comfortable returning to his job. Still, he wanted to know.

Small wonder he wasn't very good at being Amish. He seemed to be totally missing in the traditional Amish virtues like patience and humility.

He caught a glimpse of movement at the Stoltzfus farm from the corner of his eye and resolutely looked away. Seeing Sally would only remind him of how much he missed being around her. And made it doubly certain that staying away was the right choice.

If he couldn't offer her marriage, it was much better not to see her at all. Unfortunately, he couldn't block out the image that was in his mind. That clung, persistent, no matter what he did. It changed, though. Sometimes it was Sally laughing, but more often it was Sally with her eyes filled with love.

Enough. He focused on the porch railing. He'd need to reset one of the posts that had worked its way loose and then check each separate paling.

He'd been working for probably fifteen minutes when he realized he had an audience. Becky and Timothy had joined him, looking on silently. Seeing he'd noticed them, they smiled, Becky with that sweet tilt of her head and Timothy with the wide grin that seemed likely to split his face.

"We didn't make any noise. Mammi said we shouldn't bother you when you were working," Becky explained.

"We didn't bother you, did we, Onkel Aaron?" Timothy gave him a hopeful look.

"No bother at all," he said. "I'm just fixing the porch railing. It wiggles, and we wouldn't want Mammi to fall when she comes out."

"Can we help?" Becky clasped her hands in front of her, and Timothy looked eagerly at the hammer.

"Suppose you hold this for me." He tried to be tactful, but he didn't think he was ready to turn Timothy loose with a hammer.

He positioned one of them at each end of the railing, safely out of range of the tools while he went on with his work. "Did you have a gut week at school, Becky?"

"The week isn't over yet, Onkel Aaron." Her face was serious, as if he might not know that. "We still have tomorrow, and that's spelling test day."

He grinned at her solemn correction. "Okay, other than the spelling test, was it gut?"

She nodded. "I got a star on my arithmetic paper. And I studied my spelling words, so I think I know them all."

Timothy watched her, a little apprehensive. "You have a test every week?"

"Every week," she intoned. Then she smiled. "It's

not hard. You just print the words after Teacher Sally says them."

"You'll do fine when you get to school," Aaron assured Timothy.

"Yah. And Teacher Sally is the best teacher ever. Everybody says so," Becky put in. Then she paused, staring at him. "Are you mad at Teacher Sally, Onkel Aaron?"

The smile he'd had vanished abruptly. "No, I'm not." He should leave it there, but he couldn't. "What would make you think that I'm mad at her?"

"She never comes around," Timothy said.

So they'd noticed, and they had been talking about it.

"And you don't go over there anymore." Becky jerked her head toward the Stoltzfus farm.

Aaron did his best not to let his face betray him. He pounded in a nail and reached for another. "I went to the Stoltzfus place every day when I was training Star, you know that, yah? Now that he's doing so well, he's graduated. I don't need to work with him anymore, and I'm working with a new horse."

A quick glance told him they both understood, but still, they looked disappointed. What was going on in their little heads?

"Look." He gave the railing a shake, showing them that it stood firm. "We fixed it, and you were gut helpers. Denke."

Timothy grinned. "I'm going to tell Daadi that I helped." He raced off at his usual run.

Becky squatted down and helped him put the tools away. She fingered a nail before dropping it in its compartment. "You know how to fix lots of things, don't you?"

It was nice to have someone looking at him as if he

had all the answers. "Not as much as Onkel Daniel, I guess. But this wasn't a hard job."

"It was important. You said so nobody would fall. That's important."

He puzzled over that, wondering again what was in her mind. "Yah, I guess it's always important to keep people safe."

"Then you can fix the railing at school. It's wiggly just like this one was and somebody might get hurt. You can come tomorrow after school, and I'll stay and help you." She finished with a satisfied expression.

"I... I don't know." What he did know for sure was that he shouldn't go and see Sally, especially not at the place where he'd kissed her. "Maybe we should ask Onkel Daniel to do it. Or your daadi. He's on the school board."

"No, you please, Onkel Aaron. You'll let me help. They might say I'm too little. Please, please, please?"

She had the wheedling down pat. He knew perfectly well that Jessie would correct her if she heard it. He also knew that he wasn't immune to that pleading look.

He hesitated, weakening for reasons he didn't want to analyze. Finally he nodded. "All right. Tomorrow after class is over. I'll be there, and we can walk home together afterward."

Chapter Fourteen

The quiet time at the end of the school day on Friday seemed to drag even more than it usually did. For the sake of her scholars, Sally couldn't show any sign of impatience, but she felt it. Silence gave her too much time to think.

This had felt like the longest week of her life. If she'd thought the pain in her heart would become easier to bear by now, she'd been wrong. She would heal, of course, given time. She'd be able to take joy in the routine moments of her life. But the hole in her heart where Aaron had been would never change.

The only bright spot of the week had been Elizabeth's agreement to see the specialist. She still wasn't quite sure what had done it. Did the suffering Sally had experienced convince her sister-in-law that she could understand? Did it form a shared bond? She didn't know, but she was thankful. Now all she could do was pray that their appointment next week would bring good results for Elizabeth and Ben.

A glance at the schoolroom clock told her it was time at last, and a look at her scholars made her laugh.

They'd been watching the clock even more closely than she had.

"Yah, it's dismissal time. Put everything away please, and then you may get your jackets and line up by the door."

She followed the rush to the coatroom, knowing her watchful eye would ensure that the older students helped the young ones instead of rushing past them. Once they were all lined up she opened the door, standing by it to receive the goodbyes from each one.

"Goodbye, Teacher Sally." It was repeated by each scholar, and she was careful to give each one a warm smile. She'd never want a child to leave at the end of the school day without knowing that she treasured him or her, regardless of what had happened that day.

When the last one had passed her, she stepped out to the porch, as well...and nearly ran into Aaron.

For an instant her breath was gone, and she could only stare at him, unable to speak. After too long, she got control of herself.

"Aaron. Are you here to walk home with Becky?"

He nodded, his face carefully expressionless. "I am, but first I'm ordered to fix a loose porch railing."

"Ordered? By whom? I was going to ask Ben to do it this weekend."

Aaron shot a look at Becky. "It was Becky's idea. She saw me doing the job at the farmhouse and thought I should make myself useful."

Sally eyed Becky with a certain amount of suspicion and found her looking from her teacher to her uncle and back again. She'd have to put the best possible face on it, but she certainly hoped Aaron didn't think she was behind it.

"Denke. It's kind of you."

Aaron squatted, checking the railing with deliberation. "Doesn't look bad. Becky and I will have it ready to go in a couple of minutes, ain't so, Becky?"

The child nodded. "Teacher Sally can help, too, can't she?"

Aaron's lips tightened slightly. "I don't think…"

"I'll just get my schoolwork ready to go," she said, and vanished before he could complete the thought.

It only took a moment to prepare the work she'd intended to take home with her, but she lingered in the schoolroom, not wanting Aaron to think she was eager to watch him work. Only when the hammering ceased did she venture back out again.

"Finished already?" She kept her voice even and pleasant—the way she'd speak to any parent who'd stopped by to help.

"Just about." He gave the railing a shake. "It shouldn't give you any more problems. I'll just clean up, and we'll be on our way."

"I'm on my way to harness Star. I'll give you a ride back." She could hardly fail to offer, no matter how dangerous it was to her heart to be with him.

"I'll help with the harness," Becky said, and was off like a shot.

Managing a smile, Sally followed. Becky wasn't tall enough to put the harness on, but she'd find something for the child to do.

Star seemed eager to be going home, and he stood quietly while they hitched him to the buggy. Sally led him around the school to the front with Becky patting him and whispering to him the whole time, fingering the harness.

"Here we are." She stopped by the porch to find Aaron closing his toolbox. "All ready to go."

Sally focused on the buggy rather than Aaron, her hand tightening on the line as she swung herself up. In an instant Star reared, jostling the buggy. Her hand slipped and she was falling, seeing the ground rush up to meet her.

She landed hard on her right shoulder, still clutching the books she'd held. The fall jarred her so that for a moment she couldn't think. Then Becky cried out, and Aaron rushed to her, kneeling and putting his arms around her.

"Sally!" It was nearly a cry. "Are you all right? Don't try to move."

She tried to speak, but she couldn't. She could only look at Aaron's face so close to hers and the love in his eyes turned her bones to jelly.

Struggling to control his feelings, Aaron held Sally gently, relieved to see that her gaze, fixed on him, seemed normal. "Easy, don't try to move too fast. Where does it hurt?"

She blinked several times, breaking eye contact, and seemed to be assessing how she felt. She moved a little, wincing slightly.

"My shoulder is sore, but I don't think anything is broken."

His pulse slowed, steadying, and he helped her sit up, relinquishing his hold on her reluctantly. "Take it slow and easy. I'll help you get up."

Sally nodded. Biting her lip and leaning on his arm, she got to her feet. When he let go she swayed, and he put a steadying hand on her elbow.

"Let's get you over to the step where you can sit down. Then I'll deal with the horse." He glared at Star, and the animal shook himself and kicked again.

They moved slowly to the steps, and he had to forcibly resist the urge to pick Sally up in his arms and carry her. He didn't have the right to do so. He didn't have any rights where Sally was concerned, and he had to remember it.

Sally relaxed with a sigh when she was seated on the steps. "I'm all right." Her gaze went past him to Becky, who was still weeping. "Becky, will you pick up my books and papers, please? That would be a big help."

Sniffling and nodding, Becky stooped and began collecting them. Seeing her safely away from the horse and buggy, Aaron approached Star.

"Settle down now," he murmured. "It's just me. You remember me, yah?"

Star tossed his head fretfully, but stopped kicking.

Still murmuring soothing words, Aaron began stroking the lathered neck. Star had worked himself into a nervous state—that was certain. But why?

"There now. What's wrong with you today? Nothing here to be scared of."

He glanced at Sally. She'd be losing faith in his ability with horses the way things were going. She sat on the step, leaning a little to one side, and she had her arm around Becky, soothing the child in much the same manner as he tried to soothe the horse.

What on earth had caused Star to lose his head that way? He couldn't see anything around that might have frightened the animal. Besides, with his blinders on, he could only see what was in front of him.

He moved his hand toward Star's shoulder, and a shiver went over the horse's skin like a warning.

"Hush, now, don't be foolish."

He looked back at Sally again, seeing Becky staring at her with such devotion and love that it shone from her face. His heart seemed to turn over.

"You'll be wishing I'd never touched this animal to begin with," he said, trying to distract his thoughts from what he wanted to say.

"Teacher Sally doesn't think that," Becky said, rushing the words, her hands clasped tightly. "She couldn't."

"That's right." Sally patted her. "It's all right."

Aaron frowned. What was going on with Becky? Surely the sight of her teacher falling shouldn't upset her this much, at least now that she knew Sally was all right.

His hand moved along the shoulder, brushing against the strap of the harness. Star exploded again, rearing and kicking, his head tossing. Aaron caught the headstall, holding it firmly, trying not to think about those horseshoes connecting with his body.

"Stoppe. Are you ferhoodled? What's wrong with you?" Aaron fought to keep a controlled tone, not wanting to make matters worse.

Under his hands, Star settled, but he shivered all over and his ears flicked nervously.

"It's my fault!" The words came in a wail from Becky, and he spun around to stare at her.

"What are you talking about?" he demanded, but Becky only cried louder.

Sally sent him a reproving glance. "Hush, now, Becky. Don't be afraid. Just tell us what you think you did."

Becky sniffled, shivering just as Star had. Then the words spilled out. "Under the harness." She pointed a shaking finger. "There. I did it. I put a thorn from the rosebush under the strap."

Aaron's gaze met Sally's. He moved slowly, resting his palm on Star's shoulder near the harness. Star shuddered. He inched his hand along, slipping his fingers under the harness. And had to mind his tongue when he felt the sharp prick of a thorn.

Still moving deliberately, he eased the irritant out, alert for any sign of trouble from Star. But the horse seemed to know that Aaron was helping him, standing perfectly still as the thorny twig came clear. Aaron smoothed his hand along under the harness to make sure he'd gotten it all.

Star visibly relaxed. Whickering softly, he turned his head toward Aaron. Aaron patted him, murmuring soothing words while his mind spun. Caleb should be the one to cope with his daughter's behavior, but it looked as if this landed on him.

But Sally was already coping. She cupped Becky's face in her hands. "Komm, now, Becky. You must tell us why. You're not a child to be mean to an animal."

"No, no." Distraught, Becky shook her head vehemently. "I didn't know it would hurt Star so much. I just thought it would make him misbehave a little."

Sally looked toward Aaron, as if asking if he wanted to take over. But he didn't. Sally was obviously more capable than he was in this situation. He shook his head slightly.

"You wanted Star to misbehave? Why?"

Becky had been answering readily, but now she seemed to get stuck. Her cheeks grew red, and her lips pressed together. Then she put her hands over her face, hiding it.

Sally pulled the hands away, her touch gentle. "You have to answer, Becky. Why did you do it?"

Becky glanced from side to side, as if looking for a way out. Then she stared at her hands, clasping them tight in her lap.

"We... Timothy and me...we wanted to have...to have Teacher Sally for our aunt." She rushed the last few words, eager to get them out. "But Onkel Aaron hasn't even been to see you all week. He said it was because he'd finished training Star. So I thought that if Star needed more training, you would get back together again."

She felt silent, still staring at her hands. Aaron moved to her side, not knowing what to say, and certainly not wanting to look at Sally. Finally he sighed and sat down next to Becky on the step.

Heaven only knew what Sally was thinking now. And he was going to have to make Becky see...

But again Sally, with that quick perception of hers, anticipated him. "Becky, you know that what you did was wrong, don't you?"

Becky nodded, shuddering. "I hurt Star. That was wrong."

He thought for a moment she'd say that she hadn't meant to hurt the horse, but she didn't. This little niece of his was taking responsibility for herself.

"You must understand that grown-up people have to decide things like marriage for themselves." Sally paused, and he realized how difficult this must be for her. It wasn't fair of him to let her carry the burden.

"That's right." He put his arm around Becky. "Getting married to someone isn't something you decide all in a hurry or because you spent some time together. You can't make that happen for other people."

Was it his imagination, or did Sally wince at that? He rushed on, not sure he wanted to know.

"Now I think it's time we went home." He glanced at Sally. "It might be best if I drive Star. All right?"

She nodded and bent to gather up her school materials, not looking at him. He ought to say something to make this better, but he couldn't, because there wasn't anything.

Sally put her materials in the buggy and then lifted Becky up, urging her over into the middle of the seat. She'd put a child in the center in any event for safety's sake, but right now she needed Becky as a buffer between her and Aaron.

She climbed up and settled herself, preparing to endure the trip home in Aaron's company. Just when she thought the hurt couldn't get any worse, it did.

The humiliating thing was the reflection that she'd been obvious enough about her feelings that the children saw it. Shame washed over her. That should never have happened. It violated everything she believed about the relationship between teacher and scholars.

Aaron had to share the responsibility, too, and he probably realized that. Regardless, she had to be responsible for her own behavior. She certainly couldn't control his.

They rode along in silence, each occupied by his or her own thoughts. Finally she shook herself loose of her preoccupation with her feelings and glanced across the buggy seat.

Aaron was stone-faced, giving nothing away. He looked like the man he'd been that first time she saw him as an adult—the day he came home.

It hurt too much, and she switched her gaze to Becky. Poor Becky. Sympathy swept over her. The child sat with her head hanging, her hands clasped together in her lap. She had to do something about Becky.

Putting an arm around Becky, she snuggled her close. Becky looked up, startled, and then relaxed against her, the tight look vanishing from her face.

"Look how nicely Star is going along now. I think that means he forgives us, don't you?"

Becky shot a glance toward her uncle. "Maybe. I hope so."

Sally wanted to poke him in the ribs, but she didn't dare. She stared at him so intensely that she thought he couldn't help but feel it.

Whether he did or not, Aaron roused himself. "Yah, I'm sure of it. He's a gut boy. He won't hold it against anybody. An extra carrot tonight, and he'll forgive anything, ain't so?"

She nodded, giving Becky a squeeze. "He's greedy, all right. I'll make sure he knows the extra carrot is from you."

At last Becky smiled. Without moving away from Sally, she reached across to take Aaron's hand, and they traveled along toward home, linked across the seat.

Sally's heart ached with the realization of how much Becky was going to miss her uncle when he left. Aaron obviously cared about her and Timothy, too. Didn't he see how much he meant to his family? Since he'd been back, he'd fitted right into the family, secure in his proper place.

Or was that wishful thinking on her part?

They rounded the bend in the lane that brought the two farms into view, and Becky bounced on the seat.

"Look. There's a car in front of our house. Who can it be?"

They looked where she was pointing. It meant nothing to Sally, but Aaron's whole body seemed to freeze. "I know." His voice had changed. "It's someone for me." He glanced at Sally and then quickly away. "It's the man I used to work for."

It was as if a giant hand had clutched her heart. Not now. It was too soon. She wasn't ready.

But she'd never be ready for Aaron to go away again.

"I thought I might get a letter. I never expected him to come here." Apprehension was plain in his voice.

"He wouldn't have come if he were still angry with you." The impulse to reassure him was stronger even than her regret. "You know that."

Aaron looked back at the car, his eyes seeming to narrow on the man who was even now stepping out of it. His expression eased into a half smile. "Yah."

"Well, I guess you'd best go and find out." It took all she had to keep her voice from choking. "I'll let you and Becky out at the lane. Star will be fine going home."

"He will, for sure." Aaron spoke absently, all his attention on the man who waited for him.

He pulled up at the lane, getting down quickly and helping Becky down. Without even a goodbye, he strode off toward the house.

Sally turned the buggy into her lane, clucking to Star. Thank the good Lord she hadn't lost control where he could see her. Now she could let the tears flow. His employer would want him back, and in a moment he'd be gone. It was over.

Chapter Fifteen

Aaron walked toward Albert Winfield, his mind racing. Was this a good sign? The man didn't look angry, but did his presence mean he was ready to believe in Aaron? At least he wasn't wearing the furious, judgmental expression that had been stamped on his face during their final interview in his office. That was encouraging.

Becky, seeming excited about the presence of an Englisch visitor, ran ahead. Then she came to a stop, spun and raced back to Aaron. Her brief spurt of courage had vanished as her shyness took over.

Aaron took her hand, as much for his own comfort as hers. Was she picking up on his apprehension? He hoped not. Hand in hand, they walked up to Mr. Winfield. Becky studied her shoes, and Aaron met the man's eyes firmly, not willing to be the first to extend his hand.

"Aaron. I'm glad to see you." Winfield tore his gaze from Aaron and bent to smile at Becky clinging to Aaron's hand. "Who's this? Will you introduce me?"

"This is my niece, Becky. Becky, this is Mr. Winfield. I used to work for him."

Winfield had been staring because he'd never seen Aaron in Amish clothing before, he supposed. The black pants, solid blue shirt, suspenders and straw hat were pretty much a uniform here, but would seem strange to Winfield.

Becky emerged from her study of her feet to give Winfield a fleeting smile.

Aaron patted her head. "Run on in to your mammi," he said, using Pennsylvania Dutch.

Nodding, Becky scurried toward the back door, but before she could reach it, it opened. "Aaron, was ist…" Jessie let the words trail off, looking at the stranger.

Aaron filled her in quickly in Pennsylvania Dutch, and then switched to English. "Mr. Winfield, this is Jessie King, my brother Caleb's wife."

Winfield removed his ball cap, polite as always. "Nice to know you, Mrs. King."

"You are wilkom, Mr. Winfield." Her eyes were wary, and relief swept over her face when Caleb and Onkel Zeb came around the corner of the house, probably because they'd seen the strange car.

Aaron performed the introductions again, suppressing the urge to laugh. If Winfield was dismayed by the appearance of so many Amish, to say nothing of their cautious response to him, he hid it.

What was Caleb thinking? Did he suspect that his brother was about to leave them again? But Caleb's steady gaze held only support.

An awkward silence fell, and he didn't know how to break it. Finally Onkel Zeb spoke.

"You will want to talk to Aaron, ain't so? If you'll

come inside, you can be comfortable. We'll leave you two alone."

"Well, thanks, but I don't want to put you folks out. I could stand to stretch my legs after that long drive. Aaron, how about taking a walk around with me?"

A sensible solution that he should have thought of himself. It would get them away from an audience. "Sure. Let's go up toward the orchard." He gestured toward the fruit trees on the slope beyond the barn.

Winfield gave the family a polite nod, and Aaron led the way across the yard and through the field. They walked in silence for a few minutes, the grassy pathway muffling their footsteps.

When they reached the orchard, Mr. Winfield paused, smiling a little as he studied the still-laden apple trees. Aaron reached up and plucked a ripe cooking apple, inhaling the sweet scent of it.

A flash of memory went through him, triggered by the smell...a small version of himself climbing into the tree to toss down apples to his mother, standing below. She caught them in her apron, looking up at him with a carefree laugh.

The image unnerved him. He'd managed to bury the memories of a time when his mother had still been a part of his life. All three of them had, he supposed, once she'd left them.

Winfield was gazing over the farm, spread out below them. "It's a mighty pretty place. Reminds me of where I grew up. Your brother's, is it?"

He nodded. Funny, but he hadn't thought of how the property had been left. Caleb was the one who had kept it going no matter what had happened in their lives, so in that sense it was his, but in another way, it belonged to all of them—to everyone who had sprung from it and loved it.

"I guess I'd better get to the point." Winfield shoved his hands in his pockets and hunched his shoulders. "I was mighty glad to get that letter from you. I'd been looking for you, but nobody seemed to know where you'd gone."

Aaron's eyebrows lifted. "You'd been looking for me?"

"Yeah. It was this way, you see." He cleared his throat, seeming to have difficulty getting started. "Well, once I cooled down, I knew I'd been rash, accusing you before I'd looked into things on my own."

Aaron wouldn't nod agreement, but he felt his expression tighten.

Winfield probably noticed. "So I started with what I knew. The horse had been doped, no question of that. But you weren't the only one who could have gotten at him."

"No, I wasn't." He kept his voice neutral, but that, after all, was what had stung the most…that the man he'd respected had rushed to judge him without investigating.

"Sorry." Winfield sent a shamefaced look his way and went back to studying the landscape. "Well, I started asking around, and Joe Miller came to see me. He wasn't happy, Joe wasn't. Why would you do that? That's what he said, and it got me to thinking."

He hadn't even considered the question of who the guilty party was. Someone had done it, and it had to be someone with access to Winfield Stables shortly before the race.

"Only one of us who worked there could get in on race day," Aaron said.

Winfield nodded. "And nobody there had reason to want us to lose, unless they were paid off. So I started looking for someone who had more cash than he should have. Joe helped me." He grimaced. "It wasn't hard, not with Pete Foster buying drinks for everyone down at the Rusty Anchor all night, when he usually didn't have two cents to rub together."

It fit, now that Aaron thought of it. Foster was one of the few stablemen who didn't really seem to care all that much for the animals he tended. It was just a job for him, that's all.

"Did he admit it?"

"Yeah, he did. He folded as soon as the racing commission started asking questions. Ended up with sanctions against Norton Stables and a hefty fine for them. Just wish I thought it would make them act straight from now on." He shrugged, turning toward Aaron. "So, I'm here to say I'm sorry. That comes first. I acted wrongly toward you, Aaron, and I hope you can forgive me."

Aaron paused, searching for the anger and resentment he'd had when he got back to Lost Creek. It wasn't there. Smiling, he held out his hand. "It's forgotten. We're okay."

Winfield shook his hand vigorously, beaming. "I'm glad, mighty glad you see it that way. Now for the rest of it—I want you to come back. Not just as head trainer, but also manager. With a raise, of course."

Manager of an outfit as big as Winfield Stables— that meant something. It was what he'd wanted, but still, he hesitated.

"I don't expect your answer now," Winfield added. "You'll need time. Take all the time you need."

"Denke—thank you, I mean. My family... Well, I should talk to them."

He didn't quite know why he'd said that, but he realized it was true. He hadn't talked to anyone when he'd run away, and he'd left a lot of hurt behind. He couldn't do it that way again.

And there was Sally.

They started slowly back down, the grass brushing against Aaron's pant legs and the scents of autumn rising from the land. Familiar. Everything about this place was familiar, right down to the blades of grass. The day he came back he'd resented that familiarity. Now...

Now it swept over him in a flood, stopping him in his tracks. He'd left here once, called away by the lure of the unknown. He'd looked for a place for himself out there in the world.

But now he felt a call that went bone-deep, beyond any possibility of question. The land itself called to him. He knew, with a certainty that was beyond words, that what he wanted was here...here in the verdant hills, the fruitful trees and the golden wash of autumn sunlight across the fields.

Here, where he had roots, and where work waited for him that only he could do. Where people loved him and belonged to him.

And Sally. The place where he belonged had been here all along, waiting for him to open his eyes, his ears and his heart to find it. There were no more questions. He was at peace.

The sun was slipping toward the top of the ridge as Sally walked to the barn. Its slanting rays turned the leaves to brilliant shades of yellow and red where they struck. Even with her heart breaking, she could be thankful for the beauty of the valley where God had placed them.

But in a few minutes, the sun would slide behind the hill and darkness would creep over the valley. The air would grow chilly, and she'd be as cold outside as she was inside.

Sally stepped into the barn, stopping for a moment to let her eyes grow accustomed to the dim light. Star poked his head over the stall and gave a whicker of welcome.

She went to him, patting him and holding out the carrot he expected. "Greedy boy," she murmured. Her throat tightened. "Ach, I should talk. I'm greedy, too, crying over what I can't have instead of thanking God for what I do."

Star moved his head up and down, brushing against her. She'd fancy he agreed with her, but she knew he only wanted his face rubbed. Trying to smile, she complied, and his eyes closed in bliss.

"You're easily made happy, ain't so?"

She leaned her forehead against the stall post, holding back the tears that kept threatening to overwhelm her. Strange, that even Elizabeth had seemed to know this wasn't a time to try and make her feel better.

Instead, she'd given Sally an extra-large serving of potpie and shushed Ben when he started to wonder when Aaron might leave. No question but that she and Elizabeth had reached a new understanding. She just regretted that it had come at the cost of so much pain.

Sally wished she could believe that Aaron's leaving wasn't already decided. But when she'd seen the way he'd headed toward the Englischer without a backward glance, she'd known. He'd go back to that other life.

So she would stay here, filling up the hole in her heart with family, faith and the scholars who meant so much to her. It was a good life. A satisfying, useful life. But not the one she'd hoped for.

"Ach, Star, why am I so foolish?"

"What are you feeling foolish about?"

For an instant Sally stared at Star as if the gelding had spoken to her. Then she turned toward the doorway. Aaron stood there, a dark silhouette against the golden light behind him. The moment seemed to freeze into an image that burned into her mind.

Aaron moved toward her, the image becoming reality. He crossed the space between them in a few steps and then stopped an arm's length away.

"I… I thought you'd gone." It was all she could manage. She had visualized him on the road back to that other life so clearly that she could barely grasp his presence.

He shook his head. "Winfield is gone. He left after supper."

"But I thought…" she stammered to a halt. Maybe Aaron had needed time—time to make things right with his family, time to prepare for leaving.

"I would never go away without saying goodbye." He paused, his gaze on her face. "And I can't possibly say goodbye."

The truth began to dawn on her, so longed for that she didn't dare believe it. "You can't?"

"I can't, because I'm not going. This is home." There was a certainty in his deep voice that she hadn't heard before. "This is where I belong. I know that now."

Wait...take it slowly. She had to be sure. *He* had to be sure. "Are you certain sure of that?"

He smiled, ever so slightly...just a hint of that teasing smile she cherished. "Doubts, Sally? Yah, I'm certain sure." He reached across the space between them to take her hand, holding it as if it tethered him to this spot. "I didn't know myself until I had the chance to go back. And then I knew."

Quick understanding flooded her. "Your boss...your friend...he believes you now. That's what you wanted."

"He believes me, yah. It's like you said—quick to anger, and just as quick to regret. Once he cooled off, he took the time to find the truth. He asked me to come back with a raise and promotion. But I turned it down."

She could scarcely take a breath. Now it was his grasp that tethered her.

"It was just like the bishop said. If I waited and listened with an open heart, the Lord would show me what was right." Aaron's voice thickened with emotion. "I stood there looking at the farm with his offer in my ears, and all I could hear was the call to stay—as if each separate blade of grass and clump of soil was calling out that here is where I belong."

Her heart was almost too full for speech. "I... I am happy for you."

The tug of his hand brought them closer. "Don't you see? Everything I want is here...including you, if you'll have me. Will you, Sally?"

She could only look into his eyes, wordless. Her answer must have been written in her face, because he closed the gap between them in a heartbeat, and his lips found hers.

The world closed into the warm, protective, cherishing circle of Aaron's arms. The kiss spoke of shared love and tenderness. Of commitment. Of belonging to each other as long as life should last.

When their lips parted at last, she felt that everything important had been said between them. And she was sure enough to be willing to tease him, just a little.

"You know what this means, don't you? You can't get out of it. You're going to be kneeling in front of the entire church."

He dropped a kiss on the tip of her nose. "You'll enjoy that, won't you?"

He might mean it lightly, but she realized in that instant that it was even more true than he thought. "*Enjoy* might not be the right word." She tilted her face up to his. "*Rejoicing* would be better. We will all rejoice."

"Yah, I guess you will." He almost sounded surprised. "The bishop was right about that, too. He said that part came at the end, not the beginning. I see it now. He knew that once God had His way with me, asking forgiveness and accepting it would be something to look forward to, not to reject."

She nodded, heart full. "You're not dreading it any longer?"

"No, never. It was only pride that held me back, always pride." He seemed to struggle for words. "I understand now. There's no room for pride in love. I'm sorry it took me so long."

There was no room for pride in love. It was exactly what she'd learned, too. God had dealt with both of them.

"It was worth it." She put her palm against his cheek, feeling the connection that flowed back and forth between them, sure and strong. "We still have a lot to look forward to...a whole lifetime of being together."

He turned his head slightly to press a kiss against her palm. "And a lot for me to make up. I need to court you properly, don't I?"

"That's right. Every single step." Her joy was spilling over, making her want to laugh for sheer pleasure.

His arms tightened around her again. "Then we should start with another kiss, ain't so?"

Holding him close, she gave herself to the kiss...a kiss that held all the promise of a life together, blessed by God, who had brought them so surely to this moment. They were both home where they belonged.

Epilogue

"**Y**ou will be next, ain't so?" Onkel Zeb put a hand on Aaron's shoulder as they stood together for a moment, out of the crowd of people who packed the Fisher farmhouse to celebrate the marriage of Daniel and Rebecca.

"I will."

Aaron figured about a dozen people had said that to him in the past hour, and there would be many more before the day was over. Instead of annoying him, it gave him a fresh spurt of joy each time. In a few months, he and Sally would belong to each other in the sight of God and the church.

"A spring wedding will be gut, even if it's not traditional." Onkel Zeb set his seal of approval on their plans. "Sally will want to finish out the school year." He sent a cautious glance toward Aaron. "She will miss her scholars, ain't so?"

"Yah, she will." The subject didn't hold any secrets…he and Sally had discussed it thoroughly. "She hopes…we both hope that we'll start a family soon, and she'll have our own kinder to teach and care for.

And later, once they're bigger, she'll be able to go back to teaching again."

The custom was that teachers were young, unmarried women, but that was just the way it had been in their district, not the way it must be. And Sally was born to teach.

A small figure hurtled out of the door behind them, almost tripping. Aaron caught Lige before he could go headlong, and set him on his feet.

"Denke, Onkel Aaron." He said the words with a shy smile. "You're my onkel now, too, ain't so?"

"I am, for sure. We are all family now."

"Yah." The boy beamed. "I'm glad." He hurried off again, bound on some errand of his own, most likely.

"Families coming together and new families starting. That's how life is meant to be." Onkel Zeb had a satisfied look on his face. "And we will set to rest forever the idea that the King men are unfortunate in love, ain't so?"

"For sure." Aaron said the simple words with feeling. To see Daniel and Rebecca claim each other in marriage today had moved his heart. He longed for the moment when he and Sally would be the ones taking that step in the presence of the church.

His gaze, moving across the tables of guests, came to rest on Sally, who was giving some directions to those serving. As if she felt the touch of his look, she turned her head to smile at him. Their eyes met, communicating without a spoken word from across the room.

Onkel Zeb elbowed him. "What are you doing wasting time with me? Go and help your sweetheart."

"Gut idea," he said, and slipped through the forest

of chairs and tables, narrowly missing a collision with a teenager carrying a laden tray.

Coming to his rescue, Sally caught his hand and led him out a door. He found they were in a short hall between the kitchen and the pantry. Alone in the hall. Taking advantage of the moment, he stole a quick kiss.

Sally looked up at him, her face saucy. "I thought you wanted to see me."

"I did," he protested. "I needed a kiss. And maybe, since we're alone for a moment, a second one." He suited the action to the words.

After a satisfying moment, Sally reached up to drop a kiss on his chin. "Won't be long until you're growing a beard. Sure you won't miss the clean-shaven look?"

He rubbed his chin. "I think I'll look wonderful gut with a beard, don't you?"

"Fishing for a compliment? Yah, I'm so besotted with you that I'd think you looked handsome no matter what."

"That's as it should be. After all, I look considerably different now than when you were first promised to me."

For once he had the satisfaction of seeing Sally at a loss. "Different?" Her face was puzzled.

"You forgot," he said, shaking his head. "I'm surprised at you. You must have been at least eleven or twelve when I said I'd wait for you to grow up and marry you. Don't you remember?"

"Teasing again," she said in her best teacher voice. "The teacher might have to make you stand in the corner."

"That's all right." He snuggled his arms around her. "As long as you're there with me."

She responded with the gurgle of laughter he loved,

and Aaron's heart swelled. Little had he known, that day he'd walked down the road with his heart filled with bitterness, just how much joy waited for him here.

This was what their life together would be like—filled with joy and laughter and no doubt their share of sorrow. But whatever the future brought, God would bring them through it together, so long as they were faithful.

* * * * *

HIS AMISH CHOICE

Leigh Bale

Thank you to Janet Pulleyn for infecting me with the soap-making bug. I have had a blast learning and consulting with you on new colors and fragrances. And thanks to Paul for letting me invade your home on more than one occasion. You are dear friends. Now, where shall we go out to dinner next time?

The Spirit itself beareth witness with our spirit,
that we are the children of God.
—*Romans* 8:16

Chapter One

Elizabeth Beiler set her last crate of honeycrisp apples into the back of the buggy-wagon and took a deep breath. Picking the fruit was hard work but she could never get enough of its fresh, earthy-sweet smell.

Brushing the dust off her rose-colored skirts and black apron, she adjusted the blue kerchief tied beneath her chin. Because she was working outside, she'd left her white organza *kapp* at home. She arched her back, her gaze scanning the rows of apple trees.

Finally, they were finished. Not that Lizzie begrudged the work. It brought her a sense of accomplishment and security. She was just tired and feeling jittery with Eli Stoltzfus's constant presence.

At that moment, he emerged from the orchard, carrying two heavy crates of fruit in his strong arms. His blue chambray shirt stretched taut across his muscular chest and arms. His plain broadfall trousers and work boots had dust on them. Wearing a straw hat and black suspenders, he looked unmistakably Amish. His clean-shaven face attested that he was unmarried. Lizzie was dying to ask if he'd had any girlfriends during the four years he'd been living among the *Englisch*, but kept her questions to herself. It wasn't her business after all. Not anymore.

His high cheekbones and blunt chin gave him a slightly stubborn look. With hair black as a raven's wing and gentle brown eyes, he was ruggedly handsome. Not that Lizzie also was interested. Not in this man. Not ever again.

As he approached, she turned away, conscious of his quiet gaze following her. She often found him watching her, his intelligent eyes warning that there was an active, gifted mind hidden beneath his calm exterior.

"Come on, Marty and Annie. It's time to go home," she called to her two sisters in *Deitsch*, the German dialect her Amish people used among themselves.

The girls came running, the long ribbons on their prayer *kapps* dangling in the wind. At the ages of ten and seven, neither girl was big or strong, but they were sturdy and a tremendous help on the farm. Their happy chatter also alleviated *Daed*'s quiet moods. He hadn't been the same since *Mamm* died almost five years earlier. The union of Lizzie's parents had been one of love. The perfect kind of marriage she had once dreamed of having with Eli.

"What are we having for *nachtesse*?" seven-year-old Annie asked, slightly breathless from her run.

"*Ja*, I'm starved." Marty was right behind her, biting into a crisp, juicy apple from the orchard.

"I'm going to make slumgullion," Lizzie said, thinking the meat and pasta dish was easy to make and very filling. "And we've also got leftover apple crisp from yesterday."

She was conscious of Eli adjusting the crates of apples in the back of their buggy-wagon, no doubt listening to their conversation. He must be ravenous too, but he would eat at home with his parents.

"Yum! I'm so hungry I could eat Billie." Annie leaned toward the bay gelding and made gobbling sounds. The gentle animal snorted and waved his head. Everyone except Marty laughed.

"You couldn't eat Billie. He's a horse. Don't be *dumm*," Marty said.

"No calling names, please. Be nice to your sister," Lizzie reprimanded in a kind voice. "As soon as *Daed* gets here, we'll go home."

They didn't have long to wait. Jeremiah Beiler emerged from the orchard, walking with their *Englisch* truck driver. *Daed*'s straw hat was pushed back on his head. Sweat-dampened tendrils of salt-and-pepper hair stuck to his high forehead. Dressed almost identically to Eli, *Daed*'s long beard was a light reddish shade with no moustache, signifying that he was a married man, now a widower.

The truck driver nodded, said something Lizzie couldn't hear, then climbed into the cab of his tractor trailer and started up the noisy engine. A rush of relief swept over her. The back of the 18-wheeler was loaded with crates of apples from their orchard and the driver would deliver them safely to the processing plant in Longmont. Their harvest was secure.

Because of Eli.

As the truck pulled away, *Daed* turned and smiled at them, but frowned when his gaze met Eli's. Lizzie knew her father didn't approve of Eli. He feared the younger man's worldly influence on his children and had hired him only at the bishop's urging.

"You all did *gut* work," Jeremiah said.

Eli gave a slight nod, then went to hitch his horse to his buggy. Lizzie watched him for a moment. Out of the blue, he had returned just over three weeks ago, asking to be reinstated in the *Gmay*, their Amish community.

If he had been a full member of the church before his decision to live among the *Englisch,* his choice to leave them would have been seen as a breaking of his faith and he would have been shunned. But because he'd never been baptized into their faith, he'd been welcomed back with open arms, no questions asked. Just a blind acceptance that he really wanted to be here. But Lizzie wasn't convinced. Eli had broken her heart. Leaving her the day before they were to be baptized together.

When they'd been only fourteen, he'd proposed marriage and she'd accepted. But long before then, he'd whispered about attending college to learn more about science and biology. Their eighth-grade education had never been enough for Eli, yet she had thought he'd made peace with the life they had. The life they'd intended to share. Lizzie hadn't believed he'd really leave. At least not without saying goodbye.

Annie and Marty beamed at their father's praise. They all felt a great weight lifted from their shoulders. The warm weather was an illusion. When they'd first settled in Colorado eight years earlier, they hadn't realized the growing season was much shorter than their previous home in Ohio. A killing frost could strike at any time. With their apples picked, they could now turn their efforts to other pressing matters.

To the south, the alfalfa was ready for cutting. The last of the season. They would store the hay in their barn to feed their own livestock through the long winter. *Daed* would mow it tomorrow. The weather should hold long enough for the hay to dry, then Lizzie would assist with the baling. Between now and then, she planned to bottle applesauce. They no longer needed Eli's help and she wouldn't have to see him every day. Though it wasn't charitable of her, she counted that as a blessing.

"*Komm*, my girls. Let's go," *Daed* called.

Annie giggled as her father swung her into the buggy. Marty scrambled inside with Lizzie. *Daed* gathered the leather leads into his hands and slapped them against Billie's back, giving a stiff nod of parting to Eli.

"*Sehn dich schpeeder,*" Eli called as he lifted one hand.

See you later? Lizzie hoped not, then felt guilty for being mean-spirited. The little girls waved goodbye, but not Lizzie. It still hurt her deeply to think that Eli had loved worldly pursuits more than he'd loved their faith and *Gott*. More than he'd loved her.

"*Heemet!*" *Daed* called.

Home! With a cozy barn and hay awaiting him, Billie had plenty of incentive to take off at a brisk walk. The buggy-wagon wobbled as they traveled along the narrow dirt road leading out of the orchard.

Glancing over her shoulder, Lizzie noticed that Eli had his horse hitched up to his buggy and wasn't far behind them.

When they reached the paved county road, *Daed* pulled the horse up and looked both ways. A couple of cars whizzed past, spraying them through their open windows with a fine mist of grit. Once it was clear, he proceeded forward, setting the horse into a comfortable trot along the far-right shoulder. Within minutes, they would be home. Marty and Annie leaned against Lizzie and yawned. The gentle rocking of the buggy and the rhythmic beat of hooves lulled Lizzie to close her eyes.

She awoke with a start as the buggy-wagon jerked forward. A sickening crash filled her ears. Apples went flying, peppering the road. Lizzie reached for Marty, but found herself airborne. Bloodcurdling screams split the air. The hard ground slammed up to meet her. Pain burst through her entire body, a lance of agony spearing her head. She cried out, then choked, the air knocked from her lungs. Her brain was spinning, her limbs frozen with stinging shock. One thought filled her mind. Her *familye*! She had to help them.

Lifting her head, she stared at the remnants of the wood and fiberglass buggy-wagon, strewn across the county road. The fluorescent slow-moving-vehicle symbol that had been affixed to the back of their wagon now lay broken beside her. In a glance, she saw a blue sedan parked nearby, the right front fender smashed in. She blinked as a teenage boy got out of the car, his eyes wide with panic. In his hand, he held his cell phone. Had he been texting while driving?

Lying below Lizzie in the ditch, Billie snorted and thrashed in his harness. Giving a shrill whinny, the horse lunged to his feet, the laces hanging limp from his back. The poor beast. At least he didn't appear to have a broken leg.

Lizzie wiped moisture from her forehead, then gasped when she discovered it was blood. She scanned the road, looking for *Daed* and her sisters. From her vantage point, she couldn't see any of them. Her vision swam before her. She couldn't focus. Falling back, she lay there for a moment, trying to fight off the woozy darkness, but despite her best efforts, it crowded in on her.

When she came to, Lizzie realized she must have fainted. She had no idea how long she'd been out. A rush of memory made her jerk upright, then cry out with anguish. Her entire body hurt, a searing pain in her head. She must get up. Must find her father, Annie and Marty.

"*Schtopp!* Just rest." A soft, masculine voice came from above her.

Blinking her eyes, she saw Eli kneeling over her. In a glance, she took in his somber expression filled with concern. He must have come upon them right after the crash.

"*Vie gehts?*" he asked in a soothing tone roughened by emotion.

"*Ja*, I'm fine. Marty and Annie. *Daed*. Help them," she said.

"They're all alive. The *Englischer* has called for help on his cell phone. An ambulance is coming from the hospital in town," he said.

"Where…where is my *familye*?" She sat up slowly to look for them, her head whirling from another dizzy spell.

"I didn't want the girls to see you until I was certain you were all right. They're very frightened as it is. I'll bring them to you now." He stood, looked both ways, then hurried across the road.

He soon returned, holding the hands of her sisters as he crossed the busy road. He hesitated as a car and truck whipped past, swerving to avoid the debris scattered across the asphalt. One of the vehicles stopped and asked if they needed help. The *Englisch* boy went to speak with the driver.

"Lizzie!" Annie cried.

Both little girls fell into her arms, sobbing and hugging her tight. Cupping their faces with her hands, she looked them over, kissing their scratched cheeks, assuring herself that they were safe. Their faces and arms were covered with abrasions, their dresses soiled, but they otherwise seemed fine.

"There, my *liebchen*. All will be well," Lizzie soothed the girls for a moment. Then, she looked at Eli. "But where is my *vadder*?"

"He cannot be moved just now. He has a serious compound fracture to his lower left leg. I believe his tibia is all that is broken. I have splinted the leg and stopped the bleeding, then wrapped him in a warm blanket I had in my buggy."

A broken leg! But how did Eli know what to do? A blaze of panic scorched her. They'd already lost *Mamm*. What would they do if they lost *Daed* too?

"I must go to him." She tried to stand.

"*Ne*, just sit still a moment. There's too much traffic on the road and you are also hurt. I believe you have a concussion." Eli held out a hand to stop her.

Lizzie recoiled, fearing he might touch her. How could he know she had a concussion? He wasn't a doctor. Or was he? She no longer knew much about this man. Was four years long enough for him to go to medical school? She had no knowledge of such things.

She reached up and touched her forehead. A wave of nausea forced her to sit back. When she drew away her hand, fresh blood stained her fingers. No wonder a horrible pain throbbed behind her eyes and her brain felt foggy. Maybe Eli was right.

"May I…may I wrap a cloth around your head? It's

important that we stop the bleeding. I've already done all I can for Jeremiah," Eli said, his voice tentative.

"*Ja,*" she consented, giving in to common sense.

She sat perfectly still as he removed her blood-soaked kerchief. Her waist-length hair had come undone from the bun at the nape of her neck and she felt embarrassed to have him see its length. It was something special she was keeping for her husband on their wedding night. Thankfully, he politely averted his gaze as he opened the first aid kit.

"Where did that come from?" She pointed at the box.

He answered without looking up. "My buggy."

"How do you know so much about medical care?"

He shrugged, his gaze briefly meeting hers. "I went through the training and am a certified paramedic. I'm specially trained to help in critical situations like this."

So, he wasn't a doctor, but he might as well be. Although she'd heard about Amish paramedics and firefighters working back east in Lancaster County and Pennsylvania, she'd never met one before and was fairly certain her church elders wouldn't approve. Higher learning was shunned by her people because it often led to *Hochmut,* the pride of men.

"Is…is that what you've been doing among the *Englisch*?" she asked.

He nodded. "*Ja,* it's how I earned my living."

So now she knew. He must have worked hard in school to learn such a skill. She couldn't blame him for wanting to know things, but neither did she approve of him casting aside his faith for such worldly pursuits.

Eli cleansed her wound with an antiseptic towelette. His touch was warm and gentle as he wrapped her head with soft, white gauze.

"You will need three or four stitches in the gash." He gave her a soulful look, as if he could see deep inside her heart and knew all the hurt and longings she kept hidden there.

She looked away.

Sirens heralded the arrival of two ambulances and some police cars. Lizzie lost track of time as the officers set up a roadblock with flares and took their statements. She watched Eli untangle the harness and lead Billie out of the ditch. Speaking to the distressed horse in a low murmur, he smoothed his hands over the animal's trembling legs. He then salvaged the bruised apples and put the filled crates into his own buggy.

When the medics loaded them into the two ambulances, Annie leaned close against Lizzie's side, her eyes red from crying. "Is *Daedi* going to be all right?"

Lizzie reached over and took the child's hand. "The Lord's will be done, *boppli*. We must trust in Him to get us through."

As she spoke these words, she tried to believe them. If *Daed* died, could she forgive the boy who had caused the accident? Christ had forgiven all and she must do likewise, but she wasn't sure her faith was that strong.

"I'll look after Billie." Eli stood at the foot of the ambulance, holding the lead lines to the horse's halter. His expressive eyes were filled with a haunting unease, as though he were anxious to leave.

"Danke." Lizzie gave a brisk nod.

He stepped back and the medics closed the double doors. Lizzie laid her head back and closed her eyes. And in her heart, she carried a silent prayer that they would be all right.

* * *

The following day, Eli tugged on the leather leads as he veered Jeremiah Beiler's three draft horses slightly to the left. The big Percherons did as he asked, plodding steadily down the row of alfalfa as they pulled the hay mower. The low rumble of the gas-powered engine filled the air. Eli glanced at the position of the sun, unable to believe it was afternoon already. Another hour and he would finish this chore. Jeremiah's hay would be secure. It would take a few more days for the hay to dry, and then he would gather it into bales.

"Gee!" he called, turning the team to the right.

A movement brought his eye toward the red log house where Lizzie and her *familye* lived. Turning slightly, he saw her and two men heading toward him, stepping high as they crossed the rutted field. Even from this distance, Eli recognized the slant of Bishop Yoder's black felt hat. His companion was Darrin Albrecht, the deacon of their congregation. Both men were dressed identically in black frock coats and broadfall pants. Eli had gotten word of the Beilers' accident to the bishop late last night. No doubt the elders had come to check on Jeremiah's *familye*.

Lizzie accompanied them, wearing a blue dress and crisp black apron. As they drew near, Eli saw a fresh gauze bandage had been taped to her forehead, no doubt hiding several stitches from her visit to the hospital. She and the little girls must have just gotten home. He'd seen the *Englisch* midwife's car pull in the driveway an hour earlier. She must have given them a ride from town.

Sunlight glinted against Lizzie's golden hair, the length of it pinned into a bun beneath her starched prayer *kapp*. One rebellious strand framed her delicate oval face and she quickly tucked it back behind her ear. Her blue eyes flashed with unease, her stern expression and brisk stride belying her injuries. Eli was eager to hear how she was feeling and also receive news of her father's condition.

Pulling the giant horses to a standstill, he killed the engine and hopped down off his seat. As he walked the short distance to meet them, he rolled his long sleeves down his forearms.

"Hallo," he called.

He glanced at Lizzie, trying to assess her mood. Their gazes clashed, then locked for several moments. As always, he blinked at the startling blue of her eyes. Her expression showed a fierce emotion he didn't understand. A mingling of repugnance and determination.

"Guder nummidaag," Bishop Yoder said.

"It looks like you've been busy today." Deacon Albrecht surveyed the cut field, as though evaluating the quality of Eli's work.

After being gone four years, Eli was surprised at how easily farming came back to him. It felt good to work the land again. It felt good to be needed. Holding the lead lines in his hands as the powerful horses pulled the mower had given him a sense of purpose he hadn't felt since Shannon's death seven months earlier.

Thinking of his sweet fiancée made his heart squeeze painfully and a gloomy emptiness filled his chest.

"You have done *gut* work for the Beilers," Bishop Yoder said. "They will need the strength of a man on this place for a few more months, until Jeremiah is back on his feet. He will have surgery today and will be in the hospital awhile longer, until the swelling goes down so they can cast the leg."

Eli nodded, wondering what the bishop was getting at.

Bishop Yoder placed his hand on Eli's shoulder, his gray eyes filled with kindness, but also an intensity that couldn't be ignored. "I've spoken with your father. He agrees that you should work here for the time being, caring for Jeremiah's farm as if it were your own. But with this request comes a great responsibility and commitment to your faith. I know you have told me you are recommitted to *Gott*. Are you certain our way of life is what you want?"

Eli hesitated. With Shannon gone and his confidence shattered, he had needed to get away from Denver and all the reminders of her death. Here in Riverton, he hoped to find the peace he so desperately longed for and a way to forgive himself for what had happened.

His heart still felt unsure, but he was determined to stay the course and wait for certainty to come. He couldn't go back, so he'd have to find a way for himself here.

"I am." Eli nodded, his throat dry as sandpaper. Speaking the words out loud helped solidify his commitment.

"I just spoke with your *mudder*. She is inside the house, almost finished bottling applesauce for Lizzie," the bishop said.

Eli nodded, forcing himself to meet the man's gaze. "*Ja*, and my *vadder* was here earlier this morning, helping with the milking."

"You all have been most kind." Lizzie stared at the ground, her words low and uncertain.

Eli felt a wave of compassion. "It's our pleasure to help. You would do the same for us."

Or at least, he hoped she would. Her manner was so offish toward him that he wasn't sure. When he'd left four years earlier, he'd written to her often, at first. Not once had she replied. That alone told him she wanted nothing to do with him. After a year and a half of trying, he'd finally moved on with his life, meeting and falling in love with Shannon.

"Gut," the bishop continued. "Tomorrow at church, I will announce your plans to be baptized, so you can participate in the instruction classes again. They've already begun, but since you took them once before, I think we can catch you up. Then you'll be prepared for your baptism in a few months."

Lizzie looked at him and a rush of doubt speared Eli's chest. The last time he'd attended the classes, he'd been a rebellious kid and hadn't paid much attention. In those days, all he could think about was getting out of here. Was he ready for such a commitment now? Once he was baptized, there would be no turning back. But he had the next few months to decide.

"I'm happy to assist the Beilers," he said.

A sudden hesitation struck him. A quick glance in Lizzie's direction told him that she didn't want him here. Her expression held a heavy dose of disapproval. As if she thought he was tainted now, because he'd been living among the *Englisch.*

He'd loved her so much when they were teenagers, but he'd had to leave. Had to find out what the world could offer. He'd desperately wanted a *rumspringa*— that rite of passage during adolescence when Amish teenagers experienced freedom of choice without the rules of the *Ordnung* to hold them back. But he'd never meant to hurt Lizzie. In fact, he'd tried to get her to come join him. If only she had responded to his letters. Instead, each one had been returned unopened.

The bishop smiled. *"Ach*, we'll see you tomorrow then. *Willkomm* back, my brother."

Eli nodded, but didn't speak. A hard lump had lodged in his throat. He felt grateful to be here, but the reasons for the gratitude were murky. Was he truly glad to be back among his people, or was he just relieved to be away from reminders of Shannon? He'd talked to other paramedics who had lost a patient in their care, but it hadn't prepared him for the shock. And to make matters worse, the first patient he'd lost had been someone he dearly loved. Someone who was counting on him to keep her safe. And he'd failed miserably. That's when he realized how much he missed his *familye*. Seeking respite from the world, he'd come home. But thus far, peace of mind had continued to elude him.

Reaching up, he tugged on the brim of his straw hat where a letter from Tom Caldwell was safely tucked away. Tom had been Eli's former boss at the hospital in Denver. His letter was a silent reminder of the *Englisch* life Eli had left behind. And though it felt good to be back in Riverton, whenever Eli thought of never being a paramedic again, a sick feeling settled in his gut.

"If you have faith, all will be well with your *familye*. Never forget that," the bishop spoke kindly to Lizzie.

"Ja. Danke, Bishop," Lizzie said, her voice holding a note of respect.

The church elders walked away, leaving Eli and Lizzie alone. A horrible, swelling silence followed.

Lizzie looked at the ground, looked at the mountains surrounding the valley, looked anywhere but at Eli.

"You are truly all right?" Eli finally asked, peering at Lizzie's forehead.

"*Ja*, I'm fine," she said, briefly touching the bandage as if it embarrassed her.

"I didn't expect this." He gestured toward the retreating men.

"Neither did I." Her voice wobbled.

"Are you sure you're okay with me working here?" he asked.

She glanced at him. "I don't have much choice."

True. With her *daed* in the hospital and the bishop's stamp of approval, she would have to accept Eli's aid.

"I never meant to hurt you, Lizzie. I know I left rather suddenly," he said.

She snorted and stepped back in exasperation. "*Ja*, you sure did."

"I know I should have spoken to you about it first, but I feared you might tell my *eldre* or the bishop and they would have tried to make me stay."

"*Ach*, so you ran away. You took the coward's route and fled."

He stared in confusion. He'd been gone four years. Why was Lizzie still so angry at him?

"We were only fourteen when I first proposed to you," he said. "I'm sure you agree that was way too young for marriage. When I left, neither of us was ready to start a *familye*. If only you had come and joined me."

"To Denver?" she asked with incredulity.

He nodded.

"*Ne*, I would never leave my people. You knew that."

Chapter Two

"I like Eli. He's so nice," Annie said later that night.

Lizzie jerked, her fingers losing their grasp on the tiny rubber band she was using to tie off the end of Annie's braided hair.

The little girls had both had their baths and Lizzie was finishing their hair before going to bed. Each child sat on the wooden bench in the kitchen, the gas lamp above the table shining down upon their heads. Their bare feet peeked out from beneath the hems of their simple flannel nightgowns. The air carried a slight fruity smell from the detangler she'd used on their hair to get the snarls out.

"Eli is nice, but you can't like him," Marty said. She tugged the comb through a particularly stubborn knot in her own damp hair.

"Why not?" Annie asked, her forehead crinkled in a frown.

"Because he hurt Lizzie's feelings, that's why."

Both girls turned and looked at Lizzie, as if waiting for a confirmation.

"Of course you can like him." Lizzie laughed it off,

not wanting to explain how much she'd loved the man and how he'd broken her heart. Everyone in the *Gmay* had known they'd been going together and planned to marry one day.

"We can? You're okay with it?" Marty asked.

"*Ja*, it's not our place to judge," Lizzie reiterated, trying to believe her own words.

"But you were gonna get married to him. Emily Hostetler said he left you to become an *Englischer* instead," Marty said.

"You were gonna marry Eli?" Annie asked.

Lizzie inhaled a sharp breath and held it for several moments before letting it go. Hearing Eli's betrayal put so bluntly made her mind scatter and she had to regather her thoughts before responding. As he had pointed out, they'd only been fourteen when he'd proposed. Way too young to marry. Because they'd been so young, he hadn't taken it seriously, but Lizzie had. When he left, they were seventeen and she'd thought they would wed the following year. It's what they had talked about. But he'd obviously changed his mind—and hadn't felt the need to tell her.

"That was a long time ago. It was Eli's choice to leave. When the time comes, we each must make that decision for ourselves, but I dearly hope both of you will stay." She placed Annie's *kapp* on her head, then hugged the girl tight.

"I'll never leave," Marty said.

When Lizzie released her, Annie stood, her inquisitive gaze resting on Lizzie. "Is that true, Lizzie-*bee*? Eli really left you to become *Englisch*?"

Lizzie-bee. The nickname Eli had given her when she'd been barely thirteen years old because he thought she was always as busy as a bee. Back then, Lizzie had loved Eli to call her that name. Now, it was a reminder of all that she'd lost.

"Where did you hear that name?" Lizzie asked a bit too brusquely.

"It's what Eli called you when he came into the house to take Fannie home after she bottled our applesauce. You were upstairs," Annie said.

Fannie was Eli's mother and a dear friend. She was as generous as the day was long. It had hurt her deeply when Eli left.

Lizzie sat very still, looking at her two sisters. Marty had been six when Eli had left, so she undoubtedly remembered him. Annie had been only three. Lizzie didn't want to discuss what had happened, but neither would she lie. Nor did she have a right to speak ill of Eli.

"Is it true?" the girl persisted.

"*Ja*, it's true," she said, tucking an errant strand of hair beneath Annie's *kapp*.

The child's eyes crinkled with sadness. "But everyone loves you. Why would Eli leave?"

She said the words as if she couldn't understand why Eli couldn't love her too.

"He…he wanted other things, that's all," Lizzie said.

"Did he hurt your feelings when he left?" Annie persisted.

"Of course he did." Marty flipped her long hair over her shoulder.

"*Ja*, he did," Lizzie admitted. She didn't look at the girls as she parted Marty's tresses and quickly began to braid the lengthy strands. Perhaps it was good for her sisters to learn early that a man could break your heart.

"But he's back now. You don't need to have hurt feelings anymore. You can forgive him and all will be well. Maybe he'll even want to still marry you now," Annie said.

If only it were that simple. Right now, Lizzie didn't want to marry Eli. And she certainly couldn't believe Eli wanted to marry her—not after the way he'd abandoned her. But sweet little Annie had always had such a calm, quiet spirit. Honest and trusting, the girl always exemplified a childlike faith in the good of others. Lizzie never wanted to see that faith shattered. But more than that, Lizzie had to set a good example for her sisters. With *Mamm* gone, they deserved to feel safe and loved. They were both looking to her for guidance and she didn't want to let them down.

"The Lord wants us to forgive everyone. We should never judge others, because we don't know what's truly in their heart or what their circumstances are. Plus we each have our own faults to repent from," Lizzie spoke in a measured tone, believing what she said, though she still struggled to apply it to Eli.

Annie nudged Marty with her elbow. "See? I told ya so."

Marty accepted this without question and Lizzie breathed with relief. She quickly finished her chore. Upstairs, she tucked the girls into bed, feeling like a hypocrite. She told her sisters to forgive, yet she hadn't done so herself. But honestly, she didn't know how. Saying and doing it were two different things. Forgiveness wasn't as easy as it seemed. Especially when she'd been hurt so badly.

She secured the house for the night and turned out the kerosene lights. Alone in her room, she prayed for help, but received no answers. Lying in the darkness, she closed her eyes and tried to sleep, but her mind kept racing. If Eli hadn't left, they'd likely be married now. They would probably have one or two children too. How different their lives might have been. They could have been happy and in love and working for the good of their *familye*. Instead, she felt disillusioned and distrustful. But it did no good to dwell on such things. It would not change the present. Her *familye* needed her and that was enough.

Punching her pillow, she turned on her side and closed her eyes, gritty with fatigue. She tried to rest, but it was a long time coming.

In the morning, she felt drowsy and grouchy. Determined not to be cross with the girls, she kissed each one on the forehead to wake them up. She ensured they were dressed and sitting at the table eating a bowl of scrapple—a mixture of corn meal, sausage and eggs— before she lit the kerosene lamp and stepped out onto the back porch.

Crisp darkness filled the air as she crossed the yard. The chilling breeze hinted that winter was not far away. In the waning shadows, she tossed grain to the chickens, then gathered the eggs into a wire basket. When she went to feed the pigs, she found the chore already done, the trough filled with fresh water.

Oh, no. This could only mean one thing.

Turning, she went to the barn. A faint light gleamed from beneath the double doors as she stepped inside. A lamp sat on the railing of Ginger's stall. The chestnut palomino was old, but *Daed* still used her to pull the buggy when Billie was lame. Thinking Billie needed a few more days of rest, Lizzie planned to use Ginger today, to get to church. It was too bad they'd lost their larger buggy-wagon in the accident. Now, they'd have to use their older, smaller buggy.

"Easy, girl." Eli stood bent over the mare's left back hoof. He wore a plain white shirt and black suspenders, his nice Sunday frock jacket hanging on a peg nearby.

Releasing the animal's leg, he patted her rump as he stood up straight. Then, he flinched. "Lizzie-bee! You startled me."

She bit her tongue, forcing herself not to reprimand him. It would do no good. The name *Lizzie-bee* was too embedded in their past history.

"I came to feed the animals. I didn't expect you to be here today," she said.

He shrugged. "I figured you would still need help even on the Sabbath."

Leading Ginger out of her stall, he directed the mare over to the buggy. Glancing at the other stalls, Lizzie saw that Eli had already fed Billie and *Daed*'s six Percheron draft horses. And judging from the two tall canisters sitting near the door, he'd already done the milking too. It appeared he was taking his promise to the bishop very seriously.

"Have you eaten?" she asked, feeling obligated to use good manners.

"*Ja*, my *mudder* fixed a big meal for *Daed* and me. I'll have the horse hitched up in just a few minutes, then I'll drive you to church," he said.

He didn't look at her while he put the collar on the horse. Ginger stood perfectly still, knowing this routine by heart.

"That won't be necessary. You're very kind, but I can drive the *maed* myself," Lizzie said.

He paused, holding the saddle lacings in his big hands. "I… I don't think that's a good idea. You were nearly killed just a few days ago and I… I assured the bishop that I'd look after all of you."

His voice caught on the words and he turned away, but not before Lizzie saw his trembling hands. Or had she imagined that? Why did he seem so upset by the accident?

"*Ne*, you told him you'd look after the farm. That's not the same as driving us to church," she said.

He nodded, accepting her logic. "Still, I feel responsible for you. I don't want to have to tell Jeremiah that I was derelict in my duty."

Hmm. Maybe he was right. The horror of the accident came rushing back and she realized she wasn't eager to climb into a buggy again. If her fear distracted her while she was driving, it could put her sisters in danger. Perhaps it would be better to let Eli drive them for a time. But she hated feeling like a burden almost as much as she hated to depend on him.

"You needn't feel obligated. I've driven a buggy many times before," she argued half-heartedly.

"I know that. You're a capable, strong-minded woman, but I'd feel better if you'd let me drive today. Just until Jeremiah is out of the hospital." His gaze brushed over the clean gauze she had taped over her forehead. She hated wearing a bandage and would be glad when the wound healed enough to remove the three tiny stitches. No doubt, they'd leave a small scar to remind her that *Gott* had saved her *familye*'s lives.

"*Komm* on, let me drive you," he said, his voice coaxing.

Oh, she knew that look of his. The calm demeanor.

The slightly narrowed eyes. The softly spoken words and stubborn tilt that said he was going to do what he wanted one way or the other. Some things never changed.

But *she* had changed. Those soft feelings for Eli had been put away, and she wouldn't fall back into old habits, like smiling at him when he behaved this way. It was time for this conversation to end.

"All right, you can drive today. I'll go get the *kinder*." She picked up a canister of milk and lugged it across the yard toward the well house. Fed by a cold mountain stream coming out of the Sangre de Cristo Mountains, the stone bath had been built by *Daed* when the *familye* first moved to Colorado.

Once inside, Lizzie set the heavy can into the chilled water and realized her hands were shaking from her exertions. When she turned, she found Eli right behind her with the second can.

"They're too heavy for you to carry," he said.

Yes, they were, but she could manage. With her father gone, she'd do whatever she must. Feeling suddenly awkward, she scooted out of Eli's way as he placed the second canister into the water bath.

"Danke," she said before hurrying to the house.

The girls were standing on the front porch waiting, their *kapps*, dresses and aprons neatly in place. They smiled, looking so sweet and innocent that a feeling of overwhelming love filled Lizzie's chest.

"We even washed the breakfast dishes," Annie said with a big smile, handing Lizzie the basket they would take with them.

"You did? You're so helpful." Lizzie smiled back,

wiping a smudge of strawberry jam away from the girl's upper lip.

The clatter of hooves caused them all to turn. Eli drove the buggy toward them, his straw hat, vest and jacket now in place. Inwardly, Lizzie took a deep, startled breath. He looked more handsome than a man had a right to be and it pierced her to the core.

As he pulled Ginger to a halt and hopped out of the buggy, Annie scurried behind Lizzie, as if to hide.

"*Ne*, I don't want to ride in the buggy. Can't we walk today?" the child asked, gripping folds of Lizzie's dress as she peeked around her legs with caution.

"*Ja*, I would rather walk today too." Marty's eyes were also creased with fear as she sidled up against Lizzie.

Taking both girls' hands in her own, Lizzie knelt in front of them to meet their eyes. "It's too far to walk, *bopplin*. We'll have to ride. But I will be with you and the Lord will make sure we are safe."

Annie shook her head, her breathing coming fast, as though she'd been running. Lizzie knew a panic attack when she saw one. She pulled both girls into her arms and gave them a reassuring hug.

Eli stepped up onto the porch, removed his straw hat and crouched down so he could meet Annie's gaze. "Ginger is an old, gentle horse and she can't go very fast. You like her, don't you?"

"*Ja.*" Annie nodded.

"And you trust me, right?"

A pause, then another nod.

"Then I promise to pull far over onto the shoulder of the road and drive extra careful so we don't have another accident. If I hear a car coming up fast behind us, I'll pull completely off the road until they have passed us by. I'll take good care of all of us, this I promise," he said.

A long silence followed as Annie drew her eyebrows together, signaling that she was thinking it over. Lizzie didn't know what she'd do if her sisters refused to get into the buggy. It was eight miles to the Geingeriches' farm—and eight miles they'd have to travel back. If they walked, they would arrive late, sweaty and tired. And the evenings were too chilly to walk home late at night. But she hated Eli's word choice. There had been a time not so long ago when she had trusted him and he had made promises to her too. Promises she'd naively believed with all her heart…until he'd broken them.

"All right. We will ride," Annie finally said in a tone of resignation.

Eli smiled wide, placed his hat back on his head, then picked the girl up. Taking Marty's hand, he walked with them to the buggy and set them gently inside. Lizzie was right behind them. Watching his tenderness with her sisters brought a poignant ache to her heart. Without Lizzie asking, he helped her into the carriage too, holding on to her forearm a bit longer than necessary. The warmth of his hand tingled over her skin and she pulled away as quickly as possible.

When he was settled in the driver's seat, he took the leather reins and slapped them against the palomino's back.

"Schritt," he called.

The horse walked forward, settling into an easy trot.

Sitting stiffly in her seat, Lizzie adjusted her long skirts and scrunched her knees as far away from Eli's as possible. She thought about her discussion with him the day before. He'd said he wanted to stay in Riverton. That he wanted to live the Amish way of life. But what if he changed his mind? She told herself she didn't care. He meant nothing to her now except that he was a member of the *Gmay*. So why did the thought of him leaving again make her feel so sad and empty inside?

Eli turned off the pavement and headed down the dirt road leading to the Geingeriches' farm. Another buggy and horse were right in front of them, with several more following behind in a short convoy. Eli followed their pace. Each *familye* waved and greeted one another like the best of friends. A faint mist had settled across the valley, but he knew the morning sun would soon burn it off and all would be clear by late afternoon when they began their journey home.

His parents should already be here. Joining them for meetings made him feel almost normal again. They were so happy to have him home that he felt good to be here. But he still couldn't help wondering if he'd made a wrong choice by returning to Riverton. He wanted to be here. He really did. But he couldn't seem to get Shannon off his mind. Her smile. Her scent. The way she'd begged him to save her life the night of the drunk driving accident. And then the stricken look on her parents' faces at the cemetery when they had buried their only child.

When the white frame house came into view, Eli breathed a sigh of relief. He'd promised the girls they'd be safe on their journey to church and he was grateful that he'd been able to keep his word. Too many automobiles flew way too fast down the roads. With drivers talking on their cell phones or texting, he could understand why the Amish were nervous as they drove their horse-drawn buggies and wagons. What was so important on the phone that it was worth risking someone's life? He'd had a cell phone when he'd lived among the *Englisch*, but he'd only used it when absolutely necessary. He'd found them a poor substitute for building relationships face-to-face. He was just grateful that a worse tragedy hadn't struck the Beiler *familye* and Jeremiah would recover from the accident.

Turning the horse into the main yard, he pulled up where two teenage boys were directing traffic. A long row of black buggies had already been parked along the fence line. Eli waited his turn, then pulled up as instructed.

"I can unhitch your horse," one of the boys offered.

"Danke." Eli handed the lines over, watching as the two teenagers removed the harness in preparation of leading the mare over to a field where she could graze and water with other horses.

Eli helped the girls out of the buggy. He noticed how Lizzie avoided his hand by gripping the edge of the carriage. She didn't meet his eyes as she smoothed her apron, then reached back into the buggy for a basket that was neatly covered with a clean dish towel. He had no idea what was hidden beneath, but surmised it was something tasty for their noon meal later on. The thought of spending the day with Lizzie made him feel warm. If he hadn't gone to Denver, they probably would have married. They'd be taking their *familye* to church like any other couple. But then he wouldn't have met and loved Shannon, and he couldn't forget that she had meant the world to him.

"Lizzie!"

A young woman with golden hair was busy spreading a cloth over one of the long tables set up outside. Eli didn't recognize her and wondered if she was a newcomer to the *Gmay*. She stood beneath the tall spread of a maple tree laden with leaves of bright yellow. The autumn air had a distinct crispness to it, but was still pleasant enough to eat outside.

As she approached, the woman arched her back, displaying an obvious rounding of her abdomen. Eli figured she must be about six months pregnant.

"*Guder mariye*, Abby. How are you feeling today?" Lizzie asked as the woman waddled toward them.

Ach, so this was Abby! Eli had heard all about her from his parents.

She rested a hand on her belly as Jakob Fisher joined them, taking her arm in a protective gesture. Before he'd left Riverton, Eli had known Jakob and his first wife, Susan, and their two small children, Reuben and Ruby. Jakob was older than Eli and they'd never been close friends, but Eli was sad to learn that Susan had died in childbirth while he was gone. Jakob had married Abby a year earlier and now they were expecting their first child together.

"I am well. The doctor has told me I'm perfectly healthy and should deliver just after the New Year," Abby said.

"*Ach*, you may deliver early. Wouldn't it be fun to have a Christmas baby?" Lizzie asked, her voice filled with jubilation.

Jakob smiled wide. "*Ja*, that would be the best Christmas gift ever."

Abby just beamed, her face glowing with an ethereal

beauty that seemed to accompany every new mother as she worked hand in hand with *Gott* to create a new life.

"*Hallo*, Eli." Jakob nodded to him. "I would like to introduce you to my wife, Abby."

Eli smiled and nodded at the pretty woman. "I'm so glad to meet you."

"Likewise," she said. "I heard you are looking out for the Beilers while Jeremiah is laid up."

"*Ja*, the bishop thought it would be best," Eli replied with a half smile.

"Because of the accident, I heard in town that they're planning to put up more Amish buggy signs along the roads," Jakob said.

"*Ach*, it's about time," Abby said.

"*Ja*, that would be *gut*. I just hope it gets the drivers to slow down," Lizzie murmured.

Eli hoped so too. He hated the thought of any other members of their *Gmay* getting hurt.

The women stepped ahead of the men, moving off toward the kitchen. Marty and Annie joined Jakob's two children, racing across the front lawn in carefree abandon. Church Sunday was a time to worship *Gott*, but it was also a time to socialize and relax from daily labors. Both adults and children alike usually looked forward to this day with happiness. But not Eli. Not when he glanced over and saw several older women watching him, their heads bent close as they chatted together. He couldn't help wondering if he was the topic of their conversation, especially when Marva Geingerich eyed him with a look of revulsion.

"Don't mind old Mrs. Geingerich. She doesn't approve of anyone," Jakob whispered.

Eli jerked, realizing that Jakob had stopped walking

and was watching him closely. "Does my nervousness show that much?"

Jakob nodded, his mouth turned up in a generous smile. "I'm afraid so. When my Susan died, Marva didn't approve of me either, simply because I was alone with two young *kinder* to raise. It didn't matter that I had no control over my wife's death or that I was grieving. Marva seems to be able to find anything and everything to disapprove of."

When Jakob put it like that, it sounded rather silly, but Eli didn't laugh.

"You must have been brokenhearted to lose Susan. How did you recover?" Eli asked, eager to know how to ease the gnawing pain he felt deep inside for Shannon.

"I'll let you know if I ever do. Right now, I doubt a person can fully heal from losing someone they have loved. But you have to keep living. And the Lord blessed me with a second chance at happiness. I never thought it possible, but I'm so deeply in love with Abby and I can't imagine living life without her." Jakob's gaze rested on Abby, his eyes filled with such wonder and devotion that Eli felt a lance of jealousy pierce his heart. Surely there would be no third chance for him.

Turning toward him, Jakob lifted a hand and rested it on Eli's shoulder before squeezing gently. "I know it couldn't have been easy for you to walk away from your *familye* when you left us, nor any easier for you to return. It took a lot of courage to come back and face your *eldre*. Now you have a second chance with Lizzie too."

Eli blinked, not quite understanding. For the first time since his return, Eli wondered if everyone believed he still wanted to marry Lizzie. After all, none of them knew anything about Shannon. But Lizzie didn't want him. Her words to him yesterday had indicated loud and clear that she didn't love him anymore.

"Facing my *eldre* was easier than you might think," Eli said. "They're both relieved I'm back. But Lizzie is a different story. I think I've burned a bridge with her that can never be rebuilt."

Jakob nodded. "No doubt she is still angry and hurt that you left, but she's refused to look at any other man since then. She has a *gut*, forgiving heart. With time, I'm sure both of you will be able to let go of the past, just as I did."

That was just it. Eli didn't want to let go of Shannon. How could he forget what she had meant to him and the part he'd played in her death? It was his fault she had died, but he didn't mention that to Jakob.

With one last smile of encouragement, Jakob turned and joined the other men as they lined up to go inside the spacious barn for their meetings. Eli followed, standing behind Martin Hostetler, who was three years older than him. With auburn hair, a smattering of freckles across his nose and blue eyes that gleamed with merriment, Martin was hardworking and filled with energy. Eli was surprised the man was still single.

Martin nodded and asked him several questions, but was cut off when they went inside, much to Eli's relief. His thoughts were filled with turmoil. As they trailed into the barn and took their place opposite the women, he considered Jakob's words. Yes, it had taken courage to return, and yet it hadn't been so difficult. Not when he'd been yearning for home—and everything in Denver had reminded him of Shannon, filling him with grief and guilt. But now that he was here, he feared he'd made a mistake. People in his *Gmay* would expect him to marry. And he couldn't do that right now. Maybe never. Perhaps he didn't belong in this world anymore.

He glanced at Bishop Yoder's pretty daughters sitting with Lizzie. The young women smiled shyly, then ducked their heads close together in a whispered conversation. Though he'd known most of them before he left, they all looked alike to Eli. Modest, chaste and pretty. With her creamy complexion and stunning eyes, Lizzie stood out among them, like a beacon of light in a sea of fog. Eli knew the Hostetlers and Geingeriches each had a daughter of marriageable age too, but he wasn't interested. Not in any of them.

He glanced at Lizzie, who stared straight ahead at the bishop. As the *vorsinger* called out the first note of the opening song, she opened her mouth and sang in German from the *Ausbund*, their church hymnal. How ironic that she was the only woman in the room who didn't seem to be looking at him.

Someone cleared their throat nearby and he glanced over to find his father's disapproving frown aimed at him. It didn't matter that Eli was a grown man. He was unmarried and still living in his father's household. Trying to refocus his thoughts, Eli joined in with the slow harmony, the words returning to his memory like a dear old friend.

Almost immediately, the bishop and deacon stood, then disappeared into the tack room to hold the *Abrot*, a leadership council meeting to discuss church business. While they were gone, the congregation kept singing, with no musical accompaniment. Eli stared at the closed door, trying to clear his mind and relax.

Forcing himself not to look at Lizzie again. Attempting to push her from his mind. But it did no good. Again and again, he glanced her way, his thoughts returning to her wounded gaze. She'd made her position perfectly clear when the bishop had asked him to work on her farm. They needn't discuss the matter further. And yet, Eli couldn't fight the feeling that they still had unfinished business between them.

Chapter Three

The congregation knelt in silent prayer until Bishop Yoder released a discreet sigh. As a body, they each rose to their feet, turned and sat on the hard, backless benches. Once they were all seated, Lizzie watched as Bishop Yoder stood at the front of the room. With such a small *Gmay*, they had only one minister... Lizzie's father. And with him still in the hospital, the bishop would probably preach to them.

"What is in your heart today?" he asked the worshippers.

The question took Lizzie off guard. Tilting her head, she listened intently as the bishop spoke, his voice soft but powerful, like the sound of rolling thunder off in the distance. He met the eyes of each person in the room as though he were speaking to every single one of them. When he met Lizzie's eyes, she looked down, feeling suddenly embarrassed.

"Do you carry peace and charity within you, or do you harbor anger and malice toward someone?" the bishop asked, pausing to give them each time to search their hearts.

Lizzie squirmed on her seat. She glanced at Eli, but found him gazing straight forward, his expression one of thoughtful introspection.

Bishop Yoder lifted a book of scriptures. "But whosoever shall smite thee on thy right cheek, turn to him the other also."

Lizzie had heard this passage numerous times and thought she understood it clearly…until now. She had no desire to be hurt again and again, especially where her heart was concerned. But wasn't that what the Lord expected? For her to humble herself and cast aside her harsh feelings.

"Over the next weeks, I hope each of you will resolve any hard feelings you might carry toward others," the bishop continued. "Examine your own thoughts and actions and bring them into line with how the Lord would have you live. I beseech each of you to hand Him your anger and pain, your shortcomings and flaws. Then, once we all are in accord with each other, we will hold our Council Services in preparation for Communion."

Communion! A sacred time when the entire congregation must be in complete harmony with one another. With all that had happened recently, Lizzie had forgotten it was nearly that time of year.

As the bishop continued speaking about the rules of their *Ordnung* and the responsibility of each member of their community, she clenched her eyes tightly closed and gripped her hands together in her lap. Surely the bishop wasn't speaking directly to her. He couldn't know the resentment she still harbored toward Eli. Could he? Yet whether he could or not, she was the minister's daughter, after all, and she knew she should set a good example of love, tolerance and forgiveness. But how could she forgive Eli after what he'd done? He had soured her toward all men. She would probably never marry now. Never have a *familye* of her own. Never live in her own house. Over time, several men had asked her out. Martin Hostetler had pursued her doggedly, but seemed to have finally given up after the first year. Now it appeared she would become an old maid. Pitied by the other members of her community.

She took a slow breath, trying to settle her nerves. Her thoughts were selfish, she knew that. She was so worried about herself and what others might think about her that she hadn't stopped to consider Eli and his well-being. Why had he returned? What had happened to him after all this time? After he'd left, she'd been worried for him, fearing that he was lost forever. But here he was, seeking a second chance. And who was she to refuse him?

She had to find a way to let go of her anger. To forgive him. But how? All her life, she'd been taught the principles of repentance and forgiveness. So, why was it so difficult to exercise those virtues now?

Puzzling over her dilemma, Lizzie was surprised at how quickly time passed before they broke for the noon meal.

"*Komm* on. You can help me serve my potato soup." Abby spoke cheerfully as she took Lizzie's arm and pulled her toward the barn door.

"Potato soup?" Lizzie said, her mind still focused on the sermon.

Abby laughed. "I know it's a bit fancier than our normal fare of bread and peanut butter, but I'm feeling extra domestic lately. All I want to do is cook and clean. Jakob says I'm *nesting*. He says it's normal for a woman in my condition to act this way."

Laughing at Abby's enthusiasm, Lizzie let herself be pulled along. She could just imagine how fun it must be to anticipate her first child. But that thought brought her another bout of confusion, sadness and guilt.

Inside the kitchen, a dozen women crowded around, helping prepare the food. Their identical dresses were simple but pretty in assorted colors of blue, burgundy, purple and green. Each woman wore a pair of black, sensible hard-soled shoes, and a starched organdy *kapp*. Lizzie thought there was something lovely and serene about their simplistic dress.

Naomi Fisher stood slicing loaves of homemade bread in front of the counter while Sarah Yoder laid dill and sweet pickles on a plate. Abby stirred an enormous silver pot on the stove as Lizzie reached for a large serving bowl.

"I'll ladle the soup into the bowl and you can serve it hot to the men." Abby picked up a long ladle and dipped it into the frothy, white soup.

Lizzie nodded, sliding on a pair of oven mitts to protect her hands from the heat. Lifting the bowl, she held it steady while Abby ladled it full. The warm, tantalizing aroma made Lizzie's mouth water.

"Um, it smells delicious," Lizzie said.

"*Danke*. I crumbled bits of bacon and shredded cheese into it. It's one of Jakob's favorite dishes. It'll go well with Naomi's crusty homemade bread," Abby said.

"Did you see Eli Stoltzfus listening to the bishop's sermon? I hope it sank in. That boy needs to mend his ways, that's for sure."

Lizzie looked up and saw elderly Marva Geingerich standing next to Linda Hostetler. The two women were unwrapping trenchers of sliced cheese and ham. Slightly deaf at the age of eighty-nine, Marva's rasping attempt at a whisper carried like a shout across the kitchen and everyone paused in their work. Especially Fannie, Eli's mother.

"*Ja*, I saw him. He's trying hard to fit back into the *Gmay* and doing a good job of it from what I can see," Linda said.

Marva's thin lips curved in disapproval. "*Ach*, I don't know why he ever came back. Once they leave and get a taste of the *Englisch* world, they never can get rid of it. I've seen it happen several times."

Something hardened inside of Lizzie. Though she was angry at Eli, she didn't like what she was hearing. It wasn't fair and it wasn't right.

"Marva! What are you saying?" Naomi paused in her slicing, her forehead creased with a frown.

"He won't stay long, you mark my words," Marva said. "As soon as that boy gets tired of living our humble way of life, he'll be off again to live among the *Englisch*."

"You don't know that. Eli returned of his own choosing. He wants to be here with us." Sarah Yoder, the bishop's wife, set a casserole dish on the wooden counter with a thump.

Marva jerked her head up, the wrinkles around her gray eyes deepening with her scowl. "*Ach*, he's been gone too long. Who knows what wickedness he's been up to? I don't know how he'll ever fit in with the *Gmay* now. No doubt he's got plenty to repent of. Mark my words, he'll leave again and that will be that."

An audible gasp filled the room and Lizzie flinched.

Turning, she saw the reason why. Eli stood in the doorway, holding an empty glass in one hand. His expression looked peaceful as a summer's morning, but Lizzie knew he'd overheard the conversation and must be upset. It was there in the subtle narrowing of his eyes and the tensing of his shoulders. Other people might not notice, but Lizzie knew him too well. For just a moment, she saw a flash of anger in his eyes, then it was gone and she thought perhaps she'd imagined it.

He cleared his voice, speaking in a composed tone. "I'm sorry to intrude, but Ezekiel has a cough. Could I trouble someone for a glass of water?"

Ezekiel, or *Dawdi* Zeke as most everyone called him, was the eldest member of the *Gmay*. Having just turned ninety-four years, he still had an active mind and was as kind and compassionate as Marva was harsh and unforgiving.

"Of course you can." Naomi, who was *Dawdi* Zeke's daughter, took the glass from Eli's hand, filled it with tap water, then handed it back to him.

"Danke." He ducked his head and left without another word.

Everyone stared in mortified confusion, not knowing what to say. A part of Lizzie felt compassion for Eli and the urge to run after him. But another part thought it was just what he deserved. That made her feel worse because it wasn't charitable to think that way.

"How could you say those things? It wasn't very nice. We should be more compassionate." Naomi shook her head, her expression showing her dismay as she gazed intently at Marva.

"I don't know what you mean. I only spoke the

truth." Marva drew back her shoulders, pursed her lips and lifted her chin a little higher.

The hackles rose at the back of Lizzie's neck. Even if it was the truth, it wasn't kind. She would never consider belittling Eli to other members of the congregation on Church Sunday. It wasn't their place to judge him or anyone. Especially right after the bishop had preached to them about forgiveness and their upcoming Communion. But she couldn't help feeling like a hypocrite since Marva had voiced aloud her very same concerns.

Lizzie's gaze shifted to Fannie, Eli's mother. She had been cutting thick pieces of Schnitz apple pie but had dropped the knife onto the table when Marva had begun speaking. Looking at her now, Lizzie saw that her face had gone white as a sun-bleached sheet, her chin quivering.

"He's *mein sohn*. Do you really think he'll leave again?" she cried with naked fear.

Naomi quickly set her bread knife on the table before wrapping her arms around the other woman in a comforting hug. "*Ne*, it's nonsense! Don't you listen to such talk, Fannie. Eli fits in here with all of us just fine. He's one of our own and a welcome addition to our community. We love him and we're blessed to have him back. Look at all the *gut* he's done already for the Beiler *familye*. Isn't that right, Lizzie?"

Naomi looked at her and Lizzie blinked in stunned silence before stuttering over a reply. "*Ja*, he…he's been very kind."

"And who are we to judge others? We all have our faults. We are all happy that Eli has returned to his faith." Sarah nodded her approval.

"*Danke.*" Fannie wiped one eye, showing a tremulous smile of appreciation.

"Humph! We'll see." Marva huffed as she carried a tray of sliced homemade bread outside.

Swallowing hard, Lizzie realized she was staring. Her mind whirled in confusion. Seeing the hurt on Fannie's face, she hurried over to comfort the woman.

"Don't listen to such talk. Eli loves you and Leroy. He wants to be here with you," Lizzie said, trying to believe her own words.

"But what if Marva is right? What if Eli leaves again? I don't know what I'd do. He's our only *sohn*," Fannie whispered.

A tremor ran down Lizzie's spine, but she fought off her own fears and tried to be brave. "If he leaves, we'll do as Christ taught and turn the other cheek. We'll exercise faith and face whatever comes our way and pray that he'll come back again. We can never give up on anyone."

Speaking these words aloud brought Lizzie a bit of courage. She meant what she said, yet her heart thumped with trepidation.

"I just don't think I can stand to lose him again." Tears shimmered in Fannie's eyes.

"We'll all be here for you, no matter what happens," Lizzie said.

Fannie nodded, but her sad expression still showed her unease as she returned to her chore of slicing pie.

Lizzie watched her, her own hands shaking.

Abby laid a hand on her arm. "Lizzie, are you all right?"

She gave a stuttering laugh. "*Ja*, I'm fine."

What else could she say? Only Eli knew if he would

stay or go. Any member of their community could leave at any time, including her. Lizzie just wished she could be certain she wouldn't be hurt by his decisions.

"Don't worry," Abby said to her. "It'll be all right. *Komm* on. Let's get out of here. I need some fresh air."

Lizzie followed her friend outside, the screen door clapping closed behind them. They paused beneath the shade of the back porch. Children raced across the yard in a game of chase. Teenaged boys stood in a group, watching the teenaged girls. The afternoon sun sparkled in an azure sky. Lizzie wanted to cherish such a day…one of the last warm ones before the cooler weather rolled in. As she gazed at the rows of men sitting at the long tables, she let their subdued laughter soothe her ruffled feelings.

"I can't believe Marva said those horrible things. What was she thinking? She has such a waspish tongue," Abby whispered, her hands gripping the soup ladle like a hammer. "She's never been happy since her son brought the *familye* here from Ohio after his *vadder* died. She understands about repentance and forgiveness and should know better than to speak that way."

"Marva is rather stern," Lizzie agreed in a vague tone, once again feeling like a hypocrite.

"Jakob told me you and Eli were engaged once. I hope her words didn't upset you too badly," Abby said.

Lizzie shrugged as she gripped the serving bowl tighter, letting the soup warm her chilled hands. "That was a long time ago."

"Are you still friends with him now that he's returned?" Abby peered at her, as though looking deep inside her heart.

Biting her bottom lip, Lizzie couldn't meet Abby's gaze.

"Oh, Lizzie. I'm so sorry." Abby squeezed her arm. "His return must be difficult for you. And to have him working at your farm every day… But don't forget to keep an open heart and have faith. *Gott* will care for you both and all will work out fine. I know it will."

Lizzie couldn't manage to muster a smile in return. "I'm not so sure."

Resting her palm against her baby bump, Abby rubbed gently. "With my past history, I never would have believed *Gott* could make my life turn out so well. I thought I could never trust men and would never marry. But I soon learned that I was wrong. Give *Gott* a chance and He'll work so many blessings in your life, just as He did mine."

Lizzie understood. Since her marriage to Jakob, Abby had confided that she'd been physically and verbally abused by her father and elder brother. Abby was so happy now and Lizzie was glad. But she almost dropped the serving bowl when Abby turned and headed straight over to the table where Eli was sitting.

Breathing a sigh of resignation, Lizzie followed her friend, but couldn't help wondering if this day could get any worse. She wanted to turn the other cheek. To forget her pain and humiliation and believe that Eli truly was back for good. But she couldn't help thinking that Marva was right about one thing. Eli wouldn't stay.

"When did you cut your leg on the hay baler?"

Eli sat at the table next to Darrin Albrecht, their deacon. The autumn sun beat down on the men, but they'd each removed their black felt hats for their noon meal. They spoke in companionable friendship, waiting as the women set the food before them.

A rather hefty and somber man, Darrin was middle-aged with a thick head of salt-and-pepper hair and a long beard to match. As the deacon, it was his job to assist the bishop in disciplinary issues, to ensure that all members of the *Gmay* were following the rules of the *Ordnung* and to announce upcoming marriages.

"It's been two months since it happened and it wasn't even a bad cut. I can't understand why it's taking so long to heal," Darrin said.

Out of his peripheral vision, Eli caught sight of Lizzie standing just behind his left shoulder. She held a large, steaming dish, the aroma tantalizing. He leaned back, giving her and Abby room to scoop soup into his bowl. Along with the other women, they worked in silence, seeing to everyone's needs before their own. Glancing up, he saw Lizzie's face looked pale. She'd been in the kitchen earlier and he couldn't help wondering if she agreed with Marva Geingerich's opinion of him.

He clamped a hard will on his anger. When he'd returned, he'd known he might face disapproval from some of his people. It didn't change anything. He wanted to be here. And that meant he must exercise self-discipline, control his feelings and remain passive in the face of adversity. It's what the Lord would want him to do.

"Are you all right?" he asked Lizzie, worried that she and his mother were both overly upset by what had transpired.

"*Ja*, of course. Why wouldn't I be?" Before he could answer, she ducked her head and moved on to Deacon Albrecht's bowl.

Turning, Eli faced Darrin. "May I see your wound?"

He was conscious of Lizzie moving to the other side of the table as she served the other men, still close enough to overhear his conversation.

Beneath the table, Darrin hiked up his homemade pant leg to the knee. A gauze bandage had been affixed to the side of his lower calf with white tape. Eli ducked down and Darrin lifted the gauze to reveal a thin, jagged cut no more than an inch long. Though it didn't look deep, the wound was swollen and angry red.

"*Ach*, I have no doubt it's infected." Eli wasn't a medical doctor, but he recognized a septic injury when he saw one.

"Norma cleans it for me every day with hydrogen peroxide and ointment, but it doesn't seem to make any difference." Darrin pressed the bandage back in place and pulled his pant leg down.

Sitting up straight, Eli considered the man for a moment. "Have you seen a doctor about it?"

"*Ne*! There's no need for that. I don't trust those *Englisch* doctors." Darrin waved a hand in the air, then buttered a thick slice of bread.

Eli watched the man as he lifted his glass and smiled at Lizzie. Setting the serving bowl of soup down, she picked up a pitcher of water and refilled his glass…which Darrin had emptied for the third time since they'd sat down twenty minutes earlier. Several women from the congregation hovered nearby to keep the men's plates and glasses filled.

"You seem overly thirsty today," Eli said as he lifted a spoonful of soup to his mouth.

"*Ja*, he's always thirsty lately, even when he's not working in the fields." Linda Albrecht set a plate of sliced ham in front of them. She must have come outside while they were engaged in conversation.

"What about fatigue? Are you feeling more tired than usual?" Eli asked.

Darrin inclined his head. "Now that you mention it, I am more tired, even when I've had a full night's sleep. And sometimes, my feet feel numb too. Do you think the cut could be causing that?"

Eli took a deep inhale and let it go. This didn't sound good. "I'd feel better if you saw the doctor as soon as possible."

"That's what I suggested, but he won't go," Linda said, resting her hands on her hips as she tossed her husband an *I told you so* look.

"*Ach*, I'm fine. I'm sure the wound will heal eventually," Darrin insisted.

Eli met the man's eyes and touched his arm to make his point clear. "I think you're wrong, Deacon Albrecht. Please, go see the doctor. I don't want to alarm you, but you should ask him to test you for diabetes. If you've got diabetes, chances are it's probably keeping your wound from healing, which could cause other serious problems down the road. Don't take chances with your health. You want to be around to take care of your *familye* for many years to come."

Linda widened her eyes and pressed a hand to her chest. "Oh, my! Diabetes?"

Eli nodded. "He has some of the symptoms, but don't take my word for it. Let the doctor diagnose it for you. He'll be able to run some blood tests and let you know for sure. If the test is positive, he'll prescribe medication to control the problem. At the very least, he can ensure that wound on your leg doesn't turn gangrenous."

Linda gasped. "Gangrene?"

Darrin pursed his mouth, looking doubtful. Because Eli believed the man had a serious health problem, he pressed the issue further. "I'm dead serious about this, Deacon Albrecht. Go to the doctor first thing tomorrow morning. Please, do as I ask."

Darrin must have heard the urgency in his voice because his mouth dropped open. "You really mean it, don't you, Eli?"

Eli nodded emphatically. "I absolutely do. I want you to get some proper medical help."

"*Ja*, don't you worry. We will go first thing after our morning chores," Linda said. She was looking at her husband with a stern, wifely expression that would tolerate no refusals.

Knowing Linda would make Darrin go to the doctor, Eli felt relieved. He smiled and switched topics to the price of hay. When he reached for his empty glass, he caught Lizzie standing nearby. A disapproving expression drew her eyebrows together, but she hurried to fill his glass.

"*Danke*," he said.

"*Gaern gscheh*." She seemed both surprised and critical of what he'd told Deacon Albrecht. No doubt she disapproved.

She walked away and Eli longed to call her back. To tell her of the extensive training he'd received in order to become a paramedic and that he knew what he was talking about. But these people would not be impressed. Nor did he want to sound boastful. After all, his training was from the Lord so he could serve others. It wasn't a matter of pride.

And he was glad he had it—and could use it to help the deacon. Though Eli wasn't positive Darrin Albrecht had diabetes, he was absolutely certain of one thing. If the man didn't get quality medical care soon, his wound could fester into gangrene and he'd lose his leg and possibly his life. But how could he tell Lizzie that? How could he explain that he only had the Deacon Albrecht's best interests at heart?

"Eli, if you're finished eating, will you help us out?"

Jarred from his thoughts, Eli turned to find Martin Hostetler standing next to him, a wide smile on his face.

"Come play volleyball with us. We need another player to complete two teams and, as I recall, you are good at it." Martin tossed a white ball high into the air, then caught it.

Deacon Albrecht smiled. "Go on, Eli. You'll have more fun with your young friends than sitting here with me."

Eli stood and turned toward the lawn. A net was tied across the grass, affixed to two long poles that had been cemented into old tires. Lizzie stood in front of the net. Seeing her, a feeling of anticipation zipped through Eli. Obviously she'd been recruited too. It had been years since he'd played volleyball...back when he and Lizzie were kids and still crazy in love with each other.

Walking over to the net with Martin, Eli glanced at the other unmarried people surrounding him. They seemed to be paired up on two sides. Some were as young as eleven years, while a few were as old as him and Martin.

Lizzie stood gripping her hands together, looking suddenly shy.

"Which side am I on?" Eli asked.

"You'll be on this side." Martin pointed to Lizzie's team and Eli saw her immediate frown.

She turned away, stepping to the back row, but Martin placed Eli right beside her. From where he stood beneath the shade of a tall elm tree, Bishop Yoder showed a satisfied smile. Eli couldn't help wondering if the man had rigged this to get him near Lizzie. Everyone knew they'd been engaged once. No doubt some of the congregation was trying to pair them back together. One look at Lizzie's wary gaze told him it wouldn't work.

She turned aside, seeming to focus on the other team as they served. She jumped gracefully, her hands fisted together as she struck the ball. From there, Eli knocked it easily over the net, scoring a point for their team.

Several of their teammates clapped their hands and cheered, but Lizzie stood silent. The ball was served again and volleyed back and forth for several minutes, then it zipped directly toward Eli. He hit the ball lightly, offering a layup to Lizzie, just like he'd done when they were teenagers. Instead of spiking the ball over the net, Lizzie jumped back and let the ball hit the ground. It rolled onto the graveled driveway and one of the younger children chased after it.

The other team cheered.

"Tied points," Martin called from in front of the net. Facing Eli, the redheaded man smiled wide, but there was no malice in his expression. He was merely having fun.

"I thought you would spike the ball, like you used to do," Eli spoke low for Lizzie's ears alone.

"I... I didn't see it soon enough," she returned, sounding slightly irritated.

Eli didn't know if she was flustered by his presence, or if dropping the ball was her way of rejecting him. He couldn't help thinking about what Jakob had said earlier. Did Lizzie still harbor resentment toward him for breaking off their engagement when he left all those years ago?

"Are you sure you're all right?" he asked her while the other team readjusted their positions so they could serve the ball.

"Of course, why?"

Yes, he definitely caught a note of exasperation in her tone.

He shrugged. "No reason, really. I just noticed that you seemed annoyed when I was speaking with Deacon Albrecht and now again."

Her slim jaw hardened. "You're not a doctor, Eli. But I can see you gained plenty of *Hochmut* from going to college. You seem to think you know what is good for everyone."

So that was it. Like many of their people, she didn't approve of higher learning. She thought he was too prideful.

"I don't think that at all. I only want to help, Lizzie-bee. That's why I told Deacon Albrecht to go see a doctor as soon as possible...so he can get an accurate diagnosis," he said.

Releasing a heavy sigh, she turned away and focused on the game. She did an admirable job of ignoring him. No doubt she agreed with Marva Geingerich, that he would leave again. And how could he persuade her that he really wanted to stay in Riverton when he hadn't yet convinced himself?

They won the game, but Lizzie hurried off to help in the kitchen before a second match began. Karen Hostetler, who was Martin's eighteen-year-old sister, and Ellen Yoder, the bishop's daughter, both smiled prettily at him. In between serving the ball, they engaged Eli in conversation. He tried to show interest, but his gaze kept roaming over to the house where he sought some sight of Lizzie. After the second game ended, the teams broke up. Eli was glad. He had no interest in playing volleyball. At least, not without Lizzie.

He didn't see her again until it was time to drive her and the little girls home that evening. Though he wanted to head back before it got too late, he had to stay a little longer so he could attend the instruction class with the two others who were planning to be baptized in a few months. As Eli listened to the lesson from Bishop Yoder, he liked what he heard, but felt a bit nervous when he considered its importance. Once he was baptized into the Amish faith, his life would change forever. He would not take the vows unless he was absolutely confident that he intended to live them for the rest of his life.

On their way home, Marty and Annie were eager to chat about their day. As the buggy moved along at a rapid pace, Lizzie sat quietly with her hands in her lap. Eli longed to talk with her about his class, to get her opinion on several issues, but whenever he tried to engage her in conversation, her response was rather abrupt. Finally, he gave up trying.

As they pulled into the farmyard, dusk was settling

over the western sky with clouds of pink, orange and gray. He looked up at the tall Sangre de Cristo Mountains and thought he'd never seen anything so beautiful in all his life. He had just enough time to milk the cows and head home to his parents before it turned dark.

"*Danke* for driving us safely," little Annie said.

"*Ja, danke* for keeping your promise," Marty agreed.

The girls both smiled and hugged him, but Lizzie simply nodded, then went inside the house.

Watching her go, a feeling of melancholy blanketed Eli and he wondered what he could do to improve her opinion of him. It seemed that she'd lost all faith in him, and he couldn't really blame her. But that's when he made a promise to himself. No matter how long it took, he was determined to regain her trust. He just wasn't certain how.

Chapter Four

By noon the following morning, Eli had almost finished raking the alfalfa. Dust sifted through the air as
the two-horse hitch plodded along with the patience of
Job. The tines connecting to the four horizontal bars of
the side rake moved in a circular motion as they rolled
the hay into straight, tidy windrows. The action also
fluffed and turned the hay, so it would dry well before
they baled it tomorrow. Eli was eager to get the hay
in as quickly as possible. The unseasonable warmth
wouldn't hold much longer. He figured they had one or
two more days before the clouds rolled in and brought
rain to the valley.

Glancing toward the farmhouse, he saw Lizzie outside hanging clothes on the line. They hadn't spoken
since church and he felt the tension between them
reaching clear across the field.

Annie was helping her older sister, lifting damp
clothes out of the white laundry basket to hand over
to Lizzie. Marty stood nearby, gathering seeds from
the dried marigolds that had grown all summer long
in the flowerbeds surrounding the house. Above the

rattling noise of the hay rake, Eli could catch hints of the happy sound of their laughter.

The rake gave a little bump and he turned to face forward, focusing on his work. When he finished twenty minutes later, he pulled the draft horses to a halt, lifted the horizontal bars, then drove the Percherons toward the barn. Lizzie was no longer in the yard and he figured she'd gone into the house with the girls.

He deposited the rake in the barn, then cared for the horses. After watering the Percherons, he checked each of their hooves, bodies and heads. If one of them picked up a stone or had a wound of some kind, they wouldn't be much use in baling tomorrow morning. It'd take all six draft horses to pull the heavy baler and hay wagon.

Satisfied the animals were in good condition, he turned them loose in the pasture. Before he went up to the house for some lunch, he entered the cool shadows of the barn. Removing his straw hat, he wiped his forehead on his shirtsleeve and sat on a tall stool.

Another letter had arrived from Tom Caldwell, his old boss at the hospital in Denver. Pulling the short letter from the envelope, Eli read it one more time. Tom knew about Shannon's death and understood that Eli had been badly shaken by the accident. Tom had encouraged him to take and break and go home for a visit. But now, Tom was shorthanded and badly needed qualified paramedics. In his letter, he'd offered Eli a raise if he would return to work by the end of October. Eli had already sent his regrets. He was not at all certain he'd ever return to Denver—but he definitely wouldn't be going back that soon. After all, Jeremiah wouldn't be healed enough to work by that time and

Eli had given his word to the bishop that he would care for the farm until then.

"Eli?"

He jerked around, dropping the letter in the process. The paper wafted to the ground and he scooped it up, shoving it into his hat.

"What's that you're reading?" Lizzie stood in front of the double doors, holding a tray with a plate of food and tall glass of milk. A shaft of sunlight glimmered behind her, highlighting her in beams of gold.

"Nothing of consequence."

A flush of heat rose in his face. It was bad enough that his parents knew he was receiving letters and were worried his *Englisch* friends might draw him back to Denver. If only he didn't feel so conflicted. Helping Deacon Albrecht yesterday had felt so good and familiar, but he couldn't tell Lizzie that, nor his parents either. Not after what Marva Geingerich had said. They might judge him harshly. If only Shannon were here. She would advise him in that soft, understanding manner of hers. But if she were still alive, he would never have come home.

"Is it a letter?" Lizzie stepped closer, setting the tray on a low ledge of timber.

He placed the hat on his head. "*Ja*, a letter."

Her eyes crinkled with concern. "A letter from whom?"

"An old friend in Denver," he said, trying to sound unruffled.

She tilted her head to one side, her eyes narrowing. "An *Englisch* friend?"

He nodded, unwilling to lie. Except for his love for Shannon, it seemed he couldn't keep any secrets from this woman. When they'd been young, she was the only one who had known of his desire to go to college. She hadn't told a soul and, because of that, he'd thought she'd understand when he left. That she might even join him. But he had been dead wrong.

She took a deep breath, then let it go in a slow sigh. "What do they want?"

The moment she asked the question, she blinked and flushed with embarrassment. She lifted a hand to nervously adjust her white *kapp*. He almost laughed at the feminine gesture, unable to keep from admiring her graceful fingers, or the way her blue eyes darkened.

"I'm sorry. I shouldn't have asked that. It's none of my business. I brought you something to eat." She turned and gestured to the tray.

He cleared his throat, feeling like he'd swallowed sandpaper. "Was there…was there something else you wanted?"

She nodded, meeting his eyes again. "*Ja*, I was waiting until you finished raking the hay. I know that's the priority right now. But I was wondering if you might have time to drive the *maed* and me into town to visit our *vadder* at the hospital this afternoon."

Ah, so she still wasn't over the shock of the accident and still didn't feel confident enough to drive herself. He thought about teasing her, but sensed it was difficult for her to confide this weakness to him. Besides, he liked having something normal and mundane to distract him from the conflict waging a war inside his mind.

"Of course. I'd be happy to drive you and the *kinder*," he said.

"*Gut*. We'll be ready to leave as soon as you've

eaten. I also wanted to stop off at Ruth Lapp's house. She wasn't at church because she has bronchitis, so I thought I'd take a meal to her *familye*. Nothing fancy. Just a casserole and some pumpkin muffins."

Yum! Pumpkin muffins. His mouth watered at the thought. He glanced at the plate she'd brought him, noticing she'd included a muffin with thick cream cheese icing for him too. "That's very kind of you."

In fact, her generosity reminded him of why he'd returned. Because he loved this way of life. The way his people looked after one another. Their generosity and devotion to what they believed was right. He realized that even old Marva Geingerich's biting comments were made out of fear that he might leave again, which would hurt those he left behind. A part of him wanted to stay, just to prove her wrong. To show the *Gmay* how much he loved it here.

"But I'll need to leave early tonight," he said.

"Oh?" She cocked an eyebrow.

"I need to drive to Bishop Yoder's house. He's helping me make up for lost time, so I can catch up with the other students planning to be baptized in a few months. I still need to read the articles of the Dordrecht Confession."

"*Ach*, you didn't read them the last time you took the classes, before you left?"

"*Ne*, I'm afraid not."

"Then of course you must go. That's very important. You won't want to be late. We'll only be gone long enough to pay a quick visit to *Daed* and drop off the meal," she said.

"*Gut*."

They gazed at each other and the silence lengthened. In the past, they'd never had a lack of things to say to each other. Even silences had been comfortable between them. But not anymore.

Putting her hands behind her back, Lizzie scuffed the toe of her shoe against the ground. "*Ach*, I guess I'd better get back to the house and get the *kinder* ready to leave."

"*Ja*, I'll bring the buggy out in a few minutes."

With one final nod, she whirled around and was gone, leaving him feeling suddenly very empty inside.

As Lizzie hurried to the house, she thought it might have been a mistake to ask Eli to drive her and the girls into town. It seemed silly that she couldn't drive herself. And yet, she still felt too nervous. But more than that, she hated to admit that Eli's presence brought her a great deal of comfort. She liked having him here and that was dangerous on so many levels. More than anything, she had to protect her heart. Because she couldn't stand the pain of loving and losing him again.

Within ten minutes, she had the kitchen tidied and the children ready to leave. Standing on the front porch with Marty, she held a large basket containing the promised meal for the Lapps inside. She'd also tucked a couple of pumpkin muffins in for her father, although she wasn't sure if he had any diet restrictions. If so, she'd give them to the nurses.

The rattle of the buggy brought her head up and she saw Eli driving Ginger toward them from the barn.

"*Komm* on, Annie. We're going to see *Daed*," Marty called excitedly.

Annie came running, a huge smile on her face. In

her excitement, she slammed the front door behind her. "*Ach*, I can't wait. It's been forever since we saw *Daed*."

Lizzie smiled at her exuberance and tugged playfully on one of the ribbons to her *kapp*. "It's only been a few days, *bensel*."

The child hopped on one foot with excitement. "It feels like forever. I can't wait for *Daed* to come home."

Neither could Lizzie. For some reason, she felt more vulnerable with him gone. More dependent upon Eli. She'd have to correct that problem soon. She couldn't rely on Eli forever.

They settled into the buggy with Eli holding the lead lines in his strong hands. There was something restive in watching him work with the horse. Though he displayed self-confidence, he was quiet and respectful, seeming lost in his own thoughts.

"When do you think Billie will be ready to drive again?" she asked.

He stared straight ahead as he responded. "Physically, I think he's ready now, but I'm not sure how he'll respond up on the county road. Tomorrow, I'll take him out alone, to make sure he doesn't panic when cars and trucks whiz by us."

How insightful. It hadn't occurred to Lizzie that the horse might also be skittish around motorized vehicles now. It figured that Eli was perceptive enough to realize this and considerate enough to drive the horse alone, so no one else would get hurt if the animal bolted.

"I appreciate that," she said.

He shrugged one shoulder. "It's no problem. I'm happy to help out."

Yes, that was just the problem. His kindness and

generosity to her *familye* made it difficult to be angry with him. Yet, she didn't dare forget.

Marty scooted forward from the back seat and leaned against Lizzie's shoulder. "Do you think *Daed* will be able to come home with us today?"

"I don't know, *boppli*. I doubt it. We'll have to see what the doctor says."

Not to be left out, Annie nudged her way in and leaned against Eli. "How long will *Daed* have to stay in the hospital? I miss him."

Lizzie reached up and squeezed Annie's hand. "Like I said, we won't know until we talk to the doctor. I know we all miss *Daed*, but he's going to be all right and we'll see him soon. Now, sit back and give Eli room to drive."

Satisfied with this reassurance, the girls smiled and sat back. Eli glanced Lizzie's way and his soft smile made her heart skip a couple of beats in spite of herself.

Along their way, they stopped off at the Lapps' modest farmhouse to deliver the food. As Eli pulled up out front, Lizzie faced him.

"Since Ruth is so sick, will you keep the *kinder* out here with you, please? I don't want them to catch her illness. I'll only be a minute," she said.

Marty and Annie frowned, but didn't say anything. No doubt they were hoping to play with Ruth's children.

Eli ducked his head in assent. "Of course."

Lizzie nodded and hopped out of the buggy. When she reached back, Eli handed her the basket.

Moments later, Ruth answered the door. She was fully dressed, but her apron was stained and slightly crooked. There were dark circles beneath her eyes, her hair coming loose from her *kapp*, and her nose was bright red. In one hand, she clutched several tissues. With her other hand, she bounced her toddler on her hip, the little boy holding a full bottle of milk.

"Lizzie! It's nice of you to visit." Ruth covered her mouth as she gave a hacking cough that sounded like it rattled something deep down in her lungs. "I don't dare let you in. I fear I'd only give you my cold and then you'd pass it on to your entire *familye*."

"You should try a humidifier. That might help you to breathe easier," Lizzie suggested.

Trying not to be obvious, she glanced behind Ruth, noting that everything inside the house looked in fairly good order. Two older children sat on the sofa, quietly reading books. The baby seemed well cared for too. Except that she didn't feel well, Ruth seemed to be coping and seeing to the needs of her *familye*.

"*Ja*, I have one running now," Ruth said.

"*Gut*. I won't stay, but I wanted to help in some way. At least you won't have to cook *nachtesse* tonight." Lizzie handed over the basket.

"*Ach*, that's so kind of you. You're a *gut* friend." Ruth took the basket with her free hand and smiled as she jutted her chin toward the buggy. "Is that Eli Stoltzfus I see in the buggy?"

Lizzie nodded, her senses flaring. "*Ja*, it is."

"You're back together then?"

Lizzie automatically stiffened. "*Ne*, he's just helping out at the farm while my *vadder* is laid up."

"*Ja*, I heard something about Jeremiah being injured. I'm so glad you and the girls are safe and hope Jeremiah is better soon." Ruth set the basket on a table before shifting the baby to her other hip. "It'd be so nice if you and Eli got back together, though."

Lizzie didn't know what to say, so she chose to ignore the comment by smiling brilliantly. "If you need anything at all, you just let me know."

"I will." Ruth nodded.

"I'll check on you again in a few days," Lizzie promised, stepping down off the porch.

"*Danke* so much." Ruth waved to the occupants of the buggy before going inside and shutting the door.

Whew! Thankfully, Ruth didn't push the issue. Lizzie wasn't prepared to answer questions about her and Eli. They weren't getting back together, but it poked at old wounds to go around telling everyone that.

As she climbed into the buggy, Eli reached out and pulled her up. The grip of his hand around hers felt strong yet gentle. She quickly sat and smoothed her skirts before he clicked his tongue and the horse took off again.

"What you just did was very *gut*. You're a kind example for your *schweschdere*." He glanced back at the two little girls.

"*Danke.*" Lizzie didn't know what else to say. She hadn't sought his approval and yet she couldn't help feeling suddenly very happy inside. She told herself it was because she'd just done an act of service to someone in need, but she knew it was something more. Something she didn't understand.

They didn't speak for most of the remaining journey into town. Following the traffic light on Main Street, Eli pulled up in front of the hospital and climbed out.

As he took Lizzie's arm to help her down, he looked

rather stoic. "I'll let you go inside to visit your *vadder* while I tie the horse."

Hmm. Obviously he wasn't eager to see Jeremiah. That suited Lizzie just fine.

"Danke." She beckoned to her sisters.

As they hurried up the steps, the automatic double doors whooshed open. Lizzie glanced over her shoulder and saw Eli back inside the buggy and pulling away.

Inside the small hospital, the air smelled of overdone meatloaf and antiseptic. Several people sat in the reception area, gawking at Lizzie and the girls. No doubt they found their Amish clothing a bit strange. Lizzie was used to such stares and ignored them as she approached the front reception desk.

"We're here to visit our father," she spoke in perfect English.

A nurse wearing a blue smock and pants smiled pleasantly. "Oh, I'll guess you're Jeremiah Beiler's daughters."

"Yes, that's right," Lizzie said.

"The doctor is with him right now. Room eighteen just down the hallway." The nurse pointed the way.

Taking Annie's and Marty's hands, Lizzie led them down the hall, the click of her shoes echoing behind. A man wearing a white smock stood just inside the room, a stethoscope hanging from his neck.

"Ach, here are my girls now."

Jeremiah lay in a hospital bed covered with a white sheet. His broken leg lay flat on the mattress, but cradled by pillows and a blanket.

"Daedi!" Both Annie and Marty ran to their father, hugging his neck tight.

He chuckled and kissed them each on the forehead. "I'm so glad to see you *maed*. Have you missed me?"

"*Ja*, something fierce, *Daed*," Marty said.

"And have you been *gut* for Lizzie?"

"*Ja, Daed*. We're helping her all we can," Annie said.

He laughed again and glanced at the doctor, who grinned at the two little imps. Lizzie smiled and nodded respectfully as her father introduced her to Dr. McGann. She'd heard good things about the man from other members of the Amish community. He wasn't pushy and seemed genuinely concerned for their welfare. Just the kind of man she wanted to care for her father.

"When can you come home?" Marty asked, her voice anxious.

Jeremiah looked at the doctor and lifted one hand. "You see? I told you I have a lot of support at home. Can't I go there to recuperate?"

Dr. McGann shook his head. "I'm afraid not yet. The swelling needs to go down before we can cast your leg. The orthopedic surgeon did a fine job in aligning the broken bones, but it was a serious break and you mustn't put any weight on the leg yet."

"How long will he need to stay here, Doctor?" Lizzie asked, wanting to do what was best for her father, but anxious for him to be where she could care for him.

"We'll have to see. Let's give it a few more days and go from there. Otherwise, your father is doing well and I see no reason why we shouldn't be able to rehabilitate his leg. But he won't be able to put any weight on the broken bones for at least six more weeks."

"Six weeks! So long?" she asked with amazement, thinking of all the chores awaiting them at home and how difficult it would be to keep her father down. Perhaps it was best for him to remain here at the hospital awhile longer.

Dr. McGann nodded. "I'm afraid so."

"Danke." Lizzie reminded herself that the results of the accident could have been much more serious.

Dr. McGann smiled at Marty and Annie. "Now, if it's all right with your sister, how would you two like a nice lollipop? I happen to know that Nurse Carter keeps a jar of them by her desk just for pretty girls like you."

The children looked at their elder sister, their eyes round and hopeful. "Can we have one, Lizzie? Please?" Annie said.

"Ja, I think that would be all right. But be sure to say thank you," Lizzie said.

The girls hurried toward the door and Dr. McGann accompanied them out of the room. "I'll bring them right back," he called over his shoulder.

"Thank you." Lizzie smiled her gratitude, then faced her father, grateful to have a few moments alone with him.

She moved in close to his bed and took his hand. He squeezed her fingers affectionately.

"How are you doing, really?" he asked.

She released a pensive sigh. *"Gut.* All is well, *vadder.* You needn't worry."

She quickly told him that the bishop had asked Eli to work their farm and all that the Stoltzfus *familye* had done for them.

"Ja, Bishop Yoder came to see me. He thinks having Eli work at the farm is the best thing for us right now."

"Eli and his *familye* have all been very kind."

Jeremiah listened quietly, his brows furrowed in a subtle frown. "I'm grateful to them, but I'm worried too."

"About what?"

He met her gaze, his expression austere. "You. Eli was always much too ambitious and prideful. He wants too much of the world. Don't forget that he left us once. He could do so again. Be wary of him."

Hearing these words, a dark foreboding settled over Lizzie.

"But he's returned now. He says he wants to stay this time. He's even taking the baptism lessons." She didn't know why she defended Eli, but it seemed an automatic response.

"I hope he does stay. But I've seen this happen before. Once members of our faith leave the first time, it's easier to leave a second and third time. Just be careful. I don't want to lose you or see you get hurt again, Elizabeth."

Elizabeth. That alone told her that her father was quite serious. With good reason. Lizzie agreed that her father's concerns were legitimate, but his words sounded too much like Marva Geingerich's. Lizzie couldn't help thinking that everyone deserved a fair, ungrudging second chance. Even Eli. Of course, that didn't mean she loved him and wanted to marry him now. Both of them had grown far apart over the past four years. But she did hope that he found happiness and peace in service to the Lord.

"Has Eli raked the hay yet?" Jeremiah asked.

Lizzie nodded, relieved to change the topic. "He raked it just this morning, before we came into town. Even Deacon Albrecht complimented his work."

Jeremiah nodded. "*Gut.* I'm glad Eli hasn't forgotten how to farm."

They talked for several minutes more, then the girls

returned with red-and-green lollipops. They stuck out their tongues, to show how they'd changed colors and they all laughed.

Remembering that Eli had to meet the bishop, Lizzie kept their visit short. They kissed their father goodbye, then walked out into the hall. Eli stood leaning against the wall, holding his black felt hat, his ankles crossed as he stared at the floor. When Lizzie and the girls appeared, he stood up fast, his brows drawn together in a thoughtful frown. Lizzie couldn't help wondering how long he'd been standing there and if he'd overheard her conversation with her father.

"Are you ready to go?" he asked, his voice subdued as he put his hat on his head.

"Ja, danke." She headed toward the outer door.

The two girls skipped along happily beside her as they licked their lollipops.

As always, Eli helped them into the buggy before walking around to the other side. Once they were all settled, he released the brake and called to the horse. As they lurched forward, they each seemed lost in their own thoughts. For the first time since the accident, the girls seemed comfortable riding in a buggy. They finally dozed off, a compliment to Eli and his safe driving. Lizzie felt drowsy too, but couldn't let down her guard enough to sleep. She wasn't really worried they might get hit by another car, but rather she couldn't stop thinking about what her father had said.

Be wary of Eli. It's easier to leave a second and third time.

Would Eli stay or go? Lizzie would never know for certain. Which was exactly why she intended to keep her distance from him.

Chapter Five

As planned, Lizzie and Eli baled hay the following morning, just as soon as the sun had evaporated the glistening dew from the earth. Standing on the baler, she tugged hard on the leather leads to turn the six-hitch team to the right.

"Gee!" she called.

The wagon lurched as the horses stepped forward. The baler trembled. Lizzie widened her stance on the platform to keep from tumbling over the thin railing onto the hard-packed earth.

She was thankful for Tubs and Chubs. As the two strongest horses, Lizzie had hitched them in the middle, providing an anchor and stability to the other four Percherons. The powerful animals leaned into their collars and plodded along without complaint. The soft jingle of their harness mingled with the dull thuds of their heavy hooves as they pulled the baler and hay wagon behind them.

The rattling hum of the gas-powered engine filled Lizzie's ears. The smell of freshly mowed hay was mingled with dust and chaff. She inhaled a slow breath and promptly sneezed. As she reached with one hand for the tissue she kept tucked inside the waist of her black apron, her hip bumped against the guardrail. Not a lot of protection, but it helped steady her on the baler.

She looked over her shoulder. With his legs planted firmly beneath him, Eli swayed easily on the flatbed hay wagon. Taking advantage of the brief lull while they turned the corner, he'd popped up the spout of a blue jug and drank deeply. Water droplets ran down his chin and corded throat before he wiped them away with the back of his hand. As he closed the spout, he looked up and met her gaze. She spun around, embarrassed to be caught staring. But honestly, she just couldn't help herself.

Straightening the horses out to pick up the cut alfalfa, she looked back at the baler. It started up again, churning and spitting out tidy square bales tied together with two strands of heavy twine. She stole a quick glance at Eli again, noticing how he pulled each bundle with ease, the muscles in his shoulders and arms flexing as he tossed the hefty bales onto the quickly expanding stack behind him.

Down one row and up the next, the hay bales piled up and soon filled the wagon. Only a few more rows to go and the hay would be in. No more worries about storm clouds. No more fears of not having the necessary feed for their livestock when the winter snows came deep and cold. No more fretting over...

"Ready to halt!" Eli called above the rumbling of the engine.

"Whoa!" Caught off guard, Lizzie tugged on the leads and the solid horses came to a smooth stop.

They seemed unconcerned by this brief interlude, their docked tails swishing back and forth.

The baler and wagon jerked slightly and she looked back to make sure Eli was all right. He had no railing to keep him from falling off the wagon. If he couldn't keep up with the baler, it was her job to slow the horses. But Eli never seemed to have any problems and she couldn't believe how easily he had stepped back into the role of a farmer. If not for the constant ache in her heart, she could almost pretend that he'd never left at all.

He jumped down from the wagon and sauntered over to turn off the baler. "*Ach*, we've done fine work today. Another couple of hours and we'll be finished with the baling."

He flashed a dazzling smile that made his dark eyes sparkle and showed a dimple in his left cheek. Lizzie blinked and turned away, ignoring the swirl of butterflies in her stomach. She was not going to renew her feelings for this man. No, she was not.

She breathed steadily, trying to settle her nerves and enjoying the quiet break for a few moments. By nightfall, they'd be finished with the baling and she could relax. Almost. She wished she had a quiet heart, but worries about her father and all the work still needing to be done weighed heavily on her mind…not to mention her riotous feelings about Eli. In spite of her upbringing and learning to maintain a constant trust in the Lord, her mind felt burdened by doubts. Of course, she would never confess any of that out loud. She didn't want to worry her father or the bishop…or anyone else in the *Gmay*. She must have faith. All would be well. The Lord would care for them. Wouldn't He?

Eli hopped up onto the platform, standing shoulder-to-shoulder with her. She tried not to notice the warmth of his tall frame against her side, but found herself scrunching her arms so she didn't have to feel his sleeve brushing against her.

"May I?" he asked, reaching in front of her to take the lead lines.

She didn't argue as she handed them over. He flashed another smile and her heart gave an odd little thump.

"Schritt!" he called, slapping the leathers lightly against the horses' rumps.

The Percherons stepped forward and the baler gave a sudden wobble. Gripping the guardrail, Lizzie held on with whitened knuckles until they were moving at an even pace. For several moments, she stared at Eli's hands. His fingers were long, graceful and steady, the kind a surgeon would have in a medical office.

Mentally shaking herself, she adjusted the kerchief tied around her head. Because of their grimy work, she'd left her delicate prayer *kapp* in her room earlier that morning.

Within minutes, Eli pulled the horses up in front of the barn. He'd already opened the double doors in the top of the loft and the gas-powered hay elevator sat waiting for them. Marty and Annie came running from the house, but knew to stay out of the way. They watched from a safe distance, sitting on the rail fence in the shade by one of the corrals.

Looping the lead lines over the guardrail, Eli hopped off the baler platform. Lizzie went to join him, but was returning Annie's wave and not paying attention. She lost her balance and felt herself fall. Reaching out, her hands clasped at something, anything to break her fall.

"Oof!" She gasped as she dropped right into Eli's outstretched arms.

She felt the solid wall of his chest against her cheek and heard his steady heartbeat in her ear. Her legs were twisted and she struggled for a moment to regain her footing.

"Are you all right?" he asked, the sound of his deep voice echoing through her entire body.

"I...*ja*, I'm fine."

She looked up and found his face no more than a breath away. Her gaze locked with his and she felt held there by a force she didn't understand. Nothing else existed but them.

Gradually, the farm sounds invaded her dazed brain. The mooing of a cow, the cluck of chickens scratching in the yard. She became aware of the horses and her sisters watching with avid interest. She was also highly conscious of Eli's solid arms clasped around her in a most improper display.

"Are you okay?" Marty called.

"*Ja*, I just lost my balance, that's all."

Lizzie pulled away from Eli and readjusted her apron and kerchief, trying to gather her composure. Trying to pretend she wasn't shocked to discover that she was still highly attracted to this man she could neither forgive nor forget.

Eli stepped back, but she caught the glint of hesitation in his eyes. His startled expression told her that he'd felt the physical attraction between them too. So. He wasn't as unaffected as he portrayed. Which gave her even more reason to keep her distance from him.

Turning aside, he tightened his leather gloves on his finger, then moved over to the hay elevator and started it up. The rattling sound jangled Lizzie's nerves even more. She longed to run to the house and seek sanctuary in her room until her body stopped quaking. But she couldn't leave. There was still work to be done.

That's when she realized why she was in such a foul mood. For some reason, she couldn't bring herself to remain detached from Eli. She told herself it was simply because of what they'd once meant to each other, but somehow she knew it was something more. Something she was having difficulty fighting. And she couldn't help thinking it would be a very long autumn working beside Eli until her father recuperated.

The following morning, Eli scooted the three-legged stool closer to the black-and-white Holstein and sat down. Hunching forward, he applied disinfectant, then set a sterilized silver bucket beneath the cow. With firm squeezes of his fingers, he shot darts of smooth white milk into the bucket. He soon set up an easy rhythm, the metallic whooshing sounds of milk hitting the pail easing the tension in his mind.

Lizzie sat adjacent to him, milking another cow. Marty and Annie were nearby, waiting to assist with pouring the full buckets into the tall canisters. Eli kind of enjoyed the little girls' incessant chatter and spurts of giggles. In the coziness of the barn, it was almost a tranquil moment, except that Lizzie had barely said two words to him.

"Meowww."

The lazy call of a gray barn cat drew his attention. Without changing his pace, Eli glanced over as the feline slinked its way into the barn. It moved languidly before sidling up against Eli's legs and rubbing its furry head against him in a cajoling manner. When Eli didn't acknowledge the cat, the feline lifted a paw and clawed several times at the hem of his broadfall pants.

Eli chuckled. "Look here, *maed*. Milo is trying to sweet-talk me into giving him some milk."

"Shoo, Milo! This milk isn't for you." Marty rushed at the cat, clapping her hands loudly.

Milo darted over to Lizzie, who had paused long enough to look up. She spared the cat barely a glance before returning to her milking. Milo stayed close by, watching them intently with green eyes.

Luna, a yellow tabby cat, came quickly into the barn with her tail high in the air. She nudged Milo, who greeted her by swatting at her face. Obviously, he didn't want competition in his quest for milk.

Undeterred, Luna sat close by, licking her chops and giving a disgruntled *yowl*. Both cats eyed the milk greedily. Eli smiled, but continued with his work. It soon became difficult to ignore the impatient squalls and growling coming from deep in the back of Milo's throat.

"Meow!"

"What a mournful cry. So pathetic. You'd think they were starving." Lizzie spoke without looking up.

"*Ach*, go away, Luna. You too, Milo. Scat, both of you!" Little Annie copied her sister by clapping her hands, but the felines barely spared the child a glance.

Neither cat was prepared to budge. When both animals started crying repeatedly, Eli finally took pity on them. With perfect aim, he shot a stream of milk, striking Milo directly in the face. The cat sat up on his hind legs and lapped milk off his whiskers. Eli was soon shooting jets of milk into both cats' mouths, one after the other.

Annie squealed with glee. "Look what Eli's doing."

Marty laughed openly at the sight. "How do you do that?"

Eli paused in feeding the two cats and noticed that Lizzie had stopped her milking and was watching him quietly.

"I've had a lot of practice over the years. Doesn't your *vadder* spray milk at the cats?" Eli asked.

"*Ne*, he doesn't," Annie said.

"He'd probably say it was a waste of good milk," Marty said.

Eli shrugged as he shot another gush at the felines, catching them perfectly in the mouth. "The cats have to eat too."

"But they eat mice. That's their job and why they live out here in the barn," Marty said, placing one hand on her hip in a perfect mimic of Lizzie.

Eli laughed out loud. Both children glanced at Lizzie, as if seeking her opinion on the subject.

Lizzie blinked for a couple of moments, then showed a half smile. "It won't do any harm. Milo and Luna won't take enough milk to keep us from making our cheese and cream. And Eli is right. They have to eat too."

Eli was relieved. Though he knew she didn't approve of him, he didn't want to antagonize Lizzie.

He offered a bit more milk. The cats held their front paws aloft and greedily lapped up the treasure. The liquid dripped down the fronts of both animals and dampened their fur, but they didn't seem to mind. One shot caught Milo on the side of his face. He shook his head and made a funny expression before using his paws to wipe and lick off the milk.

Lizzie chuckled out loud. "I think Milo may have had too much already."

Her bright laughter caught Eli off guard. It did something to him inside…a reminder of what they'd once meant to each other and how much he'd loved her. But that was when they were little more than children. He hesitated, feeling mesmerized by her quiet beauty. Loose wisps of hair had come undone from beneath her prayer *kapp* and framed her delicate face. Her blue eyes danced with amusement, her soft lips curved in a smile.

This was the Lizzie he remembered from his childhood. This was the Lizzie he'd fallen in love with all those years earlier. And for just a moment, it was as if he'd never left. She was his Lizzie-bee, who laughed easily and had a warm sense of humor that exposed her intelligence and kindness. He couldn't help thinking of Shannon, who rarely laughed, but had a dry wit that could leave him in stitches. With her short chestnut curls and heavy features, she was so different from Lizzie. And yet, he'd loved them both at separate times in his life. But his feelings for Shannon had been more mature. More lasting. His love for Lizzie had been only a childish infatuation. Hadn't it?

"Do it again, Eli. Do it again," Annie encouraged.

Awakened from his mindless wandering, Eli took careful aim and shot more milk at the cats. When Luna started licking Milo's furry coat, they all laughed. Eli's attention was drawn to Lizzie's beaming face again. Her eyes were bright, her expression vibrant as she watched the barn cats' funny antics. She glanced up and her gaze locked with his. Then, she frowned, as if she'd remembered all the sadness that still lay between them.

"*Ach*, I think that's enough. We need to get back to work." Lizzie turned on her stool and returned to her milking.

Eli did likewise, noticing that the two cats had started licking themselves to clean every drop of milk off their fur.

Marty and Annie didn't complain as he handed off his filled milk pail to them. He waited patiently as the girls carried it over to the tall container, lifted it and poured the contents in. While they were occupied with that chore, he glanced over at Lizzie and found her watching him. She jerked, looking embarrassed. Her bucket was also full and she hesitated, not seeming to know what to do with herself until the girls returned for her milk.

"It's good to hear you laugh again," Eli spoke low.

She swallowed and looked down at her shoes. "I laugh all the time."

No, she didn't. Not anymore. Not the deep, hearty laughter that exposed the joy she felt inside. In fact, the absence of her laughter was very telling. Very rarely did her eyes sparkle, or her lips curve up with amusement. Eli knew she wasn't happy. Not anymore. And he wasn't certain if it was because of him or because of the added responsibilities resting on her slender shoulders.

Maybe both.

"You used to laugh all the time," he said. "Remember when we went fishing together? We had a lot of fun then."

Her frown deepened. "That was a long time ago."

"It's just been four short years."

"It's been four long years," she said.

She looked away, her expression wistful and sad. He didn't need to ask why. It had been only four years, and yet it had been a lifetime. But more than that, his reminder had crushed the tenuous humor between them. Even the two cats frolicking in the hay couldn't get a smile out of Lizzie now.

Marty returned with his empty bucket and he ducked his head, resuming his milking. Out of his peripheral vision, he watched as the little girls emptied Lizzie's bucket and she moved on to the next cow. He longed to chat about inconsequential things as he worked, but didn't know what to say anymore. Lizzie seemed to feel the same way. She was overly quiet, as if she wished she were with anyone but him. They used to be so comfortable with each other. So natural and relaxed. Their discussions and laughter were spontaneous. And he felt suddenly very sorry that he and Lizzie had lost the camaraderie between them.

While the girls remained behind to feed the pigs and collect eggs, Lizzie finished her chores, then hurried to the house. Watching her go, Eli felt an emptiness inside his chest. It reminded him of how alone he really was and he missed Shannon more than ever before. His ruined relationship with Lizzie seemed to make his solitude even worse.

Chapter Six

A number of days later, Lizzie shook out a damp sheet and hung it over the clothesline. She quickly attached it at each end and put a couple of pins in the middle, to keep it from sagging to the ground. In spite of the chill in the air, morning sunlight gleamed across the yard, a mild breeze coming from the east. Red, gold and brown leaves fluttered to the ground. Maybe later that afternoon, she could get the girls to rake the front yard.

By noon, the laundry should be dry and ready to be ironed and put away. She took a deep inhale, enjoying the momentarily peaceful interlude and the beauty of the autumn leaves. Once the weather turned, she'd have to hang their clothes on racks inside the house to dry.

The rattle of a buggy caught her attention and she lifted her head toward the dirt road. Mervin Schwartz pulled into the front yard. Wiping her hands on her apron, Lizzie went to greet him. She held the horse steady while Mervin heaved himself off the buggy seat. A portly man of perhaps forty-five years, he winced as he tried to step down.

"Let me help you." Lizzie took his arm, noticing he

wore a work boot on his right foot and only a heavy wool sock on his left.

"Danke," he spoke in a breathless wheeze once he stood on the ground. He favored the shoeless foot as he hobbled toward the front porch.

"Do you have an injury?" she asked, helping him climb the steps to the front door. Instead of going inside, he dropped down into one of the low Adirondack chairs *Daed* had made with his own hands.

"Ne, but I've got the gout something terrible." He groaned, easing himself back as he gripped the armrests of the chair.

"I'm so sorry. What can I do? Can I get you something?" she asked, feeling a bit helpless and wondering why he'd come all the way out here to their farm when he should be home, resting.

Mervin shook his head, his face flushed with sweat in spite of the cool day. "I came to see Eli Stoltzfus. He helped Deacon Albrecht with his leg wound and I'm hoping he'll know what I can do to ease the pain in my foot."

Lizzie blinked, thinking Mervin had lost his mind. "But Eli isn't a doctor."

"I don't want a doctor. Eli is one of us and yet he's had schooling and will know what to do for me."

His obvious faith in Eli astonished Lizzie. A number of her people served one another according to their specialties. Amos Yoder was the best blacksmith in their community. Linda Hostetler dried plants to make special teas, ointments, tonics, salves and liniments. Everyone valued their contributions. But their skills had been learned at home, as part of the community. Not through a fancy education in the *Englisch* world.

To have a member of their congregation ask for Eli's help specifically because he'd received a college education seemed odd to Lizzie, especially since her people shunned higher learning.

"I… I'll see if I can find Eli," she said.

Stepping down from the porch, she rounded the house and hurried toward the barn. Inside, the musty scent of clean straw filled her nose as she blinked to let her eyes become accustomed to the dim interior. Eli sat on the top of an old barrel, a harness spread across his lap as he mended the leather straps. Lizzie wasn't surprised to find Marty and Annie helping him. The girls both liked Eli and he was kind to them. Wherever he was, they were usually there too. Just now, her sisters were pulling the lead lines out of the way, holding them straight so he could make sense of the melee of straps, hooks and buckles.

"*Ach*, that's good. Hold it steady now."

Eli bent his dark head over the mess, his long, graceful fingers pulling apart a particularly stubborn knot. His black felt hat hung from a hook on the wall, his short hair curling against the nape of his neck.

In the quiet of the barn, no one seemed to notice Lizzie. For a few moments, she stood watching from the shadows, enjoying the serenity of the scene. Then, she cleared her throat.

"Eli?"

He looked up, his handsome mouth curved in a ready smile, his sharp gaze seeming to nail her to the wall.

"Lizzie-bee." He said her name softly, like a caress, and she couldn't help shivering.

She folded her arms. "Um, Mervin Schwartz is up at the house. He's hoping you can help him with his gout."

Eli's forehead crinkled as he stood and laid the harness on the ground before looking at the little girls. "Well then, my two good assistants, it seems we will have to mend the harness later on. Right now, someone needs our help."

He smiled and tugged playfully on the ribbons of their prayer *kapps* before whisking his hat off the hook and heading toward Lizzie. He paused at the door, pushing it wide while he waited for her to precede him outside. She did so, feeling suddenly flustered by his good manners. The little girls exited as well, and then raced ahead of them. As Lizzie walked toward the house, she was more than conscious of Eli following behind. She could almost feel his steely eyes boring a hole in her back.

The girls greeted Mervin and initially watched with curiosity as the two men discussed the problem, but the girls soon disappeared when Mervin removed his sock and revealed a rather hairy foot with a large, red bump on the side of his big toe. Even Lizzie could tell it was inflamed. The skin looked red and dry, with an odor like Limburger cheese emanating from his toes. Trying to hide her grimace, Lizzie stood back, feeling a bit repulsed. But not Eli.

With infinite gentleness, he knelt before Mervin and cupped the front of the man's foot in both hands. When Eli lightly touched the bump with his fingertips, Mervin inhaled a sharp breath through his teeth.

"It hurts, huh?" Eli asked without looking up.

"*Ja*, a lot. I can hardly stand to walk on it and I've

got chores needing to be done. Can you do something to help me?" Mervin asked.

Lizzie could hardly believe Eli didn't draw back in disgust. A vision of the Savior washing the feet of His disciples suddenly flashed inside her mind and she couldn't help respecting Eli for not shying away.

Looking up, Eli met Lizzie's gaze. "Do you have a bag of frozen peas and a clean dish towel I can use?"

She nodded, thinking of all the foods they had stuffed inside their propane-powered refrigerator. She wasn't naive enough to ask why he needed the peas.

Whirling around, she hurried inside and opened the small freezer box. She rummaged around until she found what she was after, snapped up a dish towel, then raced back outside.

The screen door clapped closed behind her as she handed the items to Eli. After scooting another chair close in front of Mervin, Eli wrapped the cloth around the bag of frozen peas. With gentle precision, he lifted Mervin's foot to the chair and laid the cold compress across his big toe.

Mervin laid his head back and groaned, closing his eyes for several moments.

Sitting next to Mervin, Eli met his gaze. "You know I'm not a doctor, right?"

"*Ja*, but you know what I need, don't you?" Mervin responded in a half-desperate voice.

"*Ja*, you need a qualified doctor," Eli said. "Someone like Dr. McGann can prescribe some medicine to help reduce the uric acid in your joints. All I can suggest is that you take an anti-inflammatory medication, drink lots of water and eat a handful of cherries every day."

Mervin blinked, taking in every word. "Cherries?"

"*Ja*, they're a natural way to reduce the uric acid. But a doctor can give you a complete list of other foods to eat or avoid eating."

Tilting his head to one side, Mervin's jowls bobbed. "Like what kinds of foods to avoid?"

Eli shrugged. "Things like bacon, fish, liver, beef, corn syrup…"

Mervin's eyes widened. "Liver? Bacon?"

"*Ja*, they're high in purine, which contributes to the uric acid in your blood. They'll make the gout worse."

"*Ach!*" Mervin lifted a hand to his face as he shook his head. "I eat liver almost every morning. I love it covered with fried onions."

"I'd recommend you no longer eat it. I'd also recommend you lose twenty pounds."

Mervin frowned.

Eli rested a consoling hand on the man's arm. "You may need to give up a few foods and watch your portion sizes, but I guarantee it'll help you feel better. But more than anything, it's important for you to go see Dr. McGann as soon as possible."

Mervin pursed his lips, his face slightly flushed with repugnance. "But he's an *Englischer*."

He said it as if it were a dirty word. Although they all lived among the *Englisch* and did business with them, some of their people didn't like to mingle with them any more than absolutely necessary.

"*Ja*, Dr. McGann is *Englisch*. But he's also experienced, capable and kind. He won't force you to do what you don't want to do, but he can ease a lot of your pain. Go see him. I wouldn't send you to him if I didn't believe he could help."

A deep frown settled across Mervin's forehead. "All right. I'll go. But only because you trust him."

"I do. Explicitly," Eli said.

His concession seemed to ease the tension in Mervin's shoulders. Lizzie quickly made a pitcher of lemonade for them to enjoy and they talked about inconsequential things for a short time. When Eli removed the bag of peas, Mervin announced that his big toe felt a bit better.

"It's just a dull throb. I believe I can even stand the drive home now," Mervin said with delight.

"Good. But I fear it won't last long. The pain will return," Eli said.

"That's all right. I'll go see Doc McGann tomorrow and buy some cherries at the grocery store on my way home. And I'll ask Hannah to fix something else for breakfast besides fried liver."

Eli chuckled and Lizzie couldn't help smiling too. They assisted the man to his buggy and she couldn't help noticing Eli's caring compassion. He ensured the man was seated comfortably before handing him the lead lines.

"You drive safely. And I'll check back with you at church on Sunday," Eli said.

"*Danke.* You've been a lot of help, my friend. It's *gut* to have you back home where you belong." Mervin tipped his hat, then clicked to the horse.

As the buggy pulled away, Lizzie couldn't help shooting a sideways glance at Eli. She studied him for just a moment, then flinched when he turned abruptly and caught her watching him.

"*Ach*, look how the time has flown," she said. "I've

still got so much work to do. I shouldn't have visited so long."

Turning, she hurried toward the house, trying to ignore the weight of his gaze following her. Her brain churned with confusion. Though she disapproved of Eli's worldly knowledge, she could see how it could benefit their people. That was good, wasn't it? But such knowledge often led to *Hochmut*. And pride was never a good thing. It kept a person from being humble and receptive to *Gott*'s will. And the fact that Eli had gotten his education prior to committing to their faith seemed a bit like cheating to Lizzie. He'd known all along that he could make peace with his people as long as he got his education before being baptized. It seemed he'd gotten what he wanted from the *Englisch* world, which meant it likely cost him little to return. So, how could she accept Eli and his higher learning now? She couldn't. It was that simple.

An hour after Mervin left, Eli had finished repairing the harness and taken Billie out for a drive with the buggy. He wanted to see if the horse was skittish around passing cars and trucks. He was delighted when the animal didn't even flinch.

Now, Eli stood at the side of the barn chopping wood. Wielding an ax, he split the last piece of kindling, then sank the blade of the tool into the top of the chopping block. Arching his back, Eli wiped his forehead with his shirtsleeve, thinking he'd have this cord of wood split by the middle of next week. As he eyed the neatly stacked pile of kindling, he felt satisfied that the Beilers wouldn't run out of fuel for their cookstove this winter.

"Oh, no you don't. Get out of here. Shoo!"

Eli jerked around, wondering what had caused such a frenzy of shouts. Wielding a broom, Lizzie chased two fat pigs across the backyard. Her laundry basket sat on its side beneath the clothesline. Obviously, she had dropped it there when she came out to collect the laundry…and found pigs in the yard. One of the swine raced toward the garden just beyond the clothesline.

"Ne!" Lizzie tore after the animal, swatting its hindquarters with the broom.

The pig squealed and veered right, barely missing the clean sheet. Understanding how the animals could ruin Lizzie's hard work if they tangled with the laundry, Eli raced forward to help her.

"Haw! Haw!" he yelled, waving his arms to direct the swine back toward their pen.

The pigs snorted and oinked as they pattered in the right direction, their short legs moving fast.

Flanking them on the right, Lizzie helped Eli herd them into the pen.

Victory!

Before the animals could escape again, Eli shut the gate. In the process, his boots slipped in the mud and down he went, landing on his backside.

Lizzie gasped. "Eli! Are you hurt?"

Standing just inside the gate, she gripped her broom like a savage warrior. She looked so fierce and endearing that he couldn't contain a chuckle.

Sitting in the mud, he bit his tongue. The cold muck seeped through his pants, soaking him to the skin. Lifting his hands, he flung great dollops of black sludge off his fingers. Now what would he do? He had an afternoon of chores left to complete with no clean change of clothes.

A chortling sound caused him to look up. Lizzie stood in front of him, trying—and failing—to hide her laughter behind her hand.

Eli tilted his head. "May I ask what is so funny?"

She hunched her shoulders, no longer laughing, but her smile stayed firmly in place. "You are. I think you are a bit too old to play in the *dreck*."

He looked down at himself, noting how long it would take to get the mud off, then looked back at her. "*Ja*, I agree. When you can quit laughing, would you mind helping me up?"

He held out his arm and waited. Leaning her broom against the pen, she took firm hold of his hand, braced her feet and pulled hard.

A heavy sucking sound heralded his freedom from the mud. As he stood before her, he felt absolutely dismayed by his predicament…until he heard her laughter again. When he glanced up, her laughter cut off, but her eyes twinkled with mirth. Being near her made his heart rate trip into double time. In spite of her frequent looks of disapproval, he felt happy being around her and figured it must be because they'd been so close once.

"You have *dreck* on your face." He reached his free hand up to wipe a streak of mud off the tip of her nose.

She gave an embarrassed giggle. "At least I'm not wearing it all over my clothes."

He chuckled helplessly and indicated her nose. "I'm sorry, but I just made it worse."

She wiped at her face, removing most of the muck. Looking into her sparkling blue eyes, he felt thoroughly enchanted. She stared back at him, her lips slightly parted. Then he remembered that Shannon's eyes were a dark amber color and his heart gave a painful squeeze.

He stepped back, feeling flushed with shame. It was disloyal for him to flirt with another woman, wasn't it? Shannon was gone, but his heart was still tied to her. He couldn't seem to let go of the pain or the guilt. It was on the tip of his tongue to tell Lizzie about his fiancée. To confide his heartache over Shannon's death. But Lizzie's expression changed to a doubtful scowl.

She turned toward the house. "I'd better get the laundry gathered in and finish making sandwiches. I'll lay out some of *Daed*'s clothing on the back porch if you'd like to get cleaned up. Then you can join us for lunch."

Without waiting for his reply, she walked fast toward the clothesline. He watched as she rinsed her hands with the garden hose, then jerked the pins from the clean sheets and haphazardly folded them and the other clothing before dropping each piece into the laundry basket. Without a backward glance, she went inside. Only when the door closed behind her did he realize he was still staring.

Swallowing heavily, he shivered as a cool breeze swept over him. He headed toward the house, eager to get out of his damp clothes. When he'd stared into Lizzie's eyes, he'd felt the attraction between them. But it wasn't right. Shannon should be here with him, not Lizzie. He'd been Shannon's fiancé and would have soon been her husband. It had been his job to look after her, to protect her, but he'd failed miserably. And it occurred to him that he'd failed Lizzie too. Twice, he'd lost the opportunity to marry the woman he loved.

And both times, it had been his own fault. Though he longed to have a *familye* of his own, maybe he'd let the chance for happiness pass him by.

Pushing his morose thoughts aside, he went to the outside faucet and rinsed himself off. He gasped and trembled in the frigid water. After he'd rinsed the muck off his work boots, he stepped up onto the back porch in his bare feet and found a pile of clean clothing waiting for him along with a fluffy towel. He quickly retired to the barn where he got cleaned up. When he returned to the kitchen, Marty and Annie were already seated at the table. The spicy aroma of allspice and cloves filled his senses.

"We waited for you, Eli. Lizzie made pumpkin bread," little Annie chirped in a happy tone.

"First, you must eat a sandwich." Lizzie stood in front of the counter, slicing homemade bread. She didn't spare him a glance as she set a plate of bologna and cheese on the table beside a bowl of sliced melon.

"We're real hungry and you took a long time," Marty added, her forehead creased with impatience.

He smiled, noticing that Annie's *kapp* was crooked. As he took his seat, he straightened it, then brushed his finger against the tip of her nose. "*Ach*, I'm famished too. Let's eat."

Once Lizzie sat down, they each bowed their head for a silent prayer. After a few moments, Eli breathed a quiet sigh and they all dug in.

"Lizzie says she's gonna cook a turkey for Thanksgiving," Marty said.

"But I want ham," Annie said. She swiveled around to look at Eli. "What's your favorite? Ham or turkey?"

He hesitated before answering truthfully. "I think

I prefer stuffed turkey for Thanksgiving and ham for Christmas dinner. Now, what's your favorite pie?"

Annie tilted her head and looked up at the ceiling, as if contemplating this deep subject. "Hmm, I think I like pumpkin the best. But Lizzie always makes pecan and apple too."

"Yum! I'd like a giant slice of each kind," Annie said.

Eli chuckled, enjoying this light conversation. If not for Lizzie being overly quiet, he would have felt completely relaxed. He had to remind himself that this wasn't his *familye* and his visit here was temporary. "That's a lot of pie for such a little *maedel*. Are you sure you can eat all of that?"

"Sure I can. I could eat it all day long." Annie nodded as she took a big bite of her sandwich to make her point.

"How come you left and didn't marry Lizzie?" Marty asked the question so abruptly that Eli choked on a bite of buttered bread. He coughed to clear his throat and took several deep swallows from his glass of chilled milk.

"Didn't you love her no more?" Annie asked before he could reply.

"Anymore," Lizzie corrected in a stern voice. "And it's none of your business."

"Well," Eli began, speaking slowly so he could gather his scattered thoughts. "We were both very young at the time and I wanted to know more about the world before I committed to our faith and settled down to raise a *familye*."

There, that was good. He'd rehearsed the explanation more than once, not wanting to admit that he'd been too frightened to marry so young. He'd wanted to go to school instead. To see and learn more about this world he lived in before he settled down for the rest of his life.

He was about to enlarge on his explanation when Lizzie set her fork down and rose slowly to her feet. Her eyes were narrowed and flashed with an emotion he couldn't name…a mixture of despair and anger.

When she spoke, her voice sounded hoarse with suppressed emotion. "It would have been nice if you had explained all of that to me instead of disappearing without a single word."

Eli stared at her, his mind a riot of thoughts he didn't know how to express. How could she say he hadn't explained? He'd told her everything in his letters. Why hadn't she replied? Why had she ignored his efforts to reach out to her? She could have written back to him.

Before he could think of a satisfactory response, Lizzie walked out to the backyard, pulling the door closed quietly behind her.

The little girls stared after their sister, their gazes round with uncertainty.

"Is Lizzie mad at us?" Annie's lip quivered, her eyes welling up with tears.

"*Ne*, she's not angry at you. Please don't cry." Eli set his sandwich on his plate.

Lizzie wasn't mad at her sisters. She was mad at him.

"I'll go check on her and see if I can get her to come back inside." He stood and smiled, speaking in a light tone he hoped would soothe them. "You two finish your lunch and I'll smooth everything over. Okay?"

They both nodded. He went outside, wondering if

he should simply take his muddy clothes and go home. It had been a difficult day and he wasn't sure what to expect when he found Lizzie.

She stood leaning against the tool shed, staring out at the stubbled fields. Tomorrow, he planned to harrow and smooth out the small ruts in preparation for spring planting. When he approached, she quickly wiped her eyes. *Ach*, did she have to cry?

"Lizzie?" He spoke gently, not sure what to say. He didn't want to create more friction between them.

She faced him, her eyes damp and filled with such misery that it nearly broke his heart.

"Why did you have to go away to school? And why are so many people asking for your help?" she asked.

Taken off guard by her questions, he shrugged. "You know why I went to school. And I suppose people come to me because they think I can make their ailments better."

"Can't you stop it?"

"Would you rather I sent them away?"

She looked down at her feet. "*Ne*, that wouldn't be right. You have to help them if you can."

"I don't *have* to help them, but I *want* to, Lizzie. I believe it's what the Savior would have me to do."

"*Ja*, you're right. It's just that…just that…"

She didn't finish her statement, but she didn't have to. Finally they were getting at the crux of the problem.

"It's the fact that I went to college that bothers you, isn't it? That I lived among the *Englisch* and became a paramedic. Right?"

She nodded. "On the one hand, your skills are so beneficial. But on the other hand, it was wrong for you to leave. Higher learning can cause too much *Ho-chmut*."

"Is that what you think? That I'm filled with pride?"

"*Ja, ne… Ach*, I don't know anymore. When you left so suddenly, I didn't know what to think. I can't even tell you how badly you hurt me. I thought we were going to marry."

He sighed and looked away. "We were too young, Lizzie. At the time, I truly loved you. But we both needed time to become adults. You know that."

Her mouth dropped open. "So you just forgot about your promises to me? You didn't even have the common courtesy to say goodbye."

Confusion fogged his brain. "I… I left you a long letter explaining everything. And I wrote to you many times afterward. Not once did you respond to me."

Her forehead furrowed in bewilderment. "You wrote your *eldre*, Eli. Your *mudder* shared some of your letters with me, but you never wrote directly to me. Not once."

Taking a step closer, he lifted a hand, forcing himself to be slow to anger. His faith had taught him to be a better man than to yell and say things he'd regret later on. His father had also taught him that a soft answer turned away wrath. So, he spoke in a gentle voice, hoping it worked.

"I wrote to you dozens of times, Lizzie. I… I didn't dare say goodbye to anyone in person because I feared you and my *eldre* would stop me from going. It's hard to explain, but I wanted to know more about the world. I couldn't stay. But I am wondering why you never responded to my letters. Why would you pretend they never existed?"

She shook her head, looking miserable. "I never received any letters from you. Not ever."

Doubt clogged his brain. He'd never known her to lie, so why would she do so now? There had to be another explanation.

"I don't know what to say," he said. "I wrote you many times, but every letter was returned unopened. I told you that I loved you and asked you to join me in Denver, but I never heard back from you."

She snorted. "Even if I had received these letters from you, it would have made no difference in my decisions. I would never have abandoned my faith to become an *Englisch* woman."

Though she spoke softly, he caught the contempt in her voice. The disdain. To her, the *Englisch* were worldly and ungodly…everything she didn't want to be.

"I know that now," he said. "But it took a long time for me to realize you would not agree to come to me. After a year, when I didn't hear from you, I finally accepted that I had lost you for good and moved on with my life."

But he didn't tell her about Shannon. If Lizzie knew he'd fallen in love with an *Englisch* girl, it might deepen her disgust for him.

"You moved on without me the moment you left," she said. "You loved worldly pursuits more than you loved me. More than you loved *Gott*. And that is because you had too much *Hochmut*. I don't know what has brought you back home, but it doesn't change anything between us. And now, I have work to do."

Lifting her chin, she brushed past him and headed toward the house, her spine stiff and unapproachable. Watching her go, he couldn't help wondering what had happened to all of his letters. They'd been returned, they were now in his possession, but who had sent them back to him? Perhaps Jeremiah? He didn't know for sure.

It didn't matter. He and Lizzie no longer loved one another. Time had drawn them apart and they'd found other lives and other loves. There could be nothing else between them. Not now, not ever.

Chapter Seven

Lizzie slid a canister of freshly made cheese curd into the chilled water of the well house. Vague sunlight gleamed through the open doorway, the air filled with the pungent scent of rain. Higher up in the mountains, it had snowed last night. Just a light dusting, but enough to lower the temperature substantially.

Brr! Lizzie snuggled deeper into her heavy black coat and tightened the blue hand knitted scarf around her neck. The chores were finished and it was time to go inside for the evening. Eli should be leaving to go home soon. For two days, she'd purposefully avoided him after their last discussion. Tomorrow, they'd pay another visit to *Daed* in town. Maybe the doctor would even let him come home. While they would still need Eli to continue on the farm during *Daed*'s recovery, she'd feel more secure with her father's presence.

Stepping outside, she secured the door, then crossed the yard. She glanced toward the barn, noticing a light gleaming beneath the double doors. Eli was still working. She thought about going to see what was keeping him so late, but decided against it. After all that had happened between them, she needed to keep her distance.

A few days earlier, during Church Sunday, he'd been surrounded by several members of their congregation. They each sought guidance on how to cure their various ailments...everything from a persistent cough to shingles. Eli had insisted he wasn't a doctor, but offered his best advice. He then encouraged each person to go into town and visit Dr. McGann as soon as possible.

"Eli! Eli Stoltzfus!"

Lizzie whirled around and saw David Hostetler driving his horse and buggy at a breakneck speed along the dirt road. Gravel flew into the air as the horse pulled into the main yard. The animal was breathing hard and Lizzie ran to see what was the matter.

In a rush, David jumped out of the buggy, then reached back to lift out his seven-year-old son, Timothy. The boy was wrapped tightly in a quilt with only his face visible. He groaned and Lizzie instantly noticed the child's rasping breath, his eyes fluttering open and closed, and his lips a bluish color.

"What is wrong?" she asked.

"Can I help?" Eli startled her when he reached to press a hand to his forehead. Dressed in his warm winter coat and black felt hat, Eli must have just been preparing to go home when he heard David's cries and came running from the barn.

Standing back, Lizzie gave Eli room as David headed toward the front porch.

"He...he breathed in pesticide. He spilled it down his front," David said, his voice sharp and slightly breathless from his exertions.

"Bring him inside," Eli said, his voice and manner urgent.

Without a backward glance, he opened the door and they hurried into the front room. Lizzie followed, anticipating they might need her help. Eli led David straight through to the kitchen.

Startled by the commotion, Annie and Marty hopped up from the couch where they had been reading by lamplight. Standing barefoot in their warm flannel nightgowns, they gazed at the group with a mixture of alarm and shock.

"Lizzie?" Always sensitive to other people's troubles, Annie took her hand.

Lizzie wrapped one arm around the girl's shoulders and pulled her close. "It's all right, *boppli*. Timmy is sick, but we're going to help him get better."

They followed the men into the kitchen.

"Lay him on the table," Eli ordered.

David did so. The boy moaned, his voice a scratchy gurgle.

Eli glanced her way. "Do you have some rubber gloves I can use?"

She nodded, opened the cupboard door beneath the sink and handed him the items. Eli quickly tugged them on, then pulled the quilt aside. Timmy was still dressed in his work clothes. Lizzie's nose twitched as the heavy odor of pesticide struck her. She crinkled her forehead, understanding why her father rarely used such volatile chemicals on his farm. If they were dangerous to bugs, they were dangerous to humans.

Eli looked up at her. "Lizzie, please have the *maed* leave the room immediately. I don't want anyone to touch Timmy or his clothes except me. Not until we can get the poison off him. The quilt and Timmy's clothes should be burned. I doubt anyone can get them clean enough to use again. Don't handle them except with rubber gloves. I don't want you to get hurt. Do you understand?"

She nodded, realizing the gravity of the situation. But for him to say he didn't want her to get hurt made her heart thud. She told herself it meant nothing. That he was only looking out for her the same as he would do for anyone. But for just a moment, she secretly wished it meant a bit more. Then, she reminded herself that they were barely even friends.

"David needs to wash his hands and arms with soap and hot water. He's been holding Timmy and probably has poison on his skin. Lizzie, you'll need to clean the sink afterward with cleanser. Be sure to wear rubber gloves."

She nodded stoically. Without a word, she ushered her sisters out of the room. David followed, leaving his son in Eli's care.

"But I wanna stay," Marty complained.

Understanding the problem very well, Lizzie didn't back down. Just breathing in pesticides or getting them on the skin could do grave damage. Besides, the girls would only be in the way if they stayed.

"*Ne*, my *liebchen*. The poison could hurt you too. In fact, it's time for you and Annie to go to bed." Taking each girl's hand, Lizzie pulled them along.

"*Ach!* I don't wanna go to bed," Annie whined.

Without a word, Lizzie pointed toward the bathroom and spoke to David. "There are clean towels in the cupboard and plenty of soap by the sink. You can borrow one of *Daed*'s clean shirts too. Remember not to touch anything you don't need to as it will spread the poison."

He nodded and headed that way.

Lizzie walked up the stairs with her sisters. "I'm sorry, but it's time to sleep and I need to help the men with Timmy."

"But what if Timmy di-dies?" Annie's voice trembled.

"No one is going to die. We must trust in *Gott* and Eli is going to do everything he can to help." Lizzie tried to make her voice sound calm and soothing, but her pulse pounded with trepidation. Even she could see that Timmy was having difficulty breathing. He obviously needed serious medical care and she wondered what Eli could do with their limited resources.

"Don't worry," Marty said. "Eli will make Timmy better. He knows what to do."

Her sister's confidence in Eli surprised Lizzie. And in her heart of hearts, she said a silent prayer, hoping her sister was right.

When Lizzie returned to the kitchen a few minutes later, David was just coming out of the bathroom. He rolled the sleeves of one of *Daed*'s shirts down his damp arms as he walked swiftly with her to the kitchen.

"I cleaned everything I touched, so we wouldn't have poison spread around your bathroom," he said.

Eli looked up as they entered the room. He held Timmy's wrist, taking his pulse with his bare hand. As soon as he finished, he pulled the rubber glove back on. "Lizzie, would you fill the bathtub with warm water? Timmy still has poison on him and we've got to wash it all off. He'll need some warm, clean clothes to wear too."

"Of course," she said, racing into the bathroom.

Over the next twenty minutes, they did what they could for Timmy. Lizzie found some fresh though rather large clothes for him to wear. By the time he was cleaned up, his breathing came a little easier, but he still had a dry, hacking cough. Eli doffed the rubber gloves, which he'd washed off. When he handed them to Lizzie, his warm fingers touched hers. She looked up and their eyes met for a few brief moments.

"It'll be all right," he whispered for her ears alone, then turned back to the boy.

Lizzie shivered, trying to ignore how Eli's kind words impacted her. He was worried about Timmy, that was all.

She put on the rubber gloves, then carefully folded Timmy's contaminated clothes inside the quilt. As she carried them outside to burn later on, she turned her face away from the heavy stench of poison.

Back inside, she provided a clean quilt and helped Eli wrap it around the boy to alleviate his trembling.

"Daedi," Timmy called in a weak voice, his eyes closed. In spite of the chill air, he was sweating profusely.

"I'm here, *sohn*." David smoothed his fingers through the boy's slightly damp hair, his big hands trembling.

"I'm sorry. I didn't mean to spill the poison. Are you *bees* at me?"

David gave a laughing scoff, which sounded more like a low sob. *"Ne,* I'm not angry with you. Don't worry, *sohn*. I just want you to get better."

Eli checked the boy's eyes again, then checked his

pulse. With pursed lips, he looked at David. "He's breathing better, but not good enough. This *kind* needs a hospital right now. His heart rate is too slow and his pupils are still contracted."

David lifted his hands. "But can't you make him better? I don't want to take him to the hospital if we can avoid it. They're all *Englisch* there and don't understand our ways."

Eli shook his head emphatically. "I've done all I can for him. The hospital has antidotes and respirators to help Timmy. If you want him to live, we need to take him there immediately."

Lizzie hated to admit it, but she thought Eli was right. If they didn't take Timmy to the hospital, he would die. But were it not for Eli, he would be dead already. The quick, capable care Eli provided had eased the symptoms. Hopefully that would be enough to give them time to get Timothy to the hospital. In all these years, she'd condemned Eli for leaving her to seek higher learning. But now, watching him trying to save Timmy's life, she realized his profession was a great benefit.

"What pesticide were you using?" Eli asked.

"Malathion. I sprayed my cornfield, hoping to kill the earworms so I'll have a bigger crop next year. When my back was turned, Timmy tried to mix some of the concentrated poison himself. He was only trying to help, but he spilled it down his shirtfront and breathed in a lot of fumes. I've got the container outside in my buggy."

"*Gut*. That was smart to bring it with you. The hospital will need to know exactly what chemicals we're dealing with. *Komm*, let's go." Taking for granted that

David would follow, Eli picked up Timmy and carried him through to the living room.

Lizzie followed, grasping the handle of a gas lamp and holding it high as David opened the front door and they all stepped out onto the porch. A brisk wind made Lizzie gasp. Night had fallen, the frosty air thick with the promise of snow. At some point during the melee, she'd doffed her warm coat and now wrapped an arm around herself. Darkness shrouded the farm in shadows and she hated to let the men leave without her. Hated not knowing the outcome of this frenzied night. But she would have to remain behind with her sisters.

She held the lamp high as the men climbed into the buggy and settled Timmy comfortably. With a frantic yell, David slapped the lead lines against the horse's back and they took off at a swift trot. Before the buggy turned onto the main road, Eli threw a quick look back at Lizzie. In the vague moonlight, she saw him lift one hand in farewell and mouth the word *danke*. Or at least, she thought that's what he said. She wasn't certain.

She waved, but felt haunted by Eli's gaze. In his eyes, she saw something that she'd never seen there before. Complete and utter fear. But what did it mean? Was he afraid Timmy might die? Or was his fear connected to something else? She had no idea, but sensed it had a deeper meaning than just the possibility of losing Timmy.

Lizzie hurried into the waiting warmth of the house. Thankfully, it wasn't snowing yet. It would normally take thirty precious minutes for the men to make it to the hospital in town…twenty minutes at the swift speed they were traveling. She only hoped and prayed the horse could stand the rapid pace.

* * *

Timmy trembled and Eli tucked the quilt tighter around him. Gazing at the boy's ashen cheeks, Eli feared the worst. A vision of Shannon's pale face filled his mind. Her weak voice as she begged him to save her life chimed in his ears. Her cries of fear as he tried to stop the bleeding seemed to haunt him. Her brown eyes as they closed for the last time never left his mind for long. He'd failed her. He couldn't save her life. And what if he lost Timmy too? He loved being a paramedic. Loved helping others. But he couldn't lose another patient. He just couldn't!

"Can't we go any faster?" he asked.

David slapped the leads hard against the horse's back. The animal plunged onward at a breakneck speed. "I don't dare push Ben any harder for fear he'll collapse and leave us afoot. I'm also worried a car might come up from behind and crash into the back of us."

Of course. What was Eli thinking? This was a horse and buggy, not an automobile. He'd grown too used to the *Englisch* world where he'd ridden everywhere in cars, trucks and buses. The rapid speed had spoiled him for this slower pace. He had to remember that he was in the Amish world now, where he should rely on faith and *Gott*'s will to get them through. Above all else, they needed to arrive safely. It'd do Timmy no good if the horse dropped dead of exhaustion, or if they collided with a car. Then they'd have to carry the boy into town on foot and they might arrive too late.

Minutes passed slowly until they finally crested a hill and the lights of Riverton came into view. A fresh pulse of anxiousness swept over Eli. Just a few more minutes now.

"Timmy, *vie gehts*?" he asked the boy, trying to keep him awake...to ensure he was still alive.

"Uh-huh." The child's voice sounded vague and his eyes barely fluttered.

"We're almost there now. You're doing fine. Soon, you'll be up and running around your farm with your *brieder* and *schweschder*."

Eli spoke to Timmy over and over again, trying to encourage the boy. Trying to encourage himself. He mustn't give up hope. He must exercise faith. And for the first time since Shannon's death, he offered a silent prayer for help.

When David pulled the buggy in front of the small emergency room, no orderly came out to greet them like they did at the large hospital where Eli had worked in Denver. Overhead lights gleamed brightly in the covered driveway with very few cars in the dark parking lot...not surprising in this small community. As he climbed out of the buggy, Eli figured they'd have one doctor on duty tonight. He just hoped he was inside and not at home waiting for a call.

"I've got Timmy. You should see to your horse, then come inside." Eli spoke quickly to David as he held the little boy in his arms.

David looked panicked. Eli knew the man didn't want to leave his son's side for even a moment. But reason won out over instinct. Since Eli was already turning with Timmy toward the doors and the horse's sides were lathered and heaving from exertion, David nodded his assent.

Without a word, David directed the buggy out of the

way of possible traffic. Eli felt the power of David's trust like a heavy mantle resting across his shoulders. A flash of memory swept over him and he remembered the trust in Shannon's eyes too.

He hurried inside, the wide double doors whooshing open then closing behind him.

"I've got a code blue pediatric case here. We need a rapid response team. Now!" Eli called loud and urgently to the receptionist.

A plump, older woman rushed around the reception counter and reached to look at Timmy's face. She didn't seem to notice Eli's Amish clothing, but a few other people sitting in the waiting room stared with open curiosity. Eli ignored them.

"He's a poison victim. Malathion," Eli spoke to the nurse.

Seeing the urgency of Timmy's condition, the woman waved a hand. "This way."

As Eli followed her, a man wearing a white doctor's coat and a name badge that read *Dr. Graham* ran toward them.

"He's got a shallow pulse, contracted pupils and is breathing with difficulty." Without being asked, Eli rattled off the information, just as he would have done as a paramedic in Denver.

They entered a treatment room and a nurse reached for an oxygen mask. Eli laid Timmy on the bed and opened the quilt so the doctor could get a better look at him.

"What poison are we dealing with here?" Dr. Graham asked in a serious tone, flashing a small handheld light into Timmy's eyes to see how his pupils reacted.

"Malathion," Eli said. "We changed his clothing

since it was spattered with pesticide and bathed him to get the poison off. After that, he started breathing a bit easier."

With a nod, the doctor ordered an antidote while the nurse hooked up an IV. Even being poked by a needle, Timmy didn't move, remaining as still as death. The slow rise and fall of his chest was the only indication that he was still alive.

Eli stepped back, letting the hospital staff take over. Though he was certified, they didn't know him and now wasn't the time to explain. Bracing his back against the wall, he prayed he wasn't too late. As he listened to the doctor giving instructions for the boy's care, Eli had mixed feelings. A part of him missed this action. The thrill of being able to use his expertise to help others. The joy of saving a life. But another part of him was terrified. He might have done something wrong. It had taken so long to get Timmy here.

"Has your son had any convulsions?" Dr. Graham asked, glancing at Eli from over his shoulder.

"He's not my son, but I'm not aware of any convulsions."

The nurse touched Eli's shoulder. "Why don't you wait outside? I'll bring word to you as soon as I can."

He got the message loud and clear. He was in the way.

Stepping out into the reception room, he saw David standing in front of the desk holding his black felt hat in his hands. He looked helpless and confused, glancing around for some sign of his son. When he saw Eli, he showed a relieved expression and hurried over to him. Eli quickly told him what he knew, which wasn't much.

They sat down to wait. Time passed slowly and Eli had too much time to think about his regrets. Leaving Lizzie four years ago was at the top of the list, followed by losing Shannon. But if he hadn't left Lizzie, he never would have met and fallen in love with Shannon. He wouldn't have had his paramedic training or be sitting in this emergency room now.

He wouldn't have known what to do to save Timmy's life.

"I don't know what I'll do if I lose my *sohn*." David leaned forward and covered his face with his hands.

Eli laid a comforting hand on the man's shoulder. He considered the unconditional love of a father and wondered if he would ever have a child of his own. First, he would have to find a wife—and he'd already ruined both of his chances at that. Even though he'd lost both of the women he'd wanted to marry, he could never regret loving them. And that realization surprised him. Loving someone else was deeply personal. Something to be cherished and protected. It was a conscious decision to hold them in your heart for always. And recognizing this gave Eli hope that he might find love a third time. But when he tried to imagine taking a wife, the only one he could picture by his side in the Amish life he'd chosen was Lizzie—and he held very little hope that Lizzie might love him again.

Chapter Eight

Lizzie pulled Ginger into the parking lot of the town park and headed toward a hitching post where a sign read Buggy Parking Only. With the number of Amish families increasing in the area, the town had accommodated them by providing a safe and convenient place with a carport cover for their horses.

Eli had tested Billie and deemed the animal ready for buggy driving again, but Lizzie still felt unsure of the horse. Ginger was older and calmer, so that's the animal she chose for this journey.

Bundled in her heavy winter coat, she hopped out of the buggy. As she tightened the scarf around her neck, she could see puffs of her breath on the chilly air. A skiff of snow that morning hadn't stopped her from coming into Riverton to visit her father and see how Timmy was doing. She'd also stopped off at Ruth Lapp's house for a short visit, happy to find that the woman was over her bronchitis and feeling much better.

Lizzie tied the horse securely, then stepped over to the sidewalk skirting the street. She had just dropped the girls off at school. It hadn't been easy to coax them out of the buggy. They hadn't heard any word on Timmy's condition and were eager to know if the boy was all right. They also were missing their father and wanted to see him. Lizzie couldn't blame them. She also wanted her dad safely at home.

As she walked up the steps to the front of the white brick building, the double doors swished open and she stepped inside. The doors closed and the welcoming warmth enveloped her. She doffed her coat and wiped her damp feet on the large floor mat and looked up.

"Lizzie!"

Linda Albrecht stood in front of the reception counter with her husband, Darrin. He was deep in conversation with the receptionist.

"Have you heard about little Timmy Hostetler?" Linda rushed over to her.

Lizzie nodded eagerly as she removed her gloves. "*Ja*, David brought him to our house last night for Eli's help before coming to the hospital. Is Timmy all right?"

Linda released a deep breath and placed a hand over her heart. "*Ja*, thank the dear Lord. But Eli told us a moment ago that it was a close call."

Darrin Albrecht joined them, folding some papers before tucking them inside the front of his coat.

"Eli is still here?" Lizzie asked.

"He is." The deacon smiled. "He refused to leave Timmy's side until he was sure the boy was okay."

Lizzie wasn't surprised. Eli would undoubtedly want to stay and offer comfort to David if little Timmy had taken a turn for the worse.

"Were you here to visit Timmy?" Lizzie asked.

"*Ne*, we came for a follow-up visit with Dr. Mc-Gann," Linda said. "It turns out that Eli was right and

Darrin has diabetes. Dr. McGann also prescribed an antibiotic for the wound on Darrin's leg."

Deacon Albrecht nodded. "That's right. Thanks to Eli, the cut is almost completely healed now. Linda has changed our diet, and between that and my diabetes medication, I feel better than I have in months."

Lizzie blinked at this news, remembering that day at church when Eli had advised Deacon Albrecht to go see a doctor soon. Apparently Darrin had accepted Eli's advice and was doing much better because of it.

"I'm so glad the *gut* Lord has blessed you," she said, feeling reluctant to give the credit to Eli. After all, *Gott* provided everything, including Eli's education and knowledge.

"*Ach*, we'd best get moving. We're supposed to have more snow this afternoon and we still have shopping to do. Don't you stay in town too long," Linda admonished.

"*Ne*, I won't," Lizzie promised.

She waved as they hurried outside, both surprised and pleased that Deacon Albrecht was feeling better and Timmy was going to be okay. Thanks to Eli and the schooling *Gott* had provided him with.

She stopped at the reception counter long enough to inquire if Timmy could see visitors, then headed down the hall to his room. She'd stop in briefly before visiting her father.

"It's a good thing you were around or I doubt Timmy would have made it. But I must admit I'm surprised to discover you're a certified paramedic. We don't see many Amish paramedics."

Lizzie turned a corner and came to a dead stop. Standing in the hallway were Eli, David and Dr. Mc-

Gann. The doctor lifted a hand and rested it on Eli's shoulder.

"I heard from Dr. Graham that you saved Timmy's life," Dr. McGann continued.

Eli flushed beet red and cast a sheepish glance at the doctor. "The Lord blessed him. I just did what anyone would have done."

"No," David said, speaking in perfect English. "I didn't know what to do. If you hadn't been there, my son might have…"

David didn't finish the statement. His normally stoic expression showed both gratitude and bewilderment as he considered what might have happened to Timmy.

"Thanks to you, a number of the Amish have been coming in to receive medical help. You're a good paramedic and a credit to your people," Dr. McGann said.

"Yes, the Lord has truly blessed us all." Eli turned aside, looking uncomfortable with the praise. His gaze landed on Lizzie and he showed a big smile.

"Lizzie!" he called, looking relieved by the distraction.

She hurried forward, not knowing what to make of all that she'd overheard. Also, being near Eli caused a buzz of excitement to course through her body.

"I'm sorry I wasn't there to milk the cows this morning, but I didn't have a ride home," Eli said.

She shook her head. "Don't worry about it. You had more important things to do here. I understand that Timmy is going to be all right."

She couldn't prevent a note of cheerfulness from filling her voice. All that mattered right now was that the boy was going to live.

"Ja." David nodded happily. "He'll have to stay here

a couple of more days, just to make sure he's breathing okay on his own, but he reacted well to the antidote."

"Dr. McGann, this is Lizzie Beiler, a member of our congregation." Eli made the introductions.

"Yes, Ms. Beiler and I know each other already. I've been treating her father." The doctor showed a kind smile.

"That's right. How is he doing?" she asked.

"Very good. The swelling has gone down and I think we'll be able to cast his leg tomorrow morning. He can go home the day after that. But he'll need several more weeks of bed rest before resuming his usual activities. If you want to drive in on Thursday morning, he should be ready to go home then."

"Oh, that's *wundervoll*!" Lizzie exclaimed.

Two more days and her father would be home. What a relief!

"And now, I'd better get back to work." With a gesture of farewell, Dr. McGann headed down the hall.

"And I'm going to go back in with Timmy. Thanks again, my dear friend. And thanks to Lizzie as well." David reached out and shook Eli's hand as he winked at Lizzie, then he turned and entered a room.

Lizzie peered inside and saw Timmy lying on the hospital bed, his eyes closed in sleep. Covered by a thin blanket, he wore an oxygen mask, but she could see the easy rising and falling of his tiny chest.

"And I had better go see my *vadder*." Lizzie stepped around Eli, but paused when he briefly touched her arm.

"Would you mind giving me a ride back to your farm when you're finished? I used David's cell phone last night to call my *vadder* and tell him where I am, but I came into town with David and my horse and buggy are still at your place," he said.

"Of course. I won't be long. I heard that a snowstorm is headed our way and I need to pick the girls up from school before we go home."

He nodded and she hurried on her way, still feeling the warmth of his fingers on her arm.

Jeremiah was sitting up eating lunch when she stepped into his room. He set a carton of milk on his tray and reached out a hand to her.

"Lizzie! Did you bring me any homemade bread? I'm half-starved for your cooking," he said.

She laughed. "I'm afraid not, but it looks like you'll be home in a couple of days, so you can eat all the bread you want soon." She leaned over and hugged him tight, his words pleasing her enormously. A quick glance at his filled plate told her why he wasn't happy with the hospital food. She had to admit, she wouldn't be interested, either.

"How are the *maed*?" he asked after her sisters.

"*Gut.* They wanted to come with, to see you and how Timmy is doing, but I insisted they go to school." She quickly told him about the close call last night and all that Dr. McGann had said about Eli saving the child's life.

"*Ja*, Deacon Albrecht visited me earlier and told me Timmy will be all right."

"The doctor credits Eli with helping Deacon Albrecht get on top of his diabetes too," she said.

"Hmm." Jeremiah looked skeptical.

"The Lord moves in mysterious ways. Perhaps He used Eli to do His *gut* work here on earth," she suggested.

And if that was the case, wasn't it also possible that

the Lord had provided the opportunity for Eli to gain higher learning, so that he could serve others in such a manner? Lizzie didn't pose the question to her father. She knew better than to push the issue, even if Eli's education had saved Timmy's life and helped other members of their *Gmay*.

"*Ja*, it is possible." Jeremiah's voice sounded rather gruff and disapproving.

Sitting in a chair next to her father's bed, she chatted with him about the farm. Finally, Lizzie asked a question that had been weighing heavily on her mind of late.

"When he first went to Denver, Eli said he left me a letter of goodbye. He also said he sent many other letters to me, yet I've never received any. Do you know something about this?" she asked.

Jeremiah's eyes widened and he took a deep breath, taking time to choose his words carefully. A sick feeling settled inside Lizzie's stomach and she dreaded his answer.

"*Ja*, I know about the letters." Lifting his head, Jeremiah met her gaze, his forehead set in a stubborn frown. "I feared Eli might entice you to join him in the *Englisch* world, so I sent all the letters back to him unopened."

So. Eli had told her the truth. He'd tried to say goodbye to her after all. A part of her was relieved that he hadn't lied. That he hadn't abandoned her without a single word. And yet, another part of her was angry that she'd been denied the truth for all this time. Eli had his reasons for leaving, but her father's deception hurt her deeply. A feeling of righteous indignation clogged her throat and she gripped her hands together in her lap, trying not to be angry.

"You had no right to hide my letters," she said.

"I know. Please don't think harshly of me, *dochder*. As your *vadder*, I did what I thought was best, because I love you and didn't want to lose you."

Her heart softened. She couldn't really fault her father's actions. By hiding Eli's letters, he'd only been trying to protect her. To keep her in their faith, with their family.

"You should have trusted me more. I'm a grown woman and the choice to stay or go be with Eli was mine alone to make," she said.

He looked away, licking his dried lips. "I couldn't take that chance. Knowing how much you loved Eli, I feared you might go."

She shook her head. "You might have been surprised. I love my *familye* and my faith dearly too."

He looked at her, his gruff face lined with fatigue. "If I had given you Eli's letters, would you have left?"

She shrugged. "It doesn't matter now. It's in the past."

Yet, she didn't really know the answer. Four years was a long time and yet it was no time at all. She had only been seventeen. She had felt so grown up, and yet since that time, she had changed so much. Her heart had been broken, but her faith had grown. Her *familye* had come to mean more than anything to her, and she knew now that their community was where she belonged. Yet, she wasn't sure if she would have stayed back then. And knowing about the letters changed nothing between her and Eli. He had left. They'd grown apart. Now, their priorities were different. But she had to be honest with herself. She might have gone with Eli. Her love for him had been so strong that she might have put aside her faith and become *Englisch* in order to be with him. But it didn't matter now because she would never know.

The buggy bounced through a mud puddle in the rutted road leading to the schoolhouse. Eli gripped the lead lines tighter and breathed a thankful sigh that they were nearly there. With everything that had happened last night, he hadn't slept at all. He'd been too worried about Timmy. Fatigue hadn't set it until this morning, when he was assured the boy would recover. Now, Eli felt a mixture of lethargy and relief. A few more hours and he'd be able to rest. But first, he had to make sure Lizzie and the girls arrived home safe and all was well on their farm.

"There's Marty." Lizzie pointed as they rode into the school yard.

Eli pulled the buggy to a stop in front of the one-room red log building. Constructed by the men of their *Gmay*, the schoolhouse had come from a kit they'd ordered a number of years earlier. Surrounded by a chain-link fence, the property included a small baseball field and sat in the farthest corner of Bishop Yoder's hayfield.

"Lizzie!" The girl waved.

Taking Annie's hand, both children ran toward them. Several other kids followed along with Rebecca Geingerich, their teacher. No doubt they'd all heard from Marty and Annie about Timmy's accident and were eager to know if he was all right.

"Have you just come from town? Any news of Timmy?" Rebecca asked in an anxious tone, holding her shawl tightly around her shoulders.

Eli nodded. "*Ja*, and he is going to be just fine."

The children listened eagerly as Eli and Lizzie related all that had happened. A few parents who were picking up their kids also paused, seeking the news.

"It was *gut* you were there when David needed you," one man exclaimed.

"*Ja*, little Timmy might not have made it without you," Rebecca said.

Eli waved a hand, feeling embarrassed by the praise. "The *gut* Lord saw us through. It was *Gott*'s will that Timmy survive."

"*Ja*, it was *Gott*'s will." They all nodded in agreement.

As Eli helped Marty and Annie into the buggy, he knew word would soon spread across the entire *Gmay* about what had happened. Eli really believed what he said. Truly, the Lord had blessed them. This time.

He could take no credit for the child's recovery. In fact, he'd believed Timmy would die. At the very least, the boy should have suffered permanent damage to his lungs. Yet he was thriving and even breathing on his own. Eli never should have doubted the Lord's power. But why hadn't *Gott* saved Shannon? Why did she have to die?

Pondering the inequality, Eli slapped the leads against Ginger's back. He glanced at the gray sky overhead, which mirrored his doubtful feelings.

Marty smiled brightly. "I'm so happy Timmy is gonna be okay."

"Me too," Annie spoke with a contented sigh.

As the buggy sped along the county road, it started to snow. Big, heavy flakes laden with moisture. Reaching out a hand to wipe off the front storm window so he could see out, Eli was eager to get Lizzie and her sisters home safely. He was grateful the buggy had thin glass to protect them from the elements, but he sure missed the windshield wipers of a car.

In the back seat, the two little girls exclaimed about the snow. Cocooned by the sheltering walls of the buggy, they nestled beneath a warm blanket. Soon, their eyelids drooped and they dozed off.

Casting a quick glance over her shoulder, Lizzie smiled with satisfaction. "They didn't sleep well last night. I'm afraid everyone in the *Gmay* has been worried about Timmy."

"*Ja*, his condition was pretty serious," Eli agreed.

"My *vadder* should be able to come home on Thursday," she said, then related what the doctor had told her.

"*Gut*. The storm will have passed by then, but the roads may still be slick. I'd feel better if you let me drive you into town to pick him up from the hospital."

She nodded. "I would appreciate that. I'm not sure I can lift him in and out of the buggy by myself. He won't be able to walk for several weeks."

"It's no problem. I'll help you."

She nodded and a long, swelling silence followed.

"You seem deep in thought today. Is everything all right at the farm?" he finally asked.

"*Ja*, all is well." Her voice sounded small and she tugged her black traveling bonnet closer around her face.

They rode in quiet for several more minutes before Eli couldn't take it any longer.

"Is something troubling you?" he asked.

Finally, she glanced his way. "I… I spoke to my *vadder* about your letters."

A leaden weight settled in Eli's chest. "And?"

"And he confessed that he sent them all back to you." She hurried on. "I hope you won't think unkindly of him. He's very sorry for not telling me about them, but he feared I might leave and join you in Denver. He only wanted what was best for me."

Hmm. Just as Eli had suspected.

"But what about what you wanted?" he asked with a brief glance in her direction. In this weather, he was unwilling to take his eyes off the road for long.

She took a deep inhale and let it go. "I guess we'll never know now."

True. It was water under the bridge. But Lizzie's voice sounded embarrassed, as if she hated confessing her father's duplicity. Because of the situation, Eli couldn't bring himself to be angry over Jeremiah's misdeed. Not when he had so many faults of his own to repent from.

"It's all right," he said. "I probably would have done the same thing if you had been my *dochder*. I can't blame Jeremiah for wanting what he believes is best for you."

She looked at him. "*Danke*. I appreciate your understanding."

"When I didn't hear from you, I figured you didn't love me anymore," he said. "I felt terrible about that, but then I realized I had to move on with my life. I... I met an *Englisch* girl and...and I asked her to marry me."

The words slipped out before he could stop them. Lizzie jerked around, her eyes round with shock. He wondered if he'd made a huge mistake by telling her, but also felt relieved to finally tell someone about Shannon. Because he feared their censure, he hadn't even told his parents about her.

"You…you were engaged to be married? To an *Englisch* woman?" she asked, her voice sounding small and deflated.

He nodded and suddenly the story poured out of him. He told Lizzie everything. How he'd given up on ever hearing from her again. How he'd met Shannon when she was working at the hospital as a pediatric volunteer. How gentle, kind and reserved she was and how they'd dated some time before becoming engaged. And then about the drunk driving accident after which she'd died in his arms.

He stared straight ahead and gripped the lead lines tighter as he spoke in a low, hoarse voice. "She was driving the car that night when a drunk driver hit us head-on. She survived the initial impact and I thought she'd be all right, but I… I couldn't save her, Lizzie. She was bleeding internally and I couldn't stop it. I prayed so hard, but *Gott* didn't answer me. He let Shannon die."

Lizzie must have heard the anguish in his voice, because she pressed her gloved fingers against her lips. He was surprised to see tears shimmering in her eyes.

"*Ach*, Eli. I'm so sorry for your loss, but I have no doubt the Lord was with you that night. We don't always understand His ways, but He has our best interests in mind. There was nothing else you could have done. It wasn't your fault. You know that, don't you?" Her voice was filled with sincerity, her eyes crinkled with compassion.

No, he didn't know that. He kept replaying everything in his mind, as if in slow motion. Trying to think of what steps he might have taken to help Shannon survive.

They were quiet for several moments, listening to the gusts of wind as white swirled around them. The falling snow was getting worse. Ginger lowered her head and trudged onward, her horseshoes biting into the slick sheet of ice covering the road. Without the protection of doors and windows, they would all be truly miserable right now.

"You must have loved Shannon very much," Lizzie said.

He nodded. "I did, just as I loved you."

She stiffened beside him and he feared she might be angry. But when he glanced over, he saw nothing but sympathy in her eyes.

"It wasn't your fault, Eli. Accidents happen and you can't save everyone. We have to trust in *Gott*. He knows what is best for each of us. You must believe that."

Somehow the conviction in her voice made him feel better. Yet, knowing how he'd broken her heart, he was surprised she was offering him comfort. If anything, he deserved her anger. But that wasn't her way.

"When you left, I was hurt to think that you could forget me so easily," she continued. "But now, I understand what happened. You wanted to know more about the world, to learn and grow. It was your choice to go and I mustn't judge you for that. It wasn't your fault that *Daed* hid your letters from me. And I can't hold a grudge against Shannon and the love you shared with her either."

"I… I tried so hard to save her," he said, trying not to let his emotions show in his wobbly voice. But he couldn't seem to help it. He had to quickly wipe his eyes.

"Of course you did." She rested a gloved hand on his arm, her touch consoling. "I know you did everything you could. But now, you should hand your pain over to the Lord. Give your grief to Him and be at peace."

She withdrew her hand and became very still, her brow furrowed in a troubled frown. She seemed so understanding. So supportive. It reminded him of when they were teenagers and she'd always put everyone else first. Her generous spirit had been one of the things he'd loved the most about her.

A particularly hard gust rocked the buggy and drew his attention back to the road ahead. He had to reach outside and clear the caking snow off the window. The wind buffeted them. For just a moment, he missed the comfort of an automobile's heater and defroster, not to mention the solid security of the larger, heavier vehicles. But a car wouldn't include Lizzie. Dear, faithful Lizzie.

He felt strangely calm sitting next to her. As he drew his arm back inside, he caught her worried look.

"I'll sure be glad when we're home," she said. "I thought we could beat the storm. I have to admit I'm glad you're driving instead of me."

In spite of her smile, her body seemed stiff and her demeanor reserved. Perhaps he was reading something in her manner that wasn't really there. As she shivered and pulled a blanket over her legs, he figured she was just worried about the weather. Yes, that must be it.

"You're *willkomm*," he replied, feeling better, yet feeling worse at the same time. Oh, he was so confused. He didn't know himself anymore. Didn't know where he belonged or what he wanted.

Fearing a truck might come barreling down the road

and not see them in the storm, he pulled the horse as far over onto the shoulder as he dared. Through the white swirling around them, he could just make out the jutting edges of an irrigation ditch running parallel to the road. He eyed the reflective snowplow poles and mileage markers, using them as a guide to stay out of the ditch. As he concentrated on his driving, they didn't speak for several minutes. A comfortable silence settled over them, something he hadn't realized how much he'd missed…until now. But he had little time to consider the reason why as they came upon a car that had slid off the road.

Chapter Nine

Two thin lines on the icy road showed where the tires of the black car had skidded off the road. The vehicle's hazard lights blinked red. Through the flurries of wind gusting against the falling snow, Lizzie could make out the front fender hanging just above the irrigation ditch. Another inch and the vehicle would drop two feet and require a tow truck to drag it out.

Lizzie clutched the side of the buggy, a feeling of trepidation filling her heart. The last time she'd been involved in a car accident had not been pleasant. Even as she wished they didn't have to stop, she knew they must. They couldn't pass by someone in need.

Eli pulled Ginger to a halt just behind the floundered car. "Wait here inside the buggy. I'll see if we can help."

Pulling his black felt hat lower over his forehead, Eli opened the door and stepped out into the lashing wind and snow. Chilling air whooshed inside the buggy. As she looked out at several tall elm trees edging the road, their barren limbs covered in white, she thought the winter scene would be beautiful…if she were watching it from the safety of her kitchen window. But sitting inside a horse-drawn buggy, she couldn't help wishing they were anywhere but here.

Hunching his wide shoulders, Eli hurried toward the car. Lizzie's gaze followed him. For some odd reason, she felt desperate to keep her eyes on him. As if she'd lose him again if she couldn't see him anymore.

At the car, Eli leaned forward and someone inside the vehicle rolled down a window to speak with him. Although Lizzie couldn't hear their conversation, she saw Eli gesture toward the horse and nod several times.

"What's going on?" Awakened by the stop, Annie rubbed her eyes and sat up.

Marty leaned forward, her eyes wide with fear. "We didn't wreck again, did we?"

Lizzie swiveled in her seat and smiled. *"Ne, bensel,"* she reassured them. "There's just a car off the road and Eli is seeing if they need our help."

A strong surge of wind rocked the buggy. Staring out the thin windows, Annie shivered and her eyes welled with tears. "But I wanna go home. I don't wanna be out here anymore."

"Me either. Let's go home now," Marty cried.

Lizzie reached back and consoled both girls, pulling them close for a quick kiss on their cheeks. *"Ne, my liebchen,* we must help these people if we can. But don't worry. *Gott* will take care of us. And Eli won't let any harm befall us."

As she cuddled her sisters, she froze at what she'd said. Did she really trust Eli so much? Since he'd arrived home, he'd shown sound judgment, but she still doubted him. He'd told her about his *Englisch* girlfriend and her heart ached for all that he'd lost. But it hurt Lizzie deeply to know he'd loved someone else so much. That he'd made a life without her. Now he was back. But did she trust him to stay? She wasn't sure.

When he jerked open the door and leaned inside, she whirled around. His hat, shoulders and arms were covered with snow. Icy drops of water covered his face. He wiped them away with a brush of his hand, his breath puffing on the frigid air. Lizzie hated that he had to be out in this rotten weather.

"I'm going to see if Ginger can pull the car back onto the road. I want all of you to stay inside, out of the wet and cold," he said.

Lizzie nodded, grateful for his consideration. But something in her expression must have betrayed her thoughts.

"Don't worry. It's going to be all right. We're just making memories to laugh about later." He flashed her a confident smile, then shut the door.

Annie shivered at the blast of frigid air. "Brr! I'm glad Eli is taking care of this. I'd hate to be outside right now."

"Me too," Marty said.

Me three! Lizzie thought. Her respect for Eli grew when she saw that he didn't complain or shirk his responsibilities. He was a man who didn't flinch at what had to be done.

They watched as he unhitched Ginger from the buggy. An *Englisch* man in a pair of blue jeans and a light jacket got out of the car to help. Without a hat or gloves to protect him from the elements, the *Englischer* hunched his shoulders and mostly just shielded his face from the snow while Eli did the work. Lizzie figured he had no idea how to harness a horse let alone tie the lines to the car. In contrast, Eli moved with speed and confidence. She wondered how he could see what he was doing in the lashing storm. But soon, he had the horse hooked up and she couldn't help thinking that he'd become an amazing man.

He spoke to the *Englischer*, seeming completely comfortable around the stranger. While Lizzie preferred not to mingle with the *Englisch*, she supposed Eli was used to them and their strange ways. A part of her disapproved of his life among them, but right now, she appreciated his goodness and generosity.

Within moments, the *Englischer* climbed back into his vehicle and put it in Reverse. Through the rear window, Lizzie saw two young children peering out, their faces pale, their eyes round. A woman's face was visible, looking back from the front seat, and Lizzie realized an entire *Englisch familye* was inside the car.

With Eli directing the horse, Ginger leaned forward, her hooves digging into the snow as she pulled on the line. The animal's back was blanketed with white, but she seemed not to notice.

The vehicle's tires made a whizzing sound as they spun around. Finally, they caught traction and the car moved back a space. Eli led Ginger out of the way as the car came to a rest on the icy pavement.

"You see?" Marty nudged Annie. "Eli isn't worried one bit, so we shouldn't be either."

Annie nodded, huddling closer to her sister. "*Ja*, the *gut* Lord would want us to stop and help our neighbors, even if they are *Englisch* and we're afraid."

Tears filled Lizzie's eyes and she quickly wiped them away so the girls wouldn't see. Her siblings sounded so confident and grown-up that it touched her heart. She could learn from their generous and trusting example. Their words inspired her to have courage and believe in Eli too. After all, he'd stopped to help in spite of the hardship and discomfort to himself. He'd already done so much for her *familye* and many other people in their *Gmay* too. From all appearances, Eli was a good, devout Amish man. He'd suffered a lot recently. When he'd told her about losing his fiancée, he'd seemed so lost and hurt. Lizzie didn't have the heart to be angry with him anymore. She had to accept that he didn't love her. That he'd moved on and found another life that didn't include her. She should move on too. But would he stay? Or would he recover from his loss and decide the Amish life wasn't for him after all? Already, Lizzie cared too much about him. She told herself it was normal to care for everyone in the *Gmay*. But if Lizzie wasn't careful, she could get her heart broken again.

Eli climbed back into the buggy and breathed a sigh of relief. Conscious of Lizzie watching him, he blew onto his gloved hands, trying to warm them. Without being asked, Lizzie handed him a blanket. He wiped his damp face.

"Wrap it over your body. It'll warm you up quicker," she said.

"Danke," he murmured, startled to hear a croak in his voice. He coughed, hoping he didn't get hypothermia for his good deeds.

When he had the blanket packed tight around his upper torso and thighs, he felt better and shivered less. He cleared his voice and took hold of the lead lines. "Mark Walden and his *familye* are in the car. Mrs.

Walden is five months pregnant and they're very grateful that we stopped."

Lizzie nodded. "*Ja*, it was the right thing to do."

He swallowed, grateful to be out of the wet and cold. "The Waldens are going to accompany us to the farm, just to ensure we arrive safely. Would you rather ride in their warm car while I drive the buggy?"

Lizzie shook her head. "That's very kind of them, but I'd rather stay with you." She glanced back at the girls, still huddled together beneath a heavy quilt. "I believe we are warm enough."

Eli wasn't surprised by her decision. He'd been living among the *Englisch* and was comfortable around them. But Lizzie wasn't.

"All right. They'll drive ahead of us, so that their lights can show the way."

He wasn't sure, but he thought he saw a flicker of relief fill her eyes before she looked away. Releasing the brake, he called loudly to Ginger, fearing the horse couldn't hear him above the storm. Either she caught his command or the animal felt the leads against her back, because she leaned into the harness, dug in her hooves and pulled forward. Eli felt the grating of the buggy wheels, frozen in ice. They gave way and were soon moving at a smooth pace. The black car drove in front of them, going slow. The bright taillights of the vehicle helped Eli see the way in the falling snow.

"I'll be glad when we're home," Marty sniffled.

"Me too. I don't want to do any more good deeds today," Annie said, her voice trembling.

"*Ja*, do you think we'll make it okay?" Lizzie asked.

Focusing on the road, Eli didn't look at any of them, but he felt the girls crouched forward between him and Lizzie. A little hand rested on his shoulder and he thought it must be Annie's. He imagined each child's eyes were wide with fear and a protective feeling filled his chest with warmth and compassion. He'd do almost anything to keep these three girls safe and wanted to reassure them all.

"Of course we'll make it," he said. "We're going very slow. Don't worry. With the Waldens' car to light the way, we'll be there soon enough." But a little doubt nibbled at his mind. Even at this snail's pace, he could see the Waldens' vehicle skidding on the icy road. Now and then, he could feel the buggy doing the same and he didn't want any mishaps to make matters worse. At this pace, the worst that could happen was they'd end up on the side of the road…unless a truck or car came up too fast behind them. That could end in catastrophe and he wondered if he should have insisted the girls ride in the safety of the car.

Everyone in the buggy was incredibly quiet. They each seemed to know that he needed to concentrate on his driving. In his heart, Eli whispered a prayer for their safety.

As they rode in silence, his thoughts began to wander. He wished he had the courage to confide another serious issue to Lizzie.

The day before, he'd received another letter from Tom Caldwell, his former employer in Denver. Tom had sent a new job offer for Eli to become an EMT supervisor. Before he lost Shannon, Eli would have loved to make such a career move. When he'd first read the letter, his heart had leaped at the proposal. It would be a wonderful way to use his skills to serve others. But then, he remembered the commitment he'd made to *Gott* and his *familye*. He planned to be baptized soon. He loved the Lord and wanted to stay in Riverton. Didn't he?

If only there was a way for him to work as a paramedic and remain here among his people. But he didn't see how. To be a paramedic, he'd need to keep his certifications current, which meant taking yearly classes and using modern technology. Surely the elders of his church would never approve of that, especially Jeremiah, who was the minister of their congregation. Eli didn't even dare ask. Not when he'd been home such a short time. They might think he wasn't serious about staying. And he was. Yet, he felt torn.

By the time they pulled into the yard of the Beilers' farm, it was early evening and the snow had stopped. They'd passed two big plows up on the county road and knew the pavement would be cleared by morning.

Eli released a giant whoosh, his breath looking like a puff of smoke on the air. He hadn't realized he'd been holding his breath. They were safe. He'd kept his promise to Lizzie and the girls.

"We're home!" Marty crowed with delight.

"*Ja*, we're safe," Lizzie said, her voice a soft whisper.

Mark Walden waved as he slowly turned his car around and headed back toward the county road so he could take his *familye* home.

"But what if they go off the road again?" Annie asked, watching their red taillights fade into the darkness.

"They won't. *Gott* is with all of us tonight and they're driving nice and slow. They also have a cell phone to call for help. They'll arrive just fine," Eli said, hoping his words were true.

"*Ja*, we must trust in *Gott* to keep us safe, even when we don't have a cell phone," Lizzie said.

Eli wasn't certain, but he thought he saw her lips curve into a little smile. Her sense of humor made him chuckle.

He pulled up in front of the dark house. "You take the *maed* inside and I'll take Ginger to the barn. I want to feed and dry her off *gut*. Then I'll head on home."

Lizzie's mouth dropped open. "But it's not safe for you to travel tonight. You should stay here until morning."

"It wouldn't be appropriate. I'll be fine. The snow has stopped. Once I get up to the county road, the plows will have cleared the asphalt all the way to my *eldres'* farm. And it would be unseemly for me to stay here tonight when you and the *maed* are alone."

She looked away, her gaze suddenly shy. "*Ach*, I hadn't thought about that. But you are right."

Eli nodded, wishing he dared take just a moment to seek her advice. Her compassion over Shannon's death had touched him deeply. Lizzie had always been so empathetic and kind. So obedient and wise. But he had no illusions. Lizzie would never approve of him asking their leaders to sanction his work as a paramedic. Especially if she knew he was considering accepting another job offer in Denver. Leaving Riverton meant abandoning his faith and *familye* again, something he hated to do. Because the next time he left, he knew he would never be coming back.

Chapter Ten

A freezing rain the next day, followed by another day of warm sunshine, cleared the snow and ice off the roads. A blanket of white still covered the valley and mountains surrounding them and another storm was on its way. Since they needed the water so badly for their summer irrigation, Lizzie wouldn't complain. Especially since they had good weather right now, when she needed it most. Standing in her father's hospital room in town, she glanced out the window and noticed the morning sky was still clear. They had just enough time to get him home. The chill air made her pull her heavy cape tighter around her.

"I don't know why you let Eli drive you into town. Couldn't you have come to get me on your own?" Jeremiah grumbled. He sat on the edge of the bed, fully dressed, his casted leg extended in front of him.

"*Ne, Daedi.* The weather has been too bad and I'm not sure I can lift you alone." She'd already told him about getting caught in a blizzard the night they'd helped pull the *familye*'s car back onto the road.

"What about Martin Hostetler? Couldn't he drive you into town instead of Eli?"

Lizzie clenched her eyes shut at the thought. Tall and slender, with bright red hair and a smattering of freckles, Martin was a nice enough man, but a bit too zealous for her. His outgoing nature and forward manner always unnerved Lizzie. He was too overt and outspoken for her likes. After Eli had left, it had taken a year to convince Martin that she wasn't interested in courting with him. The last thing she wanted to do was encourage him by asking if he would drive her into town to pick up her father.

"Bishop Yoder specifically charged Eli with looking after the farm and our *familye*. I'm afraid we have no choice but to accept his help," she said.

There. That was good. Surely her father wouldn't argue with the bishop.

"Has Eli...has he been spending quite a bit of time with you while I've been in the hospital?" Jeremiah asked.

"*Ne*, he mostly works outside or in the barn."

Not to mention her numerous efforts to avoid him.

After the doctor had instructed them on some exercises Jeremiah could do at home to help quicken his rehabilitation, she'd packed her father's few belongings into a bag. Eli had taken it outside as he went to fetch the horse and buggy. Her two sisters had tagged along with Eli, holding his hands and smiling. Now, Lizzie and her father were just waiting for an orderly to bring a wheelchair so they could wheel her father outside.

"So, he hasn't spoken to you about going back to the *Englisch* world with him?" Jeremiah peered at her with a look that said he didn't want to intrude, but he couldn't help asking anyway.

She snorted. "Don't worry, *Vadder*. Eli and I have no interest in each other anymore. He's been a tremendous help and looked after the farm, but he's been nothing but completely appropriate the entire time."

She didn't dare tell him about Shannon, Eli's fiancée—the proof that he'd fully moved past his old feelings for her. Though Eli hadn't asked her to keep the information private, she got the impression he had confided in her and she didn't want to betray that trust.

"*Ach*, what's taking so long?" Jeremiah looked at the door, a surly frown on his face.

Since her father was normally a gentle, patient man, Lizzie surmised that his weariness with the hospital was the reason for his impatience.

"They'll be here soon," she soothed.

Her own composure surprised her. But something had changed inside of her since Eli had told her about Shannon. When she'd reassured him that his fiancée's death wasn't his fault, a startling realization had struck her. She must exercise what she preached and hand her own grief and anger over to the Lord. It was what *Gott* expected from her. Eli had suffered enough without her condemnation too. But her heart still ached with the knowledge that he'd gotten over his love for her, and had been ready to build a life with Shannon. And that hurt most of all.

Thankfully, a young man wearing a blue smock wheeled a chair into the room at that moment.

"All ready to go?" the orderly asked in a pleasant voice. Lizzie could see from his curious gaze that he found their Amish clothing interesting, but he didn't say anything.

"We've been ready for half an hour," Jeremiah grumbled.

The orderly stepped forward, seeming unruffled by Jeremiah's bad humor. "Then let's get you on your way home. Remember not to put any weight on your casted leg."

Jeremiah nodded, reaching out as the orderly wrapped his arms around him to take the brunt of his weight before hefting him into the seat. An extender bar was lifted into place and Jeremiah's casted leg rested outstretched on the support.

"All ready?" The orderly smiled at Lizzie.

She nodded and he pushed the chair out of the room and down the long hall. Tugging her black bonnet lower over her forehead, Lizzie followed behind. As they passed Timmy's room, she glanced inside, finding the bed vacant. Jeremiah had told her the boy had gone home just before she'd arrived. Knowing the child was healthy enough to return to his *familye* brought a buoyant feeling to Lizzie's chest.

Outside, the frigid air caught her breath and she took a quick inhale. The horse and buggy were waiting at the bottom of the steps. The orderly wheeled Jeremiah down a side ramp sprinkled with ice melt. Eli hopped out of the buggy and came to assist.

"This young man can get me in just fine." Jeremiah gave Eli the cold shoulder by turning toward the orderly.

"Of course," Eli said, gracious as always but looking a bit snubbed by the rebuttal.

While Eli stood on the sidewalk, Lizzie stared at her

father in amazement. She knew her father was suspicious of the other man, but what cause did he have to be so rude to Eli? It wasn't like her father. No, not at all. She sensed that something was bothering him and she had no idea what it was.

The orderly lifted Jeremiah into the buggy, then gripped the handles on the wheelchair and nodded farewell.

"Drive safely," he called.

Eli waved before reaching to help Lizzie into the back of the buggy with her two sisters. She looked inside and found that little Annie had twined her hand around her father's arm and beamed with pleasure to know he was finally going home.

As always, Eli took hold of Lizzie's arm so she wouldn't stumble on the wet footrest. Normally, she looked away and tried to ignore how his touch made her stomach quiver. But this time, their gazes met. In his eyes, she saw a flash of uncertainty, then it was gone and she thought she must have imagined it. After all, Eli was the strongest, most confident man she knew. Surely her father's temper hadn't rattled him.

Once Eli was inside, he took up the lead lines and slapped them against Billie's back. The buggy jerked forward as the horse took off at a slow trot out of the parking lot. While the little girls jabbered about their activities to their father, the adults were quiet. From the stiff shoulders of the two men sitting in front, Lizzie could feel the tension in the air like a thick fog. She understood *Daed*'s motives for keeping Eli's letters from her, but she didn't understand why he was offish toward Eli now. Unless *Daed* was like Marva Geingerich and feared Eli might leave again…and try to take Lizzie with him. He'd already asked Lizzie about it, so that must be the problem. But it wasn't becoming of *Daed* to be so judgmental.

The ride home seemed to take much longer than usual. By the time they arrived, all the adults seemed to be in a sour mood. The children, picking up on the tension but not understanding it, seemed anxious and confused, bewildered as to why the happy occasion of their father coming home wasn't being treated with more joy.

Without a word, Lizzie hurried up the front steps to hold the house's door open for Eli. Since she wasn't strong enough, *Daed* had no option but to let the other man help him inside. The night before, Eli had been kind enough to move *Daed*'s bed downstairs to the living room. Lizzie figured her father wouldn't be able to negotiate the stairs. Having him close at hand would make it easier to see to his needs too.

"I can remove your shoe so you can lie down," Annie offered as Eli deposited her father on the narrow bed.

Jeremiah sat straight as a board. "I don't want my shoe removed. I should be outside working."

Showing her sternest frown, Lizzie placed her hands on her hips and shook her head. "There will be no working or putting weight on your injured leg for several more weeks. The doctor said if you don't want to walk with a limp, you'll let the bones heal."

"*Ja*, and I'll take care of the farm work," Eli said.

Jeremiah glanced at the younger man. "What work have you already done?"

Eli stood in front of Jeremiah, holding his hat in his hands. While Lizzie helped her sisters doff their coats and gloves, Eli recounted a few of the things he'd done, including mending the fence, shoeing the horses and a myriad of other chores.

"And don't forget baling and putting away the hay," Lizzie said as she hung their coats in the closet. She headed toward the kitchen, wanting to be alone for some reason. With her sisters here to mind their father, she decided to start lunch.

"Humph," came her father's surly reply. "I'm glad you've been of use then. I guess you didn't forget how to bale a field during all that time you were living among the *Englisch*."

Again, Lizzie was surprised by the extent of her father's poor manners.

"*Ne*, sir. I remember very well how to plow and bale and I'm glad I could help you out," Eli replied.

Lizzie caught the teasing quality in Eli's voice. She'd never seen a man work as hard as he had worked for them. No doubt he was feeling amused by Jeremiah's skepticism. And that made her want to defend him to her father and she didn't understand why. Yes, she was grateful to Eli. His presence on the farm had brought her a lot of comfort. Because of him, her burdens had been eased but… Oh, she didn't know what to think anymore. Eli didn't love her anymore and all her crazy feelings would lead to nothing.

Whew! After getting the third degree from Jeremiah, Eli was glad to escape the house. Lizzie would call him for the noon meal soon, but he thought going hungry might be better than facing her father again. The man obviously didn't like him and Eli understood why. As teenagers, he and Lizzie had been inseparable. Everyone expected them to marry. But then, he'd left and Jeremiah had hidden his letters from Lizzie. No doubt the man feared, then and now, that Eli might contaminate her with his *Englisch* ideas.

Opening the barn door, Eli stepped inside, relieved to be alone. He wanted to feel angry at Jeremiah, but he couldn't. Losing Shannon had taught him a patience he didn't quite understand. He only knew that everyone was a child of *Gott*. Everyone made mistakes. But he deeply believed in the power of the Atonement and forgiveness. Otherwise, he wouldn't have come home. And frankly, he was tired of being angry.

"Eli?"

He whirled around and found Lizzie standing just inside the doorway. Sunlight glimmered behind her, highlighting several strands of golden hair that had escaped her prayer bonnet. Her forehead was furrowed with concern. Wearing her winter cape, her porcelain cheeks had a rosy hue, as if they'd been kissed by the cold air. And for just a moment, he thought about taking her into his arms and kissing her. And that thought confused him. He still loved Shannon, didn't he? How could he be thinking about Lizzie when his fiancée had so recently died?

"I brought you something to eat," she said.

For the first time, he noticed that she held a tray covered by a white dish towel.

She came forward and set the tray on a wooden bench. Stepping back, she smoothed her cape, looking suddenly shy.

"I figured you wouldn't want to eat in the house today. My *vadder* isn't in a very *gut* mood," she said.

How insightful of her, but he didn't say so. *"Danke."*

Now! Now he should tell her about the job offer in Denver. He'd been pondering the letter he'd received from Tom Caldwell for days now, but still had found no answers. He was alone with Lizzie and it was a perfect moment to seek her advice.

"Are you all right?" she asked, her expression earnest.

"Sure. I'm fine." He smiled, hoping to alleviate her fears. It occurred to him that he hadn't seen her smile all day. She must have a lot on her mind too and he wished he could do even more to alleviate her load. He remembered how close they'd been as teenagers and a part of him wished they could share that closeness again.

She poked a clump of hay with the tip of her shoe. "I… I'm sure *Daed* will feel better tomorrow."

He lifted his head. "He's upset because I'm here. I've been living among the *Englisch* and he thinks I might corrupt you."

Her mouth dropped open. "He doesn't think that at all."

"Doesn't he?" he challenged.

She ducked her head, a mingling of acceptance and dismay in her eyes. "*Ach*, maybe a little bit. I'll speak to him."

"*Ne*, let it go. I knew when I returned that I'd have to prove myself again."

She met his eyes. "Can you blame him for not trusting you? You ran away. You've been gone a long time."

"*Ja*, you're right. I can't blame anyone for being upset with me. In fact, you might be even more disappointed when you hear that I've received a job offer in Denver."

There. He'd finally told her. He reached inside his

hat and pulled out Tom Caldwell's letter. Handing it to her, he waited patiently while she read it through. Twice. Then, she folded the pages, put them inside the envelope and handed it back to him. The only betrayal of her apparent calm was that her hand visibly trembled.

"So you're definitely going to leave again," she said. It was a statement, not a question.

"I haven't decided yet."

She folded her arms, as if she were cold. Since she was wearing her cape and the barn was quite warm, he doubted that.

"But you must be seriously considering accepting the offer or you wouldn't have shown me the letter," she said.

She was upset. He knew it instinctively. He could tell by the way her spine stiffened and she lifted her chin slightly higher in the air. Given the circumstances, he couldn't blame her.

"*Ja*, my logic tells me the work in Denver would give me more opportunities than staying here. But I love my life here too. I love the farm work, I love my *familye* and I love…"

He shook his head, wondering what he was about to say. He wasn't sure. A muddle of thoughts filled his mind. He was still missing Shannon more than he could say, but she was gone. Now, he was here with Lizzie.

"What about your faith?" she asked.

He nodded and placed a hand over his chest. "*Ja*, I still have it here in my heart."

She quirked one eyebrow at him. "Do you? When you go back to Denver, how can you live your faith when you are apart from your *familye* and never join us at church? Just like a bright coal that is pulled away from the flames of a fire, you would eventually lose the warmth of your faith."

He caught a tone of reservation in her voice. But deep inside, he believed in *Gott*. His faith was all that had carried him through after Shannon had passed away. Before he could say so, Lizzie quoted an old Amish saying.

"If you must doubt, then doubt your doubts, not your beliefs," she said.

He heard the conviction in her voice, but no judgment. Her face looked passive, her voice so composed... just another one of her good qualities. Except when they had played volleyball or baseball, he couldn't remember hearing her raise her voice. And he wasn't sure why he'd told her about the offer or what else he expected her to say. Of course she wouldn't want him to leave. Her faith was strong and she believed families should stay together.

"You always were so straightforward and sensible," he said.

"Is that wrong? What else do you want me to say?" she asked.

He hung his head. "I don't know. On the one hand, I wish you'd tell me it's okay to live among the *Englisch*. That I'm still a *gut* man and acceptable to the Lord if I return to Denver. But a part of me also wishes you'd yell and scream at me and tell me that you want me to stay here with my *familye* and..."

You.

Now where had that thought come from? He wasn't sure.

"*Ach*, of course I want you to stay here. We are your

people. You belong here. There, I've said it. But it didn't make you feel any better, did it?"

No, it didn't. And he realized the problem wasn't with his faith, his *familye*, or his work as a paramedic. The problem was with him. He loved both worlds, but hadn't accepted himself so that he could decide where he wanted to be. Where he truly felt he belonged and where the Lord wanted him to live.

"You…you won't mention this to my *mudder* or *vadder* or anyone else, will you? It would only upset them," he said.

A deep, wrenching sadness filled her eyes and he thought for a moment that she was going to cry. "*Ne*, I won't tell a soul. But, Eli, keeping it a secret will only delay the inevitable. What do you want? Where do you want to be? Unfortunately, you can't choose both lives."

He couldn't answer. He honestly didn't know.

"I wish you felt a firm conviction of who you are and where you ought to be. Because once you know that deep inside, there will be no turning back and you will feel a deep, abiding joy and confidence in your life. I'll pray that you find that peace very soon."

She turned and left as quietly as she had come. He stared after her for a very long time, pondering her words. Wishing he could know for a certainty where he belonged. But no answers came.

Chapter Eleven

"I don't want to do it. I tell you, I don't need to exercise."

Eli heard the irritable words as he entered the back door to the kitchen and set a pail of milk on the table. Morning sunbeams glinted off the snow-covered fields and sprayed a ray of light through the window over the stainless steel sink. The little girls' happy voices carried from upstairs. Apparently they didn't have school today so the teacher could attend some meetings.

Across the countertops and table, a variety of large and small plastic bowls, brown bottles, powders, spatulas and long wooden molds covered with freezer paper had been set out in an orderly fashion. Eli recognized the molds as the same type his mother used to make soap and he figured that was Lizzie's planned work for the day. But she wasn't in here now.

"Leave me alone, I say." Jeremiah's unmistakable curt voice came from the living area.

"But, *Daed*, the doctor said you must do these exercises twice each day so you can regain your strength." Lizzie's pleading explanation was filled with frustration.

Knowing that Jeremiah didn't want him around, Eli turned toward the door. Like a coward, he planned to flee to the barn.

"And I'm not buying dumbbells either. I've lived my whole life without lifting weights. It's a bunch of foolishness, if you ask me."

"But, *Daed*, you've been in bed for weeks already. You need to move your muscles."

Eli paused at the back door, his hand on the knob. No, he was not going to interfere. This wasn't his business. He should leave them alone and return to his chores.

"*Daed*…please."

That did it. Turning, Eli walked into the living room. He had taken a couple of classes on physical therapy and understood the process. He could help, if Jeremiah and Lizzie would let him. If there was any way he could help ease Lizzie's frustration, he had to try.

Jeremiah was sitting upright on the bed, his legs extended on top of the covers with his casted leg cradled by two pillows. Except for his missing hat and bare feet, the man was fully dressed for the day. A breakfast tray, basin of water, toothbrush and shaving implements rested on the coffee table nearby, along with a towel and comb. Eli couldn't help thinking Lizzie was taking good care of her father.

Clearing his voice, he stepped near. "Can I help?"

Lizzie whirled around and the papers she was holding fluttered to the wood floor. Eli saw that they were covered with pictures, showing how to correctly perform a number of simple exercises.

"Eli! *Guder mariye*," she said as she quickly gathered up the pages.

He nodded respectfully, noticing her ruffled expression. *"Guder mariye."*

"What do you want?" Jeremiah looked away, as if dismissing him.

Since Eli had dealt with obstinate patients before, he didn't feel intimidated one bit. And knowing how hard Lizzie was trying to help her father, Eli decided to be blunt.

"I want to offer my services."

Jeremiah glared. "What are you talking about? You're already running my farm."

Resigning himself to being patient, Eli smiled tolerantly. "That's not what I mean. I'm trained and have worked with physical therapy patients before."

"You…you have?" Lizzie said, her eyes filled with startled wonder.

He nodded. *"Ja,* when I was trying to decide what field I wanted to go into, I took some extra classes. I thought perhaps I could help your *vadder* with his exercises."

"I don't need to exercise, nor do I need your help," Jeremiah replied, his tone a low rumble.

Hmm. Maybe Eli should try a different approach.

"Of course you need to exercise. As Lizzie pointed out, it'll strengthen your body. Without it, your muscles will atrophy from lack of use. Once you're able to get up and walk again, you won't be able to do the work. You'll be weak and winded. And then I'll have to stay here on your farm even longer."

Ah! That did the trick. Jeremiah's eyes widened and he stared at Eli with open shock.

Eli hated to use such tactics, but knew it was the only way to get through to Jeremiah. It couldn't be easy for a hardworking man like Jeremiah to sit around idle all day, dependent on the help of a man he didn't even like to keep the farm running. Up until the accident, he had led a vital, busy, self-sufficient life. No wonder he was so irritable.

Releasing a cantankerous sigh, Jeremiah pursed his lips together. "*Ach*, all right. Let's get on with it then."

Lizzie smiled and threw an expression of gratitude in Eli's direction. In her eyes, he could see that she understood what he'd just done. Reverse psychology, of sorts. But if it got Jeremiah to cooperate, then it was worth the effort.

"Do you have some unopened soup cans that weigh about one pound each?" Eli asked Lizzie.

"*Ja*, in the cupboard." Without asking what they were for, she hurried into the kitchen and soon returned with two cans of soup. She handed them to Eli, then stepped back.

Jeremiah eyed the cans with a belligerent scowl. "What are you gonna do with those?"

"Since you don't have any one-or two-pound dumbbells, you can lift cans of soup to exercise your arms. It's cheaper and just as effective…unless you're already too weak to lift them," Eli added, trying to needle Jeremiah into doing the exercises.

"Humph! Of course I can do it," Jeremiah said.

Eli thought he heard a muffled laugh coming from Lizzie, but didn't look her way. Jeremiah murmured something about looking silly lifting soup cans that Eli chose to ignore.

"Can you do this?" Eli proceeded to clasp a can in each hand and do several biceps curls. Then he handed the cans over to Jeremiah.

Conscious of Lizzie watching with interest, Eli waited as Jeremiah did the curls.

"That is *gut*, but what about doing it this way?" Taking the cans, Eli showed Jeremiah a variation of curls that would exercise different muscles in his neck, shoulders, arms and back.

"*Ja*, I can do all of them." Jeremiah took the cans and mimicked Eli in perfect fashion.

"That is very *gut*. But slow down just a bit and concentrate on working your muscles. Feel your movements and make them worth the effort," Eli encouraged.

Jeremiah did as asked and Eli counted out two sets of eight repetitions before they switched to a different exercise.

"I heard your doctor tell Lizzie that he wants you to aim for full weight bearing on your leg within three weeks. In order to do that, you should exercise your good leg too," Eli said.

He didn't want to confess that, while Lizzie was helping Jeremiah pack for his trip home, Eli had spoken with Dr. McGann out in the reception room at the hospital. Eli hadn't expected to help Jeremiah with his exercises, but he was naturally curious and so he'd educated himself on what the man needed to do.

When he glanced Lizzie's way, Eli discovered that she had vacated the room. The subtle sounds of tap water running in the kitchen and dishes clanking told him she was doing her morning chores. He continued to work with Jeremiah, coaxing the older man to lay flat so he could lift, push and stretch his healthy leg. Soon, they'd completed the variety of tasks the doctor had recommended.

"There, you're all done for the morning. But you

need to do the same exercises this afternoon. It wasn't so hard, was it?" Eli asked.

"*Ne*, it wasn't hard," Jeremiah responded.

But Eli knew the man was covering the exhaustion he felt. Jeremiah's breathing sounded heavy and his arms trembled as he tried to do extra repetitions of the exercises. Even just a few weeks of inactivity had left his body weaker, but Eli doubted the man would ever confess that out loud. At least, not to him.

"Tomorrow, try to do an extra set of each exercise. You'll soon find that the work gets easier and you'll be able to do more each day." Ignoring Jeremiah's cloudy frown, Eli spoke in a cheery, optimistic tone.

"*Ja*, I will do as you say," Jeremiah said.

Pleased by this admission, Eli turned toward the kitchen. "And now, I had better get on with my work. Send one of the *maed* for me if you need anything at all."

"I won't need anything from you," Jeremiah said.

Pretending not to notice the man's deep scowl, Eli hid a smile as he walked out of the room. As he entered the kitchen and saw Lizzie standing in front of the counter, he felt suddenly light of heart. The ties of her *kapp* hung loose against her shoulders and he was tempted to tug playfully on them. No, he better not. She was still on edge around him. But he had to admit it felt great to be needed.

Wearing goggles and a face mask, Lizzie set the heavy plastic bowl on the battery-operated scale and measured out the distilled water. When she finished, she reached for the jar of sodium hydroxide, or lye as it was commonly called.

As he spoke to her father, the sound of Eli's deep voice reached her from the living room. She paused a moment, trying to hear his words.

Glancing at the new recipe Abby had given her, she read through the list of ingredients again. Now where was she?

Eli's laughter caused her to glance toward the door. With a sigh, she picked up the recipe one more time. Glancing at the bowl of water, she shook her head in disgust. She'd barely started and had already made a huge mistake. She wanted to double this batch of soap, which meant she needed more distilled water. Why couldn't she seem to concentrate today?

Setting aside the lye, she picked up the water jug and added the proper amount to the bowl. She was too distracted by her father and Eli. Determined to focus on her work, she again reached for the lye. Removing the lid, she shook the container to get the white chips to fall out into the bowl.

"Lizzie?"

She jerked, splashing lye chips into the water. The caustic liquid spattered her hands and arms and she dropped the container of chips. Of all the foolish things to do…she'd forgotten to put on her rubber gloves.

Thankfully, the lye container thudded onto the counter top rather than spilling across the floor. The last thing she wanted was to clean up a big lye spill. But she flinched in pain as the corrosive alkaline solution burned her bare flesh.

"Ouch!" she cried.

Before she knew what was happening, she found herself leaning over the sink. A gush of fresh water rushed over her hands from the tap.

She stared at the stream for several moments, shocked by what had happened. Then, she looked up at Eli. He stood close, his face only a breath away. He held her hands, his touch gentle but firm.

"Is that better?" he asked.

"Um, *ja*, it is…"

She couldn't finish, barely able to gather her thoughts. Their gazes met and she couldn't have moved away to save her life. She felt locked there, held prisoner by her own suppressed longings. As if time stood still and he had never left Riverton and nothing bad had ever happened between them.

"Does it still hurt?" he asked, his voice slightly husky.

"What…?"

He repeated the question.

She blinked, trying to remember where she was. Trying to think. "*Ne*, I think it's fine now."

"Do you have some vinegar?" he asked.

"*Ja*." But she didn't move.

"Where is it? It'll help neutralize the lye and stop the burning."

"*Ach*, of course."

With water dripping down her arms, she reached into a cupboard and took out a bottle. Before she could act, he removed it from her hand and unscrewed the lid. He reached for a hand towel and tipped the bottle so that it saturated the fabric. Then he pressed it against the myriad of small splotches on her skin where the lye had burned her. Her nose twitched at the pungent scent of vinegar, but she felt instant relief.

Looking up, she found his lips were but a space away from hers. She felt his warm breath tickle her cheek. Felt the warmth of his fingers against her skin. It happened again. That magnetic attraction she'd thought was long dead.

"Lizzie-bee," he whispered, drawing nearer.

He kissed her. A soft, gentle caress that filled her with a yearning she had forgotten years ago. She closed her eyes and let herself go...

"Lizzie, *Daed* needs another pillow."

They jerked apart as Marty bounced into the kitchen.

Lizzie flinched and turned aside, clasping the dish towel with her hands. As Eli turned off the water faucet, she snuck a worried glance over at Marty, relieved to note that the girl didn't seem to notice anything wrong. But Lizzie still felt the strong emotions buzzing between her and Eli. Had the moment affected him as much as it had her?

"Of course. I'll get one right now," she said, swiveling toward the door.

This was a good excuse to get out of here right now. She stole a glance at Eli, trying to see his face and assess his mood. He ducked his head as he dried his own hands on the discarded towel, seeming completely composed. And it was just as well. After all, he was considering another job in Denver. He was planning to leave again. He had loved Shannon and didn't want her. Deep in her heart, Lizzie had always known he wouldn't stay. That the call of the *Englisch* world was too strong for him to resist. But she'd hoped and prayed he might find life in Riverton too compelling to leave.

Her decision not to let herself fall in love with him again had been wise. And yet, moments like this reminded her of how much they'd once cared for one another. It would be so easy to let down her guard and...

No! She mustn't think that way. Eli was leaving and that was that.

As she walked out of the kitchen, she didn't look back to see if Eli was watching her. But she didn't have to. She could feel his eyes on her just as surely as she lived.

Chapter Twelve

Eli lifted the full bucket of milk and moved it carefully out from beneath the Holstein. The cow stamped a foot and gave a low *moo*. A little of the frothy milk sloshed over the brim and Eli steadied his hold on the handle. He shouldn't have filled the bucket so full, but he'd been thinking about what had happened yesterday with Lizzie. He never should have kissed her. Never should have gotten so close to her. Not only was he still heartsick over losing Shannon, but he was seriously considering leaving soon. So, what had he been thinking?

Bending over one of the tall canisters, he poured the milk inside. At a sound in the doorway, he looked up, surprised to see Lizzie standing there. After what had happened between them, he would have thought she would avoid him like the plague. He blinked, thinking she was his imagination playing tricks on his mind. But no. She stood in front of the open doorway, her slender body silhouetted by morning sunlight.

"Lizzie-bee," he whispered her name, or at least he thought he did. He wasn't sure.

She wore a light blue dress, her black apron and white *kapp* both crisp and perfectly starched. He caught a brief whiff of her scent, a subtle mixture of cinnamon and vanilla. He wasn't surprised. She was always baking something delicious to eat.

"Eli," she said.

"Lizzie," he spoke at the same time.

They both laughed with embarrassment.

After setting the bucket on the ground, he stood up straight. "Sorry. You go first."

She waved a hand in the air. "*Ne*, tell me what you wanted to say. My issue will probably take longer to discuss."

Folding her hands together in front of her, she waited with a firm, but serene expression. He never should have kissed her. Now, he felt like a heel. He'd simply forgotten himself in the moment. But he didn't want Lizzie to think he was using her. She already thought he was too worldly, too filled with pride. He'd be mortified if she thought he was taking advantage of her. But how could he explain what he'd done when he didn't understand it himself?

"I… I'm sorry for what happened yesterday. So very sorry. I've regretted it ever since and wanted you to know how bad I feel…"

She stiffened, then shook her head emphatically. "I'm sorry you regret it, but you're right. It was an accident. It never should have happened."

She turned away and he hurried to clasp her arm. He didn't want to drive her away. Trying to be gentle, he pulled her back around.

"*Ne*, Lizzie. I… I didn't mean it like that. I don't really regret our kiss. *Ach*, I do, but I don't. It's just that…"

"There's no need for you to explain. We won't discuss it ever again. Please just let it drop now."

He opened his mouth to say something more. Something that didn't sound so ridiculous. But she didn't give him the chance.

"I have a small request, if you wouldn't mind." She took a step back, her hands fluttering nervously for a moment.

He stared at her in confusion. That was it? They weren't going to discuss the kiss? She'd barely let him apologize. There was more he wanted to say. To clarify and try to help her understand. After all, she deserved an explanation. But since he didn't know what to say, maybe dropping the subject was for the best.

"What is it? Anything you need. Just name it," he said.

Okay, maybe he was overcompensating now. But he realized that he'd do almost anything for this woman. Anything at all. She'd earned his admiration and respect and he considered her to be one of the best people he'd ever been privileged to know.

"I would like to attend the quilting frolic over at Naomi's farm this morning. We will be working on some new baby quilts for Abby. The *maed* would like to go with me, to play with the other *kinder*." Her voice sounded hesitant, as if she feared he might think her desires were foolish or frivolous.

He nodded, delighted that she was telling him about a normal, mundane event. "*Ja*, you absolutely should go. It would be *gut* for you to get out of here for a while. The roads are clear and you should have no problems driving the buggy."

After all, tending to the demanding needs of a grumpy man like Jeremiah couldn't be easy all the time. It might do both Lizzie and the girls good to get out and have a little fun for once.

She frowned. "*Ach*, I have one problem, though."

His hearing perked up at that. Lizzie was actually confiding in him, seeking his advice. It was like they were real friends again. He hoped.

He stood close, looking down at her sweet face. "What is it?"

"While I'm gone, would you mind checking in on *Daed* now and then? I've prepared a lunch for both of you and put it in the cooler. When the time comes, if you wouldn't mind getting it out for him and, you know, seeing to his other needs, I'd greatly appreciate it." She shrugged, her cheeks flushing a pretty shade of pink.

Without asking for more details, he understood her meaning. "Of course. I'd be happy to look in on Jeremiah from time to time. I'm sure I can help him with anything he might need. And it might be fun to eat lunch with him today."

A doubtful frown pulled at her lips and he laughed. "Don't worry. We will both be just fine."

She showed a smile so bright that it made his throat ache.

"*Danke*, that would be great. But I should warn you. He's not happy about being alone for most of the day. He has *The Budget* newspaper and plenty of other reading material close at hand, but he may be a bit grouchy with you. I think he's got cabin fever something fierce. Are you sure you're up to spending time with him throughout the day?"

Her eyes were so wide and hopeful that he wouldn't

have had the heart to deny her, even if he was so in-clined. Which he wasn't.

"*Ja*, we'll be fine. You leave Jeremiah to me." He smiled, trying to convey a self-confidence he wasn't sure he really felt. He knew Jeremiah didn't like him anymore, but was determined to win him over. Maybe this was just what they needed.

"Will you be leaving soon?" he asked.

She nodded. "As soon as the *maed* are ready. They've just finished breakfast and are brushing their teeth now."

"*Gut*. I'll get the horse and buggy hitched up and bring them outside for you," he offered.

"*Danke*."

She turned and walked away, a happy bounce in her stride. She didn't look back at him. He knew because he stared after her to see if she would. And though it made no sense to him, he couldn't help feeling a tad disappointed that she didn't.

An hour later, Eli reached a stopping point in his work and decided to check on Jeremiah. He fidgeted with his hat, feeling suddenly more wary than normal. In spite of speaking with Lizzie's father almost every day, Eli had yet to be alone with him. Since he'd re-turned from the hospital, there'd always been someone else in the room with them. Lizzie or one of her sisters. With someone else always around, there had been no opportunity for them to discuss that Jeremiah was the one who had returned Eli's letters.

Opening the back door to the kitchen, Eli stepped inside. He let the screen door clap closed behind him, purposefully alerting Jeremiah that he was here. Then he thought better of it. What if the man was napping?

"Hallo," Eli called to the house.

He stepped into the living room, automatically glancing toward the bed. Jeremiah sat reclining against a pile of pillows, a newspaper resting beside him on the mattress. His left fingers still held the page. It looked as if he'd just lowered it there. He wore a pair of black reading glasses and peered at Eli from over the narrow frames.

"Did you need something?" Jeremiah asked, his voice still filled with a disapproving curtness.

"Ne, I just wanted to check on you, to see how you're doing." Eli forced himself to put a smile in his voice. After all, this man wasn't his enemy and he wished they'd never had any hostility between them.

"I'm doing fine." Jeremiah picked the newspaper up again, as if brushing Eli aside.

"Would you like your lunch now? It's about that time. Are you hungry yet?" Eli pressed.

Because he'd eaten so early that morning, Eli was famished and ready for the yummy meal Lizzie had prepared for them.

Jeremiah again lowered the paper to his lap and removed his glasses, setting them on top of a pile of magazines that rested beside him. He gazed at Eli for a few moments, his bushy eyebrows lifted in consideration.

"Ja, I could eat now. Why don't you go see what Lizzie prepared for us?"

Really? That wasn't so hard.

Turning, Eli returned to the kitchen. He went to the gas-powered refrigerator and opened the door, leaning down so he could peer inside. Sitting on the middle rack, he found two plates covered with plastic wrap. They each contained sandwiches made with thin slices of homemade bread and moist, thick cuts of meatloaf… probably leftover from last night's supper. A note lay atop a shoofly pie that said: *Enjoy*! As he got the plates out along with a pitcher of chilled milk, Eli's mouth watered in anticipation. He never doubted Lizzie's cooking skills. She would make some man an excellent wife.

He frowned. For some crazy reason, he didn't like the thought of her marrying someone else. And because of his relationship with Shannon, that didn't seem right.

He poured the milk and carried a tray of the food into the living room. As he set it beside Jeremiah, he didn't feel as nervous as before. That changed the moment he sat in a chair next to the elder man and took a bite of his sandwich.

"*Ach*, what are your plans for the future?" Jeremiah asked.

Eli coughed and took a quick swallow of milk to clear his throat.

"Um, I plan to live and work just as before," he said.

Jeremiah took a slow bite, chewed for a moment, then swallowed. During the entire time, his gaze never wavered from Eli. "Here in Riverton? Or will you return to Denver?"

Eli blinked, wondering if Lizzie had told her father about the job offer. He doubted it—she had said she would keep his secret. Until he was baptized into their faith, everyone in the *Gmay* was wondering if he would stay or go. For most everyone, Eli was able to brush aside their blunt questions. But something about Jeremiah's piercing gaze seemed to look deep inside of him for the truth. Because he'd always respected this man and because he was Lizzie's father, Eli couldn't lie to him. But how could he admit he didn't know for sure what he would do?

"I plan to stay."

Since he hadn't decided if he wanted to leave, he thought that was an honest enough response.

"*Gut.* I've seen the way you look at my *dochder*, and I'll admit I've been concerned."

What? The way he looked at Lizzie?

Eli tilted his head to the side. "I don't understand. I don't look any special way at her," Eli said, feeling totally confused.

Jeremiah snorted, then took another bite of food, chewed calmly and swallowed before responding. "I don't want you to hurt her again the way you did last time you left. Nor do I want her to run away with you. You sent her letters before. I imagine they asked for her to join you in Denver."

So. Here it was. The topic had turned around to the letters. Eli knew it would. Eventually. And he couldn't deny that he *had* asked Lizzie to come to him in those letters.

"I didn't run away. I just left," Eli said.

One of Jeremiah's bushy eyebrows shot up. "Is there a difference?"

"I think so. But are you referring to the letters I wrote to Lizzie, which you returned to me? Unopened? Without even telling her about them?"

Jeremiah met Eli's gaze without a single drop of shame in his eyes.

"*Ja*, those would be the ones. I don't want you to do that again. It would hurt Lizzie too much. She is a gut *maedel* and deserves better from her fiancé."

"We were only fourteen years old when I asked her to marry me."

"So? Why does it matter how old you were? Are you a man of your word or not?" Jeremiah paused, waiting for a response that didn't come.

Once again, Eli felt rotten inside. The foolishness of his youth seemed to keep haunting him.

"I regret hurting her more than I can say. When she didn't write back to me, I assumed she no longer wanted me and our engagement was broken," Eli said.

Jeremiah didn't respond to that. He simply looked at Eli with that calm, unemotional expression of his. Finally, he picked up his fork and took a big bite of pie.

"I don't regret returning your letters and I'd do it again if the situation was the same," Jeremiah said.

Eli flinched at these words. He thought their conversation was over, but apparently not.

"I do regret that my *dochder* got hurt when you ran away to the *Englisch* world," Jeremiah continued. "I hope you've figured out who you are by now. Because no amount of education, no career or accolades of men, no wealth or worldly success can ever compensate for failure in your own home. Every man must live with the man he makes of himself. As you prepare for your future, I hope you'll never forget that. Especially where my *dochder* is concerned."

Every man must live with the man he makes of himself.

Eli hesitated, these words playing over and over in his mind. Since it was an old Amish saying, he'd heard it many times from his own father. But never before had it struck him with such powerful force. Such meaning.

He thought about the past, present and future, and

wanted more than anything to be content with the man he became at the end of his life. To be able to meet the Lord without shame. To know he'd done his absolute best and kept trying even when he failed. To have as few regrets in his life as he could possibly make. But what did that have to do with Lizzie? They were no longer engaged and his future no longer included her.

Or did it?

Chapter Thirteen

Over the next few weeks, Lizzie and her *familye* settled into a routine. In the mornings and early afternoons, Jeremiah grudgingly accepted Eli's help with the simple exercises the doctor had recommended. When they drove into town to visit Dr. McGann, he was more than pleased by Jeremiah's progress.

Each evening, before he went home, Eli would come into the house to sit and talk with Jeremiah about his work for the following day. No longer did Lizzie's father speak to Eli with a gruff, disapproving voice, although he was still reserved around the younger man.

On this particular afternoon, the wind and a lashing rain buffeted the house, but Lizzie felt warm and cozy inside. Because of the stormy weather, she had dried the laundry on racks set up in the living room. As she folded each piece and laid it inside the wicker basket, she couldn't help eavesdropping on the men's low conversation. The little girls sat on the couch nearby, reading quietly to one another. Outside, dark clouds filled the sky. The rain had slowed to a smattering that hit the windowpanes. Lizzie glanced that way, grateful to be inside. As she lit a kerosene lamp and set it nearby on a table so the children could see more easily, she thought the moment seemed so tranquil. So relaxed and normal, but it wasn't. Not for Lizzie.

No matter how many days passed, she couldn't forget the kiss she'd shared with Eli. Every time she saw him, she became nervous and quivery inside. When she thought of how much he must still love Shannon, she felt completely confused. Why had he kissed her? Had he forgotten who she was? But more than that, why had she kissed him back?

"What about the disc plow? Have you sharpened the blades yet?" Jeremiah asked Eli.

The older man sat upright on his bed with several pillows to support his back. Eli sat nearby in a hard chair.

"*Ja*, I took care of that as soon as Lizzie and I finished baling and putting the hay away," came Eli's even reply.

"And the baler...does it need any maintenance?"

Eli shook his head. "*Ne*, but I cleaned it out *gut* and got it ready for next season. The harness required mending and I replaced several buckles. The *maed* helped me."

Jeremiah glanced at his younger daughters, approval shining in his eyes.

"The barn roof also needed a few repairs. I found your extra shingles and did the work before the storms hit," Eli said.

"*Gut, gut.* Tomorrow, I'd like you to check the fence again, if the weather isn't too bad. I don't want any of the livestock to get out."

"I will do so," Eli confirmed.

Hefting the laundry basket, Lizzie climbed the stairs. She felt a mixture of gratitude and uncertainty. Eli had become immersed in their lives, almost as if he was a part of their *familye*. And he wasn't.

He acted as if he wanted to stay in Riverton, but Lizzie knew he was still drawn to worldly pursuits. If only he could find his *Gelassenheit* and accept that he was born to be an Amish man. She wondered how his leaving might impact his parents and the rest of the *Gmay*.

And her.

Thinking about his eventual departure made her heart pound harder. She told herself it was because she feared for his salvation. Her faith would allow nothing less. She truly believed that, if he turned his back on their faith and left Riverton, his soul would be in jeopardy. And no matter how many times she told herself it was his choice, she still longed for a way to convince him to stay.

Inside the children's room, she placed their folded clothes tidily in their dressers. She crossed the hall to her room and looked up. A shoebox she did not recognize sat on top of her chest of drawers.

Wondering what it was, she set the laundry basket on the floor, then lifted the lid to the box. A gasp tore from her throat and she stepped back, covering her lips with the fingertips of one hand. Her thoughts scattered. Inside, tied together with a bit of string, was a hefty stack of sealed letters. Each one was addressed to her, the postmark from Denver several years earlier. Without asking, she knew these were Eli's letters. The ones her father had returned.

Reaching inside, she lifted out the stack, then closed

the door to give herself more privacy. The bed bounced gently as she sat on one corner. Resting the pile of letters in her lap, she stared at them for at least five minutes. Her body trembled when she finally untied the string. She withdrew the first letter, but her shaking hands immediately dropped it to the floor. Bending at the waist, she picked it up. What was the matter with her? After so many years, these letters should make no difference in her life. They shouldn't matter. But they did.

Obviously, Eli had put the letters here for her to find. Maybe she should return them to him, or burn them and forget they ever existed.

The envelopes had been arranged in chronological order. She told herself that, if she didn't read them, nothing in her life would change. She could go on the way she was, filled with heartbreak and doubt. And that's when she realized how comfortable she'd become with those two emotions as her constant companions.

She felt compelled to read. She had to know what Eli had said to her. The letters were a part of her somehow. A part of her life—and Eli's life—that she'd missed because her father had withheld them from her.

She slid her finger beneath the flap of the first envelope. As she pulled out the crisp pages and unfolded them, she took a deep breath, trying to settle her nerves. She immediately recognized Eli's scrawling handwriting. Her gaze scanned the words, a hard lump as big as a boulder lodging in her throat. Eli conveyed his regrets over leaving her without saying goodbye. He expressed his love for her and a wish that she would join him in Denver. He still wanted to marry her, if she wanted him. He would await her reply...a response that never came.

One by one, Lizzie read the pile of letters, dazed by Eli's explanations of his fierce desire for a college education and skeptical of his declarations of love for her. Toward the end, he conveyed the deep sense of loss he felt when she didn't write back, and returned his letters unopened. In between, he discussed his schooling and work as a waiter in a restaurant to make ends meet. He looked mature for his age and had rented a studio apartment that was small but clean and had room for her. Every day, he walked to school, sitting in classes that tantalized his intellect and convinced him more and more of an eternal *Gott* who loved all his children unconditionally. Instead of weakening his faith, his education had strengthened his beliefs. Several times, he asked why she wouldn't write to him. He begged her to reconsider and join him in his *Englisch* life.

To marry him.

And then the final letter. Lizzie maintained her composure as she read Eli's deep sense of sorrow because he realized he'd lost her for good. He said he understood why she hadn't written him. That their breakup was his fault and he couldn't blame her for not wanting a life with him outside of the *Gmay*. She deserved a man of faith who never questioned their leaders or *Gott*'s will for them. It was time for them both to move on.

And that was the end.

Folding the last letter, Lizzie added it to the stack and retied the string. She put the letters back in their box and settled the lid over the top of them. Fearing her father or sisters might find and read them, she slid them far beneath her bed where they wouldn't be discovered easily.

So, now she knew. She'd finally read Eli's letters. His words were highly personal and gave her a new insight into who he really was inside. And for the first time since she'd known him, she finally understood his desire to learn new things. And she was surprised to find that it didn't make her angry anymore. Because she'd loved him so much, she couldn't condemn him. She had to let him choose for himself, no matter how much it hurt her.

Taking a deep, settling breath, she smoothed her skirt and apron. A quick glance in the tiny mirror on her nightstand caused her to tidy her hair and adjust her *kapp*. Chores were waiting. She had to go on with her life. She couldn't while away the day by sulking here in her room. She had to go downstairs and tend to her father and sisters. She had to be strong and resolute. Firm in her faith and her place in the world.

She took a step toward the door. She clutched the knob, but couldn't make it turn so she could leave. She stared at the oak panel, her vision blurring. Something gave way inside of her and she burst into deep, trembling sobs.

It was time to go. The rain had finally stopped, the evening air filled with the crisp scent of damp sage. Eli had finished his work and harnessed his horse to the buggy, but couldn't seem to get inside and drive away. Instead, he stood at the barn doors, gazing out at the damp farmyard. It was already dark with not even the stars or moon to light his way home. Without being able to see them, he knew the sky was filled with heavy, black clouds.

For the sake of safety, he should get on the road now, before it got any later. *Mamm* and *Daed* were expecting him for supper. But he hesitated, wondering if Lizzie had read the letters he'd left in her room. Wondering if she might come out to speak with him about them. He'd watched her go upstairs and knew she must have found them.

As he surveyed the house, the lights in the kitchen brightened and he knew she must be inside, preparing supper for her *familye*. Soon, Jeremiah would be up and walking again. His leg would continue to heal and he wouldn't need Eli's help on the farm anymore. Eli could leave, if he chose to do so. He could return to Denver and his old life there. No Shannon or Lizzie to welcome him. No love to share.

Completely alone.

Lizzie wasn't coming out to the barn. His stomach rumbled and he realized it was time to eat. His parents would be worried if he didn't arrive soon. Lizzie was occupied elsewhere. She probably didn't care about the letters now. He wasn't sure what he had expected. That she would read them and come running into his arms to declare that she still loved him? That she wanted to marry him and raise a *familye* with him here in Riverton? That wasn't what he wanted, was it? He was still in love with Shannon. Right?

He snorted and turned away, returning to his buggy. He'd always been so firm in what he wanted out of life. So convinced that the *Englisch* life was best for him. But now, he felt nothing but conflict. He was even starting to doubt his love for Shannon. Sometimes, he couldn't remember her face. All he could remember was Lizzie. And that wasn't right. No, it couldn't be.

Pulling on his warm gloves, he led the horse out into the yard and secured the barn doors. He climbed into his buggy seat and took hold of the lead lines.

"Schritt!" he called.

The horse stepped forward, pulling the buggy through puddles of water along the dirt road.

Eli figured his letters to Lizzie were too little, too late. In the time since he had written them, he'd fallen in love with someone else. It still hurt like a knife to his heart every time he thought about losing Shannon. But lately, he couldn't remember the shape of her eyes, or the contour of her chin. Whenever he thought about her, his thoughts turned to Lizzie. Which was foolish because she didn't care for him anymore. Not romantically, anyway. They'd both moved on with their lives. And yet, he couldn't help wishing...

He was being stupid! He had no idea why he'd kissed her. He'd been so embarrassed by what he'd done. So ashamed.

He turned the buggy onto the county road, pulling over to the shoulder. The horse trotted forward, eager to get home.

Every time Lizzie was in the room with him, Eli felt a deeper sense of guilt. Kissing her had been wrong on so many levels. His lapse in judgment hadn't been fair to either of them. It might lead her to believe there could be something between them again. That he still loved her the way he used to. And he didn't. Did he?

He remembered all the times when he'd thought Lizzie was rejecting his letters because she was disappointed in him. He thought she had returned them all to him. Because he'd turned his back on his faith and their love. And all that time, she hadn't even known that he had written to her. From her perspective, she must have thought he'd abandoned her completely, without any explanation. That he'd broken all his promises to her. That he'd chosen the world over her. And that wasn't true. He'd begged her to join him—had wanted to share the world with her. But that had been a foolish dream. Lizzie had never wanted a life anywhere other than here.

He shook his head. The letter from Tom Caldwell was still folded inside his hat. He hadn't responded to the job offer yet. For the time being, Lizzie's *familye* still needed his help. But soon, Jeremiah would be back on his feet. So, what was holding Eli back? He wasn't sure, but knew he'd have to make a decision soon. And he'd need to speak to Lizzie as well. To tell her he was deeply, genuinely sorry for how things had not worked out between them. She deserved that apology and so much more. He only hoped she could find it in her heart to forgive him.

Chapter Fourteen

The day of Church Sunday was a pleasant surprise. The Sangre de Cristo Mountains were coated with snow, but down in the valley everything had melted off the roads and fields. The sun gleamed bright and surprisingly warm in the morning sky. Not bad, considering they were only a week away from Thanksgiving. As Lizzie hurried to gather the eggs, she thought it most fitting for the *Gmay*'s semiannual Communion meeting. It should be a day of enlightenment and confidence in the Lord. But for herself, she still felt overshadowed by qualms.

"Lizzie?"

She turned. Eli stood just beyond the open doorway, his dark hair shining against his sun-bronzed face. Wearing his best clothes, he held his hat in his hands. Seeing him brought a quick leap of excitement to her chest, but she tried to squelch it. She'd avoided him for a long time now. Perhaps today of all days, it was time to speak with him and let go of her harsh feelings. Instead of nursing her own broken heart, she should think about other people for a change...starting with Eli.

Carrying the wire basket filled with eggs, she stepped outside and latched the door of the chicken coop. Then, she looked up into his eyes.

"*Guder mariye*, Eli. *Wie bischt du heit?*"

"I am *gut*, but I am worried about you," he said.

She took a deep inhale of the crisp air and let it go, reminding herself to remain calm. To trust in the Lord. And to forgive.

"Why would you be worried about me?" she asked, thinking she knew the answer, but not quite sure.

He looked at the ground, his chiseled profile so handsome that she almost reached out to touch his cheek. Almost.

"I… I owe you an apology," he said.

Yes, he did, but she didn't say that.

"For what?" she said instead.

His gaze met hers and in his eyes, she saw deep remorse there. "For so many things. For kissing you. For leaving all those years ago without saying goodbye in person. For not coming to see you when you didn't respond to my letters. For breaking off our engagement. For being a stupid, foolish kid. I was young and *dumm* and wanted a *rumspringa*."

She showed a sad little smile. "*Ach*, then you got what you wanted."

"*Ja*, but I regret putting myself first and not thinking about how my leaving might affect you and my *eldre*. I'm sorry for the pain I caused. I can't look back and regret my life, but I do deeply regret hurting you, both now and in the past."

Oh, did he have to say that?

"*Es tut mir leid.* Can you please forgive me for what I did?" he continued.

Here it was. The moment she'd been dreading. For-giveness was a requirement of her faith. If she truly believed in Christ and the Atonement, then she must pardon Eli for any wrongs he'd done to her. Repen-tance wasn't just for her. It was for others as well. But still she hesitated, her pulse quickening as she pon-dered what to say. And yet, there was really only one response she could give.

"Of course I forgive you, Eli."

As she said the words, her heart seemed to open up and a breath of fresh air cleansed her pain-filled heart.

A wide smile spread across his face. A gorgeous smile that stole her breath away and turned her mind to mush.

Placing his hat on his head, he took her hand in his. "That's the best thing I've heard since…since I don't know when. *Danke*, Lizzie-bee. You've made me very happy."

He paused for a moment, his long fingers wrapped around hers. She showed a lame smile, trying hard to be positive and friendly. She withdrew her hand, still feeling the warmth of his skin zinging up her arm.

"Will you be ready for me to drive you and your *fam-ilye* to church soon?" he asked, still smiling brightly.

"*Ja*, but I'm afraid *Daed* still needs our help to get from the house to the buggy."

"I figured as much. I'll get the horse ready and come by to help you in about ten minutes. Is that enough time?"

She nodded, her mouth too dry to speak. Instead, she whirled around and headed toward the house. Hopefully her sisters were ready and *Daed* had finished the breakfast tray she'd left for him before coming outside.

As she crossed the yard, she looked up and saw her father peering at her from the window beside his bed. His forehead was crinkled in a troubled frown.

A flush of heat scorched Lizzie's cheeks. Surely he couldn't have overheard her conversation with Eli, but he must have seen him holding her hand. *Daed* might misunderstand and think the gesture was romantic. And it wasn't. No, not at all. But the last thing she wanted was to explain to her father that Eli had merely apologized to her. No declarations of love. No new proposals of marriage. No promises for the future. It was just a simple apology so Eli could clear his conscience before he left and returned to Denver. And that was all.

"Hallo," Eli called as he entered the front door to the Beilers' house. He glanced at Jeremiah's bed, but found it vacant, the covers pulled up over the pillow in tidy order.

The house smelled of cinnamon and he wondered if Lizzie had baked something special for lunch. But where was Jeremiah?

"Eli!" Marty came running from the kitchen, her warm winter coat tucked beneath her arm.

Annie pounded down the stairs, the ties on her *kapp* whipping at her shoulders. Both girls launched themselves at him in a tight three-way hug.

"Oof!" he grunted and staggered back with their impact, then laughed. "You're not happy to see me, are you?"

"Of course we are," Marty said with a grin.

"Look! I lost another tooth last night." Annie smiled wide, showing a gaping hole in the front.

Eli leaned over to look closely, realizing how much he loved these two little girls. It would be so difficult to leave and never see them again. And what would they think of him when they found out he was gone? He hated the thought that they might be disappointed in him.

"Wow! You've lost a lot of teeth lately. How many does that make now?" he asked.

"Two in the last month. Lizzie says I'm getting my permanent teeth in because I'm growing up so fast."

"*Ach*, I suppose that's true. You're almost as tall as Marty." He glanced between the two girls, comparing their height.

Standing straighter, Marty frowned at that. "*Ne*, she's not. I'm still the tallest. That's 'cause I'm the oldest."

Annie giggled, her sweet voice filling the room. "But not for long. Lizzie says if I eat all my vegetables, I'll grow up to be tall and strong. I might pass you up one day."

"You will not," Marty said.

"I might," Annie insisted.

The two girls engaged in a harmless pushing match and Eli reached out to separate them. "*Ach*, that's no way to treat one another. When you're older, you'll be the best of friends. I promise you that. Until then, be kind and take care of one another."

As the elder, Marty nodded, looking rather serious. The thought of leaving and never seeing them grow up to be lovely young women brought a pang of hurt to Eli's chest. How he would miss them.

"I'm sorry," Annie said, hugging her sister.

A movement caught Eli's eye and he looked up, seeing Lizzie standing in the threshold to the kitchen. Dressed in her winter coat and black traveling bonnet, she held a large basket hanging from one arm.

"Annie, it's time to leave. Go get your coat," she said.

The girl did as asked, hurrying to the closet.

Eli stood straight, contemplating Lizzie. Her cheeks were flushed, possibly from baking early that morning. Her pale lavender skirts swished against her legs as she reached for a pair of gloves on the table.

"Where is Jeremiah?" he asked.

She jutted her chin toward the bathroom. "He insisted on bathing himself this morning. I couldn't stop him."

Eli widened his eyes. "He's not walking on his broken leg, is he?"

"*Ne, ne.* He's walking on crutches. He promised not to put any weight at all on his bad leg. He knows how important it is to let it heal." The concern in her voice belied her words.

Eli's gaze followed her as she walked down the short hall to the bathroom and tapped lightly on the closed door.

"*Daedi*, are you all right? Do you need any help?" she asked, leaning her cheek against the hard panel.

"*Ne!* I'm fine," came Jeremiah's muffled response.

A loud clatter and splash accompanied his words, lending doubt to his statement.

"Eli is here to take us to church," she said.

"I'll be right out."

Lizzie returned to the living room, tugging on her

gloves. She helped Annie with her coat and tidied a short wisp of hair. Watching Lizzie lovingly caress each child's cheek, Eli thought she would make an amazing mother one day. And suddenly, he saw her with new eyes. No longer was she the young teenaged girl he'd loved and left. Now, she was a fully matured woman who understood her place in the world and was confident in her choices.

The bathroom door rattled and jerked open, releasing a blast of steam. Jeremiah stood there on crutches, holding his injured leg up so it didn't touch the floor. He was fully dressed in his black frock coat, his combed hair and beard slightly damp.

Lizzie set her basket aside and both she and Eli hurried to help the man as he hobbled forward.

"Danke," he said.

Eli flinched, surprised to hear such a gracious word directed at him. Not since he'd been home had he heard anything approaching gratitude from Jeremiah. After working for the man for almost two months now, maybe Eli was growing on him. Maybe Jeremiah didn't think he was such a bad influence on Lizzie after all. Of course, that would end if Eli returned to Denver. And though he knew Jeremiah didn't approve of him, Eli hated the thought of losing the man's respect. He hated to let him and elders of their church down. He knew what people in the *Gmay* would say about him. He could just imagine Marva Geingerich's response at church.

You see? I told you he wouldn't stay with us, she would tell everyone who would listen.

He could also imagine his mother's tears. His leaving would break her heart. And though his father would never show his emotions, Eli knew it would break his heart too. But he mustn't let that be his reason for staying. Whether he stayed or left must be purely between him and *Gott*. He would have to live with his decision for the rest of his life and he must make the choice that was right for him.

Jeremiah fell back into a chair, breathing hard while Lizzie reached for his winter coat. One of his crutches dropped to the floor with a clatter while the other leaned against the side of the chair. Eli picked them up, holding both crutches at the ready.

"Vie gehts?" Eli asked the older man.

"I'm just fine," Jeremiah said as Lizzie held up his coat and he thrust each of his arms into the sleeves.

"Does your leg cause you any pain?" Eli asked.

"Ne, it feels *gut.* But I hate this weakness. I can't hardly move without being out of breath. You were right. My muscles aren't as strong anymore." The man wiped his forehead, seeming a bit out of sorts.

"Don't worry. The weakness will fade," Eli assured him.

Jeremiah looked up, his eyes filled with hope. "You really think so?"

"Ja, I know so."

"I must do more exercises, now that I'm able to get up and walk on crutches. I need to get stronger."

"That is a *gut* idea, but don't overdo. Give your body time to mend."

Jeremiah blessed Eli with a coveted smile. And that alone made him feel incredibly happy inside. But it soon faded when he thought of the stern frown that would cover the elder man's face once he learned that Eli had returned to Denver.

"Are you ready to go?" Lizzie asked her father.

He nodded, reaching for his crutches. Eli helped him as he stood.

"Marty, get the door," Lizzie called.

Both little girls hurried to open the way so that Jeremiah could pass through to the front porch. Outside, Eli lifted Jeremiah down the stairs. He had spread ice melt so the path to the buggy wasn't slick. They all moved at a slower pace, but once Lizzie had retrieved her basket and they were loaded inside, Eli breathed a silent sigh of relief.

Taking the lead lines into his hands, he released the break and called to Billie. *"Schritt!"*

The horse stepped forward in a jaunty trot, as if understanding the happy mood inside the buggy. Eli held the lead lines in his hands and thought about how much he would miss working with horses and the other livestock once he was back in Denver. Already he was yearning for the feel of a plow as it dug into the rich, fertile soil. The excitement of the harvest. The pleasure of eating one of Lizzie's home-baked pies. But if he stayed, he would long for the work he was missing in Denver. The joy of helping someone survive a heart attack, or saving their life after a bad accident. He'd put years into his schooling and couldn't let it go.

Returning to the present, he mentally calculated how long it would take to drive to Bishop Yoder's farm. Once they arrived, there would be many strong men to lift Jeremiah out of the buggy. They'd be happy to help, always working together for the good of them all. He realized how much he would miss each member of the *Gmay*.

As he listened to the girls' happy chatter in the back

seat, he was surprised that Jeremiah chimed in now and then. Yes, the man was definitely feeling better. And though he was still weak, he was growing stronger every day. Soon, he wouldn't need Eli to work his farm. Soon, Eli could leave Lizzie and her sweet *familye* behind and return to his *Englisch* life. Lizzie had helped him see that Shannon's death hadn't been his fault and while he still grieved for her loss, he was grateful he'd been privileged to know his fiancée, for however short a time. But he wouldn't let guilt hold him back from the direction his life needed to take. Being a paramedic was what he'd worked so hard for. It was what he wanted to do with his life. He had to go back to Denver. He just had to. Lizzie would understand even if his parents and the rest of the *Gmay* wouldn't.

There. He'd finally made the decision of what he should do. He would return to Denver right after Thanksgiving. It was the right thing to do. He knew it deep within his heart. So, why did he feel so gloomy inside?

Chapter Fifteen

Sitting in the back seat of the buggy with her sisters, Lizzy enjoyed this trip to church more than any other she could remember. Snuggled in her warm cape and mittens, she listened to her sisters' happy prattle and watched the beautiful scenery pass by the window. Tall mountains and wide-open fields covered with snow met her view.

Once they arrived at Bishop Yoder's farm, Eli hopped out to help her father. Without being summoned, numerous men and boys appeared, eager to assist. They lifted Jeremiah easily and carried him inside the spacious barn. Lizzie followed with her father's crutches, placing them nearby.

"Eli!"

Little Timmy Hostetler ran into the barn and made a beeline straight for Eli. The man turned, saw the boy and scooped him up and spun him around before pausing for a tight hug.

"There's my Timmy. How are you doing this fine day?" Eli asked.

Still in the man's arms, the boy drew back and

placed his hands trustingly on Eli's shoulders. "I'm great. Even *Mamm* wonders at my recovery."

David stood nearby, a satisfied smile on his lips. "That's right. Linda thought he was too wild before he got sick. Now, she can't believe how active he is."

The other men laughed, patting Eli on the back.

Nearby, Linda Hostetler nudged old Marva Geingerich. "What do you think, Marva? Look at all the *gut* things Eli has done. Isn't it *wundervoll*? Do you still think he's going to leave again?"

"Humph!" was all Marva said.

Lizzie would have laughed it if hadn't been so sad to her. Watching Eli mingle with members of their *Gmay*, she felt a burst of joy. They were a tight community, sharing one another's burdens and joys. It was so good that they had avoided several catastrophes and they were happy to have all their members here today. But more than that, she gazed at Eli, and a sudden, wrenching sadness filled her heart with pain. Because she knew he would be leaving soon.

Marva Geingerich had been right all along.

Turning away, Lizzie headed into the house where she assisted the other women with the food. Abby and Fannie welcomed her and she pasted a smile on her face, pretending all was well.

When they were called in to church, Lizzie stepped outside and walked to the barn. Taking her place opposite the men, she sang when appropriate and listened intently as the bishop explained the true meaning of *Gelassenheit*, the joy in submission to *Gott*. She'd fought her fears for so many years now, but longed for a calm heart. She'd forgiven Eli, but still felt like she needed to let go of her fears. And that's when she realized the difficulty was no longer with Eli, but rather with herself. Withholding her forgiveness had made her the sinner, but pardoning Eli had taken a giant leap of faith. In spite of her father's disapproval and knowing Eli would soon be leaving, her heart was softened and she finally let go of her anger and doubts.

Glancing over at Eli, she watched his expressions as he listened intently to the bishop's sermon. A mixture of yearning and torment filled his eyes.

Lizzie's heart reached out to him. He didn't have an easy task ahead of him. It would take a lot for him to turn his back on his parents and church and walk away again. To return to his *Englisch* life alone, without Shannon or anyone else to love and care for. Lizzie knew she could never have that kind of strength, but neither could she be angry with him for his choices. Because now, she had another huge problem to deal with.

In spite of her father's disapproval, in spite of her best efforts not to, she still loved Eli more than ever before.

So much for her vow never to let him break her heart again.

The morning before Thanksgiving Day, Lizzie walked out to the barn under cover of darkness. Planning to get an early start to her day, she would feed the chickens first. She needed the extra eggs for her pies, breads and cream fillings.

Crossing the yard, she snuggled her knitted scarf tighter around her throat. As she exhaled, she saw her breath on the air like the blast from a steam engine. The sun wasn't even up yet, but she couldn't sleep. Too many things waged a battle inside her mind. Preparation of her *familye*'s feast, finding extra time when her sisters weren't around so she could sew a new dress for each of them before Christmas and Eli's inevitable departure.

Inside the barn, she looked up, surprised to discover that Eli's horse and buggy were already here. Two tall canisters of fresh milk sat beside the door. Since he was nowhere to be seen, she figured he must have finished the milking and gone out in the field with the cows. But why was he here so early? Maybe he couldn't sleep either.

Going about her business, she removed her gloves and picked up a silver scoop. First, she dug it into the grain, then into the cracked corn before dumping it all into her bucket and mixing it together. The extra protein helped the hens keep laying eggs even with the colder, shorter days of winter.

Looking up, she saw Eli's jacket had fallen off the peg by the door. She stepped over and lifted the coat to hang it up and blinked when some papers fell open on the ground. She picked them up, surprised to discover another letter from Eli's old boss in Denver. The man named Tom Caldwell.

Glancing at the doorway, she hunched her shoulders, feeling guilty for reading Eli's personal correspondence. She should return the letter to his coat and forget she'd ever seen it.

Folding the pages, her eyes caught the words *job* and *excited for your return*. Unable to resist, she quickly scanned the contents, discovering that Tom Caldwell needed Eli's acceptance of the supervisory job with a start date of December 1.

"Lizzie?"

She whirled around and faced Eli, flustered to be caught in the act of reading his mail. "I...um, your coat was on the ground and when I picked it up, this letter fell out."

She quickly handed the pages to him. Never had she been more conscious of her lack of worldliness. Compared to the classes he'd taken at the university and the life he'd lived among the *Englisch*, she must seem so simple and unsophisticated.

He gazed at the papers in his hand, overly quiet and seemingly uncertain. "Did you...did you read it?"

She nodded, unwilling to lie. "I'm sorry. I didn't mean to pry. It was just lying there open and I..."

Succumbed.

"*Ne*, it's me who is sorry, Lizzie. I should have taken better care. I didn't want you to see this." He peered at her, his eyes filled with misgivings. "Are you angry at me?"

She hesitated, her heart filled with anguish. How she hated to lose him a second time. How she hated that he couldn't seem to find contentment here in Riverton. But she couldn't be angry with him anymore. What good would it do? She loved him and truly wanted him to be happy, even if it meant losing him.

"*Ne*, I'm not angry. In fact, I understand." Reaching out, she squeezed his hand and met his gaze with conviction.

"You do?" he asked.

She nodded, but didn't speak. Her throat felt like it was stuffed with sandpaper.

"You see why I want to go, don't you? It's a great opening for me, Lizzie. It's what I've always wanted and I'll never get this chance again. All of my schooling has been for this opportunity. I can't pass it up. You know that, don't you?" He sounded almost desperate to convince her. And for a moment, she thought he was really trying to convince himself.

She showed a sad little smile and nodded. "*Ja*, I know it's what you've always wanted the most. I wish you would stay here in Riverton, but I know you have a gift for helping others. I can't hold you back from reaching your potential, nor will I judge you or try to stop you from following your heart. You have to decide for yourself. And I promise to support you in whatever life you choose, even though my place is here in Riverton, with our people. I care so very deeply for you and I just want you to be happy. Even if that means we'll never see each other again."

Before he could respond, she leaned upward on her tippy-toes and kissed his cheek farewell, then whirled around and raced back to the house. She didn't stop until she was safely inside her room where she closed the door and lay upon her bed to have a good, muffled cry. She would send the girls out to feed the chickens and gather the eggs later on. But even if the house was burning down around her, she didn't think she could face Eli again. She meant everything she had said to him. And right now, his happiness meant more to her than anything else, even if it meant she had to let him go.

Eli stood where Lizzie had left him. He stared at the open doorway, transfixed by the sight of her slender back as she walked away from him. Knowing he would never see her again. He couldn't move. Couldn't breathe. An overwhelming feeling of deep, abiding loss and grief pulsed over him again and again, like the crashing of tidal waves buffeting the shore. Lizzie was gone. All he had to do was finish his chores and go home. And the day after Thanksgiving, he could catch a bus back to Denver. It was what he wanted.

Or was it?

Lizzie wouldn't be there. He'd never see her again. Never hear her laugh or see her smile. Never be able to seek out her advice or hear his name breathed from her lips in a sigh of happiness ever again. And it was his own fault. He'd made this happen. With his thoughtless, selfish desires to chase the world.

But maybe, just maybe, it didn't have to be like this. He had one chance to make this right. To change the outcome. And suddenly, his life came into focus. It was as if a panoramic view opened up to him with his past, present and future life right before his eyes. Finally, he could see it all and understood what he wanted most above all other things.

His heart was filled with absolute confidence in what he must do. But he must do it now.

Turning, he reached for his coat. His course was set. He'd made up his mind and knew just what he wanted out of life. But he better not blow it this time. Because his eternal happiness was depending on what he did within the next ten minutes.

Chapter Sixteen

Over an hour later, Lizzie waited until she heard her sisters rustling around in their bedroom before she went downstairs and started breakfast. Finally the sun was up and she could stop staring at the ceiling in her room. She couldn't lay on her bed feeling sorry for herself all day long. She wiped her eyes and blew her nose and took hold of her composure. Within a week, Eli would be gone back to Denver and she'd never see him again. She had to accept that and move on.

"Why are your eyes all red and puffy?" little Annie asked when she came into the kitchen.

The girl's *kapp* and apron were askew. Lizzie adjusted her sister's clothing before turning toward the stove. "I think I might be catching a cold."

Which was partly true. She'd been sniffling even before her talk out in the barn with Eli that morning.

"Guder mariye," Jeremiah called as he hobbled into the room on his crutches.

He smiled as he kissed Lizzie on the forehead, then scooted back a chair and sat down.

"Guder mariye, Daedi," Lizzie said.

She watched him briefly, wondering if it was too soon for him to be getting around on his own. But since he never put any weight on his injured leg, she figured it was all right.

When Marty joined them seconds later, Lizzie set a meal of scrapple, bacon and thick-sliced bread on the table, then took her seat and bowed her head for prayer. As they ate, she responded automatically to questions and nodded to the conversations around her, but didn't really listen. Later, as she went about her day, she felt like she was moving in a fog. Her bones were achy, her chest filled with a painful emptiness. Maybe she had caught a cold after all. Surely it had nothing to do with losing the love of her life. Again.

"Do you want me to see if we have more eggs?" Marty asked later that afternoon.

Lizzie felt a tad guilty for sending the girl on another errand, but she had been avoiding the barn at all costs. She couldn't see Eli again. She just couldn't.

"I'm afraid I do need two more eggs," she said.

Nodding obediently, Marty did as asked. She returned minutes later with three fresh eggs.

"That's all there is. I hope that's enough to make your pies," Marty said as she set the eggs carefully on the counter.

Lizzie didn't look up from the batter she was whipping with a whisk. "*Danke, boppli*. I think this will be enough."

"*Gut!*" The girl reeled around and headed back to the living room. Lizzie knew she had a new book she wanted to read and decided to let her go. After all, it was Thanksgiving tomorrow. Except for the mandatory work of milking and feeding the livestock, they all planned to take a break from their other chores.

Once her pies sat cooling on the counter, Lizzie decided she needed some fresh air. Wrapping her cape around her, she stepped out on the front porch where she wouldn't be seen from the barn by Eli. Sitting in an Adirondack chair, she took several deep breaths, letting the frosty air cool her heated cheeks. It had gotten hot in the kitchen and she was grateful for this short break.

When she finally turned to go back inside, she glanced at the mailbox sitting at the edge of the lawn. The red flag was up, signaling to the postman that he should collect a letter to mail. That wasn't right. She had placed no letters there.

Planning to lower the flag, she stepped down off the porch and hurried over to the box. Inside, she found a sealed envelope from Eli to Tom Caldwell in Denver.

Her heart sank. No doubt the letter was Eli's acceptance of the job offer. Out of a selfish desire to keep him there in Riverton, Lizzie thought about taking the letter and destroying it. But that wouldn't be honest. Her personal integrity wouldn't allow her to do such a thing. Besides, destroying the letter wouldn't change Eli's decision. Instead, she left the letter right where it was and closed the door to the box. The red flag was up and she didn't lower it. The postman would pick it up within the next few minutes. But now, her heart felt even heavier than before. She'd seen the proof with her own eyes. Eli was leaving. She would never see him again.

Turning, she returned to the kitchen where she forced herself to focus on cleaning the turkey for their big feast tomorrow afternoon. In spite of it being

Thanksgiving, she was having serious difficulty counting all her many blessings.

She tried to think of all the things she was grateful for. Her *familye* and their good health. The *Gmay* and all her many friends who genuinely cared about her. Good, nutritious food and the plentiful moisture they'd had to nourish their crops for a bountiful harvest next fall. It was all so wonderful. So grand and glorious. Other than a husband and *familye* of her own, she had everything an Amish woman could want. Perhaps she would one day meet another good man she could love and respect. Someone who would love her in return. But right now, she just couldn't feel any joy. Maybe in the near future. But not today. Not when she knew she would never see Eli again.

The following morning, Lizzie didn't feel much better. In spite of her sisters' happy banter, she carried a heavy heart as she prepared a Thanksgiving feast for her *familye*. In fact, she didn't feel like celebrating. She felt like crying. But the Lord wanted her to have joy, so she pasted a smile on her lips and forced herself to be in a good mood. But deep inside, she felt empty.

While her sisters set the table, Lizzie mixed the stuffing. It was filled with celery, sage and onion, and her nose twitched with the wonderful aromas. When it was time, her father helped her stuff the turkey. Once it was in the oven, she set the timer and glanced over at the counter. Hmm. Where had Marty gone off to? She was supposed to be peeling the potatoes. In fact, where was Annie? She had been given the task of cleaning the broccoli. Her vacant step stool stood in front of the kitchen sink, but no girls were anywhere in sight.

"Marty! Annie! *Kumme helfe*," she called, turning toward the door.

Jeremiah stood there on his crutches, his casted leg held up from touching the floor. She had to admit, she was delighted that he was getting around so well. Because of Eli, the exercises had really helped and she must thank him for...

She paused, her brain spinning. Eli was leaving. She couldn't thank him. He wouldn't be at church next Sunday, nor would he be back at the farm to help her father with his chores.

"Where are those *maed*?" she asked, her voice rather brusque as she dried her damp hands on a clean dish towel. She stepped toward the living room, trying to see past her father's shoulder. He just stood there in the way, not bothering to move at all. Of course, he wasn't very light on his feet these days, but the least he could do was step to one side and let her pass.

"Lizzie," he said.

"Ja?" She glanced at his face, trying to skirt around him.

He lifted a hand and she drew up beside him. Caught between the fingers of his right hand was an envelope.

"What is this?" she asked, peering at him.

She didn't have time for nonsense. Not if he wanted his Thanksgiving dinner to be served on time.

He rotated the envelope so she could see her name on it, perfectly written in Eli's angled scrawl. She didn't take the letter. No, she couldn't.

"This is for you," Jeremiah said. "It's from Eli."

"Ja, I can see that." She backed away, turning toward

the sink. Trying to ignore the heavy beating in her chest and the sound of her own pulse pounding in her ears.

"He wanted you to have it. Because I hid his other letters from you, I promised him that I'd deliver this one to you personally." Jeremiah's lips twitched with laughter, but she didn't find anything humorous about it.

"I don't want it. Take it away." She made a pretense of cutting more celery for the cranberry salad she was making. Why would Eli write another letter to her? It was bad enough that he was leaving right after Thanksgiving. After all, they both knew he must report to his new job by December 1. There was no explanation required this time, so there was no need for him to say goodbye in a letter too.

Jeremiah hobbled over to her, standing beside her. "Lizzie, I want to make amends for hiding your other letters from you. Please, take this letter and read it right now."

The command in her father's voice caused her to pause. She stared at the envelope, knowing it was a farewell letter. She didn't want it, but realized her father was going to hound her until she took it. Whisking it from his hand, she tucked it inside the waist of her apron and returned to her celery. Tears filled her eyes as she cut a stalk into cubes with a knife. When a new Amish bride was planning to marry, she often grew extra celery for all the many foods she would prepare for her wedding feast. But there would be no such banquet for her.

"I'll read it later," she mumbled.

"Lizzie. Read it now." Jeremiah gripped one of her hands, holding her movements still.

She flinched when she saw Bishop Yoder standing

beside the refrigerator. When had he entered the room? And what was he doing here? Why had he come here on Thanksgiving Day? It must be serious.

"Bishop Yoder?" she croaked out his name.

"Read the letter, Lizzie," he said.

Confusion fogged her brain. Something was very, very wrong for both men to be here, pushing her to read Eli's letter. Perhaps Eli had already left Riverton and the bishop wanted her to help convince him to return. But she knew that would be futile. Eli had made his choice. She would not beg him to come home. It would be too humiliating. Too pathetic for her to do such a thing. But her father and Bishop Yoder were still standing there waiting for her.

Dropping the knife and celery stalk into the sink, she again dried her hands, then reached for the envelope and slid her finger beneath the flap to break the seal. She hesitantly pulled out the single page and spread out the creased folds. As her gaze scanned the words, her heart did a myriad of flip-flops. She gasped, unable to believe what she was reading. Without a word, she brushed past the two men and hurried into the living room, then out onto the porch.

Eli! Was he here? Or had he already left the farm? She glanced around, looking for any sign of him. Hoping. Carrying a prayer inside her heart.

"Who are you looking for?"

She spun around. Eli! He was here. He'd been sitting on an Adirondack chair, but came to his feet as he spoke to her. He whisked off his hat, holding it in his hands. In his eyes, she saw a mixture of uncertainty and hope.

She stared at him, her throat too clogged to speak. Confusion filled her mind and she didn't know what to say.

"Who are you looking for?" he asked again.

"You," she croaked.

"Did you read my letter?" he asked, stepping closer. She nodded, a raft of tears clogging her throat.

"Then you know. I'm not going back to Denver," he said.

She swallowed hard, still gripping his letter in her hand. "You're...you're not?"

"*Ne*. In fact, I mailed my rejection letter to Tom Caldwell just yesterday. I'm not going to accept his job offer after all."

"You're...you're not?" she said again, thinking she must sound irrational and foolish.

"*Ne*, I'm not. That's why I invited Bishop Yoder to accompany me here today. You see, yesterday, when you turned and hurried away from me, something cold gripped my heart."

She blinked, trying to clear the tears from her eyes. "And what is that?"

"For a third time in my life, I was about to lose the woman I loved. And I couldn't allow that to happen again. I was devastated when Shannon died. And watching you walk away was like that all over again. I couldn't lose you too. Not again. I know on my deathbed I won't be thinking about my education or my career. I'll be thinking about you. And what good would my life be if you're not a major part of it?"

She shook her head, not understanding. Not daring to hope she was hearing him correctly. "What are you saying, Eli?"

"Just that I love you, Lizzie. I love you so very much."

The letter she still clutched in her hand said the same things and so much more. She hadn't heard him say those words in many long years. But now, he said he wanted to stay in Riverton. That he wanted to marry her. She licked her lips, not daring to believe his words.

"I… I don't understand."

"I know. I didn't understand myself, until yesterday. You see, over the past couple of months, I've experienced your strength and abiding faith, and I now feel a deep sense of peace in my heart. I could return to my *Englisch* life in Denver and forever lose you and the other things that matter most to me. Or I can remain here and always wonder if I made the right choice. In all honesty, I had planned to leave. But then, I started thinking about all the things I would miss. And most of all, I would miss you more than I could stand. Without you, nothing else matters to me."

He paused, taking a deep breath. She forced herself to breathe too. To remain quiet and let him finish what he was saying.

"I don't want to live without you, Lizzie."

"You don't?"

"*Ne*, I don't. I realize that each of us has been given a *wundervoll* gift. The right to choose who and what we want to be. We both have the option of staying or going. I've finally made peace with *Gott* and I want to stay. Because I love you and my faith more than anything else in the world. This is where I belong. I know that now."

A surge of joy almost overwhelmed her. She could hardly believe she'd heard him right. "Oh, Eli. Do you know how long I've waited to hear you say these things? I've never stopped loving you. I tried to pretend that I didn't, but it was no use. I'm sure that's why my heart has been in so much pain. Becoming your wife and raising a *familye* with you here in Riverton has always been my fondest dream. But…but what about your career as a paramedic?"

He showed a thoughtful frown and looked down at his feet. That alone told her he still felt misgivings about quitting his profession. Yes, he could still help others in the *Gmay* now and then with their medical ailments, but it wouldn't be the same. If he stayed in Riverton, he wouldn't be a paramedic anymore and they both knew it.

"You've worked so hard and you love your work," she said. "I can't ask you to give that up. You say you love me now, but what about five, ten or fifteen years from now? If you must abandon your career in order to be here with me, I fear you might come to resent me for it. I don't want you to settle for something you may regret later down the road. And I don't want you to have to choose between me and your career. I want you to be happy. To feel confident that you have the best life right here with me."

He didn't speak for several moments, his eyebrows drawn together as he considered her words. A heavy sense of loss settled in her chest. Yes, she believed he truly loved her. Maybe he had never stopped. But loving one another didn't mean he would stay. Not if he couldn't have all that his heart desired.

"You and the Lord are all I need to be happy," Eli insisted. "When you turned and walked away from me yesterday, I knew that more than anything. I won't lose you, Lizzie. Not again. I have made my choice. My work as a humble farmer, future husband and father are every bit as important as being a paramedic in Denver. I will remain here with you. I know deep in my heart that it's the decision the Lord would want me to make. It's what I want too."

"Ahum!"

They both turned and found Jeremiah and Bishop Yoder standing behind them on the porch. Lizzie hadn't even heard them come outside. Through the living room window, she could see her two sisters peering out at them. Could she have no privacy at all?

Annie pressed her nose against the glass pane, looking as if she might cry. Jeremiah leaned against the outer wall, his crutches beneath his arms as he held his injured leg up off the wooden floor. Both men wore serious expressions, their foreheads creased with concern.

"I'm sorry to interrupt, but I think I might be able to clear up a few fears you both might have," the bishop said.

Lizzie's ears perked up at that. Eli faced the two men, but she could see the doubt in his eyes.

Bishop Yoder lifted a hand and rested it on Eli's shoulder. "When you came to see me yesterday and told me you wanted to stay, I was worried that you might change your mind yet again. I wanted to know what was truly in your heart. Since you returned home, Deacon Albrecht, Jeremiah and I have been watching you closely. Of course, Jeremiah has had his concerns. He has feared you might hurt Lizzie again, or draw her off with you into an *Englisch* life. But it has been our fondest hope that the two of you might discover you are still in love, and then choose to marry and start a *familye* here in Riverton. Now that we know what you really want, I have a proposal for the two of you."

Lizzie blinked in confusion. What Eli really wanted was to be a paramedic. What could the bishop have to say that would impact that?

"The church elders and I have discussed your paramedic training at length," the bishop continued. "You have done so much *gut* work for our people with your healing skills. Since our farms are scattered far outside of town, we would like you to maintain your certifications and continue to assist our people as a paramedic."

Lizzie gasped. Had she heard right?

"I have taken the liberty of speaking with the hospital administrators in town. Dr. McGann and Dr. Graham have both voiced their support and I have confirmed that they will work with you. They are pleased with the impact you have had in getting the Amish to receive necessary medical care. The hospital will even pay you a fair salary to serve as a paramedic. I know for a fact that Lancaster County and Pennsylvania have Amish paramedics and firefighters who serve their people. Our need here in Colorado is just as great. *Ach*, so you see? When we exercise faith and bow to *Gott*'s will, He blesses us with more joy than we can ever hope for."

A halting laugh burst from Eli's throat. "*Ja*, Bishop Yoder. You are right. I never expected to feel so much joy. I… I can't believe this is truly happening. I can remain here and work the career I have chosen, but…"

Eli spun toward Lizzie. His eyes were filled with happiness and eager anticipation. Reaching into his hat, he pulled out the job offer from Tom Caldwell and ripped the letter in two before placing it in her hands. Lizzie gazed at him with stunned amazement. She barely noticed as her father and Bishop Yoder turned and quietly went back inside the house and closed the door. Out of her peripheral vision, she saw the men pulling the little girls away from the window. Finally, she and Eli had a moment alone together.

"Lizzie, you hold my heart in your hands," Eli said. He squeezed her fingers, his gaze searching hers. "I'm not going anywhere. I belong right here in Riverton, with you. Say you'll be mine. Make me the happiest man in the world. I want us to be married just as soon as I'm baptized. Please say yes."

A movement from the window caught Lizzie's eye. She glanced over and saw her father nodding his approval from inside the house. She almost laughed. So much for privacy. But it wasn't as if she needed his prompting to find her answer. If her father approved of this man, then so must she. Especially when marrying Eli was what she'd always wanted.

With tears of happiness dripping from her eyes, she enfolded Eli in a tight hug. "*Ja*, I will, Eli. *Ach*, I will!"

A shout of delight came from the living room. Her *familye* and Bishop Yoder were inside, celebrating this thrilling news. And what more could Lizzie want? This Thanksgiving, she had found so much to be grateful for. So much to praise the Lord for.

"I love you, Lizzie-bee." Eli pressed a gentle kiss to her lips. His eyes were filled with wonder and love.

"And I love you, Eli. So very much."

She heard the front door open and the squeak of the

screen door as her sisters rushed outside to congratulate her. With Eli's arm securely wrapped around her
shoulders, she faced her father and the bishop. Both
men smiled wide with pleasure. With Eli by her side
and her *familye* surrounding her, Lizzie felt such deep
contentment that she was overwhelmed with joy. Truly
Gott's redeeming love had mended their broken hearts.
He had made them whole again. And Lizzie could ask
for nothing more.

* * * * *

**WE HOPE YOU ENJOYED
THIS BOOK FROM**

LOVE INSPIRED

INSPIRATIONAL ROMANCE

Uplifting stories of faith, forgiveness and hope.

Fall in love with stories where faith helps
guide you through life's challenges, and discover
the promise of a new beginning.

6 NEW BOOKS AVAILABLE EVERY MONTH!

Addie kept monopolizing Evan's time. First at the B and B—though she could hardly blame herself for that. He was the one who'd insisted on helping her out. And now again at church. Surely he had better places to be than with her.

"Do you need to go?" she asked Evan. "Sorry I kept you so long."

"I'm not in a rush. I might pop out to Wilder Ranch for lunch with Jace and Mackenzie. After that I have to…" Evan groaned.

"Run into a burning building? Perform brain surgery? Teach a sewing class?"

Humor momentarily flashed across his features. "Go to a meeting for Old Westbend Weekend."

What? So much for some Evan-free time to pull herself back together. "I'm going to that, but I didn't realize you were. The B and B is one of the sponsors for the weekend." Addie had used her entire limited advertising budget for the three-day event.

"I thought my brother might block for me today. Instead he totally kicked me under the bus as it roared by. He caught Bill's attention and volunteered me for the hero thing." The pure torment on Evan's face was almost comical. "I want to back out of it, but Bill played the 'it's for the kids' card, and now I think I'm trapped."

"Look, Mommy!" Sawyer ran over to them. A grubby, slimy—and very dead—worm rested in the palm of his hand.

"Ew."

At her disgust, Sawyer showed the prize to Evan. "Good find. He looks like he's dead, though, so you'd better give him a proper burial."

"Yeah!" Sawyer hurried over to the patch of dirt. He plopped the worm onto the sidewalk and told it to "stay" just like he would Belay. That made both of them laugh. Then he used one of the sticks as a shovel and began digging a hole.

"He's like a cat, always bringing me dead animals as gifts. I'm surprised he doesn't leave them for me on the doorstep."

Evan chuckled while waving toward the parking lot. She turned to see his brother and Mackenzie walking to their vehicle.

"Do you guys want to come out to Wilder Ranch for lunch? I'm sure they wouldn't mind two more. It's a happy sort of chaos there with all of the kids."

Addie's heart constricted at the offer. No doubt Sawyer would love it. She wanted exactly what Evan was offering, but all of that was off-limits for her. She couldn't allow herself any more access into Evan's world or vice versa.

"We can't, but thanks. I've got to get Sawyer down for a nap." Addie wasn't about to attempt attending a meeting with a tired Sawyer, and she didn't have anywhere else in town for him to go.

Evan's face morphed from relaxed to taut, but he didn't press further. "Right. Okay. I guess I'll see you later then." After saying goodbye to Sawyer, he caught up with Jace and Mackenzie in the parking lot.

A momentary flash of loss ached in Addie's chest. A few days in Evan's presence and he was already showing her how different things could have been. It was like there was a life out there that she'd missed by taking the wrong path. It was shiny and warm and so, so out of reach.

And the worst of it was, until Evan, she hadn't realized just how much she was missing.

Don't miss
Her Hidden Hope *by Jill Lynn,*
available May 2020 wherever
Love Inspired books and ebooks are sold.

LoveInspired.com

LIEXP0420